HER MOTHER'S SINS

A story in the Meg Hutchinson tradition...

Elvi Lloyd is bitterly ashamed of her mother's profession – Sybil scrapes a living by holding fradulent séances for gullible middle-aged women. When Bernard Pomfrey comes into their lives, Sybil thinks that he's falling for her mature charms, but he is more evil and vicious than either can imagine. As Swansea's most successful brothel-keeper he is intent on having his wicked way with innocent Elvi before forcing her into prostitution. He also has designs on Lynnys, daughter of his helper Connie Lamar, and as he becomes increasingly violent, Connie may be the only one who can save both girls from their mothers' sins.

HER MOTHER'S SINS

HER MOTHER'S SINS

by

Gwen Madoc

Magna Large Print Books
Long Preston, North Yorkshire,
BD23 4ND, England.

British Library Cataloguing in Publication Data.

Madoc, Gwen
  Her mother's sins.

    A catalogue record of this book is
    available from the British Library

    ISBN   0-7505-2580-0
    ISBN   978-0-7505-2580-0

First published in Great Britain in 2005 by Hodder & Stoughton

Published in Large Print 2006 by arrangement with
Hodder & Stoughton Ltd.

Magna Large Print is an imprint of Library Magna Books Ltd.

Printed and bound in Great Britain by
T.J. (International) Ltd., Cornwall, PL28 8RW

1

'I won't do it, I tell you!' Elvi Lloyd faced her mother defiantly across the table. 'It's wrong, wicked, and you can't force me.'

'Elvi, you're making a fuss over nothing.' Sybil Lloyd's plump cheeks, already heavily rouged, flushed even deeper; her features were stiff with impatience, bordering on anger. 'It's a simple thing I'm asking. Even a child could do it.'

'It's thoroughly dishonest, that's what it is.' Elvi shook her head vehemently. 'Dishonest and shameful, and I'll have nothing to do with it.'

'Dishonest!' Sybil sniffed contemptuously. 'Don't be ridiculous, Elvi. Clients expect a materialisation of a spirit at a séance. It gives them a thrill and I'm just giving them their money's worth, that's all.'

'But it's fraudulent. We'll be found out!' Elvi wailed. 'You'll make us a laughing-stock in the town. I'll lose my job with Dr Howells.'

'Nonsense!' Sybil came round the table quickly and clutched at Elvi's arm. 'There's nothing to it,' she went on in a coaxing tone. 'I'll rig a make-shift curtain across the door to the passage. When you hear the word signal you glide in through the curtains, let everyone see you and then glide out again. Simple!' Sybil gave a snigger. 'With the

9

gaslight out and just a candle burning you'll look a proper spirit phantasm in Granny Lloyd's old-fashioned wedding dress, with your hair down around your shoulders and your face whitened with flour.'

'No!' Elvi shouted. 'Do it yourself.'

'Tsk! Our living room is too small. I can't move about without being spotted, can I?'

'There! You see!' Elvi exclaimed. 'You know it's wrong.'

'No such thing!' Sybil's expression showed her exasperation. 'Look, Elvi, the ladies I've got coming to my séance tonight are well known in the town. They'll spread the word if they're impressed. It's a chance to make my reputation as a strong clairvoyant.' Her grip on Elvi's arm tightened and her tone became harsh with a warning. 'You'll do this, Elvi, or I'll make you very sorry, my girl.'

Elvi felt tears sting her eyes. 'How can you even think about deceiving people and taking their hard-earned money?'

'Huh! Hard-earned money, my foot!' Sybil exclaimed loudly. 'The two coming tonight have lived the life of Riley, they have.' She sniffed with disdain. 'Mrs Cribbins, the butcher's widow, has never done a day's work in her life, and he's left her very comfortably off.'

'I expect Mr Cribbins worked hard,' Elvi observed.

Sybil ignored her comment. 'Her friend Mrs Beavis is the wife of the landlord of the Castle Arms. Plenty of money there.'

'If her husband is still alive,' Elvi asked, 'why is

she coming to your séance?'

'She lost her old father recently,' Sybil explained tetchily. 'She's anxious to get in touch with him about a mislaid will or something.' Her gaze was speculative. 'I'm telling you, Elvi, neither are short of a bob or two and if I play my cards right tonight, they'll be eager for a few more sessions. That's why I want a materialisation of my spirit guide. We need the money, God knows! It's time you earned your keep, my girl.'

Elvi had always known the time would come when Sybil would insist that she help in committing this fraud, but she could not bring herself to do it. She would rather starve first!

'I don't care,' she cried out in rebellion. 'It's trickery, Mam, and it's cruel, too.'

'Oh! Why are you so difficult, Elvi?' Sybil snapped. 'Anyone would think you were jealous of me.' She gave Elvi a baleful glance. 'And I've told you before, don't call me Mam,' she commanded. 'It makes me sound old.' She sniffed loudly and patted her blonde hair piled high on her head in a mass of curls and ringlets. 'Call me Sybil. After all, more than one of my gentleman friends has remarked that I could pass for your older sister.'

Elvi compressed her lips, knowing Sybil's vanity was something to be borne without comment, as was the string of men who professed to be family friends. She hated the way some of them leered at her behind Sybil's back, and hated it even more if one of them tried to touch her. And there seemed to be a different man each month, but none of them stayed around for long, for which Elvi was thankful.

'What you do is wrong, Ma ... Sybil.' Elvi's tongue stumbled over the name. 'Can't you see that? Even in chapel last Sunday Pastor Davies mentioned the wickedness of séances in his sermon.' Elvi felt her face flame at the memory, convinced he was directing his words of warning at her. 'I didn't know where to put myself.'

'That Pastor Davies is nothing more than a whinging old woman,' Sybil declared bitingly. 'And I don't know why you're getting on your high horse. My gift of clairvoyance pays for our daily bread and cheese.' She sat down at the table, reaching for the crystal ball that always stood at the centre, and drawing it towards her, lifted the hem of her skirts to polish its surface. 'And you're quick enough to eat them, I notice.'

Gift of clairvoyance! Elvi winced at the hypocrisy. Sybil knew what she was all right – nothing more than a scheming trickster. Elvi longed to tell her mother as much in so many words, but shrank from facing the storm of animosity it would stir up, which could last for weeks.

'My wages help provide food, too,' she reminded her mother.

She did not earn much for cleaning at Dr Howells' consulting rooms in Walter Road in the Uplands, but Sybil insisted on taking everything, leaving her not a penny to call her own. She had to be content with Sybil's unwanted clothes, cut down to fit, and always felt shabby and ill-dressed.

She was glad of the smart dark cambric uniform and cap Dr Howells had provided for her to answer the door to his patients, who often mistook her for a nurse. This always pleased her for she was passionately interested in Florence Nightingale and had read a great deal about her work during the Crimean War. To be a nurse was the only thing she wanted but her mother would not hear of it.

'Your wages at the surgery are a pittance,' Sybil said disparagingly. 'It's my clairvoyance that feeds us and don't you forget it.' She gave Elvi a stern look. 'If you won't help me tonight, then you can go without supper and breakfast tomorrow as well. See how you like that!'

Elvi jutted her chin stubbornly, but said nothing more. She had so far avoided actually attending one of her mother's so-called séances, and did not care what punishment Sybil meted out. She would not degrade herself by cheating and swindling people.

It was impossible to get any privacy in their two rented rooms in the small house in Fleet Street close to the centre of the town. They had to share the kitchen and the lavatory in the back yard with the married couple renting the upstairs rooms, with whom Sybil quarrelled incessantly.

Water for washing was boiled in a galvanised bucket on the gas ring in the kitchen, and they bathed once a week in the tin bath in front of the living room fire. And there was no getting away from Sybil at night, for Elvi and her mother occupied the same bed.

It was often at night that the Shadows came. Sybil was clearly oblivious of them, but Elvi had been aware of them even as a young child, and had been afraid and still was.

She never saw them clearly, doing her best to ignore their presence by keeping her eyes tightly shut or putting her head under the bedclothes until they drifted away. She never dared tell her mother about the nightly visitors, fearing what it meant.

Sybil had always regaled her with tales about Elvi's great grandmother, Granny Lloyd, who not only saw spirits but talked to them, and had made a reasonable living out of it, if Sybil was to be believed.

Granny Lloyd had provided for a young Sybil when her parents died of smallpox and then for Sybil's own child. Elvi often wondered why her father had not taken care of them, but Sybil refused to talk about him, not even to tell her whether he was alive or dead. Elvi liked to believe he was still alive and would one day come back, and then they could be a real family.

The Shadows were Elvi's closely guarded secret. If Sybil ever discovered it Elvi would be forced into a life that she loathed and despised and she knew she could never bear it.

'Hurry up, Elvi!' Sybil was bustling about in the bedroom the following afternoon, adjusting her best hat to a smart angle. 'We want to get there in time to nab a good table.'

It was Saturday and as usual they were to take tea and cakes at the Mackworth Hotel in High Street, although Elvi knew they could hardly afford it.

14

'I don't want to go,' she said stubbornly. 'Anyway, it's too expensive. I'd rather walk on the promenade and have an ice-cream.'

Every Saturday was an ordeal for her, having to watch Sybil make a spectacle of herself in the tea-rooms at the Mackworth, trying to talk posh and fluttering her eyelashes at any unaccompanied man. It was humiliating.

'What you want, my girl, is neither here nor there!' Sybil flung her an impatient glance. 'Being waited on every Saturday afternoon is my one bit of pleasure in the week. You don't begrudge me that, do you? Besides, you never know who'll be there. We could meet someone very nice.'

Elvi knew what Sybil had in mind. It was several weeks since there had been a gentleman caller at their rooms in Fleet Street. Sybil craved attention and Elvi felt disgusted at how far her mother was prepared to go to attract a gentleman friend, as she called them. Elvi was sure from the shifty look in their eyes that some of them were married. It did not seem to bother Sybil, who accepted their occasional gifts and lapped up their flattery as her just due.

'That's all you go for,' Elvi burst out angrily. 'To see what men are about, and they're always horrible! I'm sick of it.'

Sybil rounded on her, her face tight with fury. 'How dare you speak to your own mother like that? What are you insinuating?'

Elvi hesitated, unable to put into words what she felt, how ashamed she was of Sybil's behaviour.

'I'm not insinuating anything ... Sybil.' She

15

reached for her tam on the chair by the dressing table and put it on, flicking back her long dark hair over her shoulder. 'It's just that I don't like the way they look at me.' She gave Sybil a level defiant stare. 'One of them tried to put his hand on my bottom. Yes, he did! That ginger-headed one, the one who said he was manager at the Co-op.'

'You wicked little liar, Elvi!'

'It's true, Mam!' Elvi cried out. 'I tried to tell you at the time, but you ignored me.'

'You're lying!' Sybil exploded. 'You're jealous of me, that's what it is. You don't want me to be happy.'

'That's not true, Mam!'

Sybil sniffed angrily. 'I ought to be married, and I'd have found a good husband before this if it wasn't for you. You put men off, Elvi.' She gave an angry snort. 'Who wants a woman with a brat?'

Elvi lowered her head. She had heard it all before. Whenever one of Sybil's gentleman friends deserted her, she insisted Elvi was to blame.

She could not wait to grow up. When that day came she was determined to leave her mother behind; go to another town perhaps and become a nurse. When she got out of Sybil's clutches perhaps the Shadows would leave her alone, too.

The only pleasurable thing for Elvi on a Saturday afternoon was the walk from home up to the Mackworth Hotel in High Street. The town bustled on a Saturday. All the shops were open until late and doing a roaring trade. Elvi wanted

16

to pause now and again and window shop but Sybil would not allow loitering, as she called it.

They were halfway up High Street when Elvi spotted a familiar face across the road.

'Oh! There's my friend Lynnys,' she exclaimed. 'I'm going to have a little chat with her.' She waved her arm excitedly. 'Yoo-hoo, Lynnys!'

She tried to dart away, but Sybil caught at her shoulder.

'Just a minute, my girl,' she said severely. 'Shouting in the street and running helter-skelter is not ladylike. You're showing me up.'

Elvi pulled her shoulder free. 'I want to talk to my friend. I won't be a minute, er ... Sybil.'

Sybil glanced across the road and sniffed in disparagement. 'Surely not the girl pushing that filthy handcart?' she exclaimed disapprovingly. 'She looks like a gypsy with that untamed mane of black hair. I don't want you associating with people like that. It's bad for my profession.'

'The same could be said for having too many gentlemen friends,' Elvi burst out hotly.

'Elvi! Really!' Sybil glanced around her with chagrin, but Elvi was not contrite.

'Lynnys is very respectable,' she declared. 'She works for Mrs Phillips the Vegetables in the market. And that's honest work.'

'I won't have...' Sybil started to say but Elvi rushed away across the road towards her friend, dodging a brewer's dray and a hackney cab, her quick movement making the horse shy, causing the driver to shout a warning.

Her friend had brought the handcart to a stop and was smiling at her, hands on hips, head on

17

one side.

'Hello, Elvi. Out shopping?'

'No,' Elvi said awkwardly. 'We're going for afternoon tea at the Mackworth.'

Lynnys' eyes grew round and she grinned. 'I didn't know your family were rich.'

Elvi shuffled her feet. 'We're not.' She felt uncomfortable for a moment, ashamed of Sybil's purpose. 'It's my mother's one treat in the week,' she said by way of explanation. She did not add that they could hardly afford it.

'Well, it's a nice day for it.'

Elvi grinned back then. She was always cheered up when in Lynnys' company. They had first met when Lynnys was delivering farm produce to Dr Howells in Walter Road. Elvi had taken to her immediately and wished they could see much more of each other in their spare time.

'Have you nearly finished your rounds?' Elvi asked.

Lynnys grimaced. 'I've got one more trip with this blooming cart to the Sandfields and then I'll be serving on the stall until the market closes at half past eight.'

Elvi shook her head. 'It's a pity you have to work on Saturday afternoon. We could go for walks along the promenade and eat ice-cream.'

'We could go of an evening after I finish work, or tomorrow afternoon perhaps,' Lynnys suggested. There was corresponding eagerness in her voice and Elvi nodded approval.

'Yes, let's do that!' Elvi was elated at the prospect of time away from her mother. 'I'll meet you on Oystermouth Road by the slip bridge at

18

about half past two.'

'I'll be there,' Lynnys agreed. She glanced across the road. 'There's a lady waving frantically,' she pointed out. 'She looks a bit cross.'

'That's my mother,' Elvi said dully. 'I suppose I'd better go.'

'And I've got to get this cart back to the market,' Lynnys said. 'Or Mrs Phillips will have my head on the block.'

They giggled together at the idea and then Elvi stepped away. 'See you tomorrow,' she said, and with a wave hurried across the road to where her mother was waiting impatiently.

Elvi felt quite pleased now. At least she had got something out of the afternoon.

The tea-rooms were quite busy, but Sybil sailed in with a swish of skirts, making a big fuss about where to sit. Elvi followed head down, trying to be invisible.

A man was sitting alone at a table for four and after a brief glance of assessment Sybil sashayed up to him, and with a breathless laugh, asked if the seats were taken. Elvi cringed. There were two vacant seats at the back of the tea-rooms, and she tugged at Sybil's sleeve.

'There is a couple of seats over by there, Ma ... Sybil,' she said quietly, but her mother ignored her, shaking her hand off.

'Sit down, Elvi,' Sybil said firmly. 'I'm sure this gentleman won't object.'

He rose to his feet. 'Not at all, madam,' he said, with a wide smile, and touching his moustache with a napkin. 'The pleasure is all mine. I'm delighted to have such a beautiful companion to share my table.'

'Oh! How thoughtful!' Sybil sat with much fluttering of eyelashes and gloved hands. 'This place gets so full, doesn't it? We come every Saturday, don't we, Elvi?'

When both Elvi and her mother were seated, the man resumed his seat. He was smiling widely. Elvi could see the glint of his teeth beneath his moustache. They were too even and too white to be his own. She had a sudden image of him taking them out at night and putting them in a glass of water, and wanted to giggle.

A waitress approached and Sybil ordered the usual pot of tea and toasted teacakes. As the girl turned away to fetch the order, the man spoke to her.

'Add the cost of the ladies' tea to my bill, please, miss,' he said.

'Oh! How very kind,' Sybil exclaimed, leaning forward showing a wide expanse of décolletage. 'We ought to introduce ourselves,' she went on coyly. 'Sybil Lloyd, I'm a widow. And this...' She gave an arch smile and indicated Elvi. 'Believe it or not, sir, this is my daughter, Elvi.'

The man feigned astonishment. 'I don't believe it. Why, I took you for sisters.'

Sybil lifted one shoulder and smiled coyly at him. 'Most people do. Of course, I married young, you understand.'

'You must have been no more than a child yourself, Mrs Lloyd,' he said in oily tones which Elvi did not like. He half rose politely. 'I'm Bernard Pomfrey, Major Bernard Pomfrey, at your service.'

'Delighted to meet you, Major,' Sybil said and simpered again. 'So courteous. There aren't many chivalrous gentlemen about these days.'

'I'm of the old school,' Bernard Pomfrey said rather pompously. 'Always treat the ladies with respect. That was drummed into me as a boy by my father. He was a military man, too.'

'I do admire the old traditions,' Sybil said. She sounded as though she had a plum in her mouth, and Elvi squirmed in her seat. 'And are you presently engaged in this dreadful war with the Boers, Major?'

Major Pomfrey looked momentarily startled and putting his hand to his mouth, coughed.

'Unfortunately not,' he said. 'An old war injury has kept me out of the fray. But I long to be in the thick of it, of course. What patriotic man wouldn't?'

What war? Elvi thought sceptically. He could have been no more than a tiny baby during the Crimean campaigns, she judged if born at all. Certain he was lying, she decided she did not like him one bit.

'You're *so* brave.' Sybil's hand fluttered to her breast dramatically. 'I do find that attractive in a man.'

Major Pomfrey smiled, showing his teeth.

The waitress brought their tray of tea and Elvi was thankful for the interruption. Sybil fussed in the pouring of the tea and then sat back, sipping delicately from her cup, her little finger extended.

Elvi ate her teacake, and watched her mother make a fool of herself. Sybil gushed, talking too loudly in a prissy voice and laughing too much, but Major Pomfrey seemed enthralled, and Elvi's heart sank.

She studied him as she drank her tea. Even disliking him, she had to admit he seemed a cut above Sybil's usual conquests. He was well dressed, very tall but narrow of shoulder, and had a bit of a paunch, although Elvi knew her mother would insist it was merely a high stomach.

A heavy gold watch chain adorned his waistcoat; gold cufflinks at his wrists, and two solid looking gold rings on his fingers. He looked prosperous, Elvi decided, but she still didn't like him and certainly did not like his eyes. They were shifty.

She sat quietly, not taking part in the conversation, yet observed that his glance kept flickering over her. He did not leer openly, as had some of Sybil's other gentleman friends, but Major Pomfrey's look was a strange calculating one that Elvi did not fully understand, and it made her very uneasy. She would be glad when they parted company.

At last Major Pomfrey took out his pocket watch and glanced at it. 'My dear lady,' he said genially to Sybil, ignoring Elvi, 'I can hardly bear to tear myself away from your fascinating company, but business demands it.'

'You're a businessman at present then,' Sybil cooed. 'I should have guessed it.'

Major Pomfrey touched his napkin to his moustache briefly.

'Yes, it's a far cry from the battlefield, of course, but I own a gentleman's outfitters,' he said, not without some pride. 'You may have noticed my shop in Castle Street, Pomfrey and Payne? My partner, Mr Payne, died many years ago.'

Sybil sat back looking impressed. 'Of course! I've passed it many times. Well, well! Fancy that!'

He glanced at his pocket watch again. 'Yes, I must be off. My staff may be shirking in my absence. We're usually very busy late on a Saturday afternoon.'

He stood up, and immediately Sybil lifted her hand to him.

'I do so hope we'll meet again, Major,' she said breathlessly. 'We're here every Saturday afternoon, like I said.'

He leaned forward and to Elvi's astonishment, kissed Sybil's hand. 'I'm certain we'll meet again, madam.' Elvi felt his gaze touch her. 'Such loveliness is irresistible.'

'Oh! Major Pomfrey, you're so naughty, flirting with me like this,' Sybil gushed. 'But I'm looking forward to our next meeting already.'

With a slight bow he turned and left the tearooms.

Sybil gave a great sigh. 'There you see,' she said to Elvi. 'I said we'd meet someone nice, and we did.'

'I notice you didn't tell him what *you* do for a living,' Elvi said. 'He wouldn't think you such a lady if he knew.'

'Elvi!' Sybil hissed. 'You're a spiteful little minx. It's obvious the Major is taken with me, and you're green with envy.'

It was no use arguing with Sybil when she was in that mood, but Elvi was determined to voice her opinion of her mother's new friend. 'I'm sure he was fibbing about his war wound,' she declared. 'And he's got funny eyes. I don't like him.'

Sybil sniffed. 'What you like hardly matters, miss,' she said. 'I like him. He's quite well off by the look of his clothes. I'd say he's not married either.' She paused at Elvi's sceptical glance. 'Major Pomfrey is quite obviously a gentleman,' she went on. 'A woman of the world can spot these things. You're too young to understand men, Elvi.'

'Well I hope we never see him again!'

'Oh, we'll see the Major again all right,' Sybil declared, her chin rising determinedly. 'I'm not letting this one get away.'

2

Bernard Pomfrey sat at his desk, thinking of Elvi Lloyd. What a promising beauty she was. He had been unable to take his mind off her since returning to the shop. He caught his breath, recalling her long slender neck, her large dark eyes; her full mouth which had never known a man's kiss.

His loins stirred powerfully at the thought of possessing her lissom body. She was young, tender and untouched, ripe for picking. He had wanted her as soon as his gaze had settled on her fresh, innocent face and he was determined to have her. He would be the first man to enjoy the fruits of that young and slender body. And when he had had his fill of her, which might take some time, she could earn for him on her back like all the others.

The office door opened suddenly and Bernard looked down quickly at the file of invoices before him on the desk, pretending to be engrossed as old Dawson, his senior sales assistant, put his head around the door.

'It's eight-thirty, Major Pomfrey, sir. All the workroom staff and my assistants have left. I've locked up the back.' The older man coughed apologetically. 'Shall I stay on to lock up the front?'

Bernard looked up casually. 'No need, Dawson,' he said patronisingly. 'You get off. I'll see to things as usual.'

Dawson looked relieved and Bernard suppressed a smile. They went through the same charade every Saturday evening. Old Dawson would have the biggest shock of his life if he ever learned of Bernard's scandalous but profitable side-line, so would their customers. But they were never likely to find out, not if he remained as careful as he had been this last year.

'I'll say goodnight, then, sir.'

'Goodnight, Dawson, and be in promptly at nine on Monday, if you please.'

Dawson nodded but looked pained. 'I'm never late, Major Pomfrey, sir, never.'

'Well, see that you're not,' Bernard said shortly. 'Oh, and by the way, make sure that order for six bolts of grey pinstripe goes out to Lassiters on Monday. I see we've taken several orders for three-piece suits in that cloth already.'

'Proving very popular the grey pinstripe is this year, sir.'

Bernard did not answer, but pointedly turned his attention to the invoices again. As Dawson quietly closed the office door behind him, Bernard sat back in his chair, stroking his moustache, a wide grin on his face.

Old Dawson was as reliable as the morning sun, but Bernard could never resist taking a rise out of him. Dawson had been employed in the business for years, even before Bernard had arrived to bamboozle himself in to a profitable partnership with old man Payne.

Even if Dawson was curious about his insistence on locking up each Saturday night, he would never guess the truth, and he had more sense than to poke his nose into anything that was none of his business.

Bernard waited until he heard the shop door close and then rose and left the office himself, going immediately to the back of the premises, where the unloading bay was situated. Dawson had padlocked the heavy wooden doors leading to the yard, and had shot the bolts on the small side door.

Bernard slid these back and opened the door. Immediately a man built like a bruiser, wearing a muffler and a cloth cap stepped lightly through and closed the door behind him.

'Anyone see you, Herb?'

'No one notices me dressed like this. Who looks twice at a working man?' Herb Collins answered. 'You worry too much, Bernie.'

'I can't be too careful, a man in my position.' Bernard glanced at the canvas bag Herb was carrying. 'A good week was it? Takings up?'

'Pretty fair.'

Bernard made his way back to the office, Herb Collins following behind. Bernard sat behind the desk again while Herb emptied the contents of the canvas sack, mostly sovereigns and some bank notes, on to the desktop. He pulled up a chair and they both began counting the money.

'Three hundred pounds!' Bernard was pleased. 'A very good week! Makes the hundred and twenty-five from the shop look very thin.' He chuckled. 'There's money in the flesh trade all right.'

He handed a small portion of the money to

Herb before adding the rest to the bag containing the week's shop-takings, completed a bank paying-in slip, and tied the bag securely. He would take that down to the night safe in Wind Street on his way home. It had been a good week all round. Very profitable.

He glanced at his companion who seemed quieter than usual. 'What's the matter, Herb? Any trouble at the house?'

Herb Collins shifted in his seat. 'Couple of drunks sneaked in to harass the girls. I dealt with 'em.' He smashed his huge clenched fist into his other hand. 'In my accustomed way.'

'Bastards!' Bernard snarled. 'Trying to get something for nothing.'

Herb looked thoughtful. 'Maybe, but I wouldn't be surprised if they were Charlie Pendle's men, sent in to wreck the place if they could,' he opined. 'We're stepping pretty hard on Pendle's toes in the Moll-house trade, Bernie. I think we can expect trouble from him from now on.'

Bernard stood up abruptly, turning his back and began fiddling with the safe, not wanting Herb to see he was rattled.

He was well aware of Charlie Pendle, a vicious young thug who was running a gang in the town, expecting to monopolise all the rich pickings. Pendle was reputed to be dangerous and unscrupulous, but the profits from the flesh trade were too good to back down now, and besides, Bernard had made sure his connection with the house in Cambrian Place was well hidden. Pendle did not know of his existence let alone his connection.

Still, the kind of trouble Pendle could make might scare away clients, especially the wealthier ones, the professional men his clean, well run house was beginning to attract.

He felt angry suddenly. What was he paying Herb for anyway?

'If you can't handle any trouble from Charlie Pendle, Herb,' Bernard rasped, 'then I'll get someone who can. Not scared of his reputation, are you?'

'I'm not scared of anyone! And no one gets past me, Bernie,' Herb said darkly. 'I give the once over to every man who comes to the house, you know that, and Connie will back me there.'

'No doubt,' Bernard said dryly. He felt calmer now, knowing his anonymity kept him safe from Pendle's throat-slitting cronies.

'By the way, there's a problem with one of the girls,' Herb went on, still sounding offended. 'The kid's got herself up the duff. Connie wants to know what to do.'

'Sling her out!' Bernard said harshly. 'Connie knows the rules. I'm not keeping these sluts fed and clothed if they can't earn on their backs. If the girl is up the spout then that's her problem. She's useless to me.'

Herb put his thumb against his nose thoughtfully. 'She's only a kid, Bernie, seventeen, and no family either. Connie thought she could work in the kitchen or something like that, otherwise she'll most probably starve.'

'Well, Connie thought wrong,' Bernard snarled. 'And she's not paid to think. You tell Connie from me if the girl stays then Connie herself will have to take her place to make up for loss of takings.'

Herb's facial muscles tightened in anger again. 'That's not right! Connie hasn't done the business for years, Bernie.'

Bernard was well aware the ex-boxer had soft feelings for Connie, worshipped her in fact, but she would not give him the time of day. Connie, most of her life a prostitute, now the Madame at his house of pleasure in Cambrian Place was, nevertheless, a one-man woman in her heart and Bernie knew her heart belonged to him, although he didn't give a fig for her. He liked that power over her, and she had no right to bend his rules.

He curled his lip in disdain at the expression on his companion's face, knowing that as boss he had the upper hand.

'Then see that the stupid girl is out first thing tomorrow and find a replacement,' he rasped. 'By the way, which one is she?'

Herb hesitated. 'Trudy, Trudy Evans,' he said at last. 'Your favourite, I think, Bernie.'

Bernie was startled. 'Is Connie sure Trudy is up the spout?'

Herb nodded. 'One of the girls, Sylvia, caught the kid spewing up in the lavatory one morning. When Connie questioned her Trudy admitted she was over two months gone.'

'Damn!'

'Connie made sure the kid hadn't gone with any other man but you. It's yours, Bernie.'

Bernard felt his facial muscles tighten in fury at Herb's accusation, and he was a little jolted at the revelation.

'Damn you, Herb!' he bellowed. 'You'll go too far one day. You forget what I've got on you. The police never write off murder.'

'It wasn't murder!' Herb exploded. He moved in his chair uneasily. 'It was an accident. I told you that.'

'But the woman died nevertheless,' Bernie sneered. 'You do as you're told in future, Herb, and watch your lip around me.'

Herb was silent, looking down at his boxer's hands tightly clenched in his lap.

'But never mind that now,' Bernie went on, satisfied that he had put the man in his place. 'Let's get back to business. These girls are a penny a dozen. I can replace Trudy any day.'

He was growing tired of Trudy anyway. She was a common little piece, always on the scrounge. He thought of Elvi Lloyd again. She would make an ideal replacement for Trudy.

'Get rid of Trudy,' Bernard said harshly. 'I already have a substitute lined up.'

Herb shrugged. 'You're the boss, Bernie.'

'You and Connie had better remember it.' Bernard's glance was dismissive. 'There's no need for you to hang about here any longer. Our business is done.'

'Right you are, Bernie.'

The big man stood up and replaced the chair in the corner of the room, before turning to the door. There he paused, glancing back at Bernard.

'Oh, by the way, a familiar face from the past turned up at the house in the week,' Herb said casually. 'Remember Josh Rowlands? He's back in Swansea.'

'What?' Bernard half-rose from his chair and then sank down again, feeling winded. 'He was at the house? And you let him in?'

Herb shrugged. 'Why not? He looks as though he's doing all right. Good suit, plenty of money in his pocket. Paid up the entrance fee without a murmur. He's a punter like the rest.'

'Did he mention my name?' Bernard could feel sweat prickle on his forehead.

'No, why should he?' Herb asked. There was curiosity in his tone. 'Although, come to think of it, you and him were pretty thick at one time, weren't you?' He paused. 'I wouldn't worry. He doesn't know you own the house, Bernie. In fact, he's probably forgotten you after all this time.'

There was a smile on Herb's face which Bernard did not like.

'Get out!'

Herb got out, closing the door as quietly as Dawson had done. Bernard sat back in his chair, wiping the dampness from his face with the back of his hand.

Josh Rowlands forget? Not him! Charlie Pendle was a vicious rival who could do harm to the reputation of the house, but Josh Rowlands knew all about Bernard personally, knew too much, in fact, enough to put him in prison, even get him hanged, if he had a mind to. Josh was devious and cunning with it. Why had he returned to Swansea after all this time? What was his game? He was after something that was certain.

Bernard swallowed hard, his palms wet with sweat. No, it must be a coincidence, he told himself, yet his thoughts went back to one cold night in November more then seventeen years before, when Bernard, Josh and another man, now dead and gone, broke into a bonded warehouse near the docks. A guard had been killed that night, but the three of them had got away with a tidy sum, enough to set each man up for life if he used his brains.

Josh had plenty of animal cunning but no common sense. Straight after the robbery he went around spending like a sailor on short shore leave and then had to get out of Swansea fast when the police started sniffing at his heels.

Bernard had been ready to bolt himself at the time, he remembered, certain that if Josh was caught he would not hesitate to implicate his accomplices in the hope of a shorter sentence. But Josh had disappeared into the dark back alleys of London, never to be heard of again. Until now.

Bernard crashed his fist down on the table-top in fury and frustration. Josh had acted like a fool back then, probably lost all his share of the robbery, while Bernard had used his head, kept on the straight and narrow, biding his time until the robbery was ancient history. When the moment was right he had bought himself into old man Payne's outfitters and had prospered considerably. And with the house in Cambrian Place he was coining it hand over fist. Now Josh Rowlands was back and he could ruin it all!

'The kid's got to go, Connie,' Herb said patiently. It was later that night and they were in her private sitting room on the ground floor of the house in Cambrian Place. 'You know what Bernie's like.'

Connie Lamar nodded. She knew Bernard Pomfrey inside out, to her cost. 'I won't sling her out, Herb. It's not fair; not the kid's fault.'

'Tell that to Bernie!'

Connie said nothing, thinking of what she must do. She knew exactly what Trudy was in for. She had been there herself, and Bernard Pomfrey had been responsible then, too, but she had never let him know the truth in all these years. She loved him but she didn't trust him.

'She can't stay here,' Herb went on. 'Bernie will make you work, you know that, and I won't be able to stand it.'

He was gazing at her with that soulful look in his eyes again. He could never hide his feelings for her, and although she liked him, she could not love him in return. He did not seem to understand that.

She loved only one man; the man who, years ago, had lured her into this trade in the first place, took her virginity, made her with child. It was a sad love; sad because no matter how badly he treated her over the years, no matter how heartless he was, she could not quell her feelings for him, try as she might.

She knew she ought to hate and despise him, yet it was herself she despised for this one weakness. If she had any backbone she would get out, try to forget him, as she knew she ought to do it for the sake of Lynnys, her daughter and Bernie's too, although he did not know of her existence.

'What I do under this roof is none of your

business, Herb Collins.' Connie was curter than she intended to be, unsettled by her own thoughts and self-recriminations.

'She's not worth getting on Bernie's bad side,' Herb insisted. 'Look, I'll take her down to the Christian Mission in Rutland Street. They'll look after her.'

'The hell they will!' Connie burst out. 'They'll shove her in the workhouse, take her baby from her and then make her rub and scrub like a skivvy. I won't have it.'

'Then what are you going to do?'

'There's a woman I know in the town, a friend of a friend,' she said carefully. 'She'll take her in, look after her properly.' Connie wetted her lips. 'If I spring for her keep.'

'Why must you pay? Why do you care so much? Anyone would think she was your kid.'

Connie felt a shaft of anguish go through her. Trudy was someone's daughter. Lynnys was the same age as Trudy, and somehow she felt that in saving Trudy she could save her own daughter from the same fate. Bernie must never learn about Lynnys. Loving him though she did, she knew he had no scruples. He loved only money. He would use Lynnys as he used Connie and poor Trudy.

'Trudy's just seventeen, no more than a child; Bernie's plaything that he'll throw away without a second thought.' Connie shook her head. 'I'll not see her jump in the river Tawe in desperation.'

She had almost done that herself at the same age, and then had decided to confess all to her mother instead and throw herself on Phoebe's mercy.

'Forget about Trudy, Herb,' Connie said. 'She'll be gone tomorrow first thing. But as far as Bernie is concerned, she was thrown out and we don't know where she went.'

'What are you doing with my things?' Careless of her nakedness, Trudy Evans scrambled off the bed as Connie opened the drawers of the chest and began taking out undergarments to throw them on the bed.

'Packing them up,' Connie said shortly, reaching into the drawers for more stuff. 'Get up and dress. You're leaving the house for good. I'm taking you somewhere safe.'

'Bugger that for a lark!' Trudy subsided to sit cross-legged on the bed again, scowling at Connie, her arms folded across her breasts. 'It's the middle of the night.'

'It's half past seven on a Sunday morning,' Connie retorted, stuffing clothes into a large carpetbag. She decided to be brutal. 'Your punter, Bernie, demands you go now you're up the duff. He's got no further use for you.'

'You're lying!' Trudy shrieked. 'I've seen the way you look at him. You're jealous because he wants me and not you.'

Connie rounded on her, aware that Trudy's words might have some truth in them. 'He thinks nothing of *you*, like umpteen girls before you,' she said. 'He's used you up and now he's finished with you.'

'It's not true!' Trudy sprang off the bed. 'He

36

loves me, otherwise he wouldn't have paid a bit extra to keep me all to himself.'

'Huh!' Connie gazed at the girl, pity in her heart. 'Bernie chooses a virgin and sticks with her simply because he's avoiding getting the clap. When he's tired of her, or in your case, if she gets a bun in the oven, he throws her to the wolves.'

'I don't believe you!'

Connie snapped the carpetbag shut. 'Even if you hadn't fallen for a baby, it wouldn't be long before some other girl caught his eye, and then you'd be working the full house, like it or not.'

'I won't go. I want to see Bernie. This is all lies, I know it is.'

'He spoke to Herb last evening,' Connie said patiently. 'He wants you out. You won't see him again, Trudy.'

'But Herb doesn't have to do what Bernie says,' Trudy exclaimed. 'He's only a punter.'

'Bernie's a regular client and a good payer,' Connie said carefully. 'Herb can't afford to lose his custom, so you have to go.'

'I'm not leaving, so there!'

'All right.' Connie was tired of arguing. 'Herb can take you down to the Christian Mission. That's the only alternative. Perhaps the workhouse will suit you better?'

Trudy let out a squeal of rage. 'You can't do this, Connie.' Then she began to sniffle and sank back onto the bed. 'I want to see Bernie. He owes me that.'

Connie sat down beside her. 'Look, Trudy, kid, I'm trying to help you. Bernie wants you slung out because he's afraid you'll cause him a scandal. Punters are like that.'

'I wouldn't do that. Bernie loves me, I tell you!'

Connie shook her head. 'Punters have lives, families outside this house. He doesn't care what happens to you,' she said harshly and then her voice softened. 'But I do.'

Trudy lifted the edge of the bed sheet and wiped her eyes, still sniffling. Even with a reddened nose and eyes she is quite a beauty, Connie thought, her heart sore with compassion not only for Trudy but for herself, for she was reminded of the way she had been at that age.

It was such a crying shame that a ruthless man like Bernie could spoil a young girl's chances of a decent life. Even if Trudy survived this, she would probably drift back into the game. Connie had seen it happen many times before. Wasn't she an example herself?

'Come on. Get dressed,' Connie urged persuasively. 'I'll take you to a good place, where you'll be looked after until your baby is born. What you do after that is up to you, Trudy.'

Connie knocked on the door of her mother's rented house in Cwmavon Terrace, a narrow rundown street behind Swansea Market. She trembled a little wondering what her reception would be. Phoebe Daniels would not be pleased to see her, especially uninvited; especially with Trudy in tow. Her mother would spot the girl for what she was in a second.

Only three times in seventeen years had Connie ever been allowed to visit the house where she was born and where her daughter now lived.

That had been one of Phoebe's conditions for helping her. She must leave the baby in Phoebe's care, and never darken her doors again unless called.

She had been called once when Lynnys was ill, and a couple of times when Phoebe had found herself short of money. Her mother made sure her upkeep payments were regular. Connie was glad to pay, eager for her daughter to have all she needed. She even changed her last name to Lamar to protect the girl from any scandal.

Connie knocked again. Phoebe was sure to be up early, even on a Sunday morning. Her mother was a hard worker and always had been. She had a job in the laundry at Swansea Hospital and she had never missed a day's work. Connie might be banned from Lynnys' life, but she had made it her business to know everything that went on in that house in Cwmavon Terrace. No harm must ever come to her daughter.

The door opened and a thin woman with a prematurely lined face looked out quizzically at her. 'Yes, what do you want?'

'It's me, Mam. Connie.'

'Connie!' Phoebe looked flabbergasted and then dismayed. 'What do you mean by coming here and on a Sunday, too? Are you mad?' She stepped out and looked up and down the street to see if they were observed. 'I didn't send for you.'

'Can we come in?' Without waiting for an answer Connie bustled past her mother, pulling Trudy in with her. 'We don't want to advertise our business on the doorstep, do we?'

Connie hurried down the passage to the back

living room where a faint smell of boiled cabbage and fried onions from yesterday's dinner still lingered. The furniture was shabby as ever but the place was clean. Phoebe saw to that.

'Here, wait a minute!' Phoebe's voice was shrill. 'What's this all about?' She stared at Trudy. 'Who's this? Why've you brought her here?'

'This is Trudy, Mam. Trudy Evans. She's in trouble.'

There was disdain on Phoebe's face as she looked Trudy up and down. 'Well, she can get out now,' she exclaimed loudly. 'I don't want her sort here. And what do you mean by it, Connie?'

'Hey!' Trudy tossed her head belligerently. 'Don't talk as if I wasn't here, and I didn't ask to come to this place, mind.' She wrinkled her nose. 'It stinks, too.'

'Why, you brass-faced little trollop...'

'Mam! Please!'

'How dare you bring her kind to this respectable house,' Phoebe shouted. 'It's bad enough you turning up, but her!' Phoebe sniffed. 'Anyone can see what she is straight away.'

'I'm not standing by here listening to this,' Trudy yelled.

'All right then!' Connie lost her temper with both of them. 'Get down to Rutland Street,' she said to Trudy. 'There's always room for one more at the workhouse.'

Trudy looked uncertain but Phoebe's expression was grim. 'I hold the tenancy to this house, Connie,' she said warningly. 'And we have an agreement. I don't know what idea you've got in your head, but she's not stopping here.'

'Yes, you're the legal tenant, Mam, but I pay all the bills, remember.'

'Well, it's only right isn't it.' Phoebe sniffed. 'I've given Lynnys a good home and a decent life. She can hold her head up; look people straight in the eye and not be ashamed of who she is.'

'And, Mam, I'm so grateful,' Connie said sincerely. 'But Trudy is only seventeen, Lynnys' age. But for the grace of God...'

Connie paused, feeling a little overcome. In her time of trouble she had had Phoebe to stand by her, even if it was grudgingly done, but Trudy had no one. Someone must help her.

'Look, Mam, Trudy is in the family way. She needs a safe place.' She glanced at the young girl. 'Even if she doesn't realise it just now.'

'What are you proposing?' Phoebe looked sceptical.

'Same arrangement as with me,' Connie said, perhaps too eagerly. 'Trudy stays here until after her baby is born, then she can do as she likes.'

'Oh, aye!' Phoebe folded her arms across her thin chest. 'And we know what this is, don't we? She'll be back on the game in a flash like you were.'

Connie felt her face flush up. Yes, she might have given it up all those years ago if she had tried to find decent work straight after Lynnys was born. Phoebe might have forgiven her, too, and she would have been with her child to watch her grow into a beautiful young woman. But her feelings for Bernie had drawn her back. She had lied to him about her months of absence, declaring she had been away in London with

41

another man. He had never come near her again but had forced her into the game for his pocket's benefit and she had submitted to the life.

Now she was a stranger to her own daughter, never meeting her, only watching from afar. Connie felt her heart had been broken over and over again.

'It's Trudy's choice,' Connie said sadly. 'What little choice she has.'

'And what about the baby when it's born?' Phoebe asked scathingly. 'She'll dump it on us. I know her sort. Another blasted mouth to feed.'

'Throw it out with the cinders if you don't want it,' Trudy exclaimed acidly. 'I don't care. I don't want the little blighter, anyway. It's responsible for putting Bernie off me. I was sitting pretty before this.'

'Oh! Listen to her, will you?' Phoebe cried, scandalised. 'Unnatural, that's what she is. Hard as nails, young as she is. When I compare her with our Lynnys...'

'Mam, don't say any more.'

'Don't call me Mam again,' Phoebe blurted, glancing warily at Trudy. 'I don't want it getting about that we're related. Lynnys believes her mother and father died of the cholera when she was a baby. I don't want her finding out the truth.'

'Trudy won't say anything, will you, Trudy?' Connie asked her heart sore. 'And if she stays here you can keep an eye on her Ma ... Phoebe. She'll be company for Lynnys.'

'Oh, *Duw annwyl!*' Phoebe lifted her bony arms to heaven. 'The thought of my lovely, innocent

42

girl under the same roof as this young trollop turns my stomach.'

'I haven't got the plague, you know,' Trudy snapped furiously. 'Or the clap, either.'

'You'd be out of that door in a jiffy if you had,' Phoebe blustered. 'And who is this Bernie bloke, anyway?'

'Just another punter like all the others,' Connie said hastily.

She knew it wasn't wise to reveal to anyone, not even Phoebe that Bernie was actually the owner of the house of pleasure.

And certainly Trudy must not realise it. Even though she pitied the girl, she had to admit that Trudy was a grasping little minx, and would not put blackmail past her. She could get herself into even more trouble, dangerous trouble, if she tried to pressure Bernie. Connie knew he had a cruel, ruthless streak if baited. She had never had the courage to face him down, and was glad he knew nothing of Lynnys.

'I'll give you double what I give you now, Phoebe,' Connie said. 'And perhaps a little more for the inconvenience when the baby is born. You won't be out of pocket, I promise you.'

'How will I explain this to Lynnys?'

Connie gave a bitter smile. 'You're good at making up stories to explain things, Mam.'

Phoebe pursed her lips with annoyance. 'All right then, but this doesn't change our agreement. I don't want you back and forth here, Connie.' She sniffed disdainfully. 'You've got that look about you same as young Trudy has. It shouts out what you are. I don't want any talk hereabouts.'

Although wounded, Connie said nothing. Phoebe would never forgive her for the path she had taken in life, and perhaps she would never forgive herself.

'Now then, miss,' Phoebe said sternly to Trudy. 'You can bring in that tin bath from out the back and have a good scrub down.'

'I'm not dirty!'

Phoebe ignored her response. 'I'll burn those clothes you're wearing.'

'But these are new! It's all new.'

'Stuff only a loose woman would wear.' Phoebe looked down her nose at the girl. 'You can borrow one or two things from Lynnys for the time being. We'll see what we can get from the pawnbrokers for you.'

'I won't wear second-hand things!'

'Then you'll have to stay in bed, won't you,' Phoebe snapped. 'Under this roof, you'll do as I tell you, my girl.'

Trudy turned a furious expression on Connie. 'What sort of a place have you brought me to?'

'A place where you'll be treated like a human being, Trudy, and not some man's property and plaything,' Connie said. 'Be thankful.'

'You can't keep me a prisoner here.'

'No, that's true,' Connie agreed. 'You're free to leave any time, Trudy. But what's out there for you now? No man wants a woman heavy with child. Within a few months you'll be ready to throw yourself in the Tawe.'

Trudy made a face, but Connie could see the girl was beginning to understand her situation.

'I'd get rid of it if I had some money,' Trudy

44

said hopefully, looking at Connie. 'It would be easier all round.'

'If you lived,' Phoebe interposed.

'I'd better go now,' Connie said. 'We won't see each other for quite a while, Trudy. Phoebe doesn't like me coming here. Good luck, and try to be sensible.'

'Put your head out of the door first,' Phoebe said hastily. 'Make sure there's no one about. I don't want my neighbours seeing a fancy woman coming out of this house. I'd die of shame if anyone found out.'

Connie wetted her lips before asking the question she had been longing to ask since she arrived. 'Is Lynnys here?'

'No.' Phoebe looked cross at her inquiry. 'She's gone for a stroll on the beach first and then she's going straight to chapel.'

'How is she?'

Phoebe seemed reluctant to answer, as though Connie had no right to ask.

'Lynnys has a job in Swansea Market serving on one of the vegetable stalls,' Phoebe said at last. 'She handles the handcart like she was born to it.'

'I wouldn't want her to wear herself out with hard work,' Connie said anxiously. 'She'll lose her looks.'

'It's honest, decent work,' Phoebe said sharply. 'And it's good for the soul.' She looked at Connie through narrowed eyes. 'If you're saying I don't look after her, you've got a damned cheek, Connie. Left in your care she'd be on the streets already.'

45

Connie did not have heart enough to rise to the bait. She had chosen her path in life a long time ago and there was no going back, but if she had her time all over again perhaps she would choose differently, if she could avoid Bernie's clutches.

She took one last look at a sulking Trudy. It was so easy for a young and innocent girl to be trapped into this life, and Bernie was an experienced hunter. She guessed that, even now, he was on the lookout for Trudy's replacement.

Connie turned and left her mother's house. One thing she had sworn to herself as a sacred oath. Lynnys' future must never be tainted in the way hers and Trudy's had been, and Connie was prepared to give her very life to make sure her daughter was never put in such danger.

3

Lynnys Daniels pushed open the back door of her grandmother's house in Cwmavon Terrace, thankful it was Sunday. She was eager to make the most of her one day off in the week and was looking forward especially to meeting Elvi later and hoped their Sunday afternoon strolls would prove to be a regular outing. Elvi had an easy unassuming way about her, and Lynnys found she could relax in the other girl's company.

And she needed that. She was pleased to get the job in Swansea Market but it was hard work lugging sacks of potatoes about, and then standing all day without a break, except to go to the lavatory, and even then Mrs Phillips, her employer, frowned as though she thought Lynnys was taking advantage.

But gruelling as the work was, she was glad to do it. Gran needed all the money she could earn, especially since their landlord had upped the rent, and as Gran always said, the most important thing in life was a roof over one's head.

Lynnys took off her Sunday hat and folded her best shawl over her arm as she walked into the living room. The aroma of freshly-made *cawl* started her mouth watering, and she smiled at the irony. Even though she served customers with vegetables all day, she would still tuck into the vegetable stew with relish. No one made *cawl* like Gran.

47

The first thing that met her gaze in the small room was the tin bath before the range, full of scummy water. She and Gran had bathed that morning, ready for going to chapel. She had rinsed out the bath herself and hung it on the nail in the back yard, so who had been using it? And it wasn't like Gran to leave a chore undone.

Puzzled, Lynnys hurried down the passage and shouted up the narrow staircase. 'Gran! Gran, are you up here? Is everything all right?'

'I'll be down in a minute.'

Lynnys was relieved to hear her grandmother's voice as strong and as confident as ever, but the dirty tin bath was still a mystery.

Hungry, she fetched a basin and spooned out a portion of the stew for herself. After a few minutes Phoebe's feet could be heard descending the carpetless stairs. But there was someone else with her.

Lynnys looked up in astonishment when her grandmother came into the room in the company of a young girl about Lynnys' own age. She was very pretty, with thick auburn hair and big green eyes. What made Lynnys stare was that the girl was wearing one of her few dresses.

'Who's this, Gran?' Lynnys put down her spoon and got up from the table. 'Why is she wearing my second-best dress?'

Phoebe looked discomfited, and Lynnys found it perplexing that her grandmother would not meet her eye. 'This is Trudy Evans,' Phoebe said. 'She'll be staying with us for a while.'

'You've taken in a lodger, Gran?' Lynnys asked in surprise. 'You never mentioned it this morning.'

'Last minute thing, it was,' Phoebe said almost defensively. 'Doing a friend a favour, I am.'

'Yes, but, why is she wearing my dress?'

'I don't want to wear this bloody rag, mind,' Trudy burst out. 'But she's burnt all my stuff. Bloody cheek, I call it.'

Lynnys' mouth fell open, and Phoebe's face flushed. 'I'll have no bad language here,' she said sharply to Trudy. 'You're not in the gutter now, my girl.'

'In the gutter?' Lynnys looked from one to the other. 'Gran, what's going on?'

'Dumped here I've been by your moth...'

'Shut up!' Phoebe interjected shrilly, and looked furious. 'Keep your lip buttoned or I'll take you down the Christian Mission myself.'

Trudy's eyes sparked rebellion for a brief moment, and then she gave Lynnys a speculative glance. 'Innocent little lamb is she?' she said. 'Don't know the first thing about men.'

'I never should've agreed...' Phoebe spluttered incoherently for a moment and then got control of herself. 'Get that bath water emptied,' she commanded Trudy. 'We don't live like pigs in this house.'

'I'm not doing anything like that,' Trudy answered loftily. 'Not in my condition.'

Lynnys blinked, glancing from one to the other. The girl looked triumphant, while Phoebe's features flushed red, and she muttered something under her breath. It sounded very much like 'dirty little tart' but Lynnys dismissed it. Her gran would never say anything like that, certainly not under her own roof.

49

'You're ill, are you?' Lynnys enquired kindly of Trudy. 'Of course you must rest. I'll empty the bath.'

'Lynnys!' Phoebe shrilled. 'You stay right where you are. I'm not having you waiting on the likes of her...'

'Gran, what's got into you?' Lynnys was concerned to see her grandmother so upset, and she did not understand why. 'The landlord hasn't made you take in Trudy, has he?'

'No, of course not.' Phoebe lifted her chin. 'The truth is...' She paused and then rushed on. 'Trudy here has got herself into trouble.'

'I didn't do it on my own, mind,' Trudy put in and winked at Lynnys. 'Bernie had something to do with it.'

'Be quiet! Or I'll wash your mouth out with soap.' Phoebe looked rattled, and Lynnys could see her grandmother's hands were shaking. 'Trudy is ... well, not to put too fine a point on it ... she's in the family way. She's got nowhere to go.' Phoebe's glance slid away. 'Her family have thrown her out.'

'Oh, how terrible! I'm so sorry for you,' Lynnys began.

'Huh!' Trudy tossed her head looking offended. 'Don't you be sorry for me.' She gave Lynnys a scornful glance. 'It's you I'm sorry for, living in a hovel with this old harridan.'

Lynnys straightened her back, upset and astonished too.

'Don't you talk about my Gran like that,' she snapped. 'She's the salt of the earth.' Frowning, she looked enquiringly at Phoebe. 'How long is

50

she staying here, Gran?'

'Until her baby is born,' Phoebe said tiredly. 'I don't know what'll happen after that.'

Lynnys looked at the newcomer in some doubt. She and Gran lived very happily together and got on like a house of fire. Now this girl had come to live with them, with her abrasive attitude, so brazen and knowing. Gran was putting up with Trudy's impossible ways and Lynnys did not understand why, yet she did have a premonition that their lives had changed irrevocably.

People were making the most of the sunny afternoon; couples strolling arm in arm, nannies pushing drowsy children in prams. Lynnys and Elvi strolled too, but Lynnys was preoccupied with what had taken place at home earlier.

'You're very quiet today,' Elvi said suddenly. 'Is anything wrong?'

Lynnys roused herself from deep thought. She was supposed to be out enjoying herself. They had planned to walk around the bay as far as West Cross and back and then find a little Italian shop for some ice-cream, but she could not take her mind off the girl Trudy. 'Let's sit on this seat for a while,' Lynnys suggested.

They sat for a moment more in silence.

'Have I said or done something wrong?' Elvi asked in a small voice. 'If you'd rather we weren't friends...'

Lynnys quickly touched the other girl's arm in reassurance, regretting her subdued mood.

'Oh, no, it's not you, Elvi. It's something at home.' She paused. 'The thing is my grandmother has taken in a girl about our age to live with us, but...'

'Well, that was good of her,' Elvi remarked. 'She must be company for you.'

Lynnys shook her head. 'Something's not right. Her name is Trudy. She won't be paying rent as far as I can gather. She's rude and uncivil, especially to Gran. To be frank – well– Trudy seems rather common, not Gran's cup of tea at all. So why is she putting up with it?'

'Perhaps she's taken her in as a favour to a friend.'

'I don't think so.' Lynnys decided to voice a thought that had been niggling at her. 'Trudy tried to say something about my mother, but Gran got in a temper and shut her up. Not like Gran at all.'

'But you told me your mother is dead.'

'Yes, she is, but more and more I'm beginning to think Gran is keeping something from me.'

'Perhaps this Trudy is just trying to make trouble.'

'I don't know about making trouble, she's *in* trouble.' Lynnys gave Elvi a sideways glance, feeling Trudy's shame herself. 'She's got herself in the family way.'

Elvi's mouth dropped open and her eyes widened. Two little spots of pink lit up her cheeks, and Lynnys could see she was shocked and embarrassed.

'I know!' Lynnys said painfully. 'Normally Gran wouldn't have anyone like Trudy under her roof, so why is she allowing it now? It seems as though she has no choice. Elvi, I'm worried.'

4

The following Saturday afternoon Elvi was even more reluctant to visit the tea-rooms at the Mackworth, not wanting to see Major Pomfrey again, but Sybil carped so much Elvi finally allowed herself to be taken in tow.

This time Sybil arranged it so that they would arrive a little later than they usually did, presumably as an excuse not to take any vacant table. Elvi saw the Major sitting alone again, looking expectantly at the door as though he were actually waiting for them, and wondered if her mother had made a genuine conquest after all. This impression was reinforced when he lifted a hand tentatively as they entered. Sybil made a bee-line for him.

'Major Pomfrey!' Sybil exclaimed with a false laugh. 'What a surprise to bump into you again.'

'Yes, my dear lady, what a fortunate occurrence for me,' he said glibly as he rose to his feet. 'Please do me the honour of sitting at my table. Let me order for you.'

Sybil sat with alacrity. 'I can't allow that again, Major,' she said coyly, grasping Elvi's arm and pulling her down onto the seat beside her. 'We hardly know each other.'

'It's the least I can do, and besides.' He smiled widely, his false teeth glinting in the light from the new electric chandeliers. 'It'll give both of us a chance to get better acquainted. Please! Don't disappoint me.'

Sybil giggled girlishly and wiggled her shoulders. 'Well, if you insist, Major.'

Elvi felt like sliding down under the table, convinced everyone was watching her mother's antics and laughing at her; at them both.

The Major glanced at Elvi, and for a moment she froze at the strange glint she saw in his eyes.

'Would you like an ice-cream, Miss Lloyd?' he asked. There was something in his tone that made the hairs on the back of her neck prickle and she quickly turned her gaze away from him, shaking her head.

'Elvi!' Sybil's voice was sharp. 'Where are your manners?' She beamed at Major Pomfrey. 'Young girls today,' she complained. 'They have no sense of decorum. I blame it on outlandish women like that Mrs Millicent Fawcett. Always got her picture in the papers, so vulgar.' She sniffed. 'Elvi is quite taken with joining her silly suffrage movement. Thank heavens she's under-age.'

Elvi felt her colour rise. She was very interested in the ideas in the pamphlet she had found from the National Union of Women's Suffrage, but Sybil had thrown it on the fire.

'Women should have the right to vote,' she opined defiantly in a low voice. 'They should be equal with men.'

Sybil merely tutted but Major Pomfrey's gaze glinted on her again, and for some reason he looked angry. Elvi could not think why. Her opinions were no concern of his.

'She's so wayward,' Sybil told him archly. 'I

sometimes despair.'

The Major seemed to have got over his irritation. He smiled across at Elvi. 'She's far too pretty for such nonsense as politics,' he said.

'What!' Sybil stared, her expression suddenly wintry. 'Oh! Do you think so?' Her tone was tight, and Elvi felt her stiffen in her seat. 'Dark hair is so drab on a woman I always think, Major,' she said sulkily. 'She follows her father there. What a pity!'

'If she had your colouring, Mrs Lloyd, then she'd be a real beauty, such as yourself,' Major Pomfrey said smoothly. 'If you were on the stage, you'd be all the rage, I'm certain of it.'

'Oh, Major! You flatterer!' Sybil was in a better temper immediately. 'But do call me Sybil. I feel we're friends already.'

'How kind you are, Sybil, to a lonely man,' he went on.

'Lonely!' Sybil put her hand to her breast dramatically. 'I know the pain of that condition, Bernard, only too well. I have Elvi, of course, and my work, but they just aren't enough.'

'Your work?'

Sybil tucked a loose curl under her hat. 'I thought you might have heard of me,' she said. 'In paranormal circles I'm quite famous for my startling clairvoyance.'

Major Pomfrey blinked, looking flummoxed. Elvi could see he was stumped for a reply, and she felt mortified. From a child she had been ashamed of the way her mother earned their living; and now at seventeen was humiliated at the bare-faced trickery Sybil practised to

55

separate grieving people from their money. She was certain Major Pomfrey was laughing up his sleeve at them both, if he wasn't disgusted instead.

'People flock to my séances, you know.' Sybil must have noticed his surprise, for her tone became defensive. 'All and sundry, rich and poor, everyone wants to get in touch with their lost loved ones, and they are willing to pay.'

Interest sparked in Major Pomfrey's gaze and he stroked his moustache. 'And you make a living from it?'

'Oh yes, and my fame is growing,' Sybil lied with ease.

Major Pomfrey looked solemn. 'I'm quite recently bereaved myself,' he confided. 'My ... er ... sister, Gertrude. We were close, you know. Would you help me contact her?'

Sybil sucked in air eagerly. 'Of course! It would be a pleasure.'

Major Pomfrey's glance flickered over Elvi. 'Where do you live?' he asked. 'And when can you arrange a séance for me?'

Sybil told him the number of the house in Fleet Street.

'Would next Monday evening at seven suit you?' she went on. 'I have some ladies already booked for a sitting then. I'm sure they won't object to a gentleman such as yourself joining in.'

The Major nodded in agreement. 'Will you be among us, Miss Lloyd?'

Elvi shivered at the suggestion, and shook her head.

'Elvi has the gift of mediumship, too,' Sybil

declared loftily, and Elvi almost fell off her chair in shock. Had Sybil found out about the Shadows? 'I'm developing her clairvoyant abilities. She'll be following in my footsteps soon.'

'Oh, really?' Major Pomfrey's gaze at Elvi was penetrating and disturbing. 'I'm sure she has potential, yes, indeed, much potential.'

Under his gaze she had an unpleasant tightness in her chest and for a moment felt unable to breathe properly.

'I would guess she just needs a teacher with the widest experience to draw out her talents to the full.' He raised one eyebrow and smiled. 'A very rewarding task, I'm sure.'

Monday evening came too soon for Elvi. Sybil had become quite nasty at her refusal to join in the séance, and in the end she had to agree just for some peace and quiet.

'It'll look bad in front of the Major,' Sybil had complained bitterly. 'As if you're a disbeliever, especially after what I told him about your abilities.'

'All right, but I'm not putting on Granny Lloyd's wedding dress,' Elvi declared. 'And I'm not taking up mediumship. I don't believe in it. I'm going to be a nurse,' she went on resolutely.

'Huh! You ungrateful little wretch.' Sybil sniffed. 'Only low women take up nursing.'

It was bad enough that Major Pomfrey would be there without making a fool of herself as well. She could not like the Major. He made her feel very uncomfortable and her skin prickled whenever he looked her way. She was determined not to sit near him at the séance.

Sybil had stretched their finances by buying a bottle of port to offer around beforehand. 'It'll soften them up a bit,' Sybil confided to Elvi. 'I've also got a nice bit of ham. Perhaps the Major will stay to supper afterwards.'

Elvi prayed he'd have a previous engagement elsewhere. Of all her mother's gentleman friends, Elvi decided she disliked the Major most.

Mrs Cribbins and her friend Mrs Beavis arrived a little early. They were two well upholstered ladies and, even though still in mourning clothes, appeared overdressed. Watching them sitting on the edge of the horsehair sofa, Elvi ground her teeth with annoyance to see the way they glanced at their surroundings with open disdain.

Sybil seemed impervious to their superior attitude, and gushed a welcome. This was the third of her séances they had attended, and she was obviously convinced there was more money to be had from them.

'A glass of port, ladies?' Sybil asked sweetly.

Both nodded in unison and Sybil glided to their shabby chiffonier and poured small measures of the dark liquid into tot glasses. She was dressed in a gown Elvi had not seen before and she guessed it had come from the pawnbrokers on the corner.

'I hope we'll get through to my dear departed father tonight,' Mrs Beavis exclaimed as Sybil handed her a glass. 'The matter of his will is pressing.' She sniffed. 'My eldest brother is ready to claim everything.'

Sybil sighed dramatically. 'It's all in the hands

of the spirits, dear Mrs Beavis. We on earth have no control as to who will deign to come through and speak with us.'

Mrs Beavis snorted. 'At a guinea a time I'd have expected more.'

'Have patience, Mildred,' Mrs Cribbins told her friend loftily. 'I've spoken with my Alf on the first two occasions. Very comforting it is, too. Worth every penny.'

'It's all right for you to talk, Cissie.' Mrs Beavis sounded aggrieved. 'Your Alf did the right thing by you; left his will at the solicitors. Dad didn't believe in them.'

Elvi noticed Sybil did not take any port. She sat on a wooden chair opposite the others, spreading her skirts carefully.

'A gentleman is joining us tonight, ladies,' she told them. 'A prominent business man in the town, he is. Anxious to get through to his dear departed sister. I said I'd help him. I know you'll not mind.'

The two ladies, now sitting back comfortably on the sofa, glanced at each other and then Mrs Cribbins smiled, while Mrs Beavis merely nodded. 'I hope he'll have more luck than I'm having with Dad,' she said.

The port was having a good effect, Elvi saw.

Major Pomfrey arrived promptly at seven. He was gentlemanly and polite to the ladies, who eyed him with interest. He accepted a glass of port, but did not drink it.

They sat around the table, now covered by the green chenille cloth brought out for special occasions. The Major sat directly opposite Sybil, the two ladies on either side of him.

'Let us begin,' Sybil said in a serious voice. 'Everyone put their hands on the table in a circle, please, fingers touching.'

Elvi could see Major Pomfrey was reluctant to do so, but a nudge and a smile from Mrs Cribbins and he spread his palms on the cloth, the heavy gold rings on his fingers glinting in the gaslight.

Although she had never sat in on a séance before Elvi knew what was expected. She lit a candle and placed the holder on the chiffonier before turning down the gaslight, and then took a seat next to her mother, putting her hands on the table to complete the circle.

Elvi could not stop trembling, wondering if the Shadows would come, and what she ought to do if they did. She would ignore them, she decided, as always.

She was startled when Sybil began to sway about on the chair next to her and then began to moan loudly. Even knowing it was all false, it gave Elvi the willies and she broke the circle and clung to the seat of her chair with both hands.

Sybil began to speak then, calling on the spirits to visit them. The candle's flame flickered momentarily as though in a draught, sending bizarre shadows dancing around the room.

'I call on the spirit of Daniel O'Leary,' Sybil intoned. 'Your daughter Mildred longs to speak with you.'

'Yes, Dad. Where the devil are you?'

'Shush!' Sybil gave a little choking cough before going on in sombre tones. 'Speak to us,

Daniel. Pass through the veil and join us.'

There was an audible gasp, and Elvi realised it had come from her own lips and she stared across at Mrs Beavis. There, standing behind and to one side of that lady's chair was an elderly man. Elvi could see him clearly by candlelight. He wore an old flannel shirt open at the neck and loose at the cuffs. Wide bracers crossed his bony shoulders. He was staring fixedly at Elvi.

'Your dear father is with us, Mrs Beavis,' Sybil said suddenly and surprisingly. 'I can feel his presence.'

Shaking with fright, Elvi glanced at her mother but could see by the candle's light that her eyes were tightly shut.

'Where is it, Dad?' Mrs Beavis exclaimed loudly. 'Where is that blasted will?'

'Quietly, please!' Sybil said in a pained voice. 'The spirits will not be bullied, you know, Mrs Beavis.'

Elvi took courage and glanced again at the apparition. She swallowed hard as he gave her a toothless grin, and suddenly she felt light-headed, and would have fallen had she not been holding onto her chair so tightly. She seemed to hear a cackling laugh inside her head, and the words 'tin box' and 'allotment' came into her mind for no reason at all.

Elvi wanted to be sick. She had never felt so strange and frightened in her life. Not even the Shadows had had such an effect on her.

'You may ask your question now, Mrs Beavis,' Sybil said.

'Dad! I need that will. Our Billy is determined

to grab everything. You promised, Dad. You promised me!'

Elvi took a sideways glance at the space behind Mrs Beavis' chair, but now there was nothing more than dancing reflections of candlelight again.

Sybil cleared her throat. 'Your father says there never was a will, so it's no good searching any longer.'

'What!' Mrs Beavis stood up abruptly, almost upsetting the table. 'But there must be. He told me so himself. Why, the old devil!'

'Calm yourself, my dear lady.' Major Pomfrey spoke soothingly. He had sat silently all though the proceedings and Elvi had almost forgotten he was there.

'Shall I end the séance?' Sybil asked. Elvi could tell from her tone that she was very much annoyed.

'No, no!' Mrs Cribbins spoke. 'I want to contact Alf again. And I'm sure this gentleman is anxious about his sister.'

'My sister? Oh, yes, of course, my sister. By all means continue, Mrs Lloyd.'

'I feel faint,' Mrs Beavis murmured. She had flopped back onto her chair again. She sounded very weak.

'Elvi, get Mrs Beavis another tot of port,' Sybil commanded. 'That'll put her right.'

Somehow, Elvi managed to get to the chiffonier and pour the port all by flickering candlelight. She did not know what to make of what had just happened. Had she imagined it all?

They were seated around the table again. Sybil

called on the spirit of Alfred Cribbins, butcher of this parish, to join them. Elvi trembled, but she saw and heard nothing untoward. However, there was a message for Mrs Cribbins from her dear departed.

Elvi was astonished when Sybil began to speak in a strange mannish voice, quite unlike herself. 'You have my undying love, Cissie,' the voice said. 'And you have my blessing to marry again, if you so desire.'

This raised an embarrassed titter from Mrs Cribbins. 'Dear Alf, as if I would!'

Then it was the Major's turn.

'I call on the spirit of Gertrude ... er ... Pomfrey to contact her loving brother. Draw near, Gertrude,' Sybil cajoled in her normal voice again. 'Join us, dear Gertrude, we beseech you.'

Elvi, convinced she had imagined things previously, was totally unprepared for what happened next. Behind the Major's chair the flickering candlelight condensed into a swirling mist and then the mist took on a more solid looking form, that of a man wearing some kind of uniform. Not a soldier, not a policeman, but something similar. Elvi was too unnerved to look more closely.

She almost cried out in terror and sat transfixed as the apparition lifted an arm and pointed its finger straight at her and then at the Major. No words came into her head, but a great weight seemed to press down on her and she was filled with a sense of deep despair and misery.

'Your sister Gertrude is with us, Major Pomfrey,' Sybil's oily voice said suddenly, cutting through Elvi's nightmare. 'Ask your question.'

The apparition faded as Sybil spoke, and Major Pomfrey stirred in his chair. 'Oh, well, yes, 'um. How are you, Gertrude? I mean, I hope you're happy ... er ... on the other side.'

'Quite happy, thank you, dear Bernard.' A light girlish voice emanated from Sybil's mouth. 'There is no pain here,' the voice went on. 'No hunger, no thirst. All is light.'

The voice stopped abruptly and Sybil immediately slumped forward onto the table.

'Mam!' Alarmed, Elvi jumped to her feet, grasping her mother's shoulders to sit her upright. Unnerved by what she had seen or imagined, she was now frightened, wondering if her mother was really ill.

'It's all right, dear,' Mrs Cribbins said calmly. 'That always happens. It takes it out of her, you know.'

'A glass of port is called for,' Major Pomfrey said and went to the chiffonier to pour a small measure. The glass was held to Sybil's lips and she seemed to come round with a loud moan, taking a sip of the liquid.

'I'm all right,' she said in a low voice. 'It's the strain of keeping the connection open between our earthly plane and the spirit realm.'

Elvi hurried to turn up the gaslight and then looked apprehensively at her mother. Sybil was sitting back in her chair mopping her face with a lace handkerchief. She glanced around the others.

'Did anything happen? Was it satisfactory?'

'Very,' said Mrs Cribbins. 'My Alf came to me again, just like his old self.'

'Did your father make an appearance?' Sybil

asked of Mrs Beavis, a look of innocence on her face.

Mrs Beavis sniffed. 'Oh, yes, the wicked old devil! To think I gave him bed and board for years and this is how he repays me.'

'Well, I'm very grateful, Mrs Lloyd,' Mrs Cribbins put in. She reached into her reticule and brought out a sovereign and one shilling and placed them on the table. 'There you are. Same time next week?'

'By all means,' said Sybil, looking very pleased.

With a sigh Mrs Beavis reluctantly followed suit with her contribution. 'I suppose I'd better come, too. You never know, Dad may be having me on. He liked his little joke.'

Elvi put her knuckle against her mouth. What she had seen must have been her imagination, yet would she imagine such a thing twice? She had never felt anything emanate from the Shadows over the years. This new experience was so very strange and disturbing. She felt upset and guilty at keeping quiet, but dared not speak out in front of Sybil.

'I would most certainly like to join these ladies again next week,' Major Pomfrey said, adding his guinea to the money on the table. 'I was delighted to hear such good tidings from my dear sister Gertrude.'

Sybil rose to her feet with alacrity. 'Oh, I'm so pleased you are satisfied, Bernard. Who knows, we might get a materialisation next time.'

Elvi felt a moment of dread on hearing this, but she was determined she would not be made a fool of by her mother's silliness and greed.

On their feet now the ladies drifted towards the passage and Elvi hurried to fetch their summer cloaks from the bedroom. To her relief Major Pomfrey was excusing himself from supper with them and was preparing to leave, too.

Elvi helped Mrs Beavis with her black brocade cloak. That lady looked very down in the mouth and worried, and Elvi felt guilty again. She glanced cautiously towards the others. Sybil was just ushering them out of the front door, bidding them good night in her usual loquacious way. They were out of earshot and Elvi knew she must say something.

'Mrs Beavis, did your father have an allotment?'

Mrs Beavis turned to look at her, surprise on her face. 'Why, yes, he did. Right up to the end he would toddle down to his allotment by Singleton Park to see his cronies and smoke his pipe.'

Elvi's throat felt dry. 'Perhaps he had a shed there,' she suggested, already wishing she had kept her mouth shut. 'Where he kept his ... papers, private like.'

Mrs Beavis blinked rapidly and then looked thoughtful. 'He did have a small hut full of old rubbish. Goodness knows what he kept there.' She gave Elvi a penetrating glance. 'Whatever made you think of that, my girl?'

Elvi laughed nervously. 'Just a guess, really, you know. No need to mention it to ... anyone else.'

'Well, his message tonight from the other side said there was no will.'

'He was fond of a joke though, Mrs Beavis, wasn't he?'

'Umm.'

Elvi began to panic now. 'Oh, take no notice of me, Mrs Beavis. I'm just a silly young girl with a vivid imagination.'

Mrs Beavis remained thoughtful as Elvi steered her toward the front door. The Major had gone but Mrs Cribbins was waiting for her friend on the pavement outside.

'I hope you had good news from your father, Mrs Beavis,' Sybil said glibly. 'Of course, I can never remember what happens when I'm in a trance.'

Elvi held her breath waiting for Mrs Beavis to expose her.

'Well, I'm not giving up hope,' the older woman said. 'There might be better news next week.' She gave Elvi a quick glance. 'We'll just have to wait and see.'

'Three guineas!' Sybil chortled as she closed the door on her clients and went back in the living room. 'I think we can run to a joint of meat at the weekend. Nice bit of pork, perhaps.' She clicked her tongue. 'If that harridan upstairs lets me use the kitchen without interference.'

Elvi was still shaken. 'Why did you tell Mrs Beavis there's no will?'

Sybil looked impatient. 'Use your head, Elvi. I've no idea where her father's will is, if there was one. I've been dangling her on a string for two weeks. I had to come up with something tonight otherwise I'd have lost my credibility.' She smiled widely. 'I thought we wouldn't see her at a séance again, but I do believe she's caught the bug.'

Elvi hesitated before asking. 'Do you see anything when the spirits are called?'

Sybil laughed out loud, a genuine laugh of amusement. 'Elvi, you're as thick as two short planks. Of course I don't see anything. There's nothing to see.'

She glanced in the mirror over the fireplace and patted her blonde coiffure. 'Bernard is really taken with me, I can tell. Something good will come of this, Elvi, mark my words.'

They dined on the ham and boiled potatoes, but Elvi had trouble swallowing the food, thinking of next Monday and facing Mrs Beavis again, not to mention Major Pomfrey.

She eyed her mother covertly across the table. 'Mam, did my father ever wear a uniform?'

Sybil's shoulders stiffened. She looked up from her plate, her expression guarded. 'No, he never did. What made you ask that?'

Elvi had to think fast. 'I was thinking, if my father was here you wouldn't need gentlemen callers like Major Pomfrey, would you. I don't like him.'

That night, for once, the Shadows did not come, but Elvi could not sleep; her mind too crowded and confused with questions and conjecture. What had really happened at the séance and what had she seen, if anything? The figure of the old man, whom she had taken to be Mrs Beavis' father had not so much frightened her as filled her with astonishment.

The apparition behind the Major's chair however was another matter altogether. In her mind's eye she saw the gesture again and knew it to be a warning.

A shiver ran down her back and despite the warmth of the night, Elvi drew the bedclothes up protectively around her neck. Besides the sense of despair she had experienced she had also felt an evil presence, quite strong and lingering. It had remained with her until after the Major had left the house.

If not her father, who was the man in the uniform? What connection had he with Major Pomfrey, and why had he chosen to appear to her? Remembering the figure's grave expression and the pall of melancholy that had all but suffocated her, Elvi knew she must not dismiss the warning. But whom or what must she fear?

5

Leaving Sybil Lloyd's rooms in Fleet Street Bernard Pomfrey made the short walk to Lower Oxford Street and managed to flag down a hansom cab. He arrived at his three-storey house in Prince of Wales Road, looking forward to the supper awaiting him.

As he let himself in, his housekeeper, Minnie Dart, was ready to take his hat, cane and gloves.

'Good evening, sir. Supper will be served as soon as you're ready.'

Bernard did not bother to look at her. She was a plain, colourless woman in her fifties, with a permanently dour expression. She was a good cook and kept his house clean. That was all he required of her.

'Yes, serve it now, Dart. Then you may retire. I won't need you again tonight.'

The food was brought and, as he ate, Bernard reflected on what had happened in the house in Fleet Street.

Sybil Lloyd was a bare-faced fraud; there was no doubt about that, but to give the woman her due, she was plausible. He gauged the two other clients there tonight were completely taken in, and pitiably eager to part with their money. Seeing them fork out their guineas with alacrity had given him an idea.

He could kill two birds with one stone. If Sybil

was set up at a more fashionable address, given all the trappings, she could attract a better clientele, people with real money. It could be a profitable little side-line if handled right. Opportunities for blackmail perhaps, and certainly extortion. Lonely older women were easily parted from their wealth with the right persuasion, and he was the man to do it.

Once Sybil was embroiled in his scheme, he would have free passage to his ultimate target, Elvi. Despite the influence of that absurd mother of hers, Elvi was demure and well-spoken as well as beautiful. There was an intelligent rebellion in her dark eyes, but he would soon knock that out of her once he had her tucked away safely in the house in Cambrian Place.

But first he had to devise a plan to get her away from the mother. It should not be that hard. He had summed up Sybil Lloyd quickly enough, even on their brief acquaintance. She was vain, avaricious and obviously unscrupulous, judging by what he had seen tonight. She would be easy to manipulate and would do nothing to stop him taking Elvi for himself, as long as there was something profitable in it for her.

Thoughts of possessing that lovely young girl and what he would do to her stirred an overpowering desire in him and he could not quell it. Cursing the fact that Trudy was no longer available to satisfy his needs, he decided he must nevertheless visit the house in Cambrian Place to find relief.

As usual when visiting there he donned rough workingman's clothes, cloth cap and a muffler. Leaving through the back entrance he set off for

71

Cambrian Place, taking an out-of-way route along the Strand.

He carried a thick stick under his arm for protection, for the Strand was a dangerous way for a lone man on foot. Footpads loitered in the doorways of low drinking dens; raucous drunks staggered out of the many seedy brothels along the way, all potential assailants. High Street would have been more direct, easier and safer but he feared recognition more than he feared attack.

He entered the Pleasure Palace, as the house was known to its clientele, by the back way, passing mostly unnoticed through the kitchens, and made his way to the room on the ground floor where Herb Collins had his office and sitting room. Perhaps Herb had found a new girl, young and untouched. His mouth went dry at the thought. Trudy must be replaced and soon. His appetites could not wait.

Connie, sitting at Herb's desk, looked up as Bernard entered the room. 'Bernie! We weren't expecting you.'

He came in and took off his cap and muffler. 'Where's Herb?'

'At a card game in town.'

'He should be here in case of trouble,' he remarked tetchily.

His eyes were feverish, excited, she noticed, and the skin on his face was darkly flushed. She knew from experience why he was there.

'Trudy has really gone, I suppose?' he went on, pacing about the room like a panther.

'She's gone, Bernie. Those were your orders.'

He paused in his stride, glancing at her and wetted his lips.

'Perhaps I was a bit hasty. Should have waited until she was replaced. Where's Herb? Has he found a new girl yet?'

'No, but Dilys is free,' Connie suggested. 'You know, that girl from the Valleys. She's only been here a month.'

Bernard grimaced. 'No.'

'She's young, quite pretty, same age as Trudy.'

'I said no. She's already been used by others, God knows who, and that's enough for me.'

He paced again. Connie watched him, knowing him so well; his overwhelming paranoid fear of venereal disease. His father had died from it, a hideous death. She knew it haunted him that he might suffer a similar end, and he went to extremes to ensure the girls he bedded were virgins.

'Do you know where Trudy is?' he asked. 'I mean Herb could fetch her back temporarily.'

'He threw her out, like you said,' Connie said casually. 'Neither of us has any idea where she went; probably working the streets by now.'

He grimaced and then looked impatient. 'I need...'

Connie smiled, amused at his frustration. 'I can see what you need, Bernie. It's Dilys or no one.'

He glared at her in fury. 'That's where you're wrong, Connie. There's always you.'

'What?' She half-rose from the chair, shocked. 'Bernie, you can't mean it. I don't do the business any more, you know that.'

She still wanted him, but not this way, not to use her like some worthless vessel to be discarded when his appetites were appeased. She had once been innocent and untouched, and he had callously used her up like all the others.

He guffawed. 'At least I know you're clean, no sign of the clap. You'll do for now.'

'Bernie, I don't want to do it. Please don't make me.' Connie rose and went towards him. 'Dilys is clean, I swear it.'

His face straightened. 'What you want, Connie, is neither here nor there. It's what I want that counts. I need a tart tonight and you're a tart, always will be, so don't fool yourself.'

'Bernie, please!'

'Stop whining and get up to your bedroom and wait for me,' he demanded harshly. 'I need a drink first.'

He turned and opened the door to usher her out. Connie drew back defiantly, wishing Herb was here. 'I won't, Bernie. It's not right. I'm the Madame here, not one of the girls.'

His glance was baleful. 'You're nothing. If you won't do as you're told then pack your bags and sling your hook. Get out of this house tonight.'

'You can't do that to me. We've known each other too long.'

'Get this through your head, Connie. I don't care about you. You mean nothing to me, never have done.' His voice was as hard as granite and Connie knew there was no reasoning with him. 'I can do anything I like. I own this house. I own you. I own all of you girls. You'll jump in the dock if I tell you to.'

They stared at each other and Connie's heart was as heavy as stone as she looked into his eyes, cold and heartless. She wanted to hate him then, but hatred would not stir. She had known what kind of a man he was from the beginning, and yet she loved him.

But what he demanded now cut her to the quick. If it wasn't for Lynnys and Phoebe she might have defied him, she told herself, but she was their main means of support. If Bernie kicked her out, and he was quite capable of it, there would be no more money. Her mother and beloved daughter would suffer. She could not let that happen. Her shoulders sagged in resignation.

'All right, Bernie.'

As she passed him to leave the room he slapped her on the buttock. 'That's my girl.'

Connie left the room without another word. After all, what he was demanding was nothing more than he had demanded so many times before in years gone by. He was right. She was no more than a tart.

Connie slipped from the bed and reached for her negligee, drawing it around her shoulders. She looked back at Bernie sprawled on the bed, his eyes closed.

What was it about him that had held her heart captive for so many years? He had lost his perfect physique a long time ago; he was mean and unscrupulous, yet when he touched her, even though she knew there was no love in him, she could not help but respond with a burning desire she felt for no other man, and there had been too many in her life. It was a weakness that kept her from the arms of Herb Collins, a man who really loved her. She was not proud of the weakness.

'Bernie?'

He did not stir.

'Bernie, it's two in the morning. You'll want to get back home. It wouldn't do to be missing from your bed when Dart brings in your early morning tea.'

He opened his eyes and sat up. 'You're right, Con.'

He swung his legs off the bed and looked up at her, a smirk on his face. Now that his needs had been satisfied he was in a better mood.

'You're still the best, Con. You know all the tricks these youngsters have yet to learn, and I'm the man to teach 'em.'

He reached for his clothing and started to dress.

'I've picked out Trudy's replacement,' he went on. 'A lovely little bit, she is, too. Something of a blue stocking, I think, but I'll soon slap that out of her.'

'Where did you find her?' Connie felt a lump rise in her throat, and she forced it down. It was senseless feeling jealousy.

'The tea-rooms at the Mackworth, of all places.' Bernie pushed the tails of his shirt inside his trousers and then buttoned up his flies, grinning widely. 'Her mother is a medium.'

'A what?'

'Talks to the spirit world.' He laughed. 'A blatant fraud, of course. She's vain and avaricious. I'll play her along for a while until I can get to the girl.'

Connie leaned against the dressing table. 'She

76

doesn't sound our sort, Bernie.'

'Her mother wants the kid to follow in her footsteps,' he went on, as though she had not spoken. 'But I say her beauty would be wasted.'

'A beauty eh?'

'I won't be satisfied until the girl's installed here, where I can enjoy her beauty all to myself.' He laughed. 'I'm looking forward to her initiation.'

Connie's jealousy got the better of her. Her shriek of laughter was off-key. 'Bernie, you dirty old man! You'll never change.'

He looked furious. 'Have a care, Con. You go too far.'

She lifted her chin, flushing in anger; her glance back at him was scornful. 'But, Bernie, you've always said that women in my profession can never go too far.'

'What's got into you?'

She turned her back on him. 'I don't like being used.'

His laugh was mocking. 'Being used *is* your profession, remember?'

She swung around to face him again, still angry. 'You think it's going to be easy separating mother and daughter.' She thought of Lynnys in the same situation, and knew she would fight to the death for her child. 'You could be very wrong, Bernie.'

'I tell you the mother is a conceited fool as well as a fraud. I went to one of her séances. She got through to the spirit of my dear departed sister, Gertrude.'

'You've never had a sister.'

'Exactly!' He inclined his head as though in

77

grudging admiration. 'She's a good mimic, though. Changed her voice to sound like a man one minute and a girl the next. Strangely enough, there's money in the game. I'm looking into it. It could be a profitable side-line if handled properly.'

'Don't have too many irons in the fire, Bernie. You could get burned.'

He gave her a level stare; his eyes held a warning light. 'You stick to the bedroom, Connie, where you belong. I'll do the thinking and planning.'

It was quite late on Tuesday afternoon when Elvi answered a knock on the front door of their lodgings. She was dismayed to see Major Pomfrey standing on the doorstep. He lifted his homburg, smiling widely.

'Hello, Elvi. Is your mother at home?'

'No.' Elvi swallowed. 'She's out.'

She started to close the door but he put his foot on the threshold.

'Perhaps I can come in and wait for her?'

Elvi wetted her lips, wondering what excuse she could make. There was something about him that frightened her, made her skin crawl. She certainly did not want to be alone with him.

'It's not allowed,' she said lamely. 'My mother doesn't like her gentleman callers in our rooms when she's not here.'

'Her gentleman callers?' Major Pomfrey raised his brows. 'Are there many gentleman callers?'

Elvi put her hand to her mouth. There was amusement and curiosity in his tone and she wondered if she had spoken out of turn. 'No.'

'I'm sure your mother wouldn't mind if I waited,' he said persuasively.

He advanced forward into the passage and Elvi had no option but to give way. She quickly retreated to their small living room and he followed her in, closing the door behind him. He took off his hat to put it on the table together with his cane and gloves.

'May I sit?' he asked politely.

Elvi nodded and he chose to sit on the horsehair sofa and then patted the space next to him.

'Come and sit here with me?' he suggested in a light tone. 'We should get to know each other better, Elvi.'

'I'll stand, thank you,' she said, moving cautiously to the other side of the table. The glitter in his eyes reminded her unpleasantly of the redheaded manager of the Co-op. She needed to divert him. 'Shall I get you a glass of port, Major?'

'No, thank you,' he answered in an amused tone, smoothing back his moustaches. 'That's not the stimulus I'm looking for.'

Elvi shook her head, puzzled at his meaning. 'I'm sorry, I don't understand.'

'No, but you will, I promise you.'

Even more confused, Elvi shifted from one foot to the other in agitation. She did not like the way he was eyeing her in a sort of devouring manner.

'I don't think there's any point in waiting, Major Pomfrey,' she said trying to sound firm. 'My mother may be some time. She's gone up Oxford Street to the butcher. Meat is sometimes cheaper this time of day, but you have to wait around until he drops the price.'

He nodded as though in sympathy. 'Yes, undoubtedly money is short for Sybil.' He gave a deep sigh. 'It's such a pity that a girl as lovely as you must do without the good things in life, such as pretty baubles and fashionable clothes,' he went on. 'I don't think you realise just how beautiful you are.'

'My mother says I have drab colouring,' Elvi said, her face flushing with embarrassment. 'I take after my father.'

He smiled. 'What nonsense! Your hair is glorious. You should wear it up in the latest style.'

'My mother says I shouldn't put my hair up until I'm eighteen, otherwise people will think I'm fast.'

'I'm sure you're not,' he said and then frowned. 'But perhaps you do have a sweetheart?' He gave her a piercing look. 'You must be careful. Young men often take advantage of girls like you.'

Elvi straightened her back and lifted her chin. 'I don't know what you mean, Major.'

'These gentlemen callers who visit your mother,' he went on in a harder tone. 'Do they ever touch you, come to your bed at night?' He frowned. 'You've not done anything ... naughty have you?'

'Certainly not!' Elvi was outraged, knowing what he was hinting at. 'How dare you? I think you'd better leave now. I'll tell my mother you called.'

'I meant no offence,' he said settling back on the sofa. 'You've no one to protect you, Elvi. You need an older man to look after you.'

'My mother looks after me very well!'

'I'm sure she does,' he said dismissively, and then took out his pocket watch. Elvi glanced at the clock on the mantelpiece. It was already half past six.

'It's getting late, Major Pomfrey,' she said. 'Your shop doesn't close until eight o'clock, does it? I'm sure you've things to see to there.'

'Not at all. And, I don't mind waiting in the least.' He smiled. 'Especially with you for company. I have some good news for Sybil; for both of you.'

Elvi glanced again at the clock on the mantel. She should be preparing the table for the evening meal, but could hardly get on with her chores while he sat there never taking his eyes off her. Her legs were beginning to ache with tension and inactivity, but she would not move from her spot on the opposite side of the table.

'It must be difficult for a family without a breadwinner,' Major Pomfrey remarked. 'When did your father die?'

Elvi blinked. 'I don't know.' She bit her lip. 'I'm not even sure he is dead.'

'What?'

At that moment the living room door opened and Sybil sailed in.

'Elvi! I hope you've got that table laid, my girl.'

Sybil stopped short, staring when she saw Major Pomfrey, who had risen to his feet at her entrance. She recovered quickly and glided towards him, gloved hand raised.

'My dear Major Pomfrey – Bernard. What a wonderful surprise to find you here waiting for me. I'm so delighted.' She flung a quick glance at

81

Elvi. 'I hope you haven't been bored.'

'Elvi has been the perfect hostess in your absence,' Major Pomfrey said as he took Sybil's hand. 'I'm pleased to see you again, Sybil, and looking so fetching. It's hard to realise Elvi is your daughter.'

'Oh, Bernard! You know how to flatter a girl.' Sybil laughed and Elvi cringed to hear the obsequious ring to it.

'Major Pomfrey has called with good news for us, Ma... Sybil, or so he says,' she spoke up quickly.

'Oh, really?' Sybil cast a wide-eyed glance at the Major. 'Do sit down, Bernard, and tell me all.'

They both sat on the horsehair sofa.

'Well, Sybil, my dear,' Bernard Pomfrey began earnestly, still holding her hand. 'Let me say how impressed I am with your wonderful clairvoyance. I was touched beyond words to hear from my dear sister, Gertrude.' He cleared his throat. 'And so relieved to know she's happy on the other side.'

'I'm honoured to be of service,' Sybil answered in a quivering theatrical voice. 'I spurn mere monetary reward, Bernard. It's enough for me to know that my gift can help alleviate the grief of others.'

Elvie was silently appalled at her hypocrisy.

'Quite so, my dear Sybil, I understand,' Major Pomfrey said smoothly. 'However, I want to help you.'

Sybil sat up even straighter, eyes wide, looking utterly surprised. 'You do?' she exclaimed. 'I mean, do you? In what way, Bernard?'

Elvi waited to hear what he had to say too. What did he have in mind? He sounded benevolent enough, but she did not trust him, not after the things he had said to her. No true gentleman would talk to a young girl like that. There was something truly disquieting about Major Pomfrey, and the strange apparition she had seen at the séance still haunted her.

Bernard Pomfrey took a moment to glance around the room.

'Sybil, I'm not a snob, please don't think that I am,' he said. 'But these lodgings are far beneath you. A lady such as yourself, with such a rare gift should live in better surroundings. That's why I hope you'll consider my proposal.'

'Proposal!' Sybil sat forward and half-rose from the sofa, hands fluttering. 'Did you say proposal?'

Watching Bernard Pomfrey's face Elvi saw the brief flash of consternation that passed across it. He recovered quickly, but there remained wariness in his eyes.

Sybil was staring, her expression expectant; her hand to her throat. 'Oh Bernard, dearest, whatever do you mean?'

He wetted his lips. 'Let me explain,' he said hastily. 'I have an interest in investing money in property. I've recently acquired a house in Walter Road; a very fashionable area, as you know; sought after by the best people in the town, doctors, lawyers and so on.'

Sybil's mouth was open, her eyes wide as she gazed at him, and Elvi knew what was passing through her mother's mind, and felt almost sorry for her.

'The house is vacant at the moment,' Bernard Pomfrey went on. 'I suggest that you and Elvi rent rooms there.'

'Oh!'

'You can have the entire ground floor, if you like,' Bernard went on quickly at the very obvious disappointment in Sybil's voice. 'There'd be a bedroom each for you and Elvi. A spacious living room and a kitchen to yourself.'

'I see!'

'And perhaps, most important of all,' Bernard said in a persuasive tone, 'there's an extra, rather splendid, reception room where you could hold your séances in style.'

Sybil's features were stiff with vexation and hurt. 'Well, Bernard, I don't know,' she said uncertainly.

Elvi hoped she would turn down his suggestion immediately. The less they had to do with Major Pomfrey the better she'd like it.

'I hope I've not offended you in any way, Sybil.' His tone was creamy. 'I only want to help, my dear lady. I'd expect a mere nominal rent, in fact less than you're paying now, I dare say.'

'Well...'

Bernard looked around again. 'Might I suggest that I rent it to you fully furnished? New furniture, carpets, curtains. New beds.'

'New beds?' Sybil's features softened a little, and she patted her coiffure. 'That's very thoughtful of you, Bernard, I'm sure.'

'I want you both to be comfortable and successful.'

'Successful?'

'Residing in a more affluent part of town you'll attract a better class of clientele. The three guineas you recently received for your services could be doubled, even quadrupled, my dear.'

Sybil's eyes shone. 'Do you really think so?'

'Undoubtedly.'

'Well, in that case, Bernard...'

'Let's not be too hasty ... Sybil,' Elvi interrupted anxiously. 'Shouldn't we discuss it? I don't think I want to move.'

Sybil looked furious. 'You'll do exactly as you're told, Elvi,' she said sharply. 'I'm your mother and I know what's best.' She turned back to Bernard Pomfrey with a wide smile. 'Having dear Bernard for a landlord will be so much more intimate.'

Bernard Pomfrey cleared his throat again. 'Yes, of course. Well now, I'll see to fixtures and fittings. You could move in at the end of next week. How would that suit you, Sybil dear?'

'That would be perfect.' Sybil's face glowed with pleasure. 'Oh, how thoughtful you are, Bernard, and so kind. I can't thank you enough.' She leaned towards him, her hand to her throat, her eyes wide. 'If there's anything I can do for you in return, you've only to ask. Anything.'

Bernard glanced at Elvi. 'I'm sure I'll get my reward soon.'

'I've got some pork chops,' Sybil began hopefully. 'Perhaps you'd like to share supper with us?'

Bernard Pomfrey rose and bowed graciously. 'Unfortunately, I have another engagement, a business meeting, you know, so regretfully I must leave.'

'I will not live in that man's house, Mam,' Elvi declared loudly as her mother came back into the room after seeing the Major off. 'I don't trust him. If you'd heard the things he said to me before you came in you'd see it for yourself.'

'What things?'

Elvi hesitated, reluctant to repeat the Major's words. But she had to make her mother understand her doubts, even suspicions about the sort of man Bernard Pomfrey really was. 'He mentioned your gentleman callers and asked if I'd been naughty.'

Sybil's face went brick red. 'How did he know about them? What have you been saying to him about me? Have you been gossiping behind my back?'

'No, Mam.' But she realised now that she had been indiscreet. 'He even asked about my father.'

'What?' Sybil's face immediately lost colour. 'What did you tell him?'

'Nothing,' Elvi said shortly. 'I don't know anything, do I, not even if he's alive or dead? Why isn't my father here looking after us? What are you keeping from me, Mam? I have a right to know.'

'You're a minor. You have no rights,' Sybil said belligerently. 'And you are a stupid, thankless girl as well.'

Herb Collins sat at his desk in his office at the Pleasure Palace, running his finger down a list of regular clients with bookings for that evening. He smiled to see some well known names; respected men in the town, accountants, lawyers and one or two councillors. No doubt Bernie would be quick to pull in favours from them in payment for his discretion.

The door opened and Sylvia, one of the girls, strolled in wearing only a lace negligee, the edges held together loosely with a ribbon. Herb took no notice when she perched herself on the edge of the desk, swinging her long legs. He had seen it all before too many times. Only one woman sent his pulses racing and that was Connie.

'How's business, Herb?'

He did not look up. 'Shouldn't you be in the parlour, waiting for your punter, Sylvia?'

'I was thinking, Herb...'

'You shouldn't do that, Sylvia. It'll give you wrinkles.'

She sniffed. 'Don't try to be comical! No, I was thinking now that Trudy's gone our mysterious Mr Smith will be looking for new company, like. I've seen him look at me.'

'Mr Smith is very choosy,' Herb said. 'He won't touch used goods. Anyway,' Herb went on, 'we won't be seeing much of him until I can find a new girl, a virgin.'

'Well, he can't be all that fussy,' Sylvia sniffed again. 'I saw him on the stairs late last night, and he didn't go home until the early hours.' She leaned towards him seductively. 'Aw! give me a chance with him, Herb. He used to slip Trudy an extra quid or two. She told me.'

'Bernie ... Smith was here last night?' It was the first he had heard of it, having been at a private card game in the town. 'Which girl?'

87

Sylvia shrugged. 'Dilys was the only one free, but when I asked her she said Mr Smith hadn't come near her.'

Herb felt his collar tighten. Bernie and Connie? No, it couldn't be.

The door opened then and another of the girls came in. 'Hey, Sylvia,' she yelled. 'Get your arse out here. Your punter has arrived.'

Sylvia left in a hurry. Herb followed and went immediately to the spacious well appointed parlour where the girls waited for their clients for the evening. Bernie had spared no expense on furniture and fittings, so it was no wonder the house was attracting wealthier men.

Several girls were sprawled on sofas or chairs in various stages of undress, while Connie, dressed up to the nines in a red brocade gown, pearls and ribbons entwined in her dark lustrous hair, sat at a piano playing some of the latest songs from the music halls, and singing in a lovely contralto voice.

Normally, Herb would have been enthralled to just stand and listen, but tonight a shaft of jealousy pierced him, so sharp it made him grunt. He strode over to the piano and without warning closed the lid down. Connie managed to withdraw her hands in time, and she gazed up at him in astonishment.

'Herb! What are you doing? What's the matter, for heaven's sake?'

He took her by the arm and pulled her from the piano stool. 'I want to talk to you now, Connie. Let's go to your sitting room.'

'Let go my arm, Herb, you're hurting me.'

He was aware of the curious glances from the girls and the giggles. 'Ooh! He can't wait, Con. It's your lucky night.'

Herb ignored it all as he almost frog-marched Connie to her sitting room down the passage towards the back of the house, his fury growing each moment.

'Now,' he began when they were inside the room with the door closed. 'Sylvia tells me she saw Bernie here last night and he didn't leave until early morning. What was he doing here, Con?'

Connie turned away casually to view her reflection in a mirror.

'Why wouldn't he be here? He owns the place, Herb.'

'Don't be funny with me, Connie. Bernie was here but his piece Trudy wasn't, so who did he have?'

'I've no idea. Dilys perhaps. Business was slow so I went up to my room early.'

Standing behind her he stared at her reflected face and knew she was hiding something. It made his blood boil. He took her roughly by the arm again and swung her around to face him.

'Was he with you? I'll kill him!'

'No!'

'You're lying, Connie. I know how you feel about him, to my cost.'

Connie snatched her arm from his grasp, her face flushing.

'It's none of your business what I feel, Herb, and you've no right to question me.'

He stared down at her, feeling the muscles in

his jaw bunch in his anger. 'Did he force you?'

He had to believe that. He had to believe she wouldn't have gone with Bernie willingly. Not after all this time. 'He did, didn't he? The bloody swine!'

She turned her face away and was silent.

'I'd never force you, Con. I love you.' He turned from her to smash one fist into his other palm. 'I could kill him for this!'

'Oh, what's all the fuss about,' Connie cried out, swinging around to face him. 'I'm just a tart, like all the others. What's so special about me?'

Herb looked at her, longing to take her in his arms. 'You're the woman I love,' he said quietly. 'That's what's so special about you.'

'Please leave my room, Herb,' Connie said. 'I want to be on my own now.'

'He's not to come near you again, understand me,' he warned as he left the room.

And he would make sure of it. He would spend his nights off at the house from now on, keeping his eye on Connie, until he found another untouched girl for Bernie.

Herb went back to the office, his anger still swelling his neck, and sat for a moment brooding. The swine needed killing, but he wouldn't swing for Bernie's sort. There were other ways of dealing with him. All it needed was for one careless word to get to Charlie Pendle's ears and Bernie's life wouldn't be worth a brass farthing.

6

Josh Rowlands pushed his body gently away from the girl's. He thought she was asleep but she stirred, clutching at him.

'Hey, mister, you don't have to go yet, mind. You're nice. I won't charge you again.'

'What's your name, kid?'

'Trudy Evans.'

Josh lay back looking around the small room. It reminded him of the bedroom he had shared with his two older brothers in the house where he had been born and brought up, of poor but respectable parents. The room looked threadbare but clean; no frills or flounces. Not the sort of place a doxy would work out of.

'You live here, kid?'

'Yeah, for the time being.' She sounded evasive and it made Josh curious.

'Working on your own, eh? It's a wonder a good-looking girl like you isn't set up in some proper house.'

Trudy sniffed and sat up. 'I was until recently. At the Pleasure Palace in Cambrian Place, until Connie kicked me out. The old cow! Jealousy it was, because Bernie preferred me to her.'

'I know the Pleasure Palace,' Josh said. 'And I know Connie, too. Never met you there though.'

Trudy hugged her knees. 'That's because my punter Bernie paid extra to keep me all to himself, see. Connie didn't like it.'

'This Bernie, what's his last name?'

Trudy hesitated, frowning. 'I dunno for sure. The other girls call him the mysterious Mr Smith.'

Josh looked at her fresh young face, as yet unspoiled by her trade. Suddenly he was curious about her. 'How did you get into this game, kid?'

Trudy lowered her head and turned her face away; a childlike gesture that touched something in his heart.

'All right, kid,' he said gently. 'You don't have to tell me.'

She was silent for a moment. 'My mother died. I never knew my father. I went to live with my mother's sister, Auntie Marge.'

'Was she good to you, kid?'

Trudy looked up and pressed her lips together as though she might cry. 'It was all right when I was little but when I got older things changed.'

Josh thought he could guess what was coming next. 'My auntie's husband was always trying it on,' Trudy said in a low voice. 'I told her but she wouldn't believe me, and after that she began to treat me bad.'

Josh saw tears glistening around her lashes. 'What happened?'

Trudy gave a deep swallow as though the words had stuck in her throat. 'One day when Auntie Marge was out my Uncle Ernie cornered me in my bedroom and ... and did it to me.'

He had guessed right. It often began that way.

'Auntie Marge found out and said it was my fault,' Trudy said thickly. 'She said I was always flaunting myself. She called me a slut and kicked me out.' She shook her head. 'I don't know how I survived really. And then one day I met Herb Collins. He told me how I could make easy money and have a roof over my head.'

'How long ago was that?'

'Just over a year, I suppose.' Trudy shrugged. 'I knew what he wanted me to do but I thought, why not. I already had the name for it.'

'You've had a rough deal, kid.' Josh waved his hand around. 'Whose place is this? We seem to have it all to ourselves.'

'Some old harridan named Phoebe Daniels and her granddaughter, Lynnys. They're both at work.'

Trudy was her old self again suddenly and a malicious gleam came in to her eyes as she looked at him.

'Do you know who Phoebe is? She's Connie's mother.' She nodded when he looked surprised. 'Yes, and that's not all. Lynnys is Connie's daughter. Muddy boots and dirty fingernails, but she thinks she's a cut above me.'

'Never is!' Josh said, lifting a hand to touch the soft curling hair that fell over the girl's shoulders. 'Never in a million years.'

Trudy giggled. 'Oh, you're nice.' She snuggled against him. 'I'm ready and willing, mister. No charge.'

Josh swung his legs off the bed. 'Thanks, angel, but I have to be somewhere. Business, you know.'

'I'll do something special if you want.'

He smiled at her and then stood to retrieve his clothes on a nearby chair. 'You're a proper little tease. No wonder this Bernie wanted you all to himself. What does he look like, by the way?'

'Tall, with a moustache. He's very rich. Always slipped me a couple of extra quid for being especially nice to him.' She winked. 'Know what I mean?'

Josh adjusted his tie, hastily turning his gaze away from her lovely body. He could guess. But he had other things on his mind now.

He had a strong feeling he knew who this Bernie was, especially in connection with Connie. Even before seeing her recently at the Pleasure Palace, he remembered Connie from years back, as a kid not much older than Trudy here.

He remembered too, that even as she plied her trade, there was only one man who meant anything to her. Bernie Pomfrey. And Bernie Pomfrey was a gent with whom he had a score to settle, and he had already waited too long to settle it.

'Bernie's at the Pleasure Palace often, is he?' Josh asked casually.

'Two or three times a week when I was there.' Trudy sniffed. 'I bet he misses me.'

Josh reached for his jacket. 'Thanks, angel, for a good time,' he said. 'I'll let myself out.'

'Will I see you again, mister?' Trudy scrambled off the bed. 'What's your name?'

'Casanova.'

'Is that Italian?'

'Maybe.'

He walked out on to the small landing where an opposite door obviously led to a second bedroom. As he went down the uncarpeted stairs he heard a key being inserted in the front door and hesitated, undecided whether to go forward or retreat.

Before he could make up his mind a woman in her late fifties or early sixties entered. She was small and thinly built. As she glanced up at him, startled, he saw her lined face turn very pale.

'Who are you? What are you doing in my house?' she screamed at him. 'I'll call the constable!'

'Keep you hair on, ma,' Josh said soothingly, descending the rest of the stairs. 'I'm not after the best silver that's for sure.'

'You've got no business here. What *are* you after?' She began to back away down the passage, her voice loud with hysteria. 'Get out! Get out!'

'It's all right, ma,' Josh said calmly, taking a step towards her. 'I'm here by invitation. Trudy...'

At that moment Trudy made an appearance on the staircase behind him, without a stitch on, and the older woman let out a screech that could have rent heaven in two.

'Oh, you dirty little bitch!' she hollered at the girl. 'Under my roof!' The woman was almost gagging with rage. 'Oh! The shame! Oh! To think it's come to this.'

She stared wide-eyed at him for a moment, her mouth gaping open, her hand clutching her chest, and then suddenly with a strange sighing sound she collapsed onto the linoleum. Josh dashed forward and knelt down beside her, putting two fingers to the side of her throat to feel for a pulse.

'What's the matter with her?' Trudy asked. 'Has she had a fit?'

95

Josh glanced up at her with tightened lips. 'Get upstairs and put some clothes on,' he instructed curtly and she darted out of sight.

It was obvious to him that this old duck had no idea what Trudy had been up to in her home. She had had one hell of a shock.

He lifted up her slight form into his arms with ease as Trudy made a reappearance in a dressing gown.

'Is she dead?' Trudy looked frightened now.

'Well, it'll be thanks to you if she is,' Josh said morosely.

Trouble like this was the last thing he wanted now. But he could not walk away from it. He was through with walking away from trouble. And after all, he was partly responsible.

'Where's her bedroom?' he asked. 'We'll have to get a doctor.'

'They got no money for doctors,' Trudy said. 'A drop of brandy might do instead. I've got a half bottle hidden under the bed. I'll get it.'

'You'll put some clothes on and go for a doctor,' Josh demanded.

He'd have to do the paying by the look of it. Well, serve him right for breaking his rule and picking up a tart off the streets. But Trudy had looked a cut above the usual low-life streetwalkers.

She stood at the foot of the staircase, wringing her hands. 'But I don't know where the doctor lives around here.'

'Out of my way,' Josh said angrily. 'This poor old duck should be in her bed. I'll take her upstairs.'

96

Lynnys turned the corner into Cwmavon Terrace, glad to be home at last after being on her feet all day. She would be glad of a cup of tea and a bit of peace and quiet, although with Trudy about that was unlikely. That girl could stir up more antagonism than Attila the Hun.

The neighbour next door, Mrs Penhale, was standing on her doorstep talking to another woman. Lynnys smiled at them.

'Evening, Mrs Penhale. How's your Colin? Is his chest any better?'

Mrs Penhale sniffed and looked away without answering, but her friend had something to say.

'You and Phoebe ought to be ashamed of yourselves for allowing it. This is a respectable street, this is.'

Lynnys stopped, puzzled by their obvious hostility, wondering what on earth she and Gran could have done to offend them. They had never had any quarrels with neighbours that she remembered. 'What are you talking about, Mrs Wilkins?'

'Huh! As if you don't know.' The woman sniffed and looked her up and down. 'Men coming and going all day. It's disgusting that's what it is. I've a good mind to tell the police.'

Frowning, Lynnys shook her head. 'I haven't the slightest idea what you mean.'

'Oh, now come off it!' Mrs Wilkins' eyes narrowed. 'I wouldn't be at all surprised if you're at it yourself.'

'At what?'

'Oh! The bare-faced cheek of it!' Mrs Penhale stepped back inside, and with a glance of pure vitriol, Mrs Wilkins followed, slamming the door

97

after her.

Lynnys stood for a moment more, staring at the closed door. Then she shrugged. Perhaps Gran knew what it was all about.

Her own front door was ajar. Lynnys pushed it open and stepped into the passage, to get the shock of her life. A tall, well built man, probably in his early forties, a complete stranger to her, was halfway up the staircase carrying Gran in his arms, while Gran's head lolled to one side.

'Gran! What've you done to my grandmother?' Lynnys yelled, rushing up the stairs towards him. 'You've killed her, you thieving murderer.'

The man paused and turned. 'The old duck collapsed,' he said hastily trying to retreat awkwardly up the next stair in the face of Lynnys' assault. 'I never laid a finger on her, kid. Trudy here was just going for the doctor, weren't you, Trudy?'

Lynnys noticed Trudy then, standing in the passage, clad only in a dressing gown, and her mouth dropped open. She realised immediately what it meant and fury rose in her breast.

'You ungrateful little wretch!' she shouted at the girl. 'You've brought trouble to us, after Gran's kindness in taking you in. And you...' She turned a scathing glance at the man. 'You're a scoundrel, mister. Get out now!'

'Now look, kid,' the man said evenly. 'I know you're mad, but your grandmother needs help. Run for the doctor while I take her up to her bedroom. Trudy can help me.' He jerked his head at her. 'Go on, mun! Don't just stand there gawping.'

Lynnys stood there perplexed, staring from one to the other, but her grandmother's ashen face soon decided her. Perhaps it was a trick to get her out of the way, but she could not take a chance. Gran looked really ill.

'I'm willing to pay the doctor's fee,' the man said, as though he believe that was what was keeping her from going.

Lynnys half-turned to the door and then hesitated. 'I'll hunt you down, mister, if you're responsible for my Gran being hurt,' she told him darkly. 'You'd better be here when I get back.'

The man continued up the staircase with his frail-looking burden. There was a crooked grin on his good-looking face. 'I'll be here, kid, don't you worry.'

Lynnys returned as soon as she could with a reluctant doctor in tow.

'My fee will be a guinea,' he remarked as they approached Cwmavon Terrace. 'Having to come out at this time of an evening is an inconvenience. I'd arranged to take my wife to the theatre.'

Lynnys gritted her teeth. If he were visiting one of those posh houses in Walter Road with a fat fee to look forward too, he would not be so averse.

She pushed open the front door expecting to see no one, but surprisingly, the tall man was still there.

'Your patient is upstairs in the front bedroom, Doc,' he said quickly as the doctor entered. 'She's awake now, but she doesn't look too good.'

The doctor grunted, giving the man a speculative glance as he started to climb the stairs,

99

Lynnys right behind him. She hesitated, leaning over the banister and glowered at the tall man.

'I'm surprised you're still here,' she said pithily. 'I thought you'd have hopped it when the coast was clear.'

'Scoundrel I may be, kid, but I'm also a man of my word.'

The doctor had already gone into the front bedroom when Lynnys reached the small landing, and she was anxious to follow him, desperate to know how her grandmother was, but at that moment Trudy came out of the back bedroom with her hat and coat on.

Lynnys' hackles rose at the sight of the girl's pert face.

'Where do you think you're going, miss?' she snapped at Trudy. She could not help blaming the girl for what had happened to her grandmother.

'I'm buggering off for the moment,' Trudy answered tersely. 'I can't stand sick people, makes my stomach turn.'

'You'll get back in our room and stay there,' Lynnys said harshly. 'I know what you've been doing. You should be ashamed, too, in your condition.'

'It's my business!'

'Not while all the neighbours are talking about us,' Lynnys blurted. She was ashamed that they were the talk of the street because of Trudy. 'Gran was sorry for you, and this is the way you repay her by bringing men to our home. It's got to stop right this minute.'

'You can't order me about,' Trudy retorted, trying to push past to get down the stairs. 'I'll do as I like, see who I like.'

Lynnys lost her temper and reaching forward slapped Trudy across the face with her open palm. She wasn't given to violence, but what Trudy had done was unforgivable.

'Now, get back into your room and stay there!'

Trudy stared at her wide-eyed, speechless for once, holding her hand to her slapped cheek.

'You'll do as you're told and behave decently or you'll get out,' Lynnys went on firmly. 'If you go out again tonight you'll come home to find the door locked and your things on the pavement. It's up to you, Trudy.'

With that Lynnys turned and went into the front bedroom. She was relieved to see her grandmother was now sitting on the edge of the bed, although she looked a shrunken shadow of herself. The doctor was putting his stethoscope back in his bag.

'What is it, Doctor? Is Gran all right?'

'Mrs Daniels has had a heart attack,' the doctor said matter-of-factly.

'What? Oh, Gran!'

'I'm all right, Lynnys, love,' Phoebe said. But she did not sound at all right, and Lynnys hurried to her, and sitting on the bed next to her, put an arm around her shoulders.

'A heart attack! Oh, this is awful.'

'I'll survive, *bach*. I'm a tough old bird.'

The doctor gave a little cough and when Lynnys glanced at him he inclined his head, indicating that he wanted to have a private word with her.

'Lie down, Gran, and I'll bring you a cup of tea,' Lynnys said gently. 'You must rest.'

She helped Phoebe on to the bed and then

101

followed the doctor down the stairs again. The tall man came out of the living room and looked expectantly at the doctor.

'Well, Doc?'

'Your mother is not a well woman, I'm sorry to tell you, Mr Daniels.'

'She's not *his* mother!' Lynnys exploded. 'I don't even know his name.'

The doctor looked confused and Lynnys wished she had not spoken. She could hardly explain the reason for the man being there.

'My name is Josh Rowlands,' the stranger said. 'Now, Doc, what's wrong with the old duck?'

'She has a heart condition,' he said. 'Had it for some time by the sound of it. This attack was comparatively mild, but things can only get worse in my opinion. She needs complete rest.'

'Oh! No!' Lynnys put her hand to her mouth in distress. 'She's not going to die, is she?' She couldn't bear to lose Gran.

The doctor inclined his head. 'Well, the prognosis is not good.'

'What does that mean?'

'It means she could have another massive attack at any time.' The doctor shook his head. 'There's little can be done for her.' He coughed again. 'That'll be three guineas.'

Lynnys stared. 'You said one guinea earlier.'

'Three guineas.'

'That's steep, Doc.'

The doctor gave Josh Rowlands' three-piece suit an assessing glance. 'You look as though you can afford it.'

Josh Rowlands handed over the fee. 'You'll be

102

on tap in case you're needed again, Doc?' There was a hard quality to his voice that made it sound like a demand rather than an enquiry.

'I'm "on tap" as you put it, Mr Rowlands, as long as my fee is met. Now, good evening to you.'

As the doctor left Lynnys hurried to the kitchen to make the tea for Gran. Josh Rowlands followed her in.

'What are you hanging about for?' Lynnys spoke sharply to him. 'You've paid your debt to Gran. There's nothing more here for you. You'll see no more of Trudy.'

She wondered vaguely if Trudy had gone out after all. She was willing to make good her threat if she had. She had Gran to think of now, for it was obvious her grandmother was in need of care and could never work again.

'I'm not interested in Trudy,' Josh Rowlands said. He leaned against the kitchen sink as she fussed with lighting the gas ring standing on the draining board. 'I am interested in you, though.'

'How dare you!' Lynnys flared at him. 'What do you think I am? I'm not Trudy's sort.'

He laughed. 'Well, I can see that. Trudy was right about the muddy boots and dirty fingernails.'

Lynnys glanced at her hands. She had not had a chance to wash since she had come home from work so of course she looked grubby.

'At least it's good honest decent dirt,' she replied proudly as she poured boiling water over the tea leaves in a brown earthenware pot. 'I've nothing to be ashamed of.'

He laughed again but said nothing.

Aware that he was watching, she self-consciously rinsed her hands under the tap, and drying them, proceeded to cut a slice of bread, wondering why he was still hanging about. With a long-handled toasting fork she held the bread over the flame of the gas ring. Gran had not eaten, so she must be famished.

'I don't suppose there's a cup of tea for me in that pot, is there?' he said. 'I haven't eaten since this morning.'

She was uncertain. 'Well, I suppose so.' She buttered the toast. 'You'll have to help yourself. I'm going up to Gran.'

She was some time upstairs making Gran comfortable and felt sure he would have gone, but when she came down again he was sitting at the kitchen table, cup and saucer in front of him and a plate with a half eaten piece of toast.

Lynnys tightened her lips. He was making himself at home and she didn't like it, but he had paid the doctor, so perhaps she should give him a little leeway.

'Aren't you going to have a cup?' he asked.

She was parched for a cup of tea, but it did not seem right to sit down at the table with him as though he was a welcome guest. But she poured herself a cup and then stood near the draining board to drink it, watching him carefully.

He was good-looking and leanly built, but strong judging by the width of his shoulders; well preserved for a man of his age, she thought. She had often imagined her father must have looked like this; handsome and smart. But this man, of course, was a scoundrel, unlike her father.

'Is your father alive?' he asked.

Lynnys flashed him a look, feeling that he had read her mind.

'No, my parents died of the cholera when I was very small,' she said. 'I never knew them. All I have is Gran.'

He raised his brows. 'So your mother is dead, too?' His expression was thoughtful, almost calculating suddenly and it made her even more uneasy at his continued presence.

'Why are you asking me all these questions? My life is none of your concern,' Lynnys said sharply. 'I want you to leave now.'

'Okay.' He rose, putting his cup, saucer and plate on the draining board. 'You have a lovely speaking voice,' he remarked, surprising her. 'Do you sing?'

Lynnys was astonished. 'Why, yes, I love to sing. I've always wanted to go on the sta...' She paused, realising he had a remarkable way of charming someone, making them forget to be angry with him. 'Please go now, Mr Rowlands. I have to take care of my grandmother.'

He nodded and turned towards the passage.

'Don't expect to see Trudy again,' she said in a warning voice.

'Okay, kid.'

He walked through the door and down the passage. Lynnys followed, calling after him. 'Mr Rowlands!'

He turned and looked at her.

Lynnys swallowed. 'Thanks for paying the doctor.'

He shrugged. 'Least I could do.' He grinned. 'So long for now, kid.'

7

It was a short walk from Cwmavon Terrace to Cambrian Place and he could have done it in less than ten minutes, but passing the Cross Keys Inn, Josh decided to stop for a pint of best bitter and give careful thought to what he was about to do.

Connie needed to know about her mother and he needed to learn all he could about Bernie Pomfrey. For the moment Josh had money but knew it would not go far and wasn't enough to give him the life he wanted. He had been living easy in London but had no connections in Swansea these days and needed to make some or he would soon be on Queer Street.

Knowing Bernie as he did, Josh reckoned the man had made good from the proceeds of the robbery they had done together all those years ago, and Josh intended to put the squeeze on him. Whatever Bernie was doing these days, it was bound to be profitable and Josh was determined to get a share of it.

Finishing his drink he set off for the Pleasure Palace intent on prising the truth out of Connie. As he entered the perfumed reception hall of the house he saw Herb Collins, accompanied by another hard-faced man who he assumed was a bouncer. Herb was obviously prepared for trouble, and Josh wondered what Herb was afraid of.

'Evening, Josh,' Herb greeted him genially enough.

Josh nodded and handed over his entrance fee, five guineas. It was pricey, but then it was a good house.

'Connie about?' Josh asked.

Immediately Herb's expression lost its geniality.

'Connie's not one of the girls, Rowlands,' he said harshly. 'They're in the parlour. Take your pick.'

'It's private, Herb. All I want is a word with her.'

'What could be private between you and her? It's been years since you knew each other.'

'I've passed the time of day once or twice lately,' Josh said. 'It's about her mother...'

'Her what?'

Josh closed his mouth. It looked like Connie kept her private life secret, and that did not surprise him if Bernie Pomfrey was involved.

'Trust me, Herb.'

'Why the hell should I?'

'It's something she's got to know about her family. You can be there, too, when I talk to her, if Connie allows it.'

Herb looked undecided for a moment, and then jerked his thumb at the bouncer. 'Get Fred in here with you,' he said to the man. 'I want two men on the door at all times.'

Herb jerked his head at Josh. 'It's early yet for trade, so Connie's still in her sitting room. Come on.'

They walked down the passage together.

'Expecting a Boer invasion, Herb?'

Herb grunted. 'Nothing we can't handle,' he answered in an off-handed manner. 'A young local crook, Charlie Pendle would like to close us down.'

'Pendle? Never heard of him.'

'After your time. Like I said, we can deal with him.'

'We? Who really runs this house, Herb?'

Herb was silent, giving him a dismissive look before knocking on a door nearby and walking straight in.

Connie sat on a chair near the fireplace, crochet work in her hands. She was as lovely as ever and instantly Josh saw the likeness with the feisty girl in the house in Cwmavon Terrace. The kid was Connie's daughter all right.

She looked up in surprise when they entered. 'Connie, Josh Rowlands here wants a private word with you, so he says,' Herb began. 'And he'd better make it quick because we'll be busy this evening.'

'We won't keep you, Herb,' Josh said pointedly.

The other man glared at him. 'I'm staying.'

'Connie may want this to remain confidential.'

She stood up, putting the crochet work on the arm of the chair. 'What's going on?'

'It's about Phoebe,' Josh said. 'And her grand-daughter.'

Immediately Connie's face turned deathly pale, and she reached for the arm of the chair to sit again. 'What did you say?'

'Maybe Herb had better leave us.'

'Now look here, Rowlands,' Herb stormed. 'I've had about enough of you.'

'What about Phoebe?' Connie asked a tremor in her voice, her gaze fixed on his face. 'What do you know about her? How do you know her?'

'She's been taken ill,' he said. 'Heart attack. I was at the house when it happened.'

'What?' She stood up quickly, hands clasped to her breast. 'Lynnys...'

'Is that the kid's name? She's all right. She's a brick. A credit to you.'

She ran her tongue quickly across her lips and glanced apprehensively at Herb, who was staring from one to the other, totally baffled.

'Herb, I want to talk to Josh alone,' she said in a shaky voice. 'I'll come into the parlour when we've finished.'

'Connie, I don't want...'

'Please, Herb!'

With a thunderous glance at Josh, Herb left the room. Josh wondered if he was standing outside the door, trying to listen.

'How is my mother? Is she in hospital?'

'No, I called a doctor to her. He said her heart was bad, had been for a long time. The old duck looks pretty rough, but she's doing all right for the moment.'

Connie put a hand to her forehead. 'Thank the Lord for that, at least.' She raised her head and gave him a hostile stare. 'How do you know about my mother and Lynnys? What were you doing at my mother's home?'

'You made an enemy of that kid, Trudy,' Josh said and sat on a sofa nearby, crossing one leg over the other. 'I was on my way here earlier when she picked me up in Castle Street, and took me back to Cwmavon Terrace. Told me all about you and Phoebe.'

'Oh my God! The ungrateful little bitch.'

'Ungrateful?' Josh inclined his head. 'She says you kicked her out in jealousy because some bloke named Bernie was too fond of her. That wouldn't be Bernie Pomfrey, would it?'

Connie's gaze slid away from his. 'Our clientele is confidential, Josh, you should know that. Prominent men in the town can't have their names linked to us.' She gazed back at him defiantly. 'I wasn't responsible for kicking her out. She got herself up the spout.'

'What?' He should have guessed as much.

'Her regular client demanded that she be turned out.'

'Nice bloke! And you and Herb went along with his demands?'

Connie remained silent. Josh studied her. She was upset at the news of her mother, of course, but there was something else, something she was holding back.

'He must be an important punter, eh?' he went on.

Connie shrugged. 'We had no choice, but I took her to Phoebe's. I knew she'd take care of her.' She clasped her hands tightly before her and turned away. 'And this is the way she repays me by turning my mother's house into a brothel. Not to mention betraying me.'

'Maybe it was a good thing she did, under the circumstances.'

She whirled to face him. 'Josh, you're not going to tell anyone, are you? Herb doesn't know. I

110

don't want anyone else finding out, either.'

'You mean like Bernie Pomfrey. He's Lynnys' father, isn't he?'

Connie clapped her hand to her mouth. 'No! It's not true. Her father is dead and gone.'

'Somehow, I don't believe you, Connie.'

'What're you going to do?'

'Nothing, for the moment.' He shrugged. 'None of my business, is it? But I am interested in Bernie Pomfrey. He was Trudy's punter, wasn't he; her sole punter, if he's still as paranoid as I remember him to be.'

Connie hesitated and then nodded wordlessly.

'Bernie's got a lot of pull around here, hasn't he? I wonder why?'

'He's influential; a respectable business man in the town. He's introduced several prominent men as well. We don't want to lose his custom or goodwill.'

He stared at her white face. She was still lying, but he did not want to upset her further by forcing the issue.

'What will you do about the kid?' he asked.

Connie put her fingers to her mouth, obviously worried. 'I don't know. I've been supporting them, and I want to keep on doing that. She needs me, they both do, but it is going to be difficult now Phoebe is laid up. I can't make myself known to Lynnys.'

'Why not?'

'She thinks I'm dead, and besides I'm ashamed for her to know the truth about me.' She sat down, and Josh could see she was on the verge of tears. 'With Mam unable to work, Lynnys will find

111

money tight. And if the worst should happen...'

'Whatever work your daughter is doing now she's wasted in it.' Josh leaned forward. 'I could get her a job as a singer. She wants to go on the stage.'

Connie snapped an angry glance at him. 'How do you know that?'

'She told me.'

She sprang to her feet. 'You stay away from my daughter, Josh Rowlands. I know what you're after.'

'Don't bust your corsets, Connie.' He shook his head. 'I'm not interested in her that way.'

'Being a tart doesn't make me a fool, Josh!' Connie flared. 'You're just like any other man, but I'm warning you. I won't be responsible for my actions if you touch her.'

He shook his head. 'My interest in her is business not pleasure. Lynnys has wonderful looks.' He almost added, in spite of having Bernie Pomfrey for a father, but resisted, not wanting to bait her. 'If she's got talent to match her looks she could make it big on the halls or in cabaret.'

'I don't want that kind of life for her. It can only lead to unhappiness. The stage is just a step away from the streets.'

'Not necessarily; not with good management, Connie. It's her life, so it has to be her choice,' Josh said reasonably. 'But,' he added, 'I wouldn't do anything of which you didn't approve.'

'Josh, she's my daughter,' Connie said stubbornly. 'I know what's best for her.'

'Muddy boots and dirty fingernails.'

'What?' She frowned at him distractedly.

'Nothing.' He stood up. 'Let's talk again when you've had time to consider.'

'Swear to me you'll tell no one, Josh.'

He smiled. 'My lips are sealed.'

They left the room together and went along the passage to the parlour. Herb gave them both hard enquiring glances but, ignoring him, Connie went straight away to sit at the piano and began to play. Josh admired her aura of calm, for he realised she must be churned up inside.

With Herb's gaze on him he had more sense than to follow Connie. Instead he went to stand before the fireplace, helping himself to a cigar from the silver box there. Immediately, a pretty young girl was at his side with a lighted match. He smiled into her eyes as she lit the cigar for him.

'I'm Dilys,' she said.

'Hello, Dilys,' he answered. 'Lead the way, my pretty.'

They left the parlour to go upstairs. He admired the curve of her hip as he followed her up the staircase to go to a room on the first floor. It was time to forget everything else for the next hour; past injustices as well as future hopes, and concentrate solely on pleasure.

Connie played tune after tune without knowing what she was playing. Mam was sick and in need of her, but how could she do anything without destroying Lynnys' innocence, even her life?

She could not call at Cwmavon Terrace to see Lynnys without revealing more than she wanted to. She needed an intermediary but that would

113

mean confiding in someone, and there was no one she would trust. Josh already knew the truth or thought he did. Maybe it could be done through him, but how far could she really trust him?

'Are you all right, Connie?' Herb was at her side.

She smiled up at him. Herb would never hurt her, she knew that, but she could not be too careful where Lynnys was concerned. Herb and Bernie had too close an association, and the more people who knew, the more chance of Bernie finding out.

'I'm quite all right,' she said as lightly as she could.

'What did Rowlands want? What's this about your mother?'

'Fishing, he was,' Connie answered. 'But he had the wrong end of the stick. My mother died years ago.'

'If he bothers you again let me know,' Herb said. 'I'll deal with him.'

'I don't need you to nursemaid me, Herb,' Connie retorted. There was no one else in the parlour, all the girls having gone to entertain their clients in private. She got up from the piano.

'I may be seeing more of Josh Rowlands in future, but that's my business.'

'Connie!' Herb looked startled at her words and sharp tone. 'Why him? You know how I feel about you. I'll do anything for you, anything.'

She was sorry she had spoken so harshly but sometimes his intense feeling for her felt like a smothering blanket. 'I'm going to my sitting

114

room now. Call me if there's trouble or if any of the girls need me.'

She left him standing there. She regretted hurting him, but she had nothing to give him.

Josh wandered down the main staircase. It was almost midnight; the reception rooms below were silent of music and girls' laughter. He could have stayed with Dilys longer. Young as she was, she was an obliging girl and skilful and he felt he had had his money's worth. Now it was time for business and the real reason he had visited the house.

The bouncer was still at his post in the wide reception hall.

'Herb about?'

'In the office,' the man said. 'But he doesn't like visitors at this time of night.'

'He'll see me.'

The man paused as though he would argue and then shrugged. Josh knew he was safe. It was more than the bouncer's job's worth to manhandle a legitimate customer of the house.

Josh flipped the man a half-crown just to keep him sweet.

'Thanks, Mr Rowlands. Second door on the right.'

The door stood open. Herb was sitting back in his chair smoking a cigarette, his feet resting on the desk. He did not appear to be busy. There was a tense but pensive expression on his boxer's face, and Josh read discontent in it.

'Busy night, Herb?' Josh began as he strolled in.

'It's late, Rowlands,' Herb said harshly taking his feet off the desk. 'You've had your fun, now it's time to go.'

Josh took a seat in spite of the other man's hostility.

'Connie's a handsome woman and I don't blame you for being protective of her...'

Herb rose abruptly to his feet, almost knocking his chair over. 'Get out, Rowlands!'

'Easy!' Josh said calmly, remaining seated. 'I'm not your enemy, Herb. I've no interest in Connie, but someone else might have.'

Herb resumed his seat. 'What do you mean? What have you heard?'

'Rumour,' Josh said evasively. 'Nothing specific.'

He had promised Connie to keep quiet about Bernie being Lynnys' father, and he would, unless it suited his purpose to do otherwise. It struck him that Herb could be tipped over the edge if he discovered Bernie's bad treatment of Connie in the past. But it was too soon to play such an important card.

'I hear Bernie Pomfrey has been making trouble here,' Josh went on conversationally. 'Throwing his weight about over one of the girls he knocked up. His custom can't be that important. Or maybe he's more than a client, eh? Maybe owns the place?'

Herb's gaze at him was wary, but Josh knew he had hit on the truth. 'Maybe yes, maybe no.'

Discontent was in Herb's eyes again. He wanted to talk about Bernie, Josh could see that. He needed encouragement.

'Trying to live two lives, I suppose? Bernie will never change,' Josh went on. 'Living high off the hog, but sucking at its underbelly at the same time. Making sure he has the best, never mind about anyone else. He'll come unstuck one day.'

Herb nodded. 'He will if Charlie Pendle gets the goods on him.'

'He's in Pendle's way, then?'

'There could be trouble soon.'

'What else is Bernie into?'

Herb relaxed back in his chair. 'He's got a legitimate business in Castle Street, gentlemen's outfitters, doing very well.' He seemed ready and eager to talk now. 'What with that and proceeds from this place Bernie's making a packet. But he plays his cards close to his chest, does Bernie. He's clever and he can be a nasty bugger when the mood takes him.'

Josh said nothing. He had seen Bernie in action years ago, and a man had died. He had got away with it, and now no one knew about Bernie's past except Josh.

'He's buying up property all over the town like it was going out of style,' Herb went on. There was envy in his voice. 'He's got rich posh friends who wouldn't touch him with a barge pole if they knew about this place. He covers his tracks well though. That's why Pendle hasn't got on to him – yet.'

Josh smiled. 'He should make you a partner, Herb,' he said cunningly. 'That's what I'd do if I was in Bernie's place.'

Herb's lips tightened. 'I keep this place running smooth, but I'm no more than a doorman to him.' He got up abruptly from his chair and began to stride about. 'Why the hell do I put up with it?'

Josh watched him for a moment. 'Connie?' he suggested.

Herb paused in his stride. 'You're too sharp for your own good, Rowlands,' he said, his mood changing again. 'Goodnight!'

Josh got up, smiling. He had what he came for.

Lynnys was up early the next morning, bringing her grandmother a cup of tea and was ready to see to her other needs.

'Good morning, Gran,' Lynnys greeted, helping the older woman to get into a sitting position in bed and propping her up with pillows. 'How are you feeling this morning?'

Phoebe took the cup of tea eagerly. 'I feel better, thanks.' But she sounded weak. 'What time is it, Lynnys, *bach*? Oh! I'm late for work.'

Lynnys sat on the bed, taking Phoebe's hand and squeezing it gently. 'Gran, you can't go to work any more. The doctor said you're bad.'

'Tsk! What do doctors know, and besides, it's all right for him to say that. He won't be the one to starve when there's no money coming in.'

'Now, Gran, be sensible. If you push yourself something could happen.' Lynnys smiled into her grandmother's eyes. 'What would I do without you?'

'But, *cariad*, how are we going to manage?'

'We will, and what's more, that lazy good-for-nothing Trudy has got to do her share. She must find work.'

'Oh!' Phoebe leaned back on the pillows, the cup and saucer rattling in her hand. 'Is that little trollop still under this roof? I should never have promised...'

'Who did you promise, Gran?' Lynnys asked

118

quickly, seeing how upset Phoebe was. 'They can't hold you to that now. Tell me who it is and I'll have a word with them if you like.'

Phoebe shook her head. 'No, *bach*, it's too late.'

'Don't worry about Trudy,' Lynnys said firmly. 'I think she'll behave herself in future. I warned her she'll be booted out, promise or no promise.'

Lynnys made some porridge for Gran's breakfast, ate her own and then went up to the bedroom she shared with Trudy, walking straight in.

'Get up now if you want breakfast, Trudy,' Lynnys said. 'I'll be off to work in a minute.'

'Go away!' Trudy put a pillow over her head.

Lynnys picked up the hairbrush from the dressing table and began brushing her hair. 'I meant what I said yesterday,' she warned the other girl. 'You'll behave decently from now on, or out you go.'

Trudy mumbled from under the pillow, 'Connie wouldn't like that.'

'What?'

Trudy removed the pillow from her face and sat up, her glance wary. 'Never mind. I can't sit around here all day doing nothing.'

'Exactly,' Lynnys said. 'You'll have to find work. With Gran laid up we need as much money as we can earn.'

'Huh! I could earn plenty if you'll let me do what I do best,' Trudy blurted. 'Pots of money.'

'Tainted money!' Lynnys flared. 'Horrible! How can you lower yourself, Trudy? Have you no shame?'

'It was a good life,' Trudy declared defensively. 'Soft bed where I could sleep all day, lovely

119

clothes, plenty to eat, presents.'

Lynnys wrinkled her nose in disgust. 'Well that's over!' she said positively. 'I'll ask about and see what's going. There might be a job in the market.'

'Muddy boots and dirty fingernails! No thanks!'

'Get up!' Lynnys demanded, thoroughly annoyed at the remark, remembering where she had heard it recently. 'Make yourself useful here for the time being, looking after Gran.' She gave the other girl a stern glance. 'No more men, Trudy, understand me?'

Trudy did not answer but stuck her nose in the air. Lynnys gave her one more impatient glance and then hurried away. She could waste no more time on the girl. She had to get to work. She could not afford to lose her job now.

Josh ate luncheon in a small Italian café in Castle Street a few doors down from the gentlemen's outfitters, Pomfrey and Payne.

Sitting at a table near the window Josh looked across the busy street at the tall graceful building of light grey stone opposite. The first floor displayed the great arched windows of the Baltic Lounge, an exclusive restaurant where only the very well-to-do could afford to dine. If he played his cards right with Bernie Pomfrey today he could be in the money this time next week, and then all doors would be open to him. He would be a frequent diner not only at the Baltic Lounge but all fashionable places in the town.

With a sigh he signalled for the bill. It was brought by a harassed-looking waitress, loose locks dangling from underneath her cotton cap. Josh left a generous tip. After all, his life was taking a turn for the good.

Josh stood on the pavement looking in the window of the outfitters for a few moments before going inside. There were several assistants, some already with customers. An older, dapper little man came forward, bowing from the hip in an old-fashioned manner.

'Good afternoon, sir. And what would sir like to see? Grey pinstripe is proving very popular this season, sir.'

'I want to see Mr Pomfrey.'

The man hesitated. 'I take it you mean Major Pomfrey.' He cleared his throat as though embarrassed. 'Major Pomfrey is the proprietor, sir. He does not see customers personally.'

Josh smiled. Major Pomfrey! Bernie was up to his old tricks, passing himself off as something he wasn't.

'He'll see me. Tell him Josh Rowlands would like a word.'

The man still hesitated, as though the request baffled him.

'Now, if you please,' Josh said in a harder voice. 'It's business.'

'Very well, sir.'

He scuttled off but was back within minutes. 'This way, sir.'

Josh followed him to an office at the back of the shop where he knocked on the door and entered.

'Mr Rowlands, Major.'

'All right! I don't want to be disturbed for the next half hour, Dawson. Now get out.'

'Yes, Major Pomfrey, sir.'

Josh strolled into the room. Bernie Pomfrey was on his feet but still behind his desk, his face suffused darkly with anger. He had changed somewhat over the years, Josh saw. He still stood erect; never powerfully built, a moustache and a decided paunch were added. Easy living had made him soft physically, but not psychologically, Josh thought, judging by the killing expression on his face.

'What the hell do you want, Rowlands?'

Josh chuckled. 'Not very friendly towards an old pal. But friendship was never your strong point, was it, Bernie?'

'I don't owe you a damn thing!'

'What makes you think I'm after anything?'

'I know you, Rowlands.'

Josh sat on a bentwood chair nearby without being asked; took off his homburg and gloves, placing them on his lap and rested his cane against the wall.

'I thought we could talk over old times, Bernie. See anything of Dai these days?'

'He kicked the bucket. How did you find me?'

'Asked around. This shop has a good reputation, so I'm told, and you look prosperous, Bernie.'

Bernie stared at him for a long moment and then sat down.

'I'm doing all right. And before you ask, Rowlands, this is a legitimate business.'

'I'm sure it is.'

'Look, Josh, what is it you want?' Bernie was trying to sound reasonable but Josh knew him better.

122

'You know how it is, Bernie.' Josh gave a shrug. 'I'm down from the Smoke for good, and I'm looking for a good connection in Swansea. I thought you might help an old buddy.'

The muscles around Bernie's mouth tightened. 'Like I said, Josh, I don't owe you a bean. If you'd used your head all those years ago you'd be sitting pretty now.' He shook his head. 'But no, not you. Cheap women were always your downfall.'

Josh laughed. 'My women were never cheap, Bernie, that was the problem.'

'I can't help you.'

'You won't, you mean.'

Bernie gave a sneer. 'Why the hell should I?'

'Maybe to stay out of prison.'

Bernie was on his feet in a flash. 'What?'

Josh examined his fingernails calmly. 'You can bet the police are still interested in learning who killed that guard at the bonded warehouse. Murder is never forgotten.'

Bernie leaned forward, palms down on the desk top. He looked mean. 'Now wait a minute!' he exclaimed angrily. 'You were implicated in that up to your neck. You can't inform on me without implicating yourself.'

'I didn't kill anyone.'

'You were there. That makes you culpable in the eyes of the law.'

'You didn't have to knife the man, Bernie,' Josh said, angry himself now. 'He'd have been no match for the three of us. We could have tied him up and left him.'

That killing was something he had bitterly

regretted letting happen all his life. The murder was what had sent the police into a frenzy of activity all over town. He could not afford to be questioned, not even routinely, so he'd made a run for it, leaving behind... Josh quenched the memory. He had not thought of her in years.

'He saw our faces,' Bernie said, interrupting his musing.

'So it was deliberate.'

Bernie sat down. 'What if it was? It was my ... our one big chance.'

'It was a hanging job then, Bernie, and it still is.'

'Dai is dead and gone, so you're the only one who knows, Josh,' Bernie said scornfully. 'I'd be careful if I were you. Swansea is getting to be a dangerous place, accidents happen.'

Josh pursed his lips. 'Funny you should say that. Herb Collins was telling me about a young thug in town, Charlie Pendle. They speak his name in whispers.'

Bernie's face went a shade paler. 'What's that got to do with me?'

'Well, it's like this, Bernie. I know you own the Pleasure Palace. No, no, don't bother denying it! I want a share of the profits; a partnership, fifty per cent, maybe.'

Bernie was staring at him open-mouthed.

'Herb's all right as far as he goes,' Josh went on confidently. 'But the place needs an owner on the premises, someone who's not afraid to show his face, if you get my meaning.'

Bernie continued to stare.

'It makes sense, Bernie,' Josh continued. 'With

124

Charlie Pendle stepping up trouble the place needs someone who's not afraid to mix it.'

'No! Go to hell!'

'I'm sorry to hear you say that, Bernie.' Josh frowned in regret. 'Maybe informing on you to the police would be dicey for me, but a whisper in Pendle's ear about your connection with the Pleasure Palace would be a different matter. Respectability makes you vulnerable, Bernie.'

'You swine!' Bernie looked as though he would have an epileptic fit. 'I should've knifed you as well back at the warehouse. I did consider it.'

Josh chuckled. 'I know you did. Me and Dai were waiting for you to make your move, and we'd have done you up good if you had.' Josh straightened his face, remembering. 'You were greedy then, Bernie, and you still are.'

'Fifteen per cent.'

'Don't be stupid, Bernie.' Josh was scornful. 'I've got you over a barrel and you know it.'

'Damn you!'

'There's plenty for everyone,' Josh said pleasantly. 'You'll have fifty per cent of the house, plus the takings from this shop. What more do you want?'

'I want to see you dead, Josh.'

Josh gazed at the other man's livid face and knew that was a real threat. But he had always lived dangerously. He did not see any reason to change.

'You'd better let Herb know the situation straight away,' Josh said in a tone of utter confidence. 'Oh, and another thing. I get my pick of the girls, okay?'

Bernie swallowed hard and Josh could see he was struggling with his anger, yet knowing he was beaten.

'All right,' Bernie said at last. 'But keep your hands off *my* girl.'

'Who is she?'

'I haven't secured her yet, but I will soon.'

Josh rose from his chair, donning his hat and taking up his cane. 'I want something on account, say, fifty quid, for now.'

'Fifty! That's crazy!'

'I need some new clothes, a couple of suits.'

'That suit you're wearing looks good stuff to me.'

'Yes, but it's my only suit. I must have a dress suit for business.' Josh smiled. 'A co-proprietor at a swell house like the Pleasure Palace should look up to the mark. Even Herb wears a dress suit to impress the clients, I notice.'

'Fifty is out of the question, Josh. I don't carry that kind of money,' Bernie said harshly. 'The house doesn't make that much anyway. Profits are low after wages for the men and keep for the girls.' He hesitated. 'I can't manage more than fifteen.'

'Don't try to outsmart me, Bernie,' Josh said grimly. 'You could never do that in the old days.' Josh held out his hand, palm up. 'Pay up.'

Bernie went to the safe and with his back to Josh, opened it, and then turned with a wad of fivers in his hand. The look on his face told Josh his old associate was incensed with rage as he handed them over.

'I'd shake hands on the deal, Bernie,' Josh said,

pocketing the money. 'But I don't trust you with my fingers. You might bite them off.'

'The feeling's mutual, Josh,' Bernie answered, and there was hatred in his eyes and also a calculating look.

Josh stared at him for a moment, knowing cogs were already busy in Bernie's brain, working out a way to be rid of him. He would have to have eyes in the back of his head from now on.

8

'Get a move on, Lynnys,' Mrs Phillips said sharply. 'You've got two more deliveries to make before the market closes. I can't afford to have my customers dissatisfied.'

Lynnys had just got back with the handcart, having trundled it all the way to Brynmill with a heavy load of farm produce, and back again. It was hard going in this warm weather, and her back was aching, not to mention her feet sore. And now there were two more to do, all before half past eight, when the market closed its gates.

'I haven't eaten yet, Mrs Phillips,' Lynnys reminded her.

'Eat on your own time,' her employer said sternly. 'After you finish work.'

Lynnys stretched her back, trying to ease the persistent ache.

'Where next then, Mrs Phillips?'

'The last two orders are in the Uplands, so you can carry them together. One for Dr Howells in Walter Road, and the other for Mrs Moffat in Ffynonne Crescent. Now be quick!'

Lynnys pushed the handcart through the town, her head held high, ignoring the snooty glances of other girls and women. She knew her face was smudged with dirt and her boots dusty, but she was as good as them any day. Up Craddock Street and Mansel Street, and then the gentle incline of

Walter Road. Although the sun was lower in the sky, it was still warm and the going hard. She called at Dr Howells first, pushing the handcart around to the back entrance, and knocked on the back door.

As usual her knock was answered by her friend Elvi, looking so professional in her dark blue cambric dress and a white cap.

'Hello, Elvi,' Lynnys greeted. 'Here's the doctor's vegetable order.'

Elvi smiled at her in obvious delight. 'Lynnys, I was just thinking about you, wondering if we could have a little picnic at Mumbles next Sunday. We could catch the Mumbles Train.'

'That's a lovely idea,' Lynnys agreed brightly. 'But I'll have to make sure Gran is all right first.'

'Of course,' Elvi said and then darted forward. 'Oh, let me give you a hand with that load, Lynnys. Those vegetable sacks look heavy.'

Lynnys was glad of the help. 'Only one more load to go,' she told Elvi. 'Up Ffynonne Crescent, Mrs Moffat.' Lynnys glanced at the several sacks. 'Looks like she's bought enough to feed a regiment.'

Elvi giggled and Lynnys joined in.

'Mrs Moffat is cooking for a big dinner party,' Elvi told her. 'Her employers' wedding anniversary or something. Dr Howells and his wife are invited. I heard him complain to her that he didn't want to go. I wouldn't turn down a free dinner, would you?'

Lynnys laughed at the eager look in the other girl's face.

'No fear! Well, I'd better be off. See you Sunday, Elvi. I'm looking forward to it.'

'Wait a minute. Have a glass...' Elvi caught at Lynnys' bare arm, and then jumped back, a startled look on her face.

'What's the matter,' Lynnys asked in surprise. 'You look as though you've seen a ghost.'

Elvi's face whitened even more. 'What? No, I was just going to ask if you'd like a glass of lime cordial before you go. There's a jug in the larder.'

The other girl hurried away to fetch it without waiting for a reply leaving Lynnys mystified. She had never seen such a frightened look on her friend's face before and was concerned.

When Elvi returned with the jug she poured a good measure of the cordial into a tumbler. Lynnys saw her hand was shaking visibly, and wondered again what on earth the matter was.

'Are you all right, Elvi?'

Elvi swallowed hard. 'Yes. I'm tired I expect.'

Lynnys drank her cordial gratefully. 'You won't get into trouble giving me this, will you?'

Elvi shook her head and Lynnys prepared to leave, but Elvi seemed agitated, hovering at her elbow.

'Lynnys, you said you're an orphan, with only your grandmother,' she said hesitantly and then shook her head. 'It isn't right, you know. You're not an orphan.'

'What?' Lynnys stared at her, feeling more astonishment than she had in her life. 'Elvi, what are you talking about? Of course my parents are dead. They died when I was little.'

Elvi shook her head again, looking apprehensive. 'Your mother is alive and so is your father.'

130

She swallowed. 'Don't ask me how I know.'

Lynnys felt a little disappointed and somewhat annoyed that Elvi, her friend, would talk such rubbish.

'If this is a joke, Elvi,' she said severely, 'it's not funny.'

Elvi quickly put her knuckles to her mouth. 'Oh, please, don't be cross, Lynnys. Forget I said anything. I shouldn't have mentioned it. But the message seemed so important.'

'Message?'

'Oh, dear!'

Elvi was staring at her in alarm. Since their friendship began Lynnys had learned that there was no spite or malice in Elvi, who had the sweetest nature, and she became more puzzled than annoyed at the girl's strange outburst now.

'Don't tell anyone, will you,' Elvi went on earnestly when Lynnys did not speak. 'If my mother ever found out...'

Lynnys shook her head, utterly bewildered. 'Of course I won't, Elvi. It's our little secret.'

'Oh, thank you!' Elvi continued to look apprehensive. 'Do you still want to picnic at Mumbles with me next Sunday?'

'Of course!' Lynnys assured her quickly. 'We're friends, but I'd rather you didn't mention my parents again.'

'No, I won't! I promise I won't.'

Lynnys smiled. 'Well, I'm off to see Mrs Moffat,' Lynnys said. 'And I'll see you at the weekend. Take care, Elvi.'

There were some beautiful houses on Ffynonne

131

Crescent, but the most impressive mansion of all belonged to the industrial magnate, George Cadogan-Rees.

As she pushed the cart up the carriageway and around the back of the house, Lynnys had to admire the vast dimensions of the house and the beautifully tended gardens surrounding it.

Lynnys knew Mrs Moffat had been housekeeper with the family for many years, and she seemed glad to see Lynnys this evening.

'Come in, Lynnys,' Mrs Moffat invited as she opened the door. 'Billy will see to the sacks. Tsk! That's too heavy a load for a young girl to carry. What's Mrs Phillips thinking of?'

Lynnys was grateful to have Billy, the boot-boy, deal with the remaining sacks. She was beginning to feel very tired and was dreading the trek back to the market with the handcart.

'Sit down by here, my girl.' Mrs Moffat offered her a wooden chair near the great range. 'Rest yourself a minute.'

'You're very kind, Mrs Moffat,' Lynnys said sitting thankfully.

Mrs Moffat, a generously proportioned lady with soft kindly features, gazed at her for a moment, hands on hips.

'You're too good for this market job, you know, Lynnys,' she said. 'I don't like to see a pretty girl like you breaking her back lugging sacks about all day and chafing her hands on that cart.'

'I'm glad of the work, Mrs Moffat,' Lynnys said. 'Especially now that my grandmother is taken poorly. It's hard, but Mrs Phillips pays well, I'll give her that.'

132

'She doesn't appreciate you,' Mrs Moffat insisted.

Billy brought in the last of the sacks, and Lynnys rose ready to take her leave.

'Wait a minute,' the housekeeper said. 'Look, I need some extra help here in the house. Mrs Cadogan-Rees is giving a big anniversary dinner party at the weekend, and there'll be so much to do. Some of the guests are staying over, a few have arrived already. How would you like to be a part of the staff, my girl? It would be a step up for you.'

Lynnys was surprised at the offer. 'It's very kind of you to think of me, Mrs Moffat. What are the duties?'

'Nothing strenuous. Billy does all the heavy carrying and such like. It would be child's play for a hard-working girl like you,' the housekeeper said. 'Mostly in the kitchen, lighting the range first thing, helping to prepare food at mealtimes, and then cleaning up.'

'It sounds good.'

'And you wouldn't be out in all weathers, either. Your present job is bearable in the summertime but think about the winters, Lynnys, trundling that handcart about in the snow.'

She had been thinking about the months to come, wondering how she would cope. 'What's the wage, Mrs Moffat?'

Mrs Moffat told her, and Lynnys was disappointed. 'That's less than I'm getting now,' she said sadly. She and Gran needed every penny at the moment.

'But there's prospects in the job,' Mrs Moffat

pointed out. 'You have a good appearance and are well mannered, so you wouldn't be a kitchen maid for ever. There are a great many servants in this house. A girl like you could easily rise in the ranks.'

'Can I think about it, Mrs Moffat; talk it over with my Gran?'

'Of course, my girl,' the housekeeper said. 'You sleep on it. Oh yes, that reminds me. You'd have to live in, Lynnys. Mrs Cadogan-Rees is very strict on that. You'd have a half-day once a week.'

'Oh!' Lynnys was crestfallen. 'I couldn't live in, Mrs Moffat. My grandmother is poorly with her heart. There'd be no one to look after her.' She would never trust Trudy to do it.

'Are you sure?' Mrs Moffat looked really disappointed. 'Don't make your mind up about it yet.'

Thinking of Trudy gave Lynnys an idea. This job might be the very thing to put the girl on the straight and narrow. Of course there was the problem of the child she was carrying, but it was early days yet. There was no need to mention it, Lynnys decided, although she hated to deceive Mrs Moffat. This job was too good an opportunity to miss.

'I couldn't leave Gran,' Lynnys said, shaking her head. 'But I have a friend...'

She hesitated to call Trudy her friend, but if she did not praise her up Mrs Moffat would think it odd.

'My friend, Trudy Evans is my age and is presentable in appearance.' Trudy was nothing if not that. 'And she's in desperate need of a good

134

job. Would you consider her for the position, Mrs Moffat? She could start as soon as you like, and living in is no problem for her.'

'Well...' the housekeeper looked dubious. 'I don't usually take staff on unless I know them.' She hesitated. 'But your recommendation is good enough, I think, Lynnys. Tell your friend to come and see me tomorrow morning.'

Lynnys was eager to get home. She had been worried about her grandmother all day, left to Trudy's tender mercies. And she was excited at finding a job for their troublesome lodger.

Lynnys was disconcerted to see Phoebe fully dressed downstairs in the kitchen, making a pot of tea. A pan of stew was simmering gently over the range fire.

'Gran! You shouldn't be up.'

'Well, if I stayed upstairs I'd have starved,' Phoebe said.

'Where's Trudy?'

'In her bed, where else. That girl hasn't got a bone in her body that isn't thoroughly lazy.'

'Well, she'll have to pull her socks up,' Lynnys said. 'I've found her a job; kitchen maid in one of those houses on Ffynonne Crescent. It's a live-in position.'

Phoebe looked startled. 'Don't they mind about her interesting condition?'

Lynnys ran her tongue over her lips guiltily. 'I didn't tell them. It'll be months yet before she shows, and the work is not strenuous helping in the kitchen.'

'We won't see a penny-piece of her wages if she

135

lives in,' Phoebe warned.

'No, but at least we'll be rid of her.'

Lynnys knew that sounded uncharitable, especially as Phoebe had made a promise to someone. But the fact was that Trudy did not fit in with their way of life, and having to pull her weight to earn her bread would be the making of her.

'Besides it's for her own good,' Lynnys went on. 'She'll be safe from temptation there because apparently Mrs Cadogan-Rees is very strict about her servant girls.'

'She won't take the job, you know,' Phoebe said morosely. 'Too afraid of anything that resembles hard work.'

'This is her last chance,' Lynnys said firmly. 'She's not living off us any longer. I wouldn't say so much if she was delicate, but she's as strong as I am.'

'I think the job sounds too good for her,' Phoebe said. 'Why don't you take it, Lynnys? You're wearing yourself out in the market.'

Lynnys shook her head. 'It's not for me, Gran.' She went towards the stairs. 'I'm going up to tell her that Mrs Moffat wants to see her first thing in the morning.'

Lynnys felt impatient to see Trudy sprawled face down on the bed, still in her nightdress. She wondered if she had been too hasty in recommending her to Mrs Moffat. If Trudy proved difficult and lazy, the housekeeper would not thank her.

'Trudy, get up!' Lynnys said loudly. 'I've found a job for you.'

'Push off! I'm tired.'

'Tired! You haven't done a stroke all day, you lazy cat,' Lynnys shouted angrily. 'Now get out of bed before I pull you out.'

'Why don't you leave me alone? I didn't ask to be here.'

'Well, now's your chance to get away from us,' Lynnys said. 'You'll work in a beautiful house, with gentry. All your meals cooked for you, and clothes provided.'

'What?' Trudy sat up with a jerk, staring at Lynnys. 'What house is this?'

'Up in Ffynonne Crescent, among the *crachach*,' Lynnys told her. 'The house is set in lovely grounds; rose gardens, lawns, trees. Beautiful! Mrs Moffat, the housekeeper wants to see you tomorrow morning.'

'What kind of a job is it?'

'Live-in kitchen maid.'

'Not on your life!' Trudy exploded off the bed. 'I'm not going to drudge for anybody. You're trying to get shot of me, aren't you?'

'No, we're trying to save you from yourself, Trudy, but you're just too stupid to see it.'

'Don't be so mealy-mouthed,' Trudy snapped. 'I'm not stupid. I know you hate me.'

'I don't hate you, Trudy, and I am trying to help, if you let me,' Lynnys said. 'The life you've been leading is wrong and can only lead to the gutter.'

Trudy tossed her head. 'You don't know what you're talking about.'

'You've got your child to think of.'

Trudy looked up sharply. 'Do they know about

137

this thing growing inside me?'

Lynnys winced at the words. It was awful that Trudy thought of her baby in that way. 'No, I didn't tell them.'

'They'd soon sling me out if they knew.'

'It'll be months yet before your condition becomes obvious,' Lynnys observed. 'Meanwhile you could earn some honest money.' She hesitated. 'If they do dismiss you, you can always come back here.'

'No! I'm not interested.'

Lynnys' lips thinned with irritation at the other girl's stubbornness. 'You either try for the position, Trudy, or out you go.'

Trudy's lips curled disdainfully. 'You wouldn't do that.'

'Yes I would,' Lynnys declared firmly. 'And what will your life be like then? How will you like sleeping under Brynmill Arch down by the beach, and spending your days hanging about the docks picking up drunken sailors, entertaining them in filthy doorways?'

Trudy looked startled. 'I never pick up riff-raff, never. I can always catch the eye of some gentleman, like that Mr Casanova, who was here the other day.'

Lynnys was taken aback for a moment and then realised the girl meant Josh Rowlands. 'His sort wouldn't look twice at you when you're in rags and no roof over your head.'

Trudy's mouth drooped.

'Be sensible,' Lynnys went on quickly, sensing an advantage. 'That life is over for you, and be thankful for it, too.'

138

'But I don't know how to be a kitchen maid,' Trudy spluttered.

'You'll soon pick it up,' Lynnys assured her. 'Mrs Moffat, the housekeeper, is very kind. I promise you, Trudy, you won't regret it.'

Lynnys made sure Trudy was up early the next morning and loaned her her best dress for the occasion. The market did not open until half-past eight, so she had plenty of time to take Trudy up to Ffynonne Crescent and introduce her to Mrs Moffat.

Trudy was obviously impressed by the house and its surroundings as they walked up the carriageway and around the back of the house.

'These people are stinking rich by the looks of it,' Trudy remarked. 'What sort of family are they? I mean how many to look after?'

'The master, the mistress and four children, two sons and two daughters.'

'Sons, eh? How old are they?'

'Now, Trudy,' Lynnys exclaimed sternly. 'Behave yourself. I've recommended you for this job. I wouldn't want Mrs Moffat to think I introduced a Jezebel into the house.'

Trudy sniffed but said nothing more, and then Lynnys was knocking at the back door and in a moment the housekeeper opened it.

'Good morning, Mrs Moffat,' Lynnys greeted. 'This is Trudy Evans, the girl I recommended for the job as kitchen maid.'

'Come in both of you,' Mrs Moffat said.

'I can't stay,' Lynnys said quickly. 'I must get down to the market before it opens or Mrs

Phillips will be on the war path.'

'Of course, I understand, Lynnys. You be off then while Trudy and I have a nice chat.'

Lynnys gave Trudy a level glance. 'I know Trudy will give a good account of herself, although this would be her first job.'

Trudy gave her a crooked smile which made Lynnys nervous, but there was nothing she could do now. She just had to trust that Trudy would not give herself away.

Lynnys came home from work that evening to find the house on Cwmavon Terrace strangely quiet. Phoebe was dozing in the chair near the range looking exhausted. Lynnys hurried to make her a cup of tea.

'Where's Trudy? Did she get the job?' Lynnys asked as she watched her grandmother sip the hot sweet tea.

'Oh, yes,' Phoebe said. 'She came back here full of it.'

'Thank heavens!' Lynnys was relieved. 'When does she start?'

'Mrs Moffat wants her to move in today ready to start her duties tomorrow morning early,' Phoebe said. 'So she packed her few things, including your best dress, and was off like a hare.' She clicked her tongue. 'That girl's up to something, mark my words.'

9

Maisie Coombs had a high-pitched laugh that always sounded off-key to Bernie's ears and set his teeth on edge, but he tried to overlook it because he needed her to further his climb up the social ladder.

A middle-aged widow, Maisie was the ideal partner for society functions and dinner parties, which is where he had first met her almost six months ago and felt lucky that he had.

She had taken to him in a big way, he knew that, and he played along, for Maisie was accepted at every echelon of polite society in Swansea. She had a good sense of humour, knew everyone worth knowing; had a bob or two of her own and, most important of all, was utterly respectable.

Tonight he was excited to accompany her as her invited guest to dine with one of Swansea's most prominent townsmen and industrialists, George Cadogan-Rees. Bernie was convinced that, if he played his cards right, this occasion would be the beginning of his social acceptance and he had Maisie to thank for it.

At eight o'clock he went to fetch her at her house in Sketty, showing up in his brand new gig and pair. He rang the bell and then turned to view his new acquisition with some pride, hoping Maisie would be impressed. If she was then others would be, too.

He was gradually acquiring all the trappings of a gentleman. He had taken pains over the last few years to look the part, and would soon have the reputation to go with the class. Inclusion in the Cadogan-Rees' celebratory dinner was just the start thanks to Maisie's generosity in asking him to accompany her.

His scheme to live two very different lives was working out well. The only fly in the ointment was Josh Rowlands. It had burned him badly to concede to Rowlands' blackmail demands, but time was on his side; time to find a way of being rid of Josh permanently.

A maid answered the door and invited him inside.

'Madam is in the drawing room, sir,' she said. 'I'll announce you.'

Maisie was standing before the fireplace as he entered and turned with a smile to greet him. 'Bernard. How lovely to see you again.'

Tall, elegant and well preserved for her age, she was beautifully turned out in a gown of black lace, ropes of pearls at her throat. On her head she wore a fetching turban of some shimmering material, decorated with an ostrich feather.

'You're a picture of loveliness yourself, Maisie.'

They were on easy first name terms, which was her doing. Maisie had set her sights on him, but Bernie knew women, and knew how to string them along without making a commitment.

'Shall we have a snifter before we go?' Maisie asked.

'Why not?'

He would have preferred to have gone straight to Ffynonne Crescent. He could hardly wait to mingle with the elite of Swansea, put himself about a bit; make the connections he was looking for.

On the drive up to the home of the Cadogan-Reeses, Bernie decided he needed to prime Maisie to help get another of his money-making schemes off the ground.

'Do you remember me telling you about that marvellous clairvoyant I've discovered?' he asked casually as he flicked the reins.

'Yes.' She touched his arm. 'Bernard, you promised you'd arrange a séance at my house,' she said reproachfully. 'I've told all my friends. They are dying to meet her, especially Dolly Mathias. You remember Dolly?'

He certainly did. Dolly Mathias was exactly the sort of gullible mark he was looking for; an older widow, well-heeled, not too bright, lonely and vulnerable to charm.

'Dolly can't wait for a séance,' Maisie went on. 'She's longing to contact her Donald. He's been gone ten years but he's all she talks about. When can we arrange it?'

'I've not been able to get the woman to agree yet,' he said cautiously. 'These mediums are such strange and temperamental people. The least upset robs them of their powers, you know.'

'Really?'

'Yes. I've decided to take her under my protection,' he said.

'Oh! I see.'

He wasn't looking directly at her but he sensed

143

Maisie's hard gaze on him. It wouldn't do for her to see Sybil as a rival. More than anything he needed Maisie on his side.

'She's a poor widow woman, very badly off; working-class, you understand,' he explained quickly. 'With a child dependent on her.' He clicked his tongue at the horse. 'I can't help worrying that she'll fall into the hands of some unscrupulous man who'll exploit her and the child.'

'Oh, dreadful!'

'Yes, it would be a crying shame. Such powers, you know. Such powers.'

'I can't wait to meet her!'

'Under my protection she could help so many people,' he said persuasively. 'I'm sure you know many in your circle who would benefit, like Dolly Mathias.'

'You're right, Bernard. I shall spread the word, starting at dinner tonight.' She slipped her arm though his as he held the reins. 'My dear man, what a marvellous thing! And just when I was getting rather bored with the social rounds.'

The evening was going extremely well, Bernie decided. He had forged a few interesting business contacts, and Maisie had made the discovery of a new and amazing clairvoyant, which was the main topic of conversation among the ladies at least. They bombarded him with questions throughout dinner.

The men present took no interest, and that suited him well. His own powers of persuasion were irresistible to the weaker gender. He wanted no competition there. Besides, men were not so easily taken in.

After dinner the ladies retired to the drawing room while the men remained, putting away an excellent port. George Cadogan-Rees lived well and Bernie was envious of his status.

'Shall we join the ladies?' Cadogan-Rees suggested an hour later.

The gathering of men filed out, talking, smoking cigars and still carrying their glasses of port. Bernie needed to find the lavatory and, asking a passing footman, was directed to facilities on the ground floor along a passage just off the main hall.

He strolled down the wide spacious staircase, puffing away at his cigar, admiring the proportions of the house, wondering what it would cost to run such a place. He found the passage and proceeded down it.

Congratulating himself on the success of the evening, he was only partially aware of one of the myriad of servants in the house walking along the passageway towards him.

'Bernie! What're you doing here?'

Bernie almost fell back against the wall at recognising Trudy Evans' voice. His jaw went slack as he stared at her, unable to believe it.

'Don't you know me, Bernie?' She pulled off her mop cap. 'It's me, Trudy.'

His tongue was glued to the roof of his mouth.

'You shouldn't have let them throw me out, Bernie, just because I'm up the duff.'

Trudy paused, glanced around and then giggled.

'I'd better button my lip or I'll be thrown out of

145

here, too,' she went on and then stepped closer to him. 'Get Herb to take me back, Bernie. You've got influence. You're his best customer. Please, Bernie.' She winked at him. 'You won't regret it. I always gave you a good time, didn't I? All the little extras.'

Bernie unglued his tongue. 'Get away from me you dirty slut! How dare you approach me? I've never laid eyes on you before in my life.'

Trudy's face reddened. 'Well, that's a nice way to talk to me, I must say, after all we've been to each other. I could tell a few tales, couldn't I?'

Bernie's need to pass water was suddenly extremely urgent.

'Get out of my way!'

Unwilling for any physical contact, he tried to edge past her to get to the lavatory door, glancing fearfully up and down the passage in case they were observed.

She reached out and clutched at his arm. 'Bernie! Don't treat me like this.'

In panic, he shook off her grasp.

'I don't know who you are,' he said angrily, though still fearful to raise his voice. 'But I'll have you sacked. When your master knows you've been importuning guests he'll have the police on you.'

She was staring at him wide-eyed, anger chasing disappointment from her face.

'Why, you mucky old bugger!' she exclaimed hotly. 'I could tell him and the police a few things about you, you high and mighty bastard.'

Bernie was aware of someone at the far end of the passage and moving swiftly he managed to gain the door of the lavatory and leaped inside. He shot the bolt and stood there sweating.

It was damned bad luck! He never would have believed that the paths of his separate lives could cross, and on this important occasion of all.

He stayed behind the locked door longer than was necessary, cursing his misfortune. He should be up in the drawing room, mixing with the other guests, ingratiating himself. And Maisie must be wondering where he had got to.

What should he do about Trudy? Heaven only knew what gossip the little whore would be spreading about him to the other servants. Talk was bound to get back to Cadogan-Rees. His ambitious schemes would be scuppered; his whole life might be exposed.

Bernie ran his hand over his still perspiring face. He must get in first, report her behaviour. Demand she be sacked. That is what any gentleman would do in the circumstances.

Bernie made his way back nervously to the drawing room. Maisie made a bee-line for him immediately.

'Where have you been, Bernard, dear?'

'Chatting,' he said distractedly. 'Excuse me a moment, Maisie, but I must have a word with our host.'

The French windows to the terrace were open and Bernie spotted Cadogan-Rees in conversation with a group of guests. He made his way there, and with a little apologetic cough, touched his host lightly on his arm.

'Excuse me, Mr Cadogan-Rees, might I have a word? It's rather urgent.'

147

The man turned, thick-set and short of stature, thinning grey hair, yet keen-eyed, George Cadogan-Rees looked shrewd and successful.

'Major Pomfrey! My dear fellow, we've not had a chance to talk properly this evening.'

Bernie edged towards the steps leading down into the gardens.

'Shall we stroll, sir? I have something very grave to tell you.'

Cadogan-Rees raised his eyebrows in surprise at Bernie's serious tone, but complied by following Bernie down the steps on to a gravel path.

'I don't want what I have to say to be overheard,' Bernie began, striding out away from the terrace. 'I wouldn't want to cause you any embarrassment.'

'Good Lord, Major! Whatever is the matter?'

'Something extremely serious, I'm afraid,' Bernie said gravely. 'Not to put too fine a point on it, I've just been importuned by one of your female servants. She accosted me in the passage leading to the lavatory downstairs. She made the most crude suggestions, offering her ... um ... services, there and then.'

'What?'

'I was shocked, sir,' Bernie said, adopting an appropriate expression. 'I knew I had to make you aware of what is going on under your own roof.'

Cadogan-Rees looked nonplussed and just stared at him.

'Of course, I don't know the name of this girl,' Bernie said quickly. 'But I did notice she had red hair.'

148

Cadogan-Rees stroked his moustache. 'Thank you for bringing this to my attention, Major. You can now leave the matter with me.'

The following morning George Cadogan-Rees called his butler, Cranston, to him in his study.

'How many red-headed female servants do we have, Cranston?'

The butler looked mildly surprised at the question. 'Actually, sir, I believe there is only one. She started duties in the kitchens Friday, recommended by Mrs Moffat herself.'

'How does she strike you?'

'Green, sir. But I think she will shape up eventually. I trust Mrs Moffat's judgment, sir. Never known her to be wrong.'

'Keep an eye on this girl, Cranston, and report any unseemly behaviour.'

'Very good, sir.' Cranston paused. 'Might I take the liberty to enquire the reason for this interest, sir?'

'Something and nothing, Cranston, something and nothing. That will be all.'

'Very good, sir.'

Cadogan-Rees sat for a moment more at his desk. As he said to his wife the previous night, he was inclined to think that Major Pomfrey was given to flights of extreme fancy and lurid imaginings, egged on by that excitement-seeking Maisie Coombs. To believe that such a disgraceful happening as the Major had described could possibly occur under his roof was ludicrous.

As far as he recalled at dinner the Major had talked of nothing but clairvoyance, of spirits of

149

the dead, materialisations, ectoplasm and other clap-trap. Strange talk for a man of any substance.

Cadogan-Rees sniffed disdainfully, tweaking his moustache. The Major was no more than a shallow fool. How could one take such a fellow seriously?

10

'There's something fishy going on, I can smell it,' Herb said darkly to Connie as she sat opposite him in his office on Saturday night.

Silently, Connie had to agree.

Business was good tonight and as all the girls were occupied elsewhere she had come in to have a chat, knowing Herb was disgruntled and as mystified as she was that Josh Rowlands had persuaded Bernie to make him a partner, and an equal partner at that. Bernie was a hard man who gave no quarter, so what did that say about Josh Rowlands, a man she was about to trust with her most precious daughter?

'Bloody Johnny-come-lately!' Herb was more aggrieved than she thought. She could understand it. Herb had worked for Bernie for some time, even before the Pleasure Palace opened, and it was entirely Herb's know-how that had built the place up to the successful house it was now. Herb kept the roughnecks at bay; protected the girls from any harm, kept a disorderly house orderly. If any man deserved to be recognised it was Herb.

Connie was about to make that comment when Josh Rowlands strolled in to the room, immaculate in evening clothes. He was on the premises every evening, through to the early hours, protecting his investment, Connie thought.

'What are you two brewing up?' Josh asked, looking from one to the other.

Herb merely grunted.

'We were talking about you, Josh,' Connie said frankly. 'Talk about falling on your feet.'

He smiled at her. 'Not before time.'

'What the hell have you got on Bernie?' Herb asked savagely. 'He wouldn't give you the time of day unless he was forced to.'

Josh looked at him for a moment, cigar between his teeth. 'I've got the goods on him, Herb. That's all you need to know,' he said at last. 'A warehouse full of goods.'

'What does that mean?'

'It means it's none of your business,' Josh snapped. 'If you've got any complaints, Herb, speak up.'

Herb was sullenly silent and Josh glanced at Connie.

'I want a few words with you, Connie,' he said. 'About one of the girls. Let's go in your room.'

She went before him along the passage to her sitting room. She wanted to talk to him too. Something had to be done for Lynnys and Phoebe.

Josh made himself at home on her sofa, while Connie poured herself a small sherry. When she was seated he said:

'It's about Lynnys. I want your permission to train her.'

Connie was startled. 'For what?'

'The stage, the theatre, whatever you want to call it.' He raised a hand when Connie opened her mouth to protest. 'Hear me out. The girl has a presence. You must have noticed it, even though you are her mother.'

Connie looked away. Lynnys was beautiful, strikingly so, and it worried her. Such beauty was a magnet. Men would want to possess it, unscrupulous men. Was Josh Rowlands one of them?

'Yes, and I'm afraid,' Connie said quietly.

'I'll protect her.'

Connie gave him a scornful glance. 'I'm sure you will,' she said pithily. 'You're like all the others, Josh. You have to destroy a lovely thing.'

'You've got me wrong.' He leaned forward. 'Look, I believe she can make it big on the stage. If she's got a voice as good as yours, youth and beauty on her side, she'll go far, and I want to be her agent.'

'How can I trust you, Josh?' Connie answered. 'Herb is right. You must have muscled in on Bernie somehow, and it'll be something underhand maybe illegal, it has to be. I can't let my Lynnys be mixed up with men like you, always on the verge of criminality.'

Josh smiled thinly. 'That's rich coming from you, with your professional history.'

'I've never done anyone any harm, never stolen from anyone,' Connie said defensively. 'I've provided a service, that's how I see it.'

Josh nodded. 'Yes, of course you have, Connie. And the game probably wasn't your choice, was it? Bernie had a hand in that, as I recall.'

'We're talking about Lynnys, remember?'

'I believe in her, Connie, believe she can make good with the right management.' Josh put one knee across the other, making himself more comfortable. 'During the years I spent in London

153

I had dealings with the theatrical profession from time to time,' he went on. 'Some of those stars of the Halls made fortunes, and the men managing them made fortunes, too.'

'Money!'

'Can't go far without it, Connie.' Josh smiled. 'I'm tired of living on the edge and on the outside. I don't want to be bluffing my way through life any longer, putting the bite on men like Bernie.'

He regarded her in silence for a moment and Connie decided to say nothing, but let him talk. She had to make a decision about him. Could he be trusted to do what she could not do for herself?

'As soon as I laid eyes on Lynnys, I knew I'd found what I was looking for,' Josh went on. His expression was eager now, as though he really meant what he was saying. 'She'd be a wow in London and in the States; Broadway maybe. They call it show business there, you know.'

'The stage is the stage, no matter what you call it,' Connie said flatly. 'It's a dicey profession and bad things can happen to an innocent girl.'

'Not with me for protection. I'd treat her as though she were my own daughter. What do you say?'

Connie watched him in silence.

'It wouldn't happen for a while,' Josh continued. 'Six months maybe of training, singing lessons, elocution, deportment, dancing.'

'Who would pay for all this?'

'I will, out of my share of this place. I've prised fifty per cent out of Bernie. You have no idea

154

what this house makes in a week.'

Connie took a sip of her sherry, lifting her chin stubbornly. 'What is it you *really* want in return, Josh? And don't tell me you'd do this out of the goodness of your heart.'

'It's business only, I swear it.'

'I'll think about it.'

'Well, don't take too long. Lynnys might ruin her looks hauling potato sacks on that handcart all over town. She should be treated like a fragile flower.'

'There's nothing fragile about Lynnys,' Connie said, smiling. 'She's as strong as a horse and as graceful as a gazelle.'

She had watched her daughter at work in the market, hiding herself behind stalls, drinking in every glimpse.

'She'd make a marvellous dancer; those long legs,' Josh agreed. 'And put that grace together with a beautiful singing voice and you have a star in the making.'

'I wouldn't want to force her into anything.'

'She's eager to make good,' Josh hurried to reassure her. 'She's got ambition. I'm providing the opportunity.'

Connie got up and walked over to the mantelpiece. What else could she do but trust him? Only he knew of her connection with Lynnys. He was the only one who could act as go-between. She was afraid to take anyone else into her confidence.

'All right, Josh,' she said turning to look at him. 'I'll take your word you have no designs on Lynnys. However, if she gives up her job in the market she and my mother will need money to live on. You pay for her training and I'll bear the cost of their keep. But my part in it must remain secret from her and everyone else, except Phoebe.'

He jumped to his feet, grinning from ear to ear. 'Connie, you'll never regret it. I swear I'll take care of her as though she were my own daughter.'

'Understand me, Josh,' Connie went on. 'I haven't said Lynnys can go to London with you. That's quite another matter.'

Lynnys was astonished on Sunday afternoon when she opened the front door to a knock to see Trudy standing on the step, smiling all over her face.

'It's all right,' Trudy said quickly, as Lynnys stared at her. 'I haven't come to stay. It's my afternoon off, so I'm visiting my family, or what passes for family.'

'Come in, Trudy,' Lynnys said.

She looked different somehow, Lynnys thought; respectable in a woollen navy coat which Lynnys had never seen before, and a navy beret balanced pertly on her red hair.

Trudy shrugged out of her coat and Lynnys hung it on a peg in the passage.

'This is a nice warm-looking coat,' Lynnys observed. The weather was too warm for such wear really, but Trudy seemed proud of the coat, the way she adjusted the folds as it hung from the peg.

'It's not new mind,' Trudy said. 'One of the other maids gave it to me, and the beret. Her father had bought her a new outfit so she didn't want it any longer.'

'That was very kind of her,' Lynnys said.

'Yes. One of the other girls gave me a dressing gown she didn't want too. They're a good bunch up at Ffynonne Crescent,' Trudy agreed. 'And Old Cranston, the butler, is strict but he's fair.'

Lynnys led the way into the living room. 'You're settling in then?' She could not keep the surprise from her voice.

She indicated a chair at the table and Trudy sat down.

'Yes. I didn't think I'd like it at first, but Mrs Moffat is good to me. I share a bedroom with a girl from Llanelli, whose family have a farm. Her mother sends her a basket of pies and fruit every week, and she shares some with me. It's nice to have family.'

There was a slight catch in Trudy's voice, and Lynnys felt sympathy for her. Trudy had no true family except herself and Phoebe.

'Well, it's lucky you've got Gran and me then, isn't it?' she said cheerfully. 'We're your family now, and we'll be hurt if you don't visit us regularly and take tea.' Lynnys paused. 'And when the time comes, you know, when they discover your condition, you must move back here with us. We'll look after you.'

'Oh! Thank you.'

Lynnys thought she saw tears starting in Trudy's eyes, and jumped up. 'I'm just making a pot for Gran,' she said. 'She's taking a nap but she'll be down in a minute. You must stay a while, Trudy and take a bite with us.'

When Phoebe joined them she seemed wary of

157

Trudy at first, but as the change in the girl became obvious to her, Phoebe's manner thawed. She wanted to know all about the household at Ffynonne Crescent and how Mrs Moffat managed things.

They chatted for a while and then Trudy said: 'I saw him, you know.'

'Who?'

'The man who got me into trouble, Bernie. He was a guest at dinner one night.' Trudy fiddled with her handkerchief. 'I spoke to him, but he was horrible to me; called me names and threatened to get me the sack.'

'The scoundrel!' Phoebe said.

Trudy stared from one to the other. 'Bernie never bothered with any of the other girls, only me, and I really thought he was fond of me. But he looked as thought he hated me and said he didn't know who I was.'

'He ought to be horse-whipped,' Phoebe said. 'Trapping a young girl into evil ways.'

'Evil?'

'Not you, Trudy,' Lynnys said quickly. 'Men like this Bernie are evil, and it's a good thing you got away from him. He did you a favour turning you off. That life is all behind you now. This is a fresh start for you and your baby.'

Surprisingly Trudy burst into tears. 'Oh, what's to become of me? How will I manage? I know nothing about babies.'

'You'll learn,' Phoebe said sagely. 'Every mother has to learn. And besides, you've got us. There's nothing I don't know about babies.'

11

Major Pomfrey provided a horse and cart to take their belongings from Fleet Street to Walter Road. Sybil got Elvi up early that Monday morning, well before dawn. Sybil had sold most of their furniture to neighbours, and their bed was to go that morning.

The Major, out of the goodness of his heart as Sybil reminded Elvi, was providing all they would need in their new home as regards furniture and fittings, including a bed each, as promised.

Elvi was miserable. Pokey and dingy as their rooms were in Fleet Street, she was loath to leave. She could not help feeling that by taking the Major's beneficence they were obliged to him, almost as though it gave him control over them, an idea which troubled Elvi greatly.

But she was powerless to persuade her mother to reconsider, and so when the cart came first thing after breakfast, tea, jam and toast, provided surprisingly by the woman in the rooms above, they took their leave.

Elvi flatly refused to ride on the cart, insisting on walking up to Walter Road, a walk she did every morning anyway to her work with Dr Howells. She was making her way up Mansel Street, head down feeling very depressed, when she heard her name called and looked up in surprise to see Lynnys coming towards her pushing her handcart along in the gutter out of the way of traffic.

'Elvi!' Lynnys called again. 'Yoo-hoo!'

Elvi stopped immediately glad to see her friend.

'On your way to work, are you?' Lynnys asked.

'No.' Elvi felt suddenly uncomfortable. Even though their move to Walter Road had been on the cards for a week or two she had been reluctant to mention it to Lynnys. She hated the idea and had hoped in vain it would not happen. Now it had.

'As a matter of fact Lynnys,' Elvi said shamefaced. 'My mother and I are moving house today to Walter Road. I'm on my way there now.'

Lynnys looked astonished, as well she might, Elvi thought.

'Good gracious!' her friend exclaimed. 'There's posh!'

Elvi shuffled her feet. 'I hate the idea!'

'Why? It's one of the best parts of town.'

'It's the landlord,' Elvi admitted miserably. 'I don't like him. He gives me the shivers. He says things he shouldn't...'

Lynnys blinked. 'Such as what?'

Elvi felt heat flood her face. 'I can't repeat it Lynnys, not even to you.'

'Have you told your mother?'

Elvi bit her lip. 'She won't believe me. She says he's a gentleman and thinks he's wonderful.'

'Elvi, I'm sorry you're upset,' Lynnys said gently. 'If there's any way I can help I will. Shall I come and see your mother and have a word?'

Elvi was startled. 'Oh no! She'd go off the deep end, and I'd never hear the last of it,' she blurted

160

and then paused. 'But thank you, Lynnys for offering. I'm so glad I have you as a friend.' She smiled wanly then. 'I'd better go and face it,' she went on. 'My mother will be on pins.'

With an encouraging smile and a wave Lynnys gripped the bars of the cart and trundled off. 'See you soon, Elvi!'

Elvi stood on the pavement and watched her go, envying Lynnys' apparent contentment with her lot, and then she turned and walked on.

She arrived at Walter Road to find that the carter had taken most of their bundles and a couple of battered cases inside. Elvi stood on the pavement and looked the house over. It had a very imposing frontage, and was larger than the house where her employer lived and had his surgery, a few doors down on the opposite side.

Elvi felt nervous and the skin on the back of her neck felt cold and clammy as she stepped into the large hallway which was almost as big as their old living room at Fleet Street. This did not feel right. It was too grand for them.

'Oh, there you are, Elvi.' Sybil came out of a door nearby. 'You've taken your time I must say. Trust you to arrive when most of the moving in has been done.'

Elvi said nothing but followed her mother back into the sitting room. It was spacious and well furnished. Sybil was grinning like a Cheshire cat.

'Wait until you see the room I'll use for my séances,' she said. 'There's even a small side room off it. Oh! I'll work wonders there!'

'Don't expect me to have any part in your frauds,' Elvi said flatly. 'I shan't like living here.'

161

Sybil's expression changed to a grim one. 'You're an ungrateful little tyke, I must say. Major Pomfrey has done us proud, and I'm paying no more than I was in Fleet Street.'

'What? Why is he being so generous?'

Sybil patted her hair. 'It's obvious,' she said with a smirk. 'The Major is concerned for me, more than concerned, I'd say. My luck is changing, Elvi. I'm sure he's working up to a proposal.'

Elvi scowled. Her mother was as adept at deceiving herself as she was other people. Whatever the Major's intentions were Elvi was sure they boded ill for them.

'I don't like it here. It's too posh for us. I won't settle, I know it.'

'You'll change your mind when you see your bedroom,' Sybil said. She glanced around. 'It's all so tastefully furnished. The Major has a great sense of style, but then, he's a gentleman.'

Elvi continued to scowl. No gentleman him, judging by the things he had said to her in the past. 'I'll have to get off to work soon,' she remarked.

'And that's another thing.' Sybil nodded with satisfaction. 'Your employment is almost next door. You can't complain about that.'

When Elvi returned home after work later that day she was disconcerted to find Major Pomfrey in their sitting room, taking tea with Sybil. Her mother's face was flushed with pleasure. Elvi wondered what Major Pomfrey was up to so soon after they had moved in and was wary.

'Elvi, Bernard ... Major Pomfrey is so kind.

162

He's given us the means to rig ourselves out with new clothes. A complete wardrobe. Isn't that wonderful and so generous?'

Elvi was silent, watching him coldly.

'Your mother's clientele will be of the upper class from now on,' the Major said. 'People of quality and means. Sybil must dress their equal, and so must you, my dear Elvi.'

'I'll have nothing to do with her séances!'

His eyes glinted. 'But surely you like pretty clothes?'

Of course she did, but not from him. She longed to tell him so to his face but knew there would be severe repercussions from Sybil.

'Excuse me. I'm going to my room.'

Major Pomfrey was intruding more and more into their lives, and his so-called generosity would tie Sybil in knots. Elvi sat on her bed, biting her thumb nail. She suspected that her mother was already under his spell or rather under his thumb.

A vague shiver ran down her spine again. She was unable to shake off the feeling she had had earlier that day that the Major had a very dark ulterior motive for all this kindness, and somehow it centred on her.

Elvi had always been glad that Dr Howells' work in the surgery did not require her to work late every day, so she was back home by late afternoon the next day. Sybil had gone into town to visit the rather exclusive department store, Ben Evans, to choose some new gowns. Elvi was in the sitting room reading when the doorbell chimed.

Praying it wasn't Major Pomfrey again, Elvi

163

was at first delighted to see Mrs Beavis, and then suddenly nervous, remembering the incident of the will.

'Elvi, I'm so glad to catch you. I wanted a word,' Mrs Beavis said eagerly, stepping in to the hall. 'I know your mother's out. I saw her in town.'

Elvi led the way into the sitting room, very conscious that Mrs Beavis was glancing around her with sharp curiosity, her eyes missing nothing.

'Very nice lodgings, I must say,' the older woman said curiosity clear in her tone. 'Coming up in the world, isn't she, your mother?'

Elvi gave a weak smile. 'You wanted a word, Mrs Beavis. Do sit down.'

Mrs Beavis settled herself comfortably, and Elvi wondered whether she should offer refreshments. The thing was she did not want Mrs Beavis to linger longer than was necessary in case Sybil returned.

'I won't stay long,' the older woman said as though reading her thoughts. 'It's about my old father's will.' She beamed. 'You were right, Elvi. It was in the hut on his allotment. How clever of you.'

Elvi smiled nervously. 'It was just a guess, you know.'

'If you say so, Elvi. My brother Billy was truly knocked for six when I produced it to the lawyer. You saved my bacon, Elvi, and I'm grateful. If there is ever anything I can do for you, please ask.'

Elvi swallowed. 'Well, there is one thing. Don't ever mention this matter to my mother, Mrs Beavis.'

'Of course not. It's our little secret. Now then, my girl, my mouth is parched for a cup of tea.'

Josh called at Cwmavon Terrace early Tuesday afternoon when he knew Lynnys would be still at the market. He needed to speak to Phoebe Daniels privately, to explain his arrangement with Connie.

When Phoebe answered the door he thought she looked much better than the last time he had seen her. She glared at him when he tipped his hat and smiled.

'Afternoon, Mrs Daniels.'

'What do you want? Trudy doesn't live here any more.'

'It's you I want to talk to,' Josh said. 'Connie sent me.'

Phoebe drew in breath sharply. 'Connie? Connie who? I don't know any Connie.'

'Connie, your daughter,' Josh said dryly.

She folded her lips for a moment and then stepped back from the door. 'You'd better come in I suppose.'

He removed his hat respectfully and followed her down the passage. She faced him in the living room, a belligerent look on her prematurely lined face.

'What are you after?' she asked sourly. 'Connie must be out of her mind telling you about us.'

'She didn't. It was Trudy.'

Phoebe clicked her tongue angrily. 'Tsk! The mischievous little madam.'

'I'm glad she did,' Josh said. 'It makes my plans easier.'

'What plans? What are you talking about?'

Josh inclined his head. 'Can I sit down? And how about a cup of tea?'

Phoebe made the tea, grumbling under her breath all the while.

She pushed a cup and saucer across the table towards him, sitting down herself. 'Now, what's this all about?'

'It's about Lynnys' future,' Josh began. 'I've talked this over with Connie. She knows I'm sincere.'

Her eyes narrowed. 'I hardly think Connie is the right person to decide what's good for my granddaughter, considering how she's thrown her own life away. Degrading herself.'

'She knows she did wrong,' Josh said reasonably. 'But she wasn't entirely to blame. She came under the influence of a bad man.'

Phoebe sniffed. 'There are no excuses for her chosen way of life, young man.'

'Maybe, but Lynnys' life will be very different. She has talent, real talent, Phoebe – can I call you Phoebe?'

Phoebe sniffed again and sipped her tea. 'Connie has been paying for Lynnys' upkeep all these years,' she said. 'But there's been little put in the kitty lately.'

'That's partly why I'm here,' Josh said eagerly. 'Connie is still willing to support you and the girl, don't worry about that. She'll provide for your day to day living and for the new clothes Lynnys will need. I'll be responsible for her training.'

Phoebe jolted upright, tea spilling out of her cup. 'Training for what?'

'A career as a singer and dancer,' Josh said. He lifted a hand as Phoebe opened her mouth wide to protest. 'It'll be an utterly respectable career, I assure you, Phoebe. First she must give up her job in the market.'

He explained about the various lessons he had already arranged.

'There'll be nothing underhand, Phoebe,' Josh assured her. 'And to ensure that to your satisfaction, I want you to accompany Lynnys to these lessons, if it won't tire you. You need only watch and listen. What do you say?'

'I don't know.'

'Look, we have time before Lynnys comes home,' Josh said. 'Ask me any questions you like. I've nothing to hide.'

It had been hot in the market under that glass roof and Mrs Phillips had worked her hard. Lynnys was glad when the gates closed against further custom, and she was left to clear up.

She was looking forward to a cup of tea and a sit down with her feet up and so was annoyed to find Josh Rowlands lounging in the living room, chatting to Phoebe as though he belonged there.

'What's going on? Why are you here? You've got no business with us.'

Josh looked at Phoebe as though expecting her to explain.

'Sit down, *bach*,' Phoebe said. 'I'll get you some tea. We've got a surprise for you, a bit of good fortune.'

Lynnys sent Josh questioning looks, but he leaned back in his chair, apparently content to let

167

Phoebe do all the talking. Lynnys was astonished at Phoebe's tolerance of him, considering he was the man who had caused her heart attack! Why wasn't she ordering him out?

Her grandmother came back in a few moments, sat down and began to explain Josh Rowlands' plans for her future.

'What? Give up my job? That's madness.'

'You said you wanted to be a singer more than anything else.' Josh spread his hands. 'I'm giving you the chance of a lifetime.'

She gave him a suspicious glance. She could not forget his unforgivable behaviour with Trudy. There was only one reason a man like him would be interested in her and she was angry at his assumption.

'I told you before, mister,' she burst out angrily. 'I'm not Trudy's sort. It's no good you hanging about here. You won't get what you're looking for.'

'You misunderstand my intentions,' Josh said reasonably. 'This is entirely a business matter.' He gave a light laugh. 'Believe me, if I thought you were like Trudy I wouldn't waste my time or money on you.'

'It's all above board,' Phoebe put in, surprising Lynnys with her mild tone and composure. Her grandmother appeared to be on his side, approving of all he proposed. 'I'll be chaperoning you at all times.' Phoebe nodded. 'I won't leave your side for a minute. You'll be quite safe.'

Flummoxed, Lynnys stared at Josh. 'We have no money, nothing, so what do you hope to gain by this, mister?'

'A good living,' Josh said quickly. 'And so would you. Entertainers with your talents can make fortunes.'

Lynnys shook her head. 'It sounds too good to be true. I don't trust you.'

'Your mother does.'

'My mother is dead.'

She glanced sharply at her grandmother. For some reason she was reminded of the strange things her friend Elvi had said; that she was not an orphan.

'He means me, Lynnys, your grandmother,' Phoebe cut in quickly. 'Mr Rowlands is confused.' She flung him an angry glance which Lynnys did not understand. 'But I know that if your mother were alive she'd be glad of this opportunity for you to make something of your life,' her grandmother went on. 'She always wanted the best for you.'

'I won't ask anything of you, Lynnys,' Josh said. 'Except hard work. And it will be hard and probably boring at the start. But you've got the talent, and you're beautiful. I know you'll be successful. I'm staking everything I own on you.'

Lynnys looked from one to the other. She was still uncertain of him. But Gran, who was so sensible and level-headed approved. What had she to lose by giving this new venture a go? If there was one thing she was not afraid of it was hard work. And she would be doing something she loved. Singing.

'All right, mister,' Lynnys said at last. 'I'll give it a try. But I won't stand for any funny business, understand?'

He grinned, obviously delighted. 'Call me Josh. I'm your agent and manager now. Later, I'll have a contract drawn up between us.'

Lynnys frowned. 'What's a contract?'

'It's a legal document which will protect both of us. Trust me.'

Lynnys regarded him solemnly. It looked as though she would have to trust him. But she would also keep in mind the kind of man he was.

12

The household at Ffynonne Crescent was a hive of activity at the weekend. Mrs Moffat was roasting and baking from early morning and Trudy was kept busy helping in the kitchen. Not that she minded. Mrs Moffat was teaching her to cook, and had praised her for her light hand with pastry.

'These people have parties at the drop of a hat,' she ventured to say to the housekeeper.

'Ah! But this is a special occasion,' Mrs Moffat said. 'Master Rhodri is coming home. He's their youngest boy. He's been away on one of those European tours for the last twelve months to widen his experience of the world.'

Trudy hid a smile as she bent over the bowl of potatoes she was peeling. Most boys didn't need to go abroad for that.

'He's spent time in the art galleries and museums of Rome and Paris; the concert halls of Vienna. He's even been to St Petersburg and Athens.' Mrs Moffat sighed. 'He's such a nice boy, my favourite. He loves my apple pies.'

'Fancy letting a little kid go to all those places on his own.'

'He's not a child, dear me, no,' Mrs Moffat said. 'Master Rhodri is almost twenty-one. I expect he'll be taking his place in the business with his older brother before long.'

Trudy was rarely allowed above stairs, but sometimes sneaked up anyway when a party was on, just to look at the ladies' dresses.

On the last occasion she had run into that swine Bernie and had been afraid to risk it since, but the thought of young Rhodri Cadogan-Rees intrigued her, and made her venturesome.

She did not get a chance to dodge away during the party, so contented herself with creeping up the following morning when she thought the family would be coming down for breakfast. She just wanted a little glance at him, just one.

The large front hall was empty. No sign of Cranston or the parlour maids. Feeling bold, Trudy tiptoed to the breakfast room door and put her head around it. Empty. Although the long table was laid for breakfast there was no sign yet of the silver platters on the chiffoniers placed against the far wall.

Trudy glanced at the clock on the mantelpiece across the room. Just gone half past seven. Mr Cadogan-Rees and his eldest son were usually breakfasting at this time before leaving for business.

Hangovers, Trudy thought and giggled.

'What's so funny, young woman?'

Trudy almost jumped out of her uniform, and swung around, panic-stricken to realise she had been caught red-handed above stairs. She was bound to get the sack for this.

Stunned, she looked up into the face of a young man of medium height and broad of shoulder. She knew straight away he was a Cadogan-Rees.

It was written all over him. It occurred to her that he would not know she had no right to be there.

'Just putting the finishing touches to the breakfast table, sir.' She bobbed a curtsy. 'I'll tell Mr Cranston you're down, sir.'

She turned to make her getaway.

'Hold on a minute. What's your name, girl?'

Trudy's step faltered and she turned back. 'Trudy, sir. Oh, please don't give me away, sir.' She stepped towards him, fluttering her eyelashes. That had always worked on men in the past.

He grinned. 'You're a cheeky little imp, I must say.'

Trudy grinned back. 'What was it like in Paris?'

'Lonely and very boring,' he said flatly. He grinned again. 'It would've been nicer if I'd had someone like you to share it with.'

'Oh, go on with you, sir.' Trudy lifted one shapely shoulder, giving a coy laugh, something she practised regularly. 'There must've been plenty of girls in Paris and Rome.'

'Yes, there were,' he said, sighing. 'But my tutor, Mr Thomas, never left my side.'

'You should've got him drunk and then you could've sneaked away.'

'Now why didn't I think of that? Trouble is old Thomas is tee-tee.'

'It must've been awful for you.' Trudy realised she meant those words. Rhodri Cadogan-Rees had a nice face, not handsome, but then none of the family was. Their money made up for that, Trudy thought.

She suddenly felt quite sorry for him. His eyes

173

had a definite twinkle, as though he longed for some fun, but didn't know where to find it.

'Yes, it was,' he answered. 'But I intend to make up for it now I'm home. I'll be twenty-one next month. Then my father can't stop me from doing anything I want.'

She liked him. He was so boyish, so different from that bastard Bernie and the other men she had met briefly after been thrown out of the Pleasure Palace. Rhodri had probably never been inside a house like that, never met a girl like her.

Trudy knew a great temptation then, and eyed him speculatively.

'Well, sir,' she began, tilting her head and widening her eyes as she gazed at him. 'If you're wanting a good time...'

She did not have time to finish her proposition, for footfalls sounded on the staircase and she recognised Mr Cranston's voice giving orders to a footman.

'Oh! I'm off!'

She managed to scurry away before being seen and hurried back to the kitchen. Mrs Moffat frowned at her.

'Trudy, where have you been?'

'Outside lavatory,' she mumbled.

'Well, get a move on with your chores.'

Trudy was busy after that, but her mind was full of Rhodri Cadogan-Rees. She liked his looks, but she would probably never see him again.

She sighed as she scrubbed dirty crockery and pots and pans in hot water and soda. Perhaps it was just as well. She had been tempted into her old ways, but that would only lead to trouble, and

174

she was in enough of that already.

She spent the rest of the day speculating on what it would be like to have money; to wear fashionable clothes and to have someone like Rhodri paying court to her.

That would never happen now. She had cooked her own goose by getting herself up the duff. It was only a matter of time before they found out and then she would be slung out on her ear.

Trudy laid her head on her pillow that night, listening to the other girl snoring. She would be sorry to leave Ffynonne Crescent. It was hard work in the kitchen and yet she felt some pride in it and she was learning so much from Mrs Moffat, surprising herself with her growing skills in the kitchen.

But how would she earn a living after her baby was born? She did not want to go back to her old ways, but what else did she know?

13

'Oh, I'm so excited! I know my first séance in
these rooms will be a huge success. Dear
Bernard. We have so much to thank him for.'

Sybil inspected her coiffure in the ornately
decorated gilt mirror in the room she called her
'salon', touching her fingers lightly to one crisp
curl after another.

Elvi watched her with exasperation. Her
mother was rigged out in an expensive-looking
evening gown in a style far too young for her.

'You're deluding yourself if you believe he's
doing it out of the goodness of his heart, Mam.'

'Well, of course not!' Sybil turned to glance at
her, a supercilious smile on her face. 'It's a
prelude to courtship, isn't it? A woman knows
when a man wants her. Bernard is making it very
plain.'

'I've got a nasty feeling about him. I think he's
up to no good.'

'Oh! What a wicked thing to say about a kind
generous man.' Sybil's cheeks flushed. 'You know
nothing. You're only a child.'

She glanced impatiently at Elvi's plain dress.

'Go and get changed immediately,' she went
on. 'I've hung your new dress on the wardrobe
door. I'm sure you'll look quite nice in it, even
with your drab colouring.' She paused. 'Tsk! If
only your hair was corn-coloured like mine. You

176

might've made a good marriage, too.'

'I won't wear anything he's bought,' Elvi declared stubbornly. 'You can take it all back to the shop.'

'I despair of you, Elvi, I really do,' Sybil said in exasperation. 'We've landed on our feet here, my girl. Can't you see it? We'll be associating with the finest families in Swansea soon.'

'If we don't end up in prison first,' Elvi retorted.

'Now, that's enough!' Sybil looked furious. 'You'll go to your room immediately and stay there. No supper either.'

At that moment the doorbell rang and Sybil jumped.

'It can't be them already! Go and see, Elvi. Show them in here. Offer them some sherry. I'll make my entrance from the side room. And curtsey, mind.'

Sybil hurried away into the adjoining room with a swish of skirts, while Elvi went reluctantly into the hall to answer the door. Never mind a new dress, she'd be better off with a maid's uniform, she thought bitterly, and opened the door determined not to curtsey, no matter who was outside.

A thin woman, probably in her fifties and dressed entirely in black, stood on the step. A shapeless hat sat squarely on her head and did nothing for her plain blunted features which were set in a grim expression.

'Miss Minnie Dart,' the woman announced in a vinegary voice.

'There's no one here of that name,' Elvi said,

shaking her head. The woman did not look as though she might be a client.

'I'm Minnie Dart, you dunderhead!' the woman said pithily. She stepped forward elbowing Elvi out of the way. 'Tell your mistress I'm here.'

'There must be some mistake.'

'Where's the kitchen? Come along, girl! Don't dawdle. Dawdling is the Devil's work.'

'Look here,' Elvi said loudly. 'You can't just barge in...'

'Don't keep our honoured guests standing around, Elvi.' Sybil bustled out of the salon, a wide smile of greeting on her face. She stopped short at the sight of the woman in black. 'Oh!'

'Mrs Lloyd?' the woman asked. 'I'm Miss Dart. Major Pomfrey sent me to help with refreshments, etcetera.'

Sybil's face immediately assumed an aloof expression, and she lifted her nose in the air disdainfully. 'Yes, of course. You're late, Dart,' she said in a huffy tone. 'And next time, use the servants' entrance at the back, if you please.'

Minnie Dart made a strange little strangled sound in her throat and her eyes sparked but she said nothing.

'I have some very important people coming here this evening, Dart,' Sybil went on haughtily. 'Quality, they are, so I want no sloppiness, you understand? Or the Major will hear of it.'

Standing closer to Minnie Dart as she was, Elvi could hear a faint rumbling in the woman's chest, and her sallow face showed a tinge of pink.

Revelling in her superiority, Sybil was oblivious. 'You'll find everything you need in the kitchen, Dart. Elvi, show her the way and then go straight to your room. That's all for now, Dart. I'll ring when your services are needed.'

Sybil flounced away to return to the salon while Elvi led the way to the kitchen. Curious, she lingered, watching the woman take off her hat and coat.

'Do you work for Major Pomfrey?'

'What business is it of yours if I do?'

Elvi decided to make her position in the household clear. 'Mrs Lloyd is my mother.'

Minnie Dart sniffed. 'Not something to be proud of, I'd say.'

In all honesty, Elvi had to agree. 'How long have you worked for him? Does he have a wife?'

Minnie Dart stared. 'You're a very nosy girl, aren't you?' She took a white starched apron out of her bag and put it on and then a crisp maid's cap. 'I keep house for the Major and, no, he isn't married.'

Elvi continued to linger while Minnie Dart began to prepare for the evening's refreshments. There were so many questions Elvi wanted to ask about Bernard Pomfrey; so many things about him disturbed her.

There was something dubious about him, a feeling prompted by that strange vision she'd had. She needed to learn all she could about him not only for her own sake but her mother's, too. Minnie Dart lived under the same roof, so she must know all about him.

'Didn't your mother tell you to go to your room?' Minnie Dart asked sternly. 'I think you'd

179

better go.'

'Is Major Pomfrey a good employer?' That wasn't what she really wanted to ask.

'As good as any, I dare say.'

'Does he...?'

'Enough!' Minnie Dart waved her away with a bony hand. 'You'll get a chance to know him when he moves in.'

'What?' Elvi stared, appalled at the news.

'Major Pomfrey is taking the rooms upstairs, moving in next Thursday.'

Elvi felt as though someone had slapped her face. 'Why?'

'He owns the house, girl,' Minnie Dart said. 'He can do as he pleases.' She paused a moment. 'Although, why he's allowed that...' She gave Elvi a grave glance. 'You know holding séances is ungodly, don't you? It's the work of the Devil.'

Elvi did not know how to reply.

'I shall sleep with my crucifix under my pillow,' Minnie Dart declared. 'And a bulb of garlic on my night-stand.'

Elvi swallowed hard, and with one last glance at the woman's forbidding expression, scuttled away to her room.

Although at first a little overwhelmed at the elevated status of her new clientele, ladies who reeked of wealth and position and spoke with plums in their mouths, Sybil found herself well prepared for them, thanks to the Major, bless him.

He had furnished her with quite a few interesting details of their personal lives. Consequently, the first séance went very well and she had given a good account of herself. She could tell the ladies were impressed, and wished the Major had been there to witness her triumph.

Mrs Mathias, a dear gracious lady who insisted Sybil should call her Dolly, had been overjoyed to make contact with her late husband Donald. That had been an easy three guineas. The other two ladies, one a wealthy widow and the other a grieving mother, appeared well satisfied to have made contact with their dear departed, and paid up their fees with alacrity.

There had been a few tricky moments with that Mrs Maisie Coombs, who was too sharp for her own good.

Sybil folded her lips as she remembered the spark of scepticism in Maisie's eyes as the séance began. But judging her to be a woman who had lived a full life, Sybil invented the departed spirit of an ardent admirer of Maisie, hinting at a passionate interlude and an indiscretion. Maisie denied understanding the message but Sybil had been gratified to see a discomfited flush come to the woman's cheeks, and she appeared chastened afterwards.

Eight guineas for one evening's work. Things were turning out very well. If only Elvi would be more co-operative. She always wore such a guilty expression in the presence of clients that Sybil feared she might give the game away. Tsk! She was a liability, that one, in one way or another.

Sybil felt hard done by suddenly, thinking back to the past and the man, Elvi's father, who had deserted her. She had loved him, but could never forgive him. It had been a terrible struggle for years.

Sybil pushed those memories aside as she sat before her vanity mirror in her bedroom, and inspected her reflection. She was still attractive. Maybe she could lose a little weight, but for her age her complexion was flawless, almost as pure as Elvi's.

There was no point in dwelling in the past, she told herself. Things were looking up now. She had money and the means of making much more. And more importantly, there was a new man in her life, a man of substance who was definitely interested in her. She could almost hear wedding bells.

Elvi could tell that Sybil was as surprised as she had been to learn that Major Pomfrey was to occupy the upper floors of the house in Walter Road. Elvi felt dread at the prospect but Sybil was elated at the news.

'I knew it! What did I tell you? It's only a matter of time, my girl, before he speaks of marriage.'

Elvi bit her thumb nail anxiously. Whenever they had been alone together in the past the Major had the same look on his face as the red-headed manager of the Co-op when he had put his hand on her bottom and squeezed. She winced at the memory of the shame she had felt.

She wouldn't be surprised if the Major had a key for every lock in the house. She didn't need visions to tell her that the man was evil. From Thursday on she would sleep with a chair back under the knob of her bedroom door and, if necessary, scatter tin-tacks on the linoleum.

Connie was disconcerted on Saturday night when Bernie walked into the parlour at the Pleasure Palace, something he never did as a rule, and jerked his thumb, beckoning her outside.

She arose from the piano stool and followed him out. His visits to the house had been very infrequent since Josh had taken the partnership. She guessed he was wary of Josh's continuous presence, and his sharp prying eyes.

Bernie was waiting for her in the reception hall. Fred the doorman was standing nearby and Connie was conscious he was watching them covertly.

'Go up to your bedroom,' Bernie said in an urgent undertone. 'I'll be with you in a few minutes.'

'There's no need,' Connie said quickly. She glanced at Fred, but he was talking to a man who had just entered. 'Herb has found you a new girl. She's in Trudy's old room. Herb's in the office now. He'll take you up to her.'

'No. Herb's as peeved as all hell because of Josh Rowlands taking over.' Bernie shook his head. 'I don't trust him to find me a clean lay any longer, so get upstairs, Con.'

'Herb will make more trouble if he finds out,' Connie warned anxiously. 'You know what he's like.'

He grabbed her arm roughly and moved them further out of earshot of Fred.

'Let's not forget who owns this place,' he said in a harsh whisper. 'Herb can be replaced or he can have a nasty accident. Now do as you're told.'

183

Connie slipped into her negligee and sat on the edge of the bed, smoking a cigarette, her heart heavy as she watched Bernie dress.

In her profession she knew better than to look for respect, but she and Bernie went back a long way. They had a history. She had borne his child, although he did not know it.

It hurt her so badly to realise she meant absolutely nothing to him, not even after all this time. He couldn't make his indifference plainer than when he used her without a thought for how she felt. Prostitutes don't have feelings. She knew that was what most people believed.

'Herb wouldn't double-cross you, Bernie,' she ventured to say. 'I've talked to the girl. She's genuine. He picked her up at the railway station, fresh up from Carmarthen. She was looking for domestic work. Herb told her how she could make real money.'

'I don't need Herb to get me a girl,' Bernie said cheerfully. He was always in better temper after he had vented his lust. 'I've found one.'

Connie exhaled smoke. 'You said that a month ago or more, but you're still here with me.'

He grinned. 'I doubt I'll bother you again, Con. The girl is the daughter of that woman I was telling you about. That so-called clairvoyant, Sybil Lloyd.' He laughed with satisfaction as he shrugged into his jacket. 'I've moved into my property in Walter Road. The mother is renting the lower floor. So you see I've got the girl under my own roof. It's merely a matter of days before I take her.'

'It may not be as easy as you think,' Connie warned. 'The mother may already suspect your motives.'

'Sybil Lloyd is a vain empty-headed fool, who thinks I'm interested in her. Stupid cow! She doesn't suspect a thing.'

'How old is this girl?'

'Elvi is seventeen and luscious. I'll have her in the palm of my hand and in my bed within days.'

Connie saw the ferocious glint light up his eyes and quailed. Even after just slaking his need he was almost slavering again.

For some reason she thought of her daughter, Lynnys. She had worried herself sick over Josh Rowlands this last week or so, wondering if he was deceiving her, wondering if he was secretly planning to corrupt Lynnys in just the same way that Bernie planned to corrupt this young girl, Elvi Lloyd. It made her shudder to think so. The girl's mother should be warned.

Connie stubbed out her cigarette. 'You're old enough to be her father,' she said tersely.

'What the hell does that matter?'

Connie remained silent. Nothing mattered to him except his own pleasures.

Equally silent Bernie put on his flat workman's cap, wound a grubby cotton muffler around his neck; his disguise, and walked out of the room without another word.

Connie felt a degree of bitterness she had not experienced before. Most clients had something to say to the girl as he left her; a word of thanks, even a bawdy joke would signify feeling of some kind. But Bernie had nothing to give, not a

185

murmur, not a nod of acknowledgment, even to the woman who had stood by him for so long.

She had made her love for him plain over the years, and he had thrown it back in her face. No one mattered to Bernie except himself. She could almost hate him for it. She was a fool to still nurture tender feelings for him. It would serve him right if his plans for this kid, Elvi, were scuttled.

It was just on three o'clock in the morning. Connie clambered into the bed and lit another cigarette. Her long-suffering heart was patient no longer. It wanted revenge for all the years she had cherished a hopeless love.

And besides, she felt guilt. This Sybil Lloyd should be told about Bernie's intentions. It was only right. She would be glad of a timely warning if Lynnys were in similar danger. She would speak to Elvi's mother as soon as possible, but it would have to wait until Monday when Bernie was at business.

She thought for a moment of the risk she was taking. He must never know she had interfered, because if he did she dreaded to think what he would do. Bernie wasn't a man to cross, as Josh Rowlands might find out to his cost.

Connie smoked the cigarette to the last, and then blew out the flame in the oil lamp nearby. Maybe now she could sleep for a while.

Ten o'clock already. Trudy yawned widely as she finished off the pots and pans in the big kitchen in Ffynonne Crescent and then hung them on their respective hooks ready for the next day.

186

She was tired but felt a little disgruntled, too. Her Sunday half-day had been cancelled because of a dinner party to celebrate the eldest son's birthday. No mention had been made by Mr Cranston of an alternative half-day off.

As a result she had been unable to call on Lynnys and Phoebe as usual, and was surprised how much she missed seeing them.

Trudy dried her hands on a coarse linen cloth, turned the gaslight out and left the kitchen, closing the door carefully. The passage leading to the back stairs was very dark and she wished she had brought a candle.

She was feeling her way along the wall when suddenly there was a rustling sound in the darkness ahead of her and her heart jumped into her mouth.

'Who's there?'

'Hush! It's me, Rhodri.'

A match was struck and in the flare of light she saw him standing there in shirtsleeves, a candlestick in his other hand. He lit the candle and held it high.

'What are you doing below stairs, Master Rhodri?' Trudy asked breathlessly, feeling a little wriggle of excitement stir.

'Looking for you, my girl.'

'Why?'

'I'm lonely, Trudy.'

Trudy wanted to giggle, and managed to quell it. 'Are you drunk?'

'Certainly not!'

'If Mr Cranston catches us you'll get me into trouble, Master Rhodri.'

'I will, given half the chance.'

'Saucy!'

'Come up to my room, Trudy.'

'What kind of a girl do you think I am?'

'A kind-hearted one, I hope,' Rhodri said in a low voice. 'Call me Rhodri. I've thought about you ever since I met you in the breakfast room the other day. Please come to my room.'

Trudy sniffed. 'It's all right for you,' she said. 'But I've got to get up at five o'clock tomorrow morning to light the range fire. I need my rest.'

'I had thought you quite liked me.'

'I do, Rhodri. I like you a lot.' She had been thinking about him, too, but knew such dreams never came true for a girl like her.

'Please! Please, Trudy.'

She looked up into his face illuminated by the candlelight, plain of countenance, yet young and fresh, and she felt a rush of tenderness she had never felt for any man before.

'Oh, all right then! But I won't stay long, mind.'

14

Connie walked the length and breadth of Walter Road on Monday morning, unable to find the house to which Bernie had recently moved, until by sheer chance she saw Minnie Dart, whom she knew to be Bernie's housekeeper, emerge from a house up near the church.

She waited until Minnie was out of sight and then climbed the steps from the pavement and rang the bell. As she waited for someone to answer she wondered if she were making a big mistake. She had no idea of the kind of a woman this Sybil Lloyd was. Suppose she betrayed her to Bernie? She dreaded to think what he might do.

The fair-haired woman who opened the door was of medium height, plump, and wearing a fashionable afternoon gown which looked as though it had cost a pretty penny.

She was smiling broadly as the door opened, but after giving Connie an all enveloping glance, her expression changed to haughtiness, and her tone, as she spoke, was aloof.

'Yes, what do you want?'

'Are you Mrs Sybil Lloyd?'

The woman hesitated, looking Connie up and down, making no effort to hide her distaste and suspicion. 'I might be,' she said at last, her tone distant. 'What business can *you* have here?'

'I want to talk to you, Mrs Lloyd.'

Sybil sniffed. 'Huh! I've nothing to say to the likes of you. Go away! This is a respectable neighbourhood.'

Connie had seen that look on the faces of so-called respectable women many times, yet it always hurt and shamed her. But she would not back down now. A terrible wrong was about to be committed. She must do all she could to prevent an innocent girl being ruined.

'It's about your daughter, Elvi,' Connie persisted, resisting the urge to turn and leave.

The woman's eyes widened. 'How could you possibly know my daughter, a low woman like you?'

Connie felt her cheeks flush at the fresh insult, and bit back a sharp retort, curbing the anger that was rising in her breast. Feeling very vulnerable and exposed, she wanted to get off the doorstep.

'I don't know her personally, but I've heard talk about her. I know she's in some danger,' Connie persisted. 'Might I come in a moment to explain?'

'I hardly think so!' Sybil Lloyd said pithily, giving her another scornful look. 'Frankly, I don't know you or want to.' Her glance played disdainfully over Connie's appearance. 'I certainly don't want *your* kind in my home.'

Connie bit her lip. Her own clothes were a little more flamboyant, a little more provocative, perhaps, but they were as expensive as Sybil Lloyd's and what's more she had paid for them herself. Whereas, she guessed, Sybil's apparent affluence had come from Bernie's wallet.

'Never mind my kind,' Connie said stiffly. 'I'm here to do you a favour, to save your daughter from a life of shame and misery.'

'What nonsense!' But Sybil looked troubled. 'You'll be asking me to cross your palm with silver next.'

Connie was angered anew at the woman's stupidity. 'Are we to talk of your daughter on the doorstep for all to hear?'

Sybil's lips thinned with anger. 'I told you to go away!

'Do you want your daughter to end up like me? Earning her living on her back, at the mercy of any man with a few coins in his pocket, all because you're too stupid to listen to reason?'

Startled, Sybil's hand flew to her mouth and then she glanced up and down the street, as though afraid that Connie's words had been over-heard. Apparently satisfied that they were unobserved, she looked at Connie, her expression angry.

'What a terrible thing to say to a mother.'

'It's a terrible thing to happen to any girl, believe me, I know.'

Sybil hesitated, obviously uncertain. 'What are you up to? If you think I'll give you money you're mistaken,' she said sharply. 'I'll call a constable.'

'I'm not after money, believe me,' Connie answered hastily, feeling her throat close at the threat.

If the police were called Bernie would learn what she had done, and that meant trouble for her. The last thing he would want was the police poking into his affairs. He had a lot to hide, and

191

would undoubtedly punish her for causing it.

'I don't think your landlord Mr Pomfrey would like having the police call at his property,' Connie hurried to point out. 'And think of the neighbours. Think of your reputation.'

'How do you know the name of my landlord?' Sybil burst out. 'And it's Major Pomfrey actually.'

'I know a lot about you,' Connie said. 'More than you know.'

Sybil blinked, and after hesitating a moment, stepped aside for Connie to enter. They stood in the hall. 'This is as far as you go,' she said firmly.

'Are you afraid I'll contaminate your sitting room?' Connie could not keep the bitterness from her voice.

'Say what you have to and then leave,' Sybil said pithily. 'This is a respectable house and, as you pointed out, I have my reputation, not to mention my profession to guard. Who are you anyway?'

'My name is Connie Lamar,' Connie told her swiftly. 'I've come to warn you about Bernie Pomfrey and his intentions towards your young daughter.'

'The Major?' Sybil looked sceptical. 'How absurd! What could you know of a gentleman like him? The Major and I are close.' Her look was triumphant. 'Very close. He looks on Elvi as merely a child, a daughter even. I believe I know all there is to know about him.'

With a stab of hurt Connie wondered how close. Had Bernie already taken this woman as a lover, just to get at the girl? She would not put it past him.

'You think you know him, Mrs Lloyd, but you

don't,' she said. 'There are sides to him you wouldn't dream possible...' Connie stopped, realising her anger and hurt was loosening her tongue. 'He has a reputation,' she went on lamely.

'I don't believe you for a minute,' Sybil flared. 'The Major is a gentleman through and through. He's proved that by the way he has treated me, so generous.' Sybil lifted her nose in the air. 'One thing I do know, he'd have no truck with the likes of you.'

Connie hesitated. It would be unwise to reveal the whole truth about Bernie's activities. All she wanted was to save Elvi Lloyd.

'I don't know him personally, of course,' she lied. 'But I have been told by a male acquaintance that Pomfrey's intentions towards your daughter are bad. He's tricked you, Mrs Lloyd. He lusts after Elvi and he's determined to get her in his clutches.'

'What?' Sybil stared and spluttered with fury. 'I've never heard such balderdash in my life. How dare you slander a dear friend of mine like this? Who's put you up to such wickedness?'

'Bernard Pomfrey is not your friend,' Connie insisted. 'He's buttering you up.' Connie waved a hand at Sybil's stylish clothes and their surroundings. 'He's given you money, hasn't he? Flattered you? But it's not you he wants, believe me. He's doing all this to get to Elvi. You must listen to me.'

Sybil looked at her in stony silence. Connie guessed the woman's vanity had taken a severe blow. She did not want to believe the truth.

'I'm not lying, Mrs Lloyd. Bernard Pomfrey is

193

an evil man...'

Connie hesitated, shaken by her own words. Bernie was evil. This was the first time she had ever acknowledged it even to herself. So much in thrall to him had she been since a young girl, she had never before wanted to believe it, but it was true. He had used her, betrayed her; had nothing but contempt for her feelings. Why was she continuing to protect him?

'This male acquaintance of yours...' Sybil paused and looked Connie up and down, her lips curling with contempt. 'One of your degenerate customers, I suppose?'

It was no good beating about the bush, Connie decided.

'Yes, he's a customer of mine, as you put it.' She nodded, quelling renewed feelings of shame that welled up within her. 'But he's also a business acquaintance of Bernard Pomfrey. Pomfrey told him that he has a young girl under his roof who he intends to take to his bed. This roof, Mrs Lloyd.'

Sybil's sneering expression angered her. The woman needed to be jolted out of her complacency by straight talking.

'Pomfrey boasted that he has the girl entirely at his mercy,' she went on, watching Sybil closely. 'He described her mother as vain and empty-headed, too weak to thwart his plan to make Elvi his personal ... whore.'

'Oh!' Sybil stepped back, clapping a hand over her mouth, obviously appalled at Connie's choice of words. 'Oh! My God!'

'Yes, Elvi, Mrs Lloyd. He named the girl to my friend,' Connie went on doggedly. 'There's no mistake. You must take immediately steps to put Elvi out of harm's way.'

Sybil recovered her composure and her eyes narrowed.

'I still don't believe a word of it. It's not possible. The Major has never given me a moment's concern...' She hesitated, her eyes widening as though a disturbing thought had struck her.

'Perhaps you should question your daughter,' Connie suggested quickly. 'There may be things she's afraid to tell you.'

'I want you to leave immediately,' Sybil said, holding her head at an imperious angle and glowering at Connie. 'You're a mischief-maker, that's what you are.'

'And you *are* a vain fool, just as he said you were!' Connie glared. She clamped her lips together then, realising there was no more she could say or do, and turned towards the door.

'Yes, I'll leave, but upon your own head be it, Mrs Lloyd, if Elvi falls into his evil hands. Her young life will be ruined.'

'Get out!'

Connie went, hearing the door slammed behind her. She felt wretched. She had warned Sybil Lloyd, but perhaps she had done more harm than good.

Sybil closed the door with a slam against her unwelcome visitor, and felt outraged at the woman's impudence. Such lies!

She went back into the salon and sat trying to compose herself. This Connie Lamar had striking looks in spite of her profession. Sybil felt a

195

momentary stab of jealousy. For all she knew the woman was a rival for dear Bernard's affections.

She dismissed the idea immediately, remembering the way Connie Lamar was dressed, expensively, but at the same time, ostentatious and coquettish. She was from the gutter and no amount of finery could disguise that fact. Bernard would have nothing to do with a woman like that.

But she was unsettled for the rest of the day, and was glad there was no séance arranged for that evening. She was waiting when Elvi came home from work, and called her into the sitting room as soon as she heard her quick steps in the hall.

'Elvi, come here.'

'What is it, Mam?' Elvi said. She stood in the doorway, looking at her mother expectantly while shrugging out of her summer coat of coarse linen and taking off her tam. 'I'm hungry. I'll make some tea. Do you want some?'

'Never mind tea. Sit down, girl,' Sybil said tensely. 'I want to speak to you.'

She watched her daughter closely as the girl reluctantly took a seat, and noticed, as though for the first time, the full young breasts thrusting against the thin cotton of Elvi's dress; her slender waist and shapely hips. Her daughter was seventeen, almost a woman. There were men who hungered after such tender youth. But surely, Bernard was not one of them?

Sybil did not know how to begin the questioning.

'Mam?'

Sybil clasped her hands together tightly, feeling

196

her cheeks heat up. Men and their desires were never subjects she ever expected to discuss with her daughter. But the shocking words of Connie Lamar were still echoing in her head.

'The Major,' Sybil began hesitantly. 'Why do you dislike him?'

Elvi glowered darkly. 'He gives me the creeps,' she said frankly.

'But has he actually ever done or said anything that ... upset you?'

'Yes, he did!' Elvi exclaimed hotly. 'I tried to tell you but you wouldn't listen, as usual.'

Sybil swallowed, feeling her heart quicken. 'Well, I'm listening now.'

Elvi sniffed, but quietened down. 'It was the evening he called at Fleet Street to offer us these rooms,' she went on. 'You were at the butcher's, and I didn't want him to come in, but he pushed past me anyway. He's no gentleman!'

Sybil remembered that evening with chagrin. She had almost made a fool of herself, thinking he had come to propose marriage.

'Go on.'

'He wanted me to sit on the sofa next to him, and get to know him better, he said, but I wouldn't.'

Sybil shrugged. 'I can't see anything untoward in that, Elvi. The Major was probably being friendly.'

Elvi shook her head. 'Friendly, my foot! You weren't there, Mam. You didn't see the way he looked at me, as though he'd like to eat me. It frightened me.'

'I'm sure it was your imagination, Elvi...'

197

'You won't believe me even now, will you?' Elvi jumped to her feet angrily. 'He's no different to any of your other gentleman callers. They're all horrible!'

Sybil was startled and then annoyed. 'You had to mention them to him, didn't you? Why couldn't you have kept quiet?'

Elvi bit her lip, looking discomfited. 'It sort of slipped out, Mam. He asked if any of them had ever touched me, and if I'd been a naughty girl.' Elvi's face flamed. 'I knew what he meant, Mam, and I was disgusted and told him so.'

'Oh, Elvi…'

'He has no right to say those things to me, Mam. It's not decent.'

'No, it's not.'

Sybil took an uncertain step towards her daughter. They had never been close, but was that Elvi's fault? The years of struggling alone with a child had been hard. She felt a moment of guilt, realising she had unfairly blamed Elvi for her struggles.

But their luck seemed to have changed just lately. They had done well from the move to this fine house, and her new and affluent clientele had put some real money in her pocket. For the first time in her life she could spend and not worry.

Sybil felt suddenly angered. Now Connie Lamar's accusations were about to spoil things.

'Did the Major ever lay a hand on you, Elvi? That's the point.'

'No! I wouldn't let him get near enough,' Elvi said vigorously. 'He said I was beautiful, and

198

needed an older man to take care of me.'

She looked pleadingly at Sybil, and her mother saw real worry in the girl's eyes.

'Mam, why did he move in upstairs? What's he up to? I'm afraid.'

'Oh, Elvi, I think you're taking your dislike too far,' Sybil said, attempting to speak lightly. 'Now go and make the tea. I'm parched for a cup.'

Elvi's look was lingering and reproachful, but Sybil turned away, and then she heard the girl leave the room.

Sybil gave a sigh, and sat down, thankful that the matter was over. She was assured now that no real harm had been done. Maybe Bernard had said things he shouldn't, but that was men for you. They were all the same. Elvi was too sensitive, and inexperienced at dealing with their ways, that was the trouble.

Things were going very well. There was no point in upsetting Bernard with that woman's wild allegations. Just the same, she would keep an eye on her daughter from now on.

Bernard must never be alone with the girl again, Sybil decided, at least not until he had made known his intentions towards her.

She rose to glance in the mirror at her reflection. It was absurd! What would a man like Bernard want with an inexperienced girl, when he could have a warm understanding woman like her?

She smiled smugly into her own eyes. Perhaps she did not know men as well as Connie Lamar did, but she knew enough.

15

'Mrs Phillips didn't like it,' Lynnys said. 'She told me not to come begging for my job back when everything falls through.' She looked anxiously at the tall man sitting at the table in the living room at Cwmavon Terrace. 'I hope I'm doing the right thing, Mr Rowlands.'

'Put it this way, Lynnys,' he answered with a reassuring smile. 'I'm investing a great deal of money in you. I'd hardly do that if I thought you'd fail.'

'It's such a big step for me.' Lynnys clasped her hands together tightly.

She had yearned for such an opportunity for so long but never believed it could happen. Now this stranger had come into her life. She could not help remembering they had met under questionable circumstances. She was risking a lot in trusting him. But perhaps she doubted herself rather than him.

'Suppose … suppose I'm not good enough?'

'Your mother has … had a beautiful singing voice,' he said, surprising her. 'It's in the blood.'

Lynnys frowned, puzzled. 'How do you know that? You never knew my mother.'

'Your grandmother told me.'

Lynnys' shoulders stiffened. 'She never talks about my parents to me.'

She felt a little put out that Gran had discussed

their family with a relative stranger, but always evaded speaking of them with her, as though there was something shameful in her mother's past.

She remembered Elvi's strange outburst and her insistence that Lynnys' parents were still alive. She had dismissed it as a flight of fancy on her friend's part, but in the light of Gran's willingness to confide family history to Josh, she should perhaps take it more seriously. Lynnys made up her mind to tackle her grandmother on the matter again at the earliest opportunity.

'What else did she say about my mother?' she asked him hopefully.

He shook her head. 'Nothing, except that your parents died of the cholera when you were very young.'

'Has she mentioned my father to you, Mr Rowlands?' Lynnys persisted.

'No, and call me Josh,' he said easily. 'I'm your manager now, and I hope our association will last many years. In fact I'm counting on it.'

She looked at him, trying to see behind the winning smile and the good looks, and realised she was an innocent in the wide world.

'Why are you going to all this trouble, Josh?' She knew enough to realise men did not make generous gestures without expecting something in return. 'What do you hope to gain?'

'Money,' he said frankly, his smile widening. 'Big money. One day you'll appear on a stage in London, billed as a big star, earning more money than you ever imagined. And as you prosper so will I.'

Lynnys was sceptical. That was still only a daydream. She was concerned about the here and now. They needed to pay the rent, not to mention buying food and medicine for Gran.

'But how will we live in the meantime?' Lynnys said uneasily. 'With no job there'll be no money coming in.'

'Don't worry. You leave that to me,' Josh said. 'I'll pay for your day to day needs. And besides all that, I'll hire a coiffeur to dress your hair, and we'll get the best dressmaker in Swansea to rig you out in the most fashionable clothes.'

Lynnys put her fingers to her mouth considering. It all seemed too good to be true. Surprisingly, Gran was obviously under his spell, but Lynnys wondered if they were both being duped in some way.

'To show how much I believe in your talent, Lynnys,' Josh said, interrupting her doubting thoughts, 'I'll pay you a retaining salary.'

That seemed too much, and she stared at him suspiciously. She knew little about men, but enough to know that some preyed on young girls. She could not keep a mistrustful tone from her voice.

'You're very generous, Josh. Too generous perhaps.'

'No, I'm not,' he answered quickly, obviously understanding her mood. 'Let me assure you, Lynnys, this is strictly business.' He grinned engagingly. 'I have no designs on your body, lovely though it is.'

Lynnys felt her cheeks flush.

'There'll be a legal contract between us,' he

202

went on easily. 'I'm not doing this for nothing, mind. You'll pay me back when you start earning money. I'll expect it.'

He rose to his feet. 'I've engaged a voice coach for you, a Mr Hibbler. He has a studio in Wind Street.' He took his watch out of his waistcoat pocket. 'Your first appointment is at ten o'clock. And this afternoon you attend Madam Bonham's Dancing Academy in St Helen's Road.'

'Dancing Academy?' Lynnys felt a little bewildered. 'What on earth for? I'm a singer not a ballet dancer.'

'Ballet, no,' Josh said with a grin. 'But you need to be graceful on stage; know how to move. It doesn't hurt for an artiste to be an all-rounder, kid.'

Things were moving so swiftly she felt out of breath already.

'Phoebe will accompany you as chaperone,' Josh went on. 'A hansom will call here to take you to various lessons each day.'

She was astonished. 'I've never been in a hansom in my life. I can walk.'

'Phoebe can't,' Josh reminded her. 'I'll go with you to Mr Hibbler's this morning to introduce you, and then I must leave you, as I've a business appointment elsewhere.'

He took a folded sheet of paper from his jacket pocket. 'This is your lessons schedule, Lynnys, for several weeks to come.'

She took it from him and stared at the contents. Singing and dancing lessons three times a week, interspersed with lessons in deportment, and sessions with an elocutionist. According to this there'd be hardly a moment to call her own.

She had never been afraid of hard work, but wondered how she would cope with the strangeness of it all. Yet she wanted to succeed with all her heart.

'The hard work will be worth it, Lynnys, you'll see,' Josh said with confidence. 'I have faith in you. Don't disappoint me.'

Josh came away from Mr Hibbler's studio as soon as he could, and made his way on foot up High Street to the premises of Pomfrey and Payne, Outfitters.

Mr Dawson came to meet him as he walked into the shop. 'What can we do for you, sir? Oh! It's Mr Rowlands, isn't it?'

'You have a good memory,' Josh said with approval. 'Is Mr Pomfrey in? I'd like to speak with him.'

Mr Dawson gave a little cough. '*Major* Pomfrey is in the office, sir. I'll just see if he's available.'

'Don't bother,' said Josh swiftly. 'He'll see me. I'll announce myself.'

'But, sir...!'

Josh strode past the older man purposefully and opened the office door without knocking. Bernie looked up, an impatient expression on his face which turned to anger when he recognised his visitor.

'What the hell do you want, Rowlands?'

'I've come to do you a favour, Bernie.'

Josh took a chair from against the wall nearby and, placing it before the desk, sat down, crossing his legs comfortably. He took off his fedora, placing it on his knee and removed his gloves while studying the man before him.

'How would you like to be rid of me from the Pleasure Palace for good, Bernie?' he went on.

Bernie closed the accounts book he was examining, and leaned back in his chair. His expression was wary now.

'How much would it cost me?'

Josh laughed. 'You're quick!' He hesitated, wondering how far he could go. He decided to stretch it to the limit. 'Thirty thousand should do it.'

Bernie gave a bellow of laughter. 'You overprice yourself, Rowlands. That would buy up half of Swansea,' he said. 'You can stay at the house. It makes no odds to me.'

'You don't come by there so often as you used to,' Josh said. 'I think I worry you, Bernie. You'd like to see me gone.'

'You flatter yourself,' Bernie said, putting the account book in a drawer and locking it. 'You're a mild inconvenience, that's all.'

There was a degree of smugness in his tone which Josh found unsettling. He said nothing, but waited.

'I won't need to visit the Palace for quite a while. There was always a chance I'd be recognised anyway,' Bernie went on. 'I've found a little beauty, and she's under my own roof. She'll stay there until I've finished with her, which may be some time. I've a lot to teach her.' He grinned complacently. 'Did I tell you I've moved up to Walter Road among the *crachach*?'

'Who's overpricing himself now?'

Bernie scowled. 'Why are you here really?'

205

Josh decided to be partly truthful. 'I want to turn legitimate. Association with a flesh house won't do me any good where I'm going.'

'Then get out,' Bernie said harshly. 'No one needs you around anyway.'

'I'll go when I get what's due to me,' Josh said evenly. 'I've got plans for the big time. I need ready capital to finance a new venture in show business.'

'What?' Bernie looked disbelieving. 'You don't know the first thing about show business. It would be a waste of good money. You've been a petty hustler all your life, Rowlands, and you'll never be anything else.'

'I know a sure thing when I see it,' Josh said decisively. 'I've discovered a girl with a considerable singing talent. A real looker, too.'

'Oh, so that's it.' Bernie nodded knowingly. 'A skirt. Huh! I might've known.'

'It's not like that. This is business.'

'Yes, funny business. Who is she? Some floozy you picked up off the street?'

Josh was angered despite himself. 'No, this kid has class. She'll go far.' He looked disdainfully at Bernie. 'She's turned out well, despite the fact that her father is a dirty scoundrel.' He almost said murdering scoundrel, but stopped himself. 'And her mother ... well, let's say her mother is no better than she should be.'

Bernie laughed. 'The daughter of a tart? Forget it, Rowlands. She'll go her mother's way. They all do.'

'Not this one.'

Bernie sneered. 'You never could pick a winner.

206

You've managed to muscle your way into a share of the Pleasure Palace, but that's as far as you go.'

Josh ground his teeth. 'What value do you put on your reputation? What value do you put on your neck for that matter? You killed a man, Bernie. That'll never go away.'

Bernie scowled. 'Like I told you before,' he sneered, 'you can't give me away without implicating yourself. This girl can't mean that much to you.'

'How much does your life mean to you?' Josh asked angrily. 'I know you've been seeing Connie. I've covered up for you so far, preventing Herb from finding out because it suited me.'

'So what?'

'So, I may enlighten him. Herb is right on the edge, Bernie. He already believes you've double-crossed him, letting me have a partnership without giving him a chance at it. If he finds you've been using Connie as your personal whore again he'll crack wide open. He'll blab to Charlie Pendle.'

Bernie's face was stony.

'I may even tell him about the warehouse job. He'd give you up in a flash,' Josh went on. 'It's in your interests to get me off your back for good. Twenty thousand.'

'That's still a hell of a lot of money. I don't have it lying around, mind.'

'Herb tells me you've been buying up property all over Swansea,' Josh said. 'Sell up. Paying me is better than getting your throat slit or stretched.'

'Herb talks too much.' Bernie hesitated, the blinking of his eyes revealing he understood the truth of his own words. It was a moment before he spoke again. 'Five.'

'Fifteen, and I'm letting you off cheap.'

Bernie's eyes narrowed. 'You'd make a lot more than fifteen thousand over the years if you stayed at the Pleasure Palace.'

'I'm sick of it,' Josh said harshly. It was true. It had seemed like a good way of making easy money at first, now he felt like a pimp. 'I want out, but at a price for keeping my mouth shut. Take it or leave it, Bernie.'

There was a long silence before Bernie spoke again. Josh waited patiently, knowing he had the upper hand.

'All right,' Bernie agreed at last. 'I'll have the money for you at the end of the week.'

'No, Bernie, I'll take a cheque now.'

Bernie looked furious but after a pause took a cheque book out of the desk drawer and briskly wrote the cheque, handing it reluctantly to Josh.

'I want you out of the Palace now,' he said harshly. 'And I don't want to see your face there again. Understood?'

Josh rose, putting the cheque in an inner pocket, patting it with satisfaction. He put on his hat and reached for his gloves while giving Bernie a hard stare.

'Don't try to double-cross me, Bernie, by cancelling this cheque,' he said. 'You wouldn't survive it.'

Josh called at his bank immediately to deposit the cheque and then waited until he was sure Lynnys had finished her time with Mr Hibbler before returning to the studio. The Hungarian was just preparing for his next pupil. He smiled when he saw Josh.

'Ah! Mr Rowlands.'

'Well, what do you think, Mr Hibbler?'

The little man put his thumb and two fingers to his lips and threw a kiss into the air. 'The young woman, she is superb. What a voice! It will be an honour to train her, yes.'

'Good!' Josh was pleased that his hunch had been confirmed. 'I didn't tell her it was an assessment, Mr Hibbler. She was nervous enough.'

'Yes, I could see it.' Mr Hibbler smiled. 'But when she began to sing, it was all forgotten. Outstanding! She is an artiste of the first order, Mr Rowlands. You have done the world of the theatre a service in discovering her.'

'Our agreement is confirmed then?'

The other man shrugged 'It will not happen overnight, you understand. It will take time and money.'

Josh smiled. 'I have both.' He said this with some relief. If Bernie had not agreed to his terms the whole thing would have fallen through.

They shook hands, and Josh felt a corner had been turned in his life. Bernie was right. He had been a hustler, but from now on things would be different. He had something worthwhile to believe in and work for.

It was ironic that Lynnys was Bernie's daughter, and it seemed hard to believe, too. It pleased him to know that secret, a secret he would guard. Bernie would never know that such a treasure had been denied him.

16

'That woman is impossible!' Sybil exclaimed as she joined Elvi in the sitting room the following Saturday morning. 'Such impertinence!'

'Who, Mam?'

Sybil lifted her shoulders, feeling as though her feathers had been thoroughly ruffled. 'That Minnie Dart, of course. Her disrespectful behaviour towards me is intolerable.'

'Perhaps if you were a little more friendly she'd be more helpful,' Elvi suggested.

'Friendly? To a servant?' Sybil's lips tightened. 'Don't be absurd, Elvi.'

She held herself erect and glanced in the mirror over the fireplace, patting her hair. She had come up in the world and had no intention of hobnobbing with mere servants.

'I get along with her all right,' remarked Elvi.

Sybil gave her daughter a dismissive glance. 'You're just a child. But she knows she can't pull the wool over my eyes. Tsk! I can't understand the Major employing such a low person.'

Without a word her daughter rose from her chair and made to leave the room.

'Wait a minute,' Sybil said sharply. 'You know I have that séance at Mrs Coombs' house this evening. It's very important to me, Elvi, and I want to make a good impression. Wear that pink gown. It looks quite good on you.'

'I shan't go.' Elvi had that stubborn look at her face again and Sybil felt impatient.

'You'll do as you're told, my girl. Besides, I'm doing this for you.' Sybil stroked the back of her hand across her forehead. What it was to have a thankless daughter. 'You could at least help me.'

'I hate these séances,' Elvi said darkly. 'And you know why.'

'Don't start that again!' Sybil felt her anger rising. 'There's a chance I could earn as much as thirty guineas this evening. Thirty guineas! Think of that! That was more than I made in six months in Fleet Street. I'm telling you, Elvi, we've landed on our feet here. I won't have you spoil it. Now go and put curling rags in your hair ready for this evening.'

As Elvi left the room, Sybil heard a man's voice in the hall. Her pulses quickened as she recognised Bernard Pomfrey.

A swift glance in the mirror again told her she looked immaculate, with not a hair out of place, and she turned with a wide welcoming smile as he tapped at the door and entered.

'Bernard!' she gushed. 'I didn't expect to see you here at this time of the morning. I thought you'd be at business.'

'I had to speak with you,' he said and came forward to take her outstretched hand. 'Sybil, my dear, you look wonderful, as usual.'

Sybil smiled coyly, lowering her gaze, as she thought a well-bred lady might. 'Dear Bernard, do sit down.'

They sat on a sofa together. Sybil was conscious of his closeness, and felt a little breathless.

211

'I'm going to take you into my confidence, Sybil, my dear,' Bernard said seriously. 'I'm here on an errand of mercy. The fact is, and I know you'll never betray my confidence, Dolly Mathias is hard up.'

'What?' Sybil stared.

'Yes, I know,' Bernard nodded. 'She puts on a good front, doesn't she, the poor dear? Donald left her only a small annuity, and she's struggling.'

'Well, I never!' Sybil was astonished. On the occasions she had met Dolly Mathias she had been impressed at the older woman's fashionable elegance. 'But her pearls and diamonds?'

'Paste, Sybil dear. All paste.' Bernard looked solemnly sad. 'She had to sell her jewellery a long time ago. I know all this because my dear friend Maisie told me. She asked if I could help without embarrassing Dolly, and I thought of you, Sybil.'

'But what can I do, Bernard?' Sybil was startled. 'I'm just a poor widow woman.'

'I would never ask you to do anything underhand, of course,' Bernard said. 'But you can help with your gift of clairvoyance, Sybil.'

Sybil put her hand to her throat. 'How?'

'I know of a very profitable investment which would yield a considerable return from a small outlay,' Bernard said. 'Of course, given her circumstances Dolly would not risk it on just anyone's say-so, but if her dear departed husband were to tell her to invest, Dolly would do it. It would put her on her feet; the saving of her.'

'I see.' Sybil thought of the thirty guineas she would earn that evening. What was good for

212

Dolly Mathias was good for her. 'I would like to take advantage of that investment myself, Bernard.'

He blinked and looked flummoxed. 'Ah! Yes. Well, that may pose a problem,' he said, rather hesitantly, Sybil thought, and felt slighted for a moment.

'It's very complicated, you see, Sybil, my dear,' he went on. 'If too many people are investing in this project at the same time, it'll draw attention, and then the yield will be much lower.' He shook his head gravely. 'One could lose one's money altogether.'

'Oh!'

'We must think of Dolly on this occasion,' he said cajolingly. 'I promise I will find a good investment for you quite soon.'

'Oh, thank you, Bernard. You're so clever.'

'Tell Dolly that Donald says that a surprise opportunity to make a great deal of money will shortly come her way from a friend. She must put all she can into the project.'

'Poor woman.'

Sybil felt sympathy, having struggled all her life to make ends meet. She liked Dolly, who was friendly and not a bit stuck up, not like that Maisie Coombs, who was always ogling eyes at Bernard. The woman was after him and making no bones about it. Disgusting at her age.

'Of course, I'll help.' She smiled up into his eyes, putting as much appeal into her expression as possible. She was years younger than that Coombs woman, and that must count for something. 'Will you be there this evening, Bernard?'

213

'Unfortunately, no. I have a previous engagement; the annual dinner of the Swansea Shopkeepers Association.' He paused. 'Oh, by the way. I suggest Elvi doesn't accompany you this evening, Sybil. I believe she should stay at home. To be blunt, my dear, her scepticism on these occasions is very apparent. She may unsettle things.'

For some reason Connie Lamar's warning echoed in her mind at that moment.

'Leave her alone here?' She searched his expression keenly. 'I'm not sure...'

'She won't be alone,' Bernard said hastily. 'Dart will be here in my absence. She's very reliable.'

Sybil was tempted to speak against his housekeeper then, but decided now wasn't the time.

'Elvi will stay at home. She's reluctant to go anyway.' She put her hand on his arm. 'I'll do everything I can to help Dolly, Bernard. A friend of yours is a friend of mine.'

Elvi was surprised and relieved when her mother announced that she need not accompany her that evening. Now she could settle down to a quiet read. She had bought a second-hand book from a stall in the market. It was a novel of love, which she had kept hidden from Sybil as she suspected her mother would not approve.

After Sybil swept out to the carriage sent by Mrs Coombs, Elvi fetched her book and was taking it to the sitting room when she saw Minnie Dart come down the stairs from the apartment above, dressed to go out.

'Where are you going?'

Minnie Dart raised her brows. 'What business

is it of yours, my girl?'

'None,' Elvi admitted. 'Except that Major Pomfrey assured my mother that you'd be here to keep me company.'

Minnie sniffed. 'What nonsense! He told me this morning I could take the evening off. I'm going to see my sister.' She gave Elvi an enveloping glance. 'Besides, it's not my place to act nursemaid to a girl of your age. Afraid of the dark, are you?'

Elvi glanced up the stairs towards the Major's rooms. No, it wasn't the dark she was afraid of. The house was so big; it scared her sometimes, especially when she knew he was there.

'Is he at home?'

'No, he's gone to a function at the Guildhall. Probably won't be back until the early hours.' She clicked her tongue. 'Men and drink! It's the Devil's work.'

Minnie sounded as though she disapproved of the Major, and Elvi was surprised.

'You work for him. I thought you liked him.'

Minnie's mouth turned prune-shaped. 'I despise all men,' she said vehemently. 'The Devil incarnate.'

'Did you despise your father?'

Minnie's face turned pale. 'Impudence!' she spluttered, and without another word, strode out of the front door.

With a shrug Elvi went back to her book. It was enjoyable. She easily imagined herself to be the heroine, being wooed by the handsome hero. She sighed over the tender words.

After an hour, when she had grown used to the

215

silence in the rest of the house she decided to make a pot of tea and went into the kitchen. She was just putting the iron kettle on the gas ring when the front door opened and closed again.

Elvi was startled. It couldn't be Sybil home so soon. It must be Minnie Dart back from her sister's. Elvi hoped so. Having never known her own father, she was curious about Miss Dart's and wanted to ask more questions.

She went into the passage that led from the kitchen to the front hall and opened the baize door to call out.

'I'm in the kitchen, Miss Dart, making tea. Come in and chat.'

There was silence and then Elvi heard footsteps, heavy measured footsteps crossing the tiled floor of the hall. She knew that step. Major Pomfrey had returned home!

Elvi retreated quickly to the kitchen. Her impulse was to hide, but what was the good? He knew she was there.

She was standing on the opposite side of the big kitchen table as he pushed the door open and strode in. Attired in a formal long-tailed coat, watch chain stretched across the rise of his stomach, he seemed taller, bulkier than usual, more threatening.

'Ah! Elvi, my dear girl,' he began, smiling widely at her. 'At last we have time to ourselves, eh? And we won't be disturbed.'

Elvi swallowed down her fright and kept silent, watching him warily.

He moved purposefully towards the table.

'I've been waiting for this opportunity for a long

time, too long,' he said. 'Now I'll have what's mine at last.' His eyes flashed in that peculiar way which always made goose-bumps rise on her upper arms, and she felt fear creep up her spine. 'We have all evening,' he went on. 'I'm determined to know you, Elvi, the way a man knows a girl. And when I'm finished you'll know what a real man can do.'

Inexperienced as she was, instinct told her what he had in mind, and she could hardly believe it. Why had Sybil allowed this to happen?

'My mother will be home soon, Major.' She could not keep a quiver from her voice.

'She won't be back for some time, I've seen to that. By then I'll have done all I want to and you'll be mine for keeps.' His tone was triumphant. 'Come here, girl!'

'No!'

'Do as I say, you little tease,' he commanded. 'I can wait no longer.'

Elvi's glance went to the kitchen door standing ajar. Could she move fast enough to escape him?

'Don't try to get away, Elvi,' he warned, his tone ominous, obviously interpreting her glance. 'And don't play games with me, either. I can be very generous to a girl who's good to me. I can get nasty if I'm disobeyed. Now come here!'

There was nothing to lose, Elvi decided. She was trapped, so she might as well make a run for it. She put her knuckles to her eyes as though about to weep, hoping to distract him.

'Don't start blubbering,' he ordered harshly. 'That doesn't cut any ice with me.'

Even as he spoke, Elvi darted for the door. She

reached it as a heavy hand fell on her shoulder. He yanked her back with a snarl.

'You cunning little bitch! You can't get away from me. I will have you. Make up your mind to it.'

Elvi struggled in his grasp. 'Let go of me! Let go!'

'I'll never let you go again, girl,' he said fiercely. 'I've got plans for you. You're my doxy from now on until I get tired of you. And then it's the Pleasure Palace for you.'

She had no idea what he meant, but it sounded like a threat. She struggled fiercely again, but he was too strong.

He caught her by the shoulders and held her in front of him. She could feel his hands shake as he held her fast. In fright she looked up at him. His face was glossy with sweat and he was breathing heavily.

Without warning he thrust her backwards against the wall, pressing his body to hers so that she was unable to move.

Elvi screamed in terror. 'Get away! Take your hands off me.'

'Be quiet!'

He grabbed her chin and jaw roughly, holding her face in an unyielding grip. He bent his head so that his sweaty face was close to hers, his lips red and moist beneath his moustache. Fumes of tobacco and liquor filled her nostrils, making her want to throw up.

'Give me a kiss,' he demanded huskily. 'Come on, my lovely girl, give me what I want. You know you want it too.'

Elvi was unable to twist away and before she knew it, his mouth was pressed down hard against hers. His kiss was so savage she could not breathe properly, and began to whimper in sheer panic.

He released her mouth but still held her face captive.

'There, that wasn't so bad, was it?' he asked. 'The rest will be even better, you'll see.'

'This is wrong,' Elvi gasped, struggling. 'Let me go now or I'll tell my mother. She'll have the authorities on you.'

'Your mother will do nothing to thwart me.' He laughed in triumph. 'She's too greedy and I've got her tied up in knots.'

Releasing her face, his body still pinning her to the wall, he gripped the neck of her dress. 'Now let's see what you've got under that dress. A luscious body, I'll be bound.'

With a mighty heave, he rent the cotton material in two and it fell away.

He laughed. 'What's this? A cotton liberty bodice? You should be wearing silk next to that lovely skin.'

He tore at the bodice too and Elvi felt the buttons give way in front. She tried to lift her hands to protect herself, suddenly ashamed of her nakedness, but before she could do so, his hand closed on her left breast. He squeezed cruelly and Elvi gasped in pain.

'Don't! For pity's sake! Don't!'

He made a strange grunting sound and thrust his body even harder against hers. 'Can you feel how much I want you, you little witch?' he asked hoarsely. 'Can you feel it?'

'You're hurting me,' Elvi whimpered, now so thoroughly terrified her legs were turning to jelly. This was a nightmare and she prayed someone would arrive and rescue her.

He grasped her hand and forced it down against the flies of his trousers. 'Can you feel it, Elvi? It's hungry for you.'

Elvi was horrified and struggled to draw her hand away from the tumult she felt beneath the fabric. Sick to her stomach, she did not understand and did not want to.

'Let me go, you beast!' she screamed in disgust.

'Yes, the beast wants you, and will have you, Elvi, here and now,' he muttered heavily. 'I'll be the first man to take you, and you'll never forget me.'

She felt his hand at her skirts, pulling them up around her hips. 'No!'

He was breathing heavily as he struggled to lift her skirts, while Elvi fought back as strongly as she could, pushing at his hands but he was far too strong for her.

'Don't fight me, you bitch or it'll be the worse for you.'

She forced herself to look up at his face. There was an animal feverishness about his features, his eyes bulging from their sockets in his lust. Terrified though she was, she knew there was no reasoning with him or appealing to his better nature. He was no more than a wild beast and she was at his mercy.

Above her head was a row of copper saucepans hanging from hooks along the wall. If only she could reach one to use as a weapon.

His hand was on the elastic of her bloomers dragging them down, and he gave a triumphant throaty laugh. 'Now we'll see what you have, my pet.'

Elvi lifted an arm straining to grasp at the nearest saucepan, but it was well out of her reach. Instead, realizing her hands were her only weapons, she began to push at his chest, finding extra strength in her dread of what was to come. Her efforts had little effect, and so lifting her hand she raked her fingernails down his cheeks.

He let out a bellow of pain and leaning back struck her viciously across the face. Elvi's head jerked back and cracked against the wall and for a moment she thought she would lose consciousness, but she struggled to remain aware.

'You stupid little whore! You've marked me. I'll beat you black and blue when I've finished with you.'

His grip had slackened and Elvi took advantage to struggle wildly, risking another blow. His hand was at her bloomers again when suddenly there was a sound from the front of the house which made them both freeze. Someone had come in through the front door and had slammed it behind them.

Taking in a great breath, Elvi yelled as loud as she could.

'Help! Mam! Help!'

He clapped his hand over her mouth. 'Shut up!' he hissed fiercely.

Panting, he stood still listening. Elvi took the opportunity to struggle again. Someone was there. Perhaps her mother. She managed to free her mouth.

'Help! Mam!'

He silenced her with his hand over her mouth again. But Elvi heard the creak of the baize door. Someone had come into the passage to the kitchen, but no one appeared. He still held her in a grip of iron, but Elvi could feel his body tense as he waited. He held her immobile so that she could not move a muscle.

The door creaked again as it was released and Elvi heard faintly quick footsteps, the footsteps of a woman cross the tiles of the hall towards the staircase.

'That must be Dart,' he said, as though to himself, his voice full of fury. 'Damnation! I can't risk it now.' He glared down at her. 'You call out again or scream and I'll knock you unconscious, understand?'

She nodded her head as best she could and he released her mouth. His expression was vicious as he looked into her eyes.

'I *will* have you, you stupid whore,' he muttered darkly. 'I've made up my mind you're mine, to do with as I will.'

'I'll tell!'

'No you won't.' He lips curled in disdain as he stared at her. 'If you say a word to anyone I'll expose your mother's fraudulent séances. She'll be in real trouble, believe me.'

'You can't do that.'

'I'll tell them you helped her, so you're guilty, too. No one will believe you against *my* word. You'll both go to prison for sure.'

'You deserve to go to prison, you beast!'

He grabbed her by the throat. 'I should snap your neck here and now, but it doesn't suit me. But I'll make you pay, my girl. Wait until I get you locked up at the Pleasure Palace. You'll pay on your back, over and over, and when I've had enough of you, I'll give you to the rabble.'

Elvi understood none of it, but did recognise a serious threat. Did he mean to abduct her?

He let go of her and stepped away. She saw the damage her fingernails had done; red angry weals marked his right cheek.

'Dart coming back has changed my plans for tonight,' he said bitterly. 'But there'll be many more nights, dearest Elvi. Think about that while you're in your bed.' He smiled sneeringly. 'This evening was just a taster of things to come.'

He whirled suddenly, and striding quickly to the door left the kitchen. Weak with fear, Elvi found she could not stand upright, but slid down the wall until she was sitting on the cold stone flags of the floor, mindless now of her nakedness.

In a daze she heard the front door open and close, and knew that he had gone out. She began to cry then, huge shuddering sobs shaking her body.

She must get away from this house. Her mother must believe her now. But where could they go? He would surely send the police after them in revenge. There seemed no escape from him.

When the shakes in her body eased, Elvi rose from the floor and made her way to their bathroom on the ground floor. She felt unclean and washed herself all over, scrubbing vigorously, almost hysterically, at the places where he had touched her, yet she could still feel the vile sensation of his hands on her body and the smell of him was still in her nostrils.

She hurried to her bedroom afterwards, placed the back of a chair under the door knob in deep dread of his return and then curled up in her bed. The terror of what she had experienced tortured her, making her relive every terrible moment, and although she tried hard, could not help weeping again.

She would never forget this night, not as long as she lived.

17

Sybil returned home from the séance later than she intended, happily conscious of the thirty guineas secure in her purse. She could hardly believe her good fortune. Six months of this and their financial situation would be secure. A year and they would be rolling in it. And it was all due to dear Bernard's generosity. Sybil sighed with satisfaction. He must think a lot of her to go to all this trouble.

The gaslight burned high in the sitting room and removing her cape, Sybil breezed in expecting Elvi to be still up.

She had so much to relate. She had been brilliant tonight, even if she said so herself. Her portrayal of dear departed Donald certainly had Dolly Mathias convinced, she had wept real tears. Sybil was genuinely glad to have helped Bernard help his friend.

'Elvi! What an evening I've had. You wouldn't believe...'

She was disappointed to find the room empty, and clicked her tongue with impatience. What a waste of gas. A book was left open on the sofa and she picked it up. Tsk! One of those trashy love novels. Elvi knew she disapproved. Strange she hadn't hidden it away.

Sybil threw the book back on the sofa and walked into the hall, listening. The house was very quiet, and she felt a moment of unease, but shrugged it off. The taste of her successful evening still lingered and she wanted to savour it some more before she went to bed. But where was Elvi?

She went down the passage to the kitchen. The gaslight was on here, too. What is that girl thinking of? Her head was full of that love rubbish.

Sybil reached up and turned the gas supply low, so that only a faint glow remained. Love! She had stopped believing in that nonsense a long time ago when the man she loved deserted her. Love! Huh! Now she knew better. Only money mattered.

Returning to the sitting room she turned the gas low there too, and then made her way to the back of the house where the bedrooms were. She was still keyed up and was determined to share her excitement no matter how late it was.

She paused outside Elvi's door and listened. She thought at first the girl was probably asleep, but then noticed a faint chink of light beneath the door.

Sybil tapped. 'Elvi! You're not asleep, I know you're not. I'm coming in.' She turned the knob but the door would not budge. 'Elvi, the door is stuck. Help me with it.'

She heard a movement inside the room and after a moment the door was opened a crack. Elvi peered at her through the narrow opening.

'Are you alone, Mam?'

'Well, of course I'm alone. What on earth...?' She peered at her daughter. Elvi's face looked very pale and strained. 'Are you ill, girl?'

226

'Oh, Mam! Something terrible has happened.' Elvi opened the door wider for her mother to come in.

Sybil strode forward. 'What's got into you, Elvi, leaving all the gaslight on? You're acting like a baby, afraid of the dark.'

'Assaulted, I've been,' Elvi blurted. 'By that awful man upstairs.'

'What?' Sybil's mouth remained open in astonishment and disbelief.

Pulling her dressing gown more tightly around herself, Elvi sat on the bed and began to cry.

Sybil stared at her. 'What did you say?'

'He hurt me, Mam!' Elvi blubbed. 'He tore my clothes, even my liberty bodice. And then he put his hand here.' Elvi put both her hands over her breasts in a defensive manner. 'He was beastly! He said terrible things, called me names.'

'I can't believe it. You're making this up to upset me.'

'I'm not! It's true, I tell you. Why won't you believe me?' Elvi stood up and slipped out of her dressing gown. She lifted the short sleeves of her nightgown. 'There! Look! He did that.' She pulled down the neckline of her nightdress. 'And this.'

Sybil saw ugly bruising on her daughter's upper arms and breast. 'Where did this happen?' she demanded, uncertain how to cope with the situation. 'Not in your bedroom? Elvi, you didn't lure him in here, did you?'

Elvi gave a howl of anguish. 'I did nothing to deserve it, Mam. How could you think so?' She sat on the bed again, her face in her hands.

Completely flummoxed, Sybil sat down next to

her, catching her breath. 'Of course not. I didn't mean that. It's just that...' She glanced around the room bemused. 'The Major has always appeared such a gentleman...' She shook her head. 'It's hard to believe he'd do something like this.'

'Well, he did!' Elvi was vehement. 'He meant to do more, something very bad, I know it.'

'I'm sure he didn't mean to go as far as you think.' Sybil was floundering, confused by her cherished hopes of him now set against the evidence before her. 'Men sometimes get carried away,' she went on weakly.

'His hands were all over me, Mam!' Elvi shrieked, jumping to her feet to face Sybil. 'I told him to stop but he wouldn't. He tried to pull my bloomers down and he would have, too, if Miss Dart hadn't come home unexpectedly.'

Sybil straightened her back. 'His housekeeper went out this evening?'

Elvi nodded. 'He gave her the evening off. She told me as she was going out.' She gulped. 'Obviously he didn't expect her to return so soon. He was furious.'

Sybil folded her lips in a tight thin line. Bernard had lied to her. That was no figment of Elvi's vivid imagination.

'It was disgusting, Mam,' Elvi went on. She looked as though she might throw up. 'He forced me to ... to touch him in front ... oh! Mam! I feel sick.'

Sybil ground her teeth in ire. Bernard had deceived her, insisting Elvi stay at home when all the time he was planning this. Connie Lamar's warning came back with full force. Why hadn't she taken it seriously?

'We've got to leave this house, Mam,' Elvi went on, a touch of hysteria in her voice. 'As soon as we can. We must look for new lodgings in the morning.'

Sybil was startled. 'Now, now, Elvi,' she said quickly. 'Let's not get things out of proportion.'

Giving up everything they had seemed a step too far. They were very comfortable here and there was money to be made. She was sure Bernard could be dealt with, without giving up everything she had achieved.

'You're upset, of course, you are,' she went on in a reasoning tone. 'But he didn't really harm you, did he?'

'He mauled me and threatened me. I'm very frightened,' Elvi exclaimed hotly. 'He said he'd lock me up in a place called the Pleasure Palace. What's he talking about, Mam?'

Sybil put her fingers to her mouth. She had no idea what he meant, but the name sounded like it might be a brothel he was referring to.

No! That couldn't be right. The Major was a gentleman. Of course, even gentlemen got excited at times and acted rashly, but Bernard would never have anything to do with a house of ill-repute; not a man in his position. He was a respectable business man and had standing.

And besides, he moved in such a high social circle, dining with some of the best people in Swansea; with influential friends such as Dolly Mathias and Maisie Coombs. They would never be associated with a man of dubious character. It didn't make sense.

She glanced at her daughter. It irked her to think that Elvi was the object of his attentions and not herself, and felt deep disappointment in him which cut her to the quick.

Yet the more she thought about it the more absurd and unlikely it seemed. It must have been no more than a momentary temptation on his part, brought on by Elvi acting provocatively in some way. As for the lie he had told her about Miss Dart, well, men could say and do peculiar things in moments of foolhardiness.

'I'm sure you're exaggerating the whole thing, Elvi,' Sybil said sharply, more to convince herself than her daughter. 'You're upset, of course you are, but we mustn't lose our heads over a misunderstanding. There's a lot of money at stake.'

'Money?'

Elvi sounded outraged, but Sybil knew they must not be hasty. The way forward was to make sure Bernard never had another opportunity to molest her.

'It'll never happen again,' she said reassuringly. 'Because I shan't leave you alone for a minute while you're in this house.' She was confident she could manage things without surrendering all she had achieved so far. 'I'll have a word with him,' she went on. 'I'm sure he'll see reason.'

'You don't understand, Mam,' Elvi told her wearily. 'He's determined to have his way with me. He said he'll report you to the authorities for fraud, if I don't obey him. You'll go to prison and so will I.'

'Ooh!' Sybil was shaken for a moment, glancing

at her daughter suspiciously. 'He never said that!' Elvi might be making it up.

Elvi nodded emphatically. 'He was furious. He even said he'd break my neck. Mam, we must go somewhere where he can't find us.'

'I'm not going to be driven out!' Sybil declared. 'Do you know how much I earned this evening? Thirty guineas! Think of it. That kind of money is not to be sneezed at, my girl.'

'Mam!' Elvi sounded overwrought. 'You talk calmly of money when I'm worried out of my wits as to what he'll do to me. I'm terrified. Doesn't that mean anything to you?'

'You're a child still, Elvi. You don't understand such things,' Sybil retorted determinedly. 'I shall deal with this in my own way.' She rose from the bed. 'Now get some sleep.'

'I won't sleep tonight,' Elvi declared miserably. 'I'll never sleep peacefully in this house again.'

'Well, I need my sleep,' said Sybil firmly. She moved to the door and then looked back at her daughter hesitantly. 'Put the chair back under the door knob when I'm gone.'

With that she closed the door and made her way thoughtfully to her own room.

Tackling Bernard would be ill-advised, she saw that now. The threats of reporting her to the authorities for fraud were daunting. She would pretend nothing had happened, and would be as sweet to him as usual. It was best he did not suspect she knew how he had treated Elvi.

As to this house of ill-repute, it was hard to believe. Yet she suspected Connie Lamar knew more than she was telling. But there was no way

231

of contacting the woman, even if she wanted to.

Sybil made up her mind. She would keep silent, but would wait, watch and listen. Sooner or later, Bernard would show his hand again, but now she was doubly warned.

Trudy found it exciting, creeping above stairs in the dead of night, making her way to Rhodri's bedroom. There was always the chance that she'd be discovered and then the jig would be up. But for the time being she was enjoying herself.

At first she had been pleasantly surprised at how different Rhodri's lovemaking was to Bernie's almost frenzied assault. She had thought Rhodri a sissy at first when he did not come at her like a raging bull as Bernie had always done.

But Rhodri's patience and tender touch, his concern for her feelings reminded her of that man Casanova, who she had entertained just the once in the bedroom at Cwmavon Terrace.

Rhodri was much younger than Bernie and so kind. When they were both satisfied, he often let her sleep the rest of the night through without disturbing her. That touched her heart.

Rhodri was waiting with a glass of wine for her tonight. He always greeted her that way, as though she was someone special, like a real lady.

'Did anyone see you, Trudy?'

She shook her head, sipping the wine. It was lovely.

She allowed him to open the buttons of her maid's dress and slip it from her shoulders, followed by her cotton shift. She watched his face as he did so. Excitement sparkled in his eyes but he never hurried his task. She was getting quite fond of him and his gentle ways.

Commonsense made her check the thought. Her nights with him were just fun, she reminded herself. Their association, it could not be called a relationship, could go nowhere. She must be content with what she had and be glad while it lasted.

When they were both undressed Rhodri drew her to the bed, sat with her, and then pressed her gently back against the pillows, warm lips on hers. She clung to him, all eagerness. After a moment he released her and sat up.

'Trudy, do you like me?'

She sat up too, surprised at his serious tone. They usually made love before talking.

'Well, of course I do.' She smiled at him, fluttering her lashes. 'Otherwise I wouldn't be here, would I?'

'No, seriously, Trudy. It's important.'

He reached across for her glass of wine left on the side table and handed it to her and then looked solemnly into her eyes as she sipped it.

'It's important because I love you, Trudy,' he said softly. 'I love you really and truly.'

She giggled, more from astonishment than anything else, and did not know how to answer him.

'I want us to be together for the rest of our lives,' he went on. 'I'm going to speak to my father; tell him that I want to marry you.'

'Marry me!' Trudy jumped with shock, spilling her wine on the bed linen. 'No, Rhodri, you can't tell them anything about us. I'll get the sack.'

'Of course you won't.'

'Your mother would have a fit at the very idea!' Trudy got off the bed and reached for her shift and slipped it on. 'Your father might overlook a quick fling with a kitchen maid, but he wouldn't tolerate anything serious.'

'I'm over twenty-one. I can do as I like.'

Trudy went to him and put her hand softly against his face. He was no oil painting, but she felt tenderness for him and tried to quell the feeling.

'But he could disinherit you, leave you penniless,' she warned. 'I wouldn't want to be responsible for that. Besides ... there's something about me you don't know.'

'I know all I need to,' Rhodri said energetically. 'I know you're honest and true, and I know I love you.' He lifted his shoulders. 'And even if you don't love me now, you'll learn to. I'll be good to you, Trudy, honestly I will.'

'Let's not talk about this any more tonight,' Trudy suggested earnestly.

She could see he was serious, and was concerned. She needed someone to talk to, and thought of Lynnys and Phoebe. Until she had spoken with them and had their reaction, she wanted him to say no more.

'Let's enjoy our time together.' She pulled her shift up over her head, and threw it onto a chair nearby. 'Love me tonight like you usually do.'

With a little laugh he reached up and drew her to the bed, enfolding her in his embrace. Trudy entwined her arms and legs around him. Great barriers separated them, and she could never call him husband, but tonight he was hers.

Connie was surprised to see Josh come into the parlour of the Pleasure Palace early one evening. She had not had a chance to speak with him since he had quitted his partnership in the house, and was anxious for news about Lynnys.

'You're a stranger,' she said archly, as he strolled over to the piano where she usually sat. 'I knew you wouldn't be able to stay away though.'

He gave a laugh of chagrin. 'I'm not here for pleasure, believe it or not. I've come to see you.'

He glanced around at the few girls who were still lounging about the room waiting for clients, and jerked his head. 'Let's go somewhere more private.'

Obediently, Connie closed the lid of the piano and walked out of the room, while Josh followed in her wake. She went straight to her sitting room.

'Would you like a drink?' she offered, when he was seated on one of the plush chairs that graced the room.

'Whisky would be nice.'

She handed him a glass. 'What's wrong, Josh? Is it something to do with Lynnys?'

He took the glass from her and then raised it as though in a toast. 'Absolutely nothing's wrong,' he said. 'Everything is going splendidly, and Lynnys is fine.'

'Then why the visit? You've got something on your mind, that's for sure.'

'As you're paying your share of costs, I feel we're partners as far as Lynnys' career is

235

concerned,' Josh said magnanimously. 'I won't do anything behind your back.'

Connie watched him carefully, sipping her sherry. She still wasn't sure she could trust him. He was likeable, but he had always been just one step ahead of the law. He was probably too old to change his ways now, and that made her nervous for Lynnys.

'What are you up to, Josh?'

'It's all legitimate, Connie, don't fret. Lynnys is coming along very well with her training. You'd be proud of her.'

'I was proud of her when she was hauling potato sacks about at the market, when her fingernails were dirty,' Connie said sharply. 'It was honest, clean dirt.'

Josh smiled wryly. 'You still think I'm on the make, don't you?' he asked. 'But you're wrong, Connie. When I look at Lynnys I see a brilliant future, not only for her, but for myself too; a legitimate future.'

'Well?'

He put his whisky glass down, the liquid hardly touched she noticed. 'Lynnys is doing well, but her training, hairdresser, dressmaker are costly. I feel it's time I had some return on my investment. I'm hoping you'll agree.'

'To what?'

'I've booked an engagement for Lynnys to perform at the Palace Theatre top of High Street next week. The fee isn't that good, but it's a start.'

'The Palace Theatre?' Connie shook her head. 'I'm not sure, Josh.' The theatre was in the poorer area of town, near the Irish quarter. Unruliness and drunken fist-fights were a regular occurrence at night. The idea of Lynnys being jeered at or ogled on stage by what might well be a rabble audience disturbed her. 'She's not ready. She could be destroyed.'

'I'm her manager and I say she's ready.'

'I'm her mother. Don't forget that.'

'Look,' Josh said reasonably. 'Lynnys is sensational, Connie. Your daughter's a born star. You must come and listen to her at Hibbler's studio. See for yourself.'

Connie bit her lip. 'You know I can't do that.'

'I could introduce you as a friend of mine. Lynnys need never know the truth.'

Connie felt her heart flutter at the thought of talking with Lynnys, being near her, taking a proper part in her life. It would be a dream come true.

'You could even attend her performance at the Palace Theatre, see how she's received. I tell you, she'll have them cheering in the aisles. The Irish love a good singer.'

'If only it were the Empire Theatre in Oxford Street,' Connie said wistfully. Top performers and artists from all over the country performed there. It was a respectable venue.

Josh laughed. 'One step at a time, Connie. After appearing at the Palace Theatre Lynnys will the toast of the town, believe me.'

'Oh, Josh,' Connie felt a sob rise in her throat. 'If I could be close to my girl just now and then, it would mean so much to me.'

He rose to his feet. 'Coaching sessions start at ten o'clock,' he said. 'I'll come for you in a hansom.' He gave a little apologetic cough. 'Dress down, Con. Something inconspicuous.' He smiled ruefully. 'You understand, don't you?'

She felt a brief stab of annoyance at his implication, but then nodded. Phoebe always said she shouted her profession by the clothes she wore.

'I'll be as demure as a mouse,' she assured him.

Josh left, but Connie went on sitting, her heart singing. Perhaps Phoebe would be aghast at the idea of her becoming acquainted with Lynnys. But if she remained incognito, a friend of Josh, it could do no harm. And she could watch over her daughter, see that she came to no harm.

She was sitting in the warm glow of her thoughts when Herb came into the room without knocking first, his face grim.

'What did Rowlands want?'

Connie lifted her chin. 'Nothing to concern you, Herb.'

'I'll be the judge of that. Now what did he want? Are you seeing him behind my back, is that it?'

Connie rose hastily, furious at his demanding tone. 'Just because you say you have feelings for me, Herb, doesn't give you the right to know my every thought.'

He ground his teeth and was silent for a moment.

'You are seeing him,' he thundered at last. 'By God! You're sleeping with him.' He smashed one huge fist into the other. 'I'll do for him, I swear it. It's bad enough to know you once belonged to Bernie, but Rowlands! No, I won't have it, Con.'

'It's nothing like that,' Connie said angrily. 'But it is private, and I'll say no more. Now please leave my room, Herb.'

He hesitated stubbornly. She could see the strain in his features. He was on the verge of eruption, and she wondered what he would do if Bernie stalked in that moment demanding she satisfy his appetites. She sensed that for all his physical strength, Herb feared Bernie, and she wondered why.

'I love you, Connie,' he said more reasonably. 'Why won't you give me a chance?'

'Please, Herb! We've talked about this too often and I'm tired of it. Don't mention it again.' She flicked her skirts behind her ready to walk from the room. 'I'm going to my bedroom now,' she said determinedly. 'And I don't want to be disturbed, not for anything.'

He still stood there.

'Leave me in peace!' Connie exploded, and he turned abruptly and left.

It was nearing midnight when Bernie suddenly appeared at the Pleasure Palace, flinging open the office door and marching in.

'Where's Connie?' he barked. 'I want her tonight.'

Herb rose to his feet hurriedly. 'Connie's ill, Bernie,' he lied quickly.

He could see from Bernie's deep scowl he was in a vile mood, a dangerous, almost feral glint in his eyes. Judging by the deep fingernail scratches on his cheek Herb guessed something had gone badly wrong in his attempts to have his way with the girl in his house in Walter Road.

He wondered what had happened, but one thing he was certain of, he did not want Bernie anywhere near Connie tonight in his present furious mood or any other night for that matter.

But it was now obvious to him that Bernie had been using Connie all along and she had lied to protect him. It made him seethe to think of it. He was angry with Connie for lying but now Bernie was going too far.

'I don't give a bugger how she feels,' Bernie stormed. 'Fetch her now.'

'She's ill, I tell you. The doctor's been to see her,' Herb lied, his tone harsh. It was dangerous to thwart Bernie, particularly for him, but he must take a chance to protect Connie. 'You can see for yourself, if you like.'

Bernie hesitated, although his foul mood persisted. 'You'd better not be lying to me, Herb,' he muttered. 'I've protected you all these years.'

His anger swelled. It was time to make a stand.

'Protect me?' Herb burst out wrathfully. 'Used me, more like,' Herb snarled. 'Call it by its proper name, Bernie, blackmail. Dancing to your tune, I've been all along; watching your back, especially where this place is concerned.'

'If I thought you were double-crossing me, Herb, I'd drop a whisper in the right ears about that killing.'

'Good God, Bernie!' Herb exclaimed. 'That was fifteen years ago. And it wasn't murder. It was an accident. I didn't mean to kill her.'

'The police will still call it murder, Herb.' Bernie smiled sneeringly. 'You're liable for the drop.'

240

Herb swallowed. That one careless, violent act had haunted him for years, and he carried remorse for it, even to this day. He often wondered if Connie knew about it, or sensed it, and that was why she wouldn't let him near her.

'It was manslaughter if anything,' Herb said in a low voice.

'Well, maybe, but that would mean a long stretch in clink, so watch your step, Herb.'

'I wouldn't cross you, Bernie,' Herb said in a placating tone, deciding he must act clever. 'Look! I've done you a favour. I told you a week or two ago that I've got a girl for you. Not a day over fifteen, she isn't; straight up from the country.'

'So you say.'

'I wouldn't lie to you, Bernie,' Herb went on persuasively. 'I was hanging about the railway station looking for a likely mark, when this fresh-faced kid came up to me and asked if I knew where she could find domestic work, as innocent as you like.'

'But she's been in the house two weeks, already,' Bernie said suspiciously.

'I swear to God, I've kept her clean. No man has been anywhere near her. She's in Trudy's old room.'

Bernie was silent, thinking it over obviously. Herb sensed he might be winning.

'You could take a look at her,' he suggested. 'Judge for yourself.'

Bernie gave him a long stare and Herb held his gaze steady.

'All right,' the other man said at last. 'But heaven help you if you've lied.'

He turned and left the office while Herb sat down again relieved. Connie was safe, at least for tonight.

But this could not go on. He put his elbows on the desk and leaned his head in his hands. For Connie and him to be free of Bernie the man must die.

Herb gave a choking cough of despair. He had blood on his hands already, and deeply regretted it. It would torment him to be responsible for the death of another, but there was no other way.

'Mr Collins! Mr Collins! Wake up, for pity's sake.'

Herb was roused abruptly from sleep by someone shouting his name hysterically and thumping wildly on his bedroom door.

'Wait a minute,' he grunted as he swung his legs off the bed and grabbed at his dressing gown. He shuffled to the door and opened it.

A skinny girl, one of their domestic workers, was standing there, her eyes staring; her plain face ashen.

'What the hell are you doing, Flossie, waking me at this hour of the morning?'

Flossie gave a huge gulp. 'Oh, Mr Collins, come with me quick. It's that new girl, Eirwen. I just went in to empty her slops when I found her. She's lying on the bed. There's blood everywhere. I think she's dead.'

'What?'

Herb raced down the flight of stairs to the second floor where most of the girls' rooms were, Flossie scuttling behind him.

'Her face is all beaten,' Flossie gasped as she ran. 'I hardly recognised her. What's happened to her, Mr Collins? Have we had a burglar? Shall I call a copper?'

'Shut your mouth, Flossie, if you want to keep your job,' Herb answered curtly. 'And get Mrs Lamar up. Speak to no one else, mind.'

'Yes, Mr Collins.'

Flossie hurried along the passage to Connie's bedroom, while Herb, sweating now with apprehension, pushed open the door of the room that Trudy had once occupied. He pulled up short at the sight of the small figure sprawled on the bed, naked and covered in blood.

'Oh, my God! Bernie, you swine, what have you done?'

Tentatively he approached the bed. The girl had been badly beaten, especially about the head and face. As Flossie had said, Eirwen was hardly recognisable. It was obvious that her nose was broken, and both eyes were closed and swollen, as was her mouth. She had probably lost some teeth. Herb knew only too well what a man's fist could do.

'Poor little bitch!'

He put the tips of two of his fingers against her throat. There was a faint pulse. She wasn't yet dead!

He ran to the door and yelled. 'Flossie! Run and fetch Doc Benson. Get the old soak here any way you can, and hurry, girl.'

Connie came hurrying along the passage. 'What's happened, Herb?'

'Bernie's half killed the new girl, that's what,'

Herb told her savagely. 'The bastard wants hanging.'

Connie covered her face with her hands when she saw the state the girl was in.

'She's still alive,' Herb said, taking a sheet and covering the girl's nakedness. 'I've sent for Doc Benson. I hope he's sober.'

'We've got to get her to hospital, Herb,' Connie said.

'Bernie may not like that.'

'We must! She could die.' Connie sobbed. 'He must be out of his head to do this. And to leave her alone in this state. It's horrible, inhuman.'

Herb ground his teeth. 'And this is the man you've given up everything for,' he said bitterly. 'That could've been you lying there, Connie. He's got no feeling for you or anyone else.'

They both stayed in the room until the doctor came. Doc Benson looked bleary-eyed, dishevelled and unsteady as he came into the room, carrying a battered doctor's Gladstone bag.

He grunted when he saw the pitiable state his patient was in. 'Bloody hell! Who did this?'

'A punter but it's no concern of yours, Doc,' Herb said sharply. 'Do what you can for her.'

'She should be in hospital,' Connie suggested.

Doc Benson knelt on the bed and after an examination nodded his head. 'She's too bad for me to do much. We'd better get her to the hospital.' He glanced at Herb. 'I take it the house will foot the bill?'

Herb nodded. 'I'll call a hansom. Go with her, Doc. But if they ask questions say she was found on the street by a passerby who called you. You've no idea who she is but you feel sorry for her and you'll pay. Keep us out of it.'

'Of course I will.' Doc Benson gave a wry smile.

'It's all right, Doc,' Herb said. 'I'll make it worth your while. Just make sure the girl survives, and keep your mouth shut. If this gets around it could put us out of business for good.'

When the injured girl had been carried out to the hansom cab, the doctor in attendance, Herb and Connie sat in her sitting room on the ground floor.

'What made him do it, Herb?'

'He's gone crazy, that's what.' Herb rubbed his large hands together. 'He always had a violent streak.'

'Perhaps it wasn't Bernie.'

Herb nodded. 'It was, Connie. I knew there was something wrong when he came in.' He stared at her accusingly. 'He wanted you and it's not the first time, is it?'

She shook her head, avoiding his gaze.

'Don't lie to me again!' he went on harshly.

She turned her face away and was silent.

He was willing to let the matter rest for the moment while they sorted out the mess they were in.

'Bernie's getting dangerous, Con,' he said heavily. 'Very dangerous. That could've been you.'

'I'm sorry for that girl he has at Walter Road. If he treats her like this…' Connie hesitated. 'I warned the mother against him, you know, but she wouldn't listen.'

'Maybe she did,' Herb said thoughtfully. 'Bernie looked frustrated enough to kill someone last night. Judging by what he did to that girl, it's just a matter of time before he does kill.'

It was over a week since Elvi's dreadful experience with Major Pomfrey in the kitchen and at four-thirty, when his surgery finished, Dr Howells said she could go home as she looked under the weather.

That was an understatement, Elvi thought. She was still upset and nervous, but life had to go on. She was glad of her duties with Dr Howells and wanted to keep her job. Although money was no longer a problem for Sybil, Elvi desperately needed her own money, her independence.

On the pavement outside the surgery Elvi's pace slowed as she turned towards home. How she detested that house. Every moment she had to spend there was insufferable and the thought that *he* might be there waiting caused her to tremble with dread and loathing.

She stood a moment, gaze cast down when someone spoke her name and she looked up in anxiety to see a fashionably dressed young woman before her, smiling widely.

'Elvi, don't you know me?'

Elvi stared unable to believe her eyes. 'Lynnys? I didn't recognise you.'

'Yes, it's me,' Lynnys said. 'All done up like a dog's dinner.'

'You look really lovely, but where…'

To Elvi's surprise Lynnys flushed. 'I'm training to be a singer now,' she explained. 'And I've got a manager.' She indicated her clothes. 'All this is his idea.'

246

'When did all this happen?' Elvi asked curiously. 'You never said a word on our Sunday outings.'

Lynnys bit her lip. 'Well it was rather sudden,' she admitted with obvious embarrassment. 'And I wasn't sure it would really come true.' She pointed up the road. 'I've just come from elocution lessons with Miss Wallace a few doors up.'

Elvi was impressed and suddenly felt a little envious. 'My goodness, things are going well for you then?'

Lynnys nodded and then her glance sharpened as she looked at Elvi, who averted her gaze.

'What's wrong, Elvi?' Lynnys asked kindly. 'You look very unhappy.'

Elvi knew her misery was evident and she could not hide it. Even Dr Howells spotted it and now Lynnys.

'It's nothing,' she said lamely.

'We're friends, Elvi,' Lynnys said. 'You can tell me anything.'

'I – I had a terrible experience the other evening. Oh! Lynnys, it was awful!'

'What?' Lynnys looked startled and came forward and put her arm around Elvi's shoulders. 'What was it? You're frightened, I can see.'

Elvi opened her mouth, wanting to share her terror and distress, but suddenly she felt ashamed. Had she unwittingly caused Major Pomfrey to act in that abominable way? Was it her own fault?

She bit down on her lower lip. 'I have to go, Lynnys. My mother's waiting for me.'

'All right then,' Lynnys said uncertainly. 'I'll see you Sunday afternoon at the usual time? We can talk then.'

Elvi swallowed and shrugged unhappily. 'I don't know, Lynnys. Things are so uncertain...' She turned and began to walk hurriedly away. 'Goodbye.'

'Elvi! Wait!'

Elvi kept her back turned and quickened her pace, tears welling in her eyes. Major Pomfrey had spoiled everything for her and fear of him haunted her every waking moment. She would never be happy and carefree again.

18

Connie trembled as she entered the street door of Hibbler's studios in Wind Street much later that morning, and felt breathless as, lifting her skirts, she followed Josh up the narrow staircase to the upper floor.

She could hardly believe she would come face to face with her daughter at last, and felt extreme gratitude to Josh for this chance. She was determined to make the most of it, and if all went well, she might see Lynnys often; even become her friend perhaps.

Her mouth dry with nervousness, Connie entered a room with a high ceiling and tall windows that let in bright sunlight. The studio was sparsely furnished. At one side was a grand piano. Other musical instruments rested on a table against the wall and a few wooden chairs were scattered around on the bare boards of the floor.

Everything in the studio looked old and worn, and the thin elderly man who came forward to greet them looked very much the same way. He bowed formally to Connie and clicked his heels in an old-fashioned courtly manner.

There was no sign of Lynnys, and Connie's heart gave a little lurch of disappointment.

'This is my friend Mrs Lamar,' Josh began. 'And this is Mr Hibbler, Connie. He's Lynnys' voice coach.'

'How do you do, Mr Hibbler?' Connie said breathlessly, holding out her hand. To her surprise he lifted her fingers briefly to his lips.

'I am honoured, madam,' he said, and Connie detected a faint foreign accent. He gave her a penetrating look. 'You are perhaps related to Miss Daniels, my talented pupil?'

Connie shook her head vigorously. 'No, not at all. I've never met her. Mr Rowlands mentioned her and I was curious.' Connie hesitated. 'I'm a singer myself.'

'Ah!' Mr Hibbler seemed satisfied with that. 'Miss Daniels has not yet arrived,' he went on. 'But I expect her on the moment. Please be seated. I regret the uncomfortable furniture, madam.'

Josh took Connie's arm and led her to some chairs against one wall while Mr Hibbler fussed at the grand piano sorting out sheets of music.

'You look splendidly respectable this morning, Connie, with no artificial colour on your face,' he said in a low voice. 'And black suits you. It brings out the colour of your eyes.'

'I feel quite naked without my rouge and beauty spot,' she admitted. She removed her gloves. Her hands now devoid of rings and bracelets, still shook. 'Will Lynnys object to me being here? I'm unknown to her.'

'She must become used to strangers watching her perform,' Josh pointed out. 'She needs an audience, Connie.'

'You said Phoebe accompanies her as chaperone. What if she makes a fuss?'

'Phoebe won't be here today. There'll be just you and your child.'

'Oh, Josh!'

At that moment the door from the stairs opened and a young dark-haired girl came eagerly into the room. Connie's heart missed a beat, and she made to rise from her chair, but Josh's hand on her arm stayed her.

'Patience, Connie,' he murmured. 'Let Hibbler make the introductions.'

'Am I late, Mr Hibbler? I'm so sorry,' the girl said. Even her speaking voice was melodious, Connie noticed.

As the girl slipped out of her light summer coat she gave a glance at the seated visitors and then looked away quickly as though shy at seeing a stranger. Mr Hibbler glanced at them too as though he had forgotten they were there.

'Ah, yes!' he said. 'We have an audience today, my dear.' He drew Lynnys across the room towards them. Connie and Josh rose to their feet together. 'Mr Rowlands has brought a friend. Mrs Lamar, this is my wonderful pupil, Miss Lynnys Daniels.'

Lynnys offered her hand shyly and Connie grasped it, willing herself not to be over-zealous in her greeting.

'How do you do, Miss Daniels? May I call you Lynnys?'

'Of course, Mrs Lamar. I'm pleased to meet you too.'

Connie was aware of Lynnys' sharp gaze which took in all of her appearance, and was glad she had taken Josh's advice about dressing carefully.

He had related how he and Lynnys had first met, and Connie suspected the girl was wary of his associates. She was glad to realise her daughter was no fool.

Mr Hibbler ran his fingers over the piano's keyboard, a signal that they must waste no more time and should begin.

Connie sat down again while Josh strode over to a window to view the street below. He was giving her privacy to enjoy every moment of being with her daughter, and she liked him for it.

The music began, and Connie sat enthralled as Lynnys' powerful yet sweet voice filled the room with glorious sound. She could only gaze at her daughter in wonder and awe.

Josh was right. Lynnys' brilliant talent must be heard by as many people as possible. She had a gift that must never be left unknown. Connie made up her mind that she would do all she could to help Lynnys' career. Her daughter was all that mattered now.

The coaching session ended and it was time to leave. Connie longed to clasp Lynnys in her arms and blurt out the truth. Now that they had finally come together, she did not want to be parted from her child.

The hansom cab that was on permanent hire for Lynnys' benefit arrived as they all three stepped out on to the pavement.

'Why don't you share the cab with us, Mrs Lamar?' Josh said formally; his wink at Connie went unnoticed by Lynnys.

'Oh, thank you, Mr Rowlands,' Connie said just

as formally.

When they were seated inside Connie was eager for conversation with her daughter, but knew she must guard her tongue.

'You have a wonderful talent, Lynnys,' she began. 'I'm much impressed with your performance. Mr Rowlands tells me that shortly you're to sing before an audience for the first time. How will you like that?'

'I'm very nervous,' the girl said, and smiled shyly. 'I hope it won't turn out to be a disaster.'

Connie shook her head. 'No.' She glanced meaningfully at Josh sitting across beside Lynnys. 'I believe you're meant for great things, my dear girl. I'll follow your career with interest, and be your friend, if you'll let me.'

Lynnys looked across at her and smiled.

'I could use a friend, Mrs Lamar.' She looked quickly at Josh beside her. 'Mr Rowlands is very kind and patient, too, but it's also good to have the advice of an older woman...' Lynnys' eyes widened and she put her fingers to her mouth quickly. 'Oh, Mrs Lamar, I didn't mean to imply you are old, I just meant...'

Connie laughed, feeling how good it was to talk with her daughter in a natural way and share laughter. She leaned forward and touched the girl's arm reassuringly.

'I know exactly what you mean, Lynnys, my dear,' she said happily. 'And I want to be as much help to you as I can. I hope to see much more of you.'

Lynnys nodded agreement, her embarrassment gone. They reached Cwmavon Terrace and

Lynnys alighted.

'Goodbye, Mrs Lamar,' she said earnestly. 'I look forward to meeting you again.' And then she walked lightly to her own front door.

Josh gave the cabbie further instructions, and they set off for the Pleasure Palace.

'Why don't you move out of that place, Connie?' Josh asked. 'Find a respectable boarding-house. If you're to go on seeing Lynnys you should distance yourself from Bernie and all he stands for.'

'He'd never let me do that.'

'He doesn't own you, Con.'

Connie swallowed. 'It feels like he does.' She sighed heavily. 'If I try to break away he'll give me the heave-ho. I can't lose this job, especially if I want to help Lynnys.'

'You'd find something else.'

She shook her head. 'I don't know any other way of making a living. I've been a tart since I was sixteen.' She looked across at Josh and could not stop tears brimming in her eyes. 'If Bernie gets rid of me, I'd have to go back on the game to earn a crust. I couldn't stand that now. I'd rather be in the river.'

'He's been a swine to you,' Josh growled gutturally, and Connie realised how much he hated Bernie.

'Yes, he has,' she murmured. 'And I've loved him for years, Josh, and stuck with him even though I knew he had no real feelings for me.'

'He never deserved you, Connie.'

She nodded, having to agree. 'I know that now. Lately, after the cruel way he has used me I began to think twice about what I really felt for him. And then last night when he beat that poor girl almost to death I knew I'd had enough.'

'What?' Josh sat forward, startled. 'What girl?'

Connie hesitated. Herb had warned everyone to keep quiet, but she needed to tell someone. She could not stop thinking about the young girl Bernie had in his house in Walter Road.

It was obvious the mother couldn't or wouldn't protect her. Heaven only knew what Bernie had already done to the girl or what he would do in future if he wasn't stopped.

'This is to go no further, Josh. Swear it.'

He nodded. 'Tell me everything, Connie.' His face was grim. 'Leave nothing out.'

Connie told him all that she knew. 'From Herb's description Bernie was enraged with frustration last night,' she went on, and then told him about the girl, Elvi, who might be Bernie's next victim. 'I suspect his plans to take the poor kid went wrong. He'll have no mercy for her when he does get her in his clutches.'

'So,' Josh said thoughtfully. 'Bernie has finally made a mistake.'

'It'll be covered up,' Connie said. 'Herb will see to that. Herb's afraid of Bernie for some reason and does everything he's told.'

'So, Bernie almost killed again, did he?'

'Again?' Connie was startled. She stared at her companion. His gaze shifted for a moment as though reluctant to speak further. 'Josh! Explain what you mean.'

'He's killed before, years ago.' He gave her a direct look then and told her what had happened

255

that night long ago when Bernie had killed the guard in cold blood. 'You never really knew him, Connie. Your devotion was misplaced.'

Connie bit her lip. 'This is awful! I knew he was hot-tempered, even dangerous, but I never dreamed he was capable of murder.' She paused thoughtfully. 'But if it wasn't for Bernie I would never have had Lynnys. She's worth all the suffering and humiliation he's put me through.'

Josh gave a quiet laugh. 'That's motherhood for you.'

Connie walked into the Pleasure Palace feeling happier than she had done in years. Josh's revelations about Bernie could not dim the pleasure she felt at being close to Lynnys. She had never dreamed it could happen. Now, thanks to Josh, the future looked rosier.

As she went down the hallway towards her sitting room she softly sang part of the aria Lynnys had rendered earlier. The girl was a true artiste with a superb voice. She had always felt pride in her daughter, but now her heart was bursting with it.

As she passed the office door, Herb Collins stepped out in her path. His expression was dark and moody.

'Where've you been, Connie? And why are you dressed like a preacher's wife?'

She did not reply, tightening her lips in anger, and attempted to push past him, but he grabbed at her arm.

'You've no right to question me,' she said sharply, trying to shake off his grasp. 'Let me

256

pass, Herb.'

'You were with Rowlands,' he said. 'I just saw you get out of a cab.'

'What of it?'

Jealousy sparkled in his eyes. 'I don't know what you see in that cheap crook.' His face was grim. 'If he doesn't leave you alone he'll have me to deal with.'

'And maybe you'll get more than you bargained for. Josh can look after himself.'

She wrenched her arm free and stalked off down the passage. He followed close behind.

'Connie, why do you keep on rejecting me?' he asked in a ragged voice. 'Has Bernie been talking out of turn, accusing me of ... things?'

She turned to face him, Josh's surprising revelation of Bernie's shocking past vivid in her mind. Had Herb been mixed up in that too?

'What do you mean?'

His jaw worked for a moment and then his shoulders dropped.

'Nothing,' he murmured. 'Nothing.'

Connie whirled on her heel away from him and entered her sitting room. She would not let him spoil her new found happiness. To her annoyance he came and stood in the doorway.

'Is it serious between you and Rowlands?' he asked in a hard voice. 'Bernie won't like that.'

'There's nothing between me and Josh except friendship.'

He came further into the room, his lip curling in scorn.

'You're a whore, Connie. No man can be merely friends with you.'

257

Connie felt stunned to hear him say those words, when he continually professed love for her. She took a step closer to him, and raising her arm slapped him across the face as hard as she could.

'Get out!'

Lynnys came into the living room of her home in Cwmavon Terrace almost at a run, eager to tell her grandmother of the morning's encounter with her pleasant visitor.

'How are you, Gran? Is everything all right? I'll make you a bit of dinner now.'

Phoebe gave a snort of disgruntlement. 'Don't know why I couldn't go with you today as usual,' she said peevishly. 'I don't trust that Josh Rowlands.'

'He brought a friend with him this morning, a lady.'

Mr Hibbler, Josh Rowlands and Gran always praised her, but she felt they were doing it out of kindness. Mrs Lamar was a stranger, and that seemed to make her approval more valuable.

Phoebe raised her brows. 'Oh, yes, and what's this lady's name, then?'

'Mrs Lamar,' Lynnys said. 'Very nice she was to me, too. Praised my singing.'

'Mrs Lamar?' Phoebe started forward in her chair, her face turning pale. 'Lynnys, listen to me. You mustn't see this woman again.' She raised a hand to her mouth as though in distress. 'I don't know what in the world she was thinking of...'

'Why ever not?' Lynnys was puzzled. 'Do you know her, Gran?'

Phoebe seemed to swallow hard. 'No, but Josh Rowlands keeps dubious company,' she said. 'This Mrs Lamar isn't respectable with her painted face and gaudy clothes. Mark my words, she's a bad lot.'

Lynnys laughed out loud. 'Mrs Lamar doesn't paint her face, Gran. What ever gave you that idea?'

Phoebe looked unconvinced. 'She's Trudy's sort.'

'Nonsense! She's very respectable. A widow, I believe. She was dressing all in mourning clothes anyway.'

Phoebe stuck out her lower lip belligerently. 'They're very cunning, these low women. They call themselves your friend and the next minute you're ... in the gutter with them.' She gazed at Lynnys pleadingly. 'Don't have anything more to do with her, my girl.'

Concerned at the anxiety in her grandmother's voice, Lynnys knelt down on the mat next to her chair and put an arm around her thin shoulders.

'Gran, there's no need for you to be upset.' She kissed the older woman's cheek gently. 'You've got the wrong idea about Mrs Lamar. She's very pleasant and I like her. I hope to see her again.'

Phoebe shrugged out of her embrace. Her expression showed impotent fury. 'It's not right what she's doing!' she exclaimed. 'If I was well enough I'd put a stop to her game, the shameless tart.'

'Gran!'

She turned her head to look at Lynnys, grasping her arm urgently. 'Please be careful, *bach*,'

Phoebe said urgently. 'There are so many evil people about, ready to snare a young girl like you into bad ways. I'm a sick old woman and can do nothing. If only you had a father to protect you.'

'Mr Rowlands seems like a father to me,' Lynnys said thoughtfully.

Lately she wished he was her father. Despite her grandmother's suspicions, she felt safe with him, and that meant she must trust him.

'That wastrel!' Phoebe exclaimed wrathfully. 'Damn him for exposing you to those who belong on the muck heap. Believe me, he's no one's father.'

'I thought you liked him,' Lynnys said. 'Aren't you glad that I'm making something of myself?'

To Lynnys' concern Phoebe burst into tears. 'It's all my fault,' she sobbed. 'I should've been a better mother. I should've seen...' She clutched Lynnys' hand. 'I won't make the same mistake with you, Lynnys, *cariad.*'

'Gran, why are you so upset?' Lynnys stroked her grandmother's hand, distressed herself to see her tears. 'Are you hiding something from me? Is it about my mother?'

Phoebe gulped and shook her head. 'You mustn't mind me, *bach,*' she answered evasively, gently withdrawing her hand from Lynnys' grasp. 'I'm just a weak old fool with too much time on my hands these days, remembering bygone days.'

Lynnys could not let the matter drop. 'You never talk about my mother, Gran,' she said quietly but firmly. 'Did she do something wrong? You must tell me. I've a right to know.'

Still dabbing at her nose with a handkerchief,

Phoebe's gaze slid away. 'I'm being silly and talking a lot of old rubbish, *cariad*,' she said. 'I want you to be successful as a singer, Lynnys, but at the same time I'm afraid I'll lose you in the end. You're all I've got now.'

Lynnys reined in her urge to press harder on the matter. It was obvious her grandmother would say no more at this time. She must be patient and wait until Gran felt able to speak freely.

She understood Phoebe's fears and taking her grandmother's hand again squeezed it reassuringly. 'You won't lose me, Gran, no matter what happens,' Lynnys said. 'And you're always telling me how strong-willed I am. I'll come to no harm, believe me. No one's going to lead me astray.'

Phoebe was more herself after they had eaten. Lynnys had the afternoon free with no lessons or dressmaking sessions. She was glad because Gran seemed to need her company today.

When someone knocked on their door mid-afternoon, Lynnys was a little disconcerted to see Trudy standing on the step, her young face wreathed in smiles.

'I've got a half-day off,' Trudy announced. 'I thought I'd come for a visit.'

There was a bubbling excitement about her, and Lynnys suspected the other girl had some sort of news she wanted to share.

'Your half-day is usually a Sunday,' she remarked, stepping aside to let Trudy into the passage.

'I swapped with one of the other maids,' Trudy said. 'I couldn't wait until Sunday.'

261

She went into the living room and, taking off her coat and hat, sat down on a stool by the range. Phoebe was sitting with her feet up, and scowled when she saw Trudy. 'What do you want?'

Trudy looked astonished at the greeting and glanced questioningly at Lynnys, who had perched herself on a kitchen chair at the table.

'Gran isn't feeling well.' Lynnys made up the excuse quickly.

'Tsk! I'm the same,' Trudy said. 'Sick as a dog this morning, I was. Luckily no one noticed.'

'They will,' Phoebe warned sharply. 'Your days up at Ffynonne Crescent are numbered, I'll be bound.'

'Perhaps that won't matter.' Trudy lifted her head proudly. 'I've had a proposal of marriage.'

'What?'

'Well, don't look so surprised, the pair of you,' Trudy remarked archly. 'I'm not fat and ugly yet.'

'Who is he?'

Trudy looked as though she wanted to hug herself with glee.

'Rhodri Cadogan-Rees, the youngest son of the family. He's madly in love with me.'

Lynnys could only stare, her mouth open. Phoebe was also agape, but was the first to find her voice.

'You hussy! You've been leading an innocent boy astray.'

'I did no such thing,' Trudy protested pertly. 'It was the other way about. He chased after me, until I let him catch me.' Her face broke into a wide smile. 'Oh, he is lovely though. Not good-looking, mind, but wonderful just the same.'

'How do you really feel about him, Trudy?' Lynnys asked gently.

She felt sadness for the girl, who was obviously living in a pipe-dream. A powerful family like the Cadogan-Reeses would never entertain a kitchen maid for a daughter-in-law.

'I think I'm in love with him, too,' Trudy said softly. 'I think about him all the time.'

'What a lot of piffle!' Phoebe exclaimed derisively. 'I bet you haven't told him about your interesting condition, have you, you little minx?'

Trudy gulped. 'No, not yet.'

'Perhaps you should,' Lynnys suggested. It was hard to advise someone in Trudy's position. She was obviously much taken with this young man. But it must all end in tears for her surely.

'I'll think about it,' Trudy said hesitantly.

'Don't forget, Trudy,' Lynnys said kindly. 'Your home is here with us when the Cadogan-Reeses ask you to leave.'

'I haven't forgotten,' Trudy answered lightly. 'But I might start a new life with Rhodri.'

'Fat chance!' Phoebe interposed disparagingly. 'When he realises what you are he'll be shot of you quick enough. Everyone knows a leopard doesn't change its spots.'

'Well, I've changed,' Trudy declared staunchly. 'I've got my baby to think of, and I want a decent life, too.' She tossed her head. 'Love will find a way, just you wait and see.'

19

Bernie set off in his carriage early the next afternoon on his way to visit Dolly Mathias, his strategy for gaining her confidence clear in his mind.

But he must concentrate on what he was doing, he warned himself, and not let his acute exasperation at failing to overpower Elvi Lloyd the night before cause him to make further errors of judgment that might cost him dear.

The rage of frustration that had been seething deep inside him still simmered, but he did his best to control it, aware that he had already made a bad mistake in attacking that girl at the Pleasure Palace last night. Her efforts to resist him, her cries and struggles had reminded him of Elvi, renewing his sense of frustration at failing to subdue her, feelings which demented him to such an extent he had completely lost control.

As he beat her, he had thoughts of Elvi; his hands on her young soft flesh, tearing at her clothes, moments from ultimate domination. If it hadn't been for that stupid woman, Dart, returning so unexpectedly, Elvi would be in his power now, to do with as he liked, when he liked.

But, by God! He would have her eventually, even if it meant abducting her from the house on Walter Road. Yes! That was an excellent idea. Sybil would be helpless, not knowing where Elvi was.

When he had Elvi under lock and key he would make her pay. Once he had subjected her to the extent of his appetites she would be too ashamed of what she had become to try to escape, and too afraid of him not to obey, and would weakly submit in future.

His hands were shaking as he held the reins, thinking of what he would do to Elvi, but forced himself to calm down. Concentrate on the game, he warned himself. There was a great deal of money at stake. Dolly was old and inclined to silliness, but not a complete fool. One careless slip might make her suspicious of his motives.

By the time he had arrived at her house he had his deep seated rage in check.

'Major Pomfrey to see Mrs Mathias,' he announced importantly when the middle-aged maid answered the door.

'Come in, please, sir.' The woman looked momentarily annoyed for some reason, but stood aside to allow him to enter the hall. 'I'll see if madam is at home.'

She returned within a few seconds. 'Madam will see you in the sitting room, sir. This way.'

The maid showed him into a well appointed room, lavishly furnished, which spoke of the wealth Dolly Mathias possessed.

Dolly came forward to greet him, holding out a bejewelled hand.

'Bernard! How lovely to see you.'

He lifted her rheumaticky fingers briefly to his lips. 'Dolly, my dear. How wonderful you look.'

She wore an afternoon gown of rich blue paisley silk, a matching turban around her head.

Bernie suspected that the old girl was losing her hair.

The maid still hovered in the doorway.

'Elsie,' Dolly said airily to her. 'Fetch in a tray of tea, and then you can be off.'

The maid disappeared immediately and Dolly laughed. 'She's cross because it's her afternoon off, and I've delayed her,' she said. 'She knows I'll make it up to her, the silly woman.'

'Sack her. Get someone younger,' Bernie advised quickly. 'Her sort are a penny a dozen.'

'Elsie's been with me years.' Dolly looked shocked at the suggestion. 'She knows what I want before I even ask. Elsie suits me fine. I've no time for these flighty maids who don't know a butter knife from a corkscrew.'

Elsie brought the tea tray in at that moment and with a brief curtsy, left.

'Dear Bernard,' Dolly said as she handed him a cup of the green tea he particularly detested. 'You don't visit me often enough.' She pouted. 'You're always at Maisie's though.'

'Well, I've come especially to see you, Dolly dear,' Bernard said gushingly, putting the cup and saucer on a side table. 'A piece of remarkable information has come my way about some stock that's set to rise dramatically within weeks.' He tapped the side of his nose. 'My inside source tells me it can't fail to pay out over fifty per cent return within the month.'

'Oh, Bernard!' Dolly looked at him in astonishment. 'My Donald told me through that clairvoyant, Mrs Lloyd, that such an opportunity would come my way shortly.'

266

He feigned surprise. 'How extraordinary! I only heard of it myself this morning.'

'I can hardly believe her prediction has come true and so soon,' said Dolly. 'Dear Donald. He watches over me, you know. And Maisie said it was all nonsense.'

'I've an idea, Dolly,' Bernie said, as though inspiration had only just struck him. 'Why don't you invest too? We're bound to make a killing and that would put Maisie's nose out of joint.' He checked himself. 'But, of course,' he went on quickly, 'we must be very discreet about it. This information is not for anyone's ears.'

'You mean we won't tell Maisie about it?'

Bernie inclined his head sagely. 'This is a little too rich for Maisie's blood, I think.' He was counting on Dolly being always eager to get one over on Maisie. 'Besides, dear friend though Maisie is, she can't keep a secret for the life of her.'

He leaned forward and put his hand in Dolly's, giving a gentle squeeze.

'It's essential this be kept under close wraps, and I know you're the soul of discretion, Dolly. Money can be lost as well as gained by careless talk.'

'I'll not say a word.'

He squeezed her hand again. 'I knew I could count on you. I intend to put fifty thousand into it.' He paused as though considering. 'Perhaps you should venture less, say five thousand, just in case,' he went on artfully.

'Oh, no, Bernard. My Donald has given his approval,' Dolly shook her head vehemently.

'And besides this is a rare opportunity as well as a sure thing, as they say in horse-racing circles. I shall put in fifty thousand, too.'

'How soon can you have the money ready?'

'I can give you a cheque now.'

Bernard smoothed back his moustaches. 'The deal would be better done in cash, Dolly,' he said with a wink and then wondered if he'd gone too far. 'Discretion, remember?'

Dolly was thoughtful. 'It'll take me a few days. I must see my bank manager and perhaps my accountant.'

Bernie lifted a hand. 'Dolly, I don't think you understand the delicacy of this deal and the absolute need to keep things secret between us.' He shook his head sadly. 'I've made a mistake in telling you about it. Forget I ever mentioned it.' He rose to his feet. 'I'd best take my leave, Dolly, and forgive me for troubling you.'

'No! Bernard, please.' She rose shakily from her seat on the dark brown leather chesterfield. 'I'm not helpless, you know. I can do as I like with my own money. I'll raise cash from the bank tomorrow. Come around again in the evening, and we can settle matters. I'm sure there are papers to sign.'

'Oh, yes, and I'll have everything ready when I call.'

Bernie took the old lady's hand again and brought it to his lips. What an easy touch she turned out to be. He could keep her on the string for months until he brought the bad news that the stock had collapsed.

Bernie left, congratulating himself. As Sybil

Lloyd's clientele grew among the well-to-do of the town, this con game of his could turn out to be a profitable side-line. And there was no one with whom he need share the proceeds.

The swelling of her abdomen was now quite noticeable. Trudy tried tying her apron in various ways to disguise it, but it was becoming more and more difficult to keep her condition hidden.

One Wednesday morning, wanting to stay out of the housekeeper's sight as much as possible, she went downstairs extra early to get most of her chores done before Mrs Moffat arrived to make the family breakfast.

Trudy was coming out of the larder, having cut slices from the side of bacon hanging there, when Mrs Moffat arrived in the kitchen earlier than usual.

'Bring that fresh fish from the cold slab,' the housekeeper instructed, rolling up her sleeves. 'I'm preparing kedgeree this morning. We've got guests staying.'

'Yes, Mrs Moffat.'

Trudy put the bacon slices on a dish nearby and turned to the larder door.

'Wait!' Mrs Moffat exclaimed. 'Trudy, what have you got under your apron?'

Trudy gulped and tried to edge behind the table. 'Nothing, Mrs Moffat.'

Mrs Moffat frowned. 'Come here, girl. You're hiding something.'

Hesitantly Trudy came forward, willing her abdomen to look flat. 'It's nothing, really it isn't.'

'Take off your apron, girl.'

Reluctantly Trudy had to comply. Mrs Moffat took one look at the obvious bulge under her dress and threw up her hands in dismay.

'Trudy! What have you done, you bad girl?'

'I'm getting fat, that's all,' said Trudy quickly. 'I've been eating too much.'

'Do you take me for a fool, girl? You've got yourself into trouble.' Mrs Moffat threw up her hands again. 'Oh! To think I recommended you. What will Mr Cranston say? Trudy, you've disappointed me, really you have.'

'It isn't my fault,' Trudy said quickly.

The jig was up and it was time to play her trump card. Ever since the first time Rhodri had approached her she had been planning what to say when her condition was discovered.

She faced Mrs Moffat squarely, pulling her cap straight on her head. 'It's Master Rhodri's fault.'

'What?' Mrs Moffat looked appalled.

'He lured me to his bedroom to see his trophies from abroad.' Trudy clasped her hands before her breast. 'I'm a good girl, Mrs Moffat. I didn't know it was wrong.'

'Oh, my heavens above!' exclaimed Mrs Moffat. 'What a wicked thing to say. Young Master Rhodri. No! Never!'

'Well, speak to him, then.' Trudy pouted at not being believed. 'He'll tell you.' Rhodri said he loved her so she counted on him owning up. 'He's even asked me to marry him.'

Mrs Moffat stood stock still, mouth agape for a long moment, and then she pulled herself together.

'Go straight to your room, and stay there,' the housekeeper commanded her. 'I'll speak with Mr Cranston and he'll have a word with the master.' She glared at Trudy. 'Oh, what shame you've brought us.'

Trudy had never seen her angry before and felt suddenly unsure of herself.

'I'm the one up the spout,' she pointed out pertly. 'Not Rhodri. Why must I take all the blame?'

'You brazen girl! I've never heard the like. Now, off you go, and lock yourself in.'

Trudy did as she was told. Her room-mate had gone off about her business with the chamber pots and luckily she met no other member of staff to question her.

It was a long wait, and now the sickness had passed she felt very hungry, having missed breakfast. She sat on the bed wondering what her fate would be.

Would Rhodri stand by her and insist on marriage? She pictured his face and the light of love she had seen in his eyes. She was sure he would try, but could he overcome his parents' objections? He would put up a fight for her, she knew he would.

It was almost midday, according to the alarm clock on the mantelpiece over the fireplace in the bedroom, when she heard Mr Cranston calling her name outside her door.

She went out to face him. His features were expressionless as he looked down on her.

'Follow me,' he commanded in a cold distant voice.

271

She followed him to the master's study and went inside in his wake. Trudy had never been in this room before and was impressed with the furniture and curtains.

The master, Mr Cadogan-Rees, was sitting behind a big mahogany desk looking very important. Mr Cranston took up a position close to his master's side. There was no sign of Rhodri or the mistress of the house.

'Stand there, girl,' Mr Cadogan-Rees commanded in a severe voice, pointing to a spot before his desk.

Trudy complied obediently. Where was Rhodri? Why wasn't he here to support her?

'I'm told you stand in disgrace,' Mr Cadogan-Rees said. 'I'm not entirely surprised.'

Trudy stared at him. 'It's not my fault. Rhodri... Master Rhodri lured me...'

'Silence!' Mr Cadogan-Rees cleared his throat. 'I've been warned against you by Major Pomfrey. A few weeks ago, while a guest on this house, he was on his way to the gentleman's lavatory when you accosted him and made improper suggestions. Needless to say he was insulted and disgusted.'

'I never did!' Trudy exclaimed hotly. 'I don't even know this Major, whoever he is. Never heard of him.'

'Be quiet, girl! I'm speaking!' Mr Cadogan-Rees barked. 'Now you accuse my son of misconduct. The impudence of it!'

'Now look here!' Trudy said, standing straight with fists clenched at her sides. 'You call Master Rhodri here this minute. He'll tell you the truth.

272

We've been seeing each other regularly in his room...'

'Enough!' Mr Cadogan-Rees's face turned red. 'My son has just left on a long trip to the Argentine,' he said. 'He won't be back for a while, a long while.'

'He asked me to marry him!' Trudy squeaked, stunned to learn that her lover had deserted her.

'Don't be absurd, girl. Talk like that will get you nowhere,' the master said harshly. 'You must realise you are dismissed from our service immediately. You'll pack your bags and leave before five o'clock this evening.'

'I've nowhere to go!' Trudy lied. 'No roof over my head. You can't just throw me out. It's Rhodri's baby, I tell you.' Trudy paused for a moment as a new thought struck her. 'It's your own grandchild you're throwing out on to the streets.'

Mr Cadogan-Rees fussed with his starched collar as though it was suddenly too tight for him, his face reddening even more.

'I'm not a harsh man,' he said at last. 'And if it wasn't for your lies against my son, Rhodri, I'd feel sorry for you. Although there is no reason at all why I should assist you, I'm prepared to give you some money to help you along.'

'Want to see Rhodri, I do,' Trudy said, biting back tears. She'd been certain he wouldn't leave her in the lurch, and couldn't believe he had really gone away. 'He said he loved me.'

'Now that is enough!' Mr Cadogan-Rees exclaimed, moving uneasily in his seat. He opened a drawer of the desk and took out a small linen bag. 'Here are twenty guineas. Take the money and be thankful, my girl.'

'But...'

He threw the bag on the desk towards her. 'You are dismissed,' he said. 'Go and pack your things immediately and then leave my house.'

Trudy hesitated, uncertain. Mr Cadogan-Rees turned his face away and began fiddling with some papers on his desk, ignoring her. Mr Cranston walked to the door and held it open. He gave a sharp cough when she remained immobile.

With a sigh Trudy reached for the bag and bowing her head, walked dejectedly out of the room.

She could not stop tears falling as she crammed her few things into her canvas bag. Now Rhodri was gone she began to realise what he really meant to her. She missed him already. She had felt safe and secure listening to his promises. For the first time in her young life she understood what love was.

When Trudy turned up on their doorstep at Cwmavon Terrace at tea-time Phoebe knew immediately what had happened. Trudy's face, usually so brazen, was streaked with tears and Phoebe was momentarily taken aback.

'No good crying over spilt milk, my girl,' she said as Trudy followed her down the passage to the living room. 'You should have thought of the consequences of your bad ways a long time ago.'

Lynnys was laying the table. She took one look at Trudy and opened her arms to her. Phoebe was astonished, watching Lynnys embrace a sobbing Trudy, knowing her granddaughter had trouble liking the girl.

'Sit down by there,' Lynnys said at last, pointing to the stool by the range. 'Have a cup of tea and you'll feel better. After all, you're home now.'

Trudy's face crumpled as she looked from one to the other. 'I don't know why you're both so good to me after the bad things I've done.'

'That's in the past,' Lynnys said. 'You've got a new start now.'

'I won't sponge on you, like before,' Trudy told them eagerly. 'I've got twenty guineas. That'll pay my way here for some time to come.'

Phoebe stared, immediately suspicious. 'And where did you get that kind of money, I'd like to know– No! Don't tell me!'

'I haven't done anything wrong ... well, not very wrong, anyway.'

'Trudy!'

'I told Mr Cadogan-Rees that Rhodri is the father.' She shook her head. 'Well, he did say he loved me,' she went on hastily. 'And I love him, too, but his father has sent him away. So there's no hope of us ever getting together.'

'It's wicked blaming that innocent boy for your condition,' Phoebe said.

'He's not that innocent,' Trudy remarked. 'Anyway, they gave me the money. I'd be a fool to refuse it under the circumstances. I won't be able to work for a while, so it'll pay for my keep.'

'I suppose you're right,' Lynnys said, looking befuddled.

Trudy held the bag out to Phoebe. 'You look after it for me, Phoebe,' she said. 'I trust you.'

Phoebe gave a sniff. 'I should hope so.'

As she took the bag she looked keenly at the girl's face. Maybe Trudy was trying to change her ways. They had promised her she could stay, and if she was to change she must have a steady and respectable home life.

'It's not just about paying your way though, Trudy,' Phoebe said. 'You can't sit around all day, you know, queening it like you did before. Lynnys needs some help about the house because I can't do much now with my bad health.'

Trudy's face beamed. 'I've learned a lot from Mrs Moffat. She taught me how to cook and a lot of other things. I reckon I'd could be a house-keeper myself if I put my mind to it.'

Phoebe raised her brows. 'Well, that sounds promising.' She smiled at last. 'Welcome home, Trudy.'

20

It was a month since Major Pomfrey had attacked her in the kitchen, but Elvi was still haunted by the experience. She made sure she was never in the house when Sybil was absent, even accompanying her mother on her regular shopping jaunts, although she hated it. Anything was better than being trapped by the awful man again.

She never stopped trying to persuade Sybil that they should move out, but her mother was adamant. They were doing far too well financially for that.

Elvi knew it was true. Séances were held at Walter Road at least once a week, sometimes twice, when her mother extracted fat fees. Dolly Mathias and Maisie Coombs had introduced more of their affluent friends, and Sybil's fame was spreading.

Elvi was still disgusted with the whole thing. Just because Sybil's new victims were filthy rich did not mean they were not being defrauded of their money. She could not help feeling it would all end badly.

On Saturday Sybil announced that she had arranged to go to Dolly Mathias' home to hold a séance that evening, and Elvi must come too.

'Perhaps you'd rather stay here alone again,' Sybil said irritably when Elvi pulled a face.

'No!'

'Well, then, get ready, my girl, and try to look happy about it.'

Dolly had sent a hansom to pick them up, which Elvi thought was very generous of her, as Sybil had confided in her that Mrs Mathias was poorly off, according to Major Pomfrey.

She was surprised therefore when they reached Dolly's home in Sketty, a large detached house standing in its own grounds. The inside was even more impressive.

'She doesn't look poor to me,' Elvi whispered to her mother as they were relieved of their coats and hats.

'All show,' Sybil murmured out of the corner of her mouth. 'Hocked up to the rafters, poor old girl. Although Bernard is trying to help her.'

Elvi shuddered. She would rather spend the rest of her days in the workhouse than have any help from that dreadful man.

They waited in a side room while Dolly's guests at the séance assembled in the large drawing room, since Sybil preferred to make an entrance when all had settled.

Elvi felt tensed up with nerves. She had avoided séances at home and had not attended one since that disturbing evening when she had seen Mrs Beavis' father and that other strange apparition behind Major Pomfrey's chair. She thought she understood that warning now. Major Pomfrey was a man to be avoided at all costs.

She almost jumped out of her skin when the door to the drawing room was opened by the maid. 'Madam is ready for you now,' she announced.

Sybil walked slowly, regally and with great dignity into the room. She had bought herself yet another new gown especially for the occasion, and was immaculately turned out.

She's in her element, Elvi thought dismally, following behind, trying to be as invisible as possible. At that moment she felt she would always walk in her mother's dubious shadow.

There were too many people present to sit around a table, and so Sybil elected to sit facing her audience, gaslight dimmed and only a single candle, strategically placed, to give some light. Elvi was allowed to sit well to one side, hidden in shadows, and was thankful not to be part of the spectacle.

An hour ticked slowly by while Sybil gave several messages, using her special talent for changing the timbre of her voice. There were occasional gasps of awe from the audience from time to time, and Elvi thought it remarkable that rich people had no more sense than poor people when it came to parting with their money.

After an hour Sybil indicated that she was psychically exhausted, and needed a break, but would continue the séance later.

The gaslight was raised; buffet trolleys were wheeled in and bottles opened. Elvi was glad of a cup of coffee. She had seen nothing untoward when the lights had dimmed, and felt more relaxed.

'If you want to visit the lavatory, go now,' Sybil whispered to her after a while. 'I don't want you fidgeting later when I'm in full flight. You'll disturb my aura.'

Aura, my thumb nail! Elvi thought as, red-faced, she asked the maid quietly where the lavatory was and was directed upstairs.

Sybil watched her daughter leave the room, head down as though she had something to be ashamed of, and felt irritated and disgruntled that the weight of making a living for them both rested entirely on her shoulders.

Elvi was a liability and no mistake. She should be taking her place now, learning the trade, so to speak, earning her crusts. It was no wonder men tried to take advantage of her when she behaved like a little mouse.

Sybil pushed that thought aside. She still wasn't sure that Elvi had not encouraged the Major's attentions in some way. Young girls were so silly.

She quickly adjusted her expression as Dolly Mathias came towards her across the room.

'A quiet word, Sybil,' Dolly began, sitting down next to her, looking around as though afraid she might be overheard. 'I wanted to tell you that the message you gave me from my dearest Donald the other evening has borne fruit.'

'Oh! Really? I mean, it was inevitable.'

'Yes. A marvellous opportunity to make money has come my way, and thanks to you, I knew instantly that I must take advantage of it.'

'How wonderful.' Sybil paused. 'It wouldn't have anything to do with Major Pomfrey would it?'

Dolly looked startled. 'He's told you?'

'Well, he's explained the situation, after all, we are friends, you know,' Sybil said glibly. 'But believe me, Dolly, it'll go no further. I've been in that position myself, and I'm not one of these women who gossip to all and sundry. We all have our trials and tribulations.'

'...Er ... yes, I suppose so.' Dolly looked confused, and Sybil felt suddenly even sorrier for her. It must be awful to be elderly and virtually penniless.

'If anyone can help you Major Pomfrey can,' Sybil went on encouragingly. 'Now I think we should be getting on with the séance.' She glanced towards the doorway. 'Where is that girl?'

As she climbed Elvi had to admire the wide staircase with its curving highly polished banister and thick-pile carpet. How luxurious. It was hard to believe Mrs Mathias was in debt up to her eyebrows. Elvi had never seen carpet on stairs before, not even at Dr Howells', although it was true she had never been in their living quarters.

She took her time on the way back from the lavatory, admiring paintings on the walls of the corridor, and delicate ornaments on occasional tables.

She reached the head of the staircase and was preparing to descend, when suddenly she felt giddy and swayed, her vision blurring for a moment. Frightened, she grabbed at the banister for support, fearful of falling, rubbing her eyes with her free hand. What on earth was wrong with her?

Recovering her balance, she stared down the length of the staircase before her and almost let out a scream of horror. At the foot of the stairs a figure of a woman lay sprawled on the marble tiles, head and legs twisted at an unnatural angle.

Elvi rammed her knuckles into her mouth as she recognised Dolly Mathias. Instinct told her no body could be twisted in that way and be still alive. What had happened? Why were none of the guests coming to her aid?

She was about to let out a yell of warning when suddenly the figure on the floor vanished. Shaken to the core, Elvi clutched with both hands at the banister. Her legs suddenly weak she sank down onto the top step and stared down the staircase in shock and disbelief. Was she going mad? She must be losing her mind to imagine such a terrible thing.

And then someone came into the hall from the drawing room. It was the maid, pushing a buffet trolley towards the back of the house. Everything looked so normal now, and Elvi began to doubt her senses, yet she felt much shaken still.

After a moment, when her legs felt steadier, she made her way down the stairs and almost tottered in to the drawing room to see that the guests were finding their seats for the resumption of the séance.

Elvi hurried towards her mother at the far end of the room, relieved to see Dolly Mathias, fit and well, sitting next to her chatting.

'Elvi, where have you been?' Sybil's voice was sharp with annoyance. 'And what on earth is the matter with you? Your face is as white as a sheet.'

'I don't feel well,' Elvi muttered, taking covert glances at Dolly Mathias, who was smiling at her. 'I want to go home.'

'Elvi, don't be difficult,' Sybil commanded. She turned to Dolly. 'What it is to have an ungrateful daughter,' she said. 'When one tries one's best to provide.'

'I have no children,' Dolly said sadly. 'Donald and I were never blessed.'

'Blessed!' Sybil sniffed. 'I'd hardly call it a blessing.'

'I have two nephews, on Donald's side,' Dolly went on. 'Brynley is a very nice young man, a doctor, you know. Norman is a lawyer.' Dolly grimaced. 'He rarely visits, and only then to make sure I'm not frittering away his inheritance.'

Elvi could see by the distant look in her eyes that her mother was not the least interested in Dolly's relatives. Sybil's irritated glance fell on her again.

'Elvi, go and sit down somewhere quiet and compose yourself,' she commanded. 'I'll have a word with you when we get home.'

Elvi returned to a shadowy corner of the room, but all through the remainder of the séance she could not take her eyes off Dolly Mathias. Did her vision predict an accident? Should she warn the woman? But how could she without revealing to her mother what she had seen? Besides, people might laugh at her and scoff. It was easier to persuade herself that the vision had never happened. All she could do was pray that Mrs Mathias came to no harm.

Elvi was just preparing a tray with a pot of tea and some Garibaldi biscuits for Dr Howells which he always required after morning surgery,

283

when someone knocked at the back door. Elvi answered and was astonished to see Lynnys.

'Can I come in a minute, Elvi?' her friend asked.

She was wearing a beautiful dress of blue silk with a fitted coatee of blue velvet. Her long black hair was dressed in the latest fashion and she wore a wide-brimmed pale straw hat decorated with blue ribbons. Elvi was overawed by her friend's stunning appearance.

'Come in, Lynnys,' she said awkwardly, conscious of the fact that she had neglected Lynnys lately. 'It's good to see you.'

'I had to come, Elvi,' Lynnys began. 'I've waited at our usual place every Sunday for the last few weekends.' She paused looking anxious. 'Have I done something to offend you?'

'No, really you haven't,' Elvi assured her. She clutched her hands tightly together in front of her, wondering how she could explain her negligence. 'Things haven't been good at home. I couldn't get away. I'm sorry.'

'I'm sorry, too,' Lynnys said sadly. 'I've missed you. I've enjoyed our Sundays together very much.'

'So have I, but things have changed...'

Elvi closed her eyes and swallowed hard. She simply could not find the words to explain the constant fear and loathing which darkened her life since Major Pomfrey's attack. The experience had demoralised her completely and had sapped her confidence. She could not relax and be happy now.

'As long as there's nothing wrong between us,'

Lynnys said. 'How are you these days? You still look drawn. Elvi, are you ill?'

'No, it's not that.'

Lynnys looked at her keenly for a moment. 'Won't you tell me what's troubling you, Elvi? I might be able to help.'

Elvi glanced away wordlessly, unable to look Lynnys in the eye. Yet why should she feel shame at what had happened? She had done nothing wrong. It was that vile man.

'I hate to see you troubled like this, Elvi,' Lynnys said kindly. 'Look!' She reached in to her reticule and took out some tickets and held them out to Elvi. 'You need cheering up.'

'What are those?'

'I don't want to blow my own trumpet,' Lynnys said with a smile. 'But I'm appearing on the bill at the Palace Theatre, you know, at the top of High Street.' She held out the tickets. 'I thought you might like to attend my performance and then visit me backstage.'

Elvi took the tickets hesitantly. 'It's very kind of you, Lynnys.' She wetted her lips. 'I would like to but I don't think my mother will allow...'

Lynnys bit her lip. 'I know the Palace is not exactly on a par with the Empire, but Josh – he's my manager – says it's a start.'

Elvi felt sorry. She would have loved the experience and excitement of such an event over a month ago and would have been agog to attend. Now she could find no pleasure in anything while she still lived under Major Pomfrey's roof.

Elvi handed the tickets back to her friend. 'It's good of you to think of me, Lynnys. I do

285

appreciate it, but I won't be able to come.'

Lynnys took the tickets back reluctantly. 'I'm sorry you're unhappy, Elvi. Listen, you know where I live if you ever need me. I want us to go on being friends, despite everything.'

Elvi nodded her head silently. She needed a friend now more than ever, but the dark presence of her mother's landlord overshadowed her thoughts and her life.

'Thank you, Lynnys. I do appreciate it.'

When her friend had left, Elvi sat a moment more feeling very low and at risk. She and her mother might take precautions, but an inner voice warned her that it was not over yet. Major Pomfrey had not finished with her and she quailed in dread.

21

Connie thought she would sit in the circle at the Palace Theatre but Josh had arranged a box for her, and she was glad that he had.

The auditorium was packed with a noisy audience on this Saturday night. The so-called Italian tenor had already been booed off stage. After which a fight erupted between two women in the front stalls. The entertainment was brought to a halt while they were both thrown out.

When the comedian hastily retreated under a welter of rotting vegetables, Connie was ready to go backstage to prevent Lynnys making an appearance at all. But Josh, who was sitting in the box with her, held her back.

'It'll be all right, Connie, believe me.'

'They'll eat her alive, Josh.'

'Have faith. Lynnys has a talent beyond anything this crowd has seen or heard. They'll be eating out of her hand.'

Connie sat in trepidation. She doubted she could sit and watch her beloved daughter humiliated in this way.

'One cat-call, that's all it'll take,' Connie warned him anxiously. 'And I'll go down and get her off stage myself.'

A man in rumpled evening dress came on stage at that moment to announce the next act.

'And now, ladies and gentleman, the songbird

of the south; the nightingale of Swansea town, Miss Lynnys Daniels!'

'Bring back the comedian!'

There was another scuffle in the stalls as some man objected to this suggestion.

'Give the girl a chance,' a woman's raucous voice shouted over the din. There were further shouts of support from men.

'Yes, let's see her, mun!'

'She can show us her ankles.'

There was a roar of laughter.

'They've started already,' Connie exclaimed. 'And they haven't set eyes on her yet. Josh! You must stop it.'

'She's been announced,' Josh said. 'There'll be a real riot if she doesn't come on stage. Lynnys can handle it. There's steel in that girl's backbone.'

'I should never have let you talk me into this!'

Breath caught in Connie's throat as the curtains parted and a young delicate figure in a white dress stood centre stage, head held high, dark tresses cascading around her shoulders. There was something almost angelic about the solitary form that the audience fell silent for a moment.

'Sing!' some man commanded at last.

The ramshackle orchestra, pianist, violinist and cello, struck up a chord and played an introduction to a well known aria.

Connie felt a tremor of apprehension as Lynnys stepped towards the footlights, lifted her arms wide to the audience and began to sing.

There was complete silence as notes as pure as mountain water swirled around the auditorium, filling every square inch of the place with sounds that stirred the heart as well as the senses.

'What did I tell you?' Josh whispered in her ear. 'Lynnys is meant for great things.'

Connie had heard Lynnys sing before but was overawed at the power and the confidence in the girl's voice and manner when faced with an auditorium filled with an unruly crowd.

The aria ended and Lynnys bowed low before the stilled audience. The silence continued for a moment and then the clapping began, together with the stamping of feet.

There were yells of: 'More, more!'

The manager in rumpled evening dress hurried on stage again.

'Ladies and gentlemen,' he announced eagerly. 'Miss Daniels will now give a rendition of "Danny Boy".'

Connie glanced anxiously at Lynnys, but the girl was smiling in pleasure at her audience. The orchestra struck up again and in a moment, while all present were silent in anticipation, Lynnys sang.

Connie dragged her gaze away from her daughter to look down at the people in the stalls below and was astonished to see many, men and women, wipe tears away on sleeves or handkerchiefs.

'In the palm of her hand,' Josh murmured. He sounds choked himself, Connie thought in wonder.

When the song was finished, Lynnys bowed again and made to leave the stage, but the audience was unwilling to let her go.

'More, more.'

'Give us "The Old Rugged Cross".'

With a glance at the manager, who nodded, Lynnys sang the great hymn with warmth and much feeling. The silence was profound, the rough hearts present calmed. When the hymn was finished Lynnys bowed humbly to her public in a quietness that was worthy of a cathedral.

'Thank you, one and all,' she called out to her admirers. 'It has been an honour to entertain you.'

There was uproar as the curtains closed on her bowed form. Indignant shouts of: 'Don't go! More!' echoed around the auditorium, accompanied by stamping of boots. Men were on their feet in the aisles. Things were looking ugly.

The manager appeared from behind the curtain and held up his hands for silence. 'Ladies and gentlemen, please!'

'Fetch her back, mun!'

'We want the Songbird, so we do!'

'Miss Daniels must leave for another engagement.' He managed to dodge an over-ripe tomato. 'But I can assure you that your very own Songbird will return again next week.'

There were growls of disappointment and a few people waved fists at him. The manager gestured frantically at the orchestra leader who began to rattle out a popular music-hall tune on the piano.

'Come on, Connie,' Josh said, rising. 'We'll go backstage.'

Backstage was grubby and smelled of years of unwashed performers.

'Don't sit down anywhere,' Josh warned Connie quietly. 'Fleas!'

Lynnys' dressing-room was no bigger than a broom cupboard, but it had a mirror, over which was a gas-mantle. People were already crowded at the door, among them a man who said he was a reporter from the *Cambrian Leader*.

'I'm Miss Daniels' manager,' Josh told him importantly. 'I'll let you know when she feels inclined to give an interview. However, she may be leaving very shortly on a European tour, including Paris and Vienna.'

'What was all that?' Connie asked, appalled at the idea.

'Publicity,' Josh said. 'A few white lies will do no harm.'

Josh pushed their way into the dressing-room. Lynnys rose from her seat before the mirror to greet them, her eyes shining.

'Did I do all right, Josh?' Her glance fell on Connie and she blushed. 'Mrs Lamar, it was very good of you to attend. I hope you enjoyed it.'

Connie grasped the girl's hands and squeezed. 'You were wonderful, Lynnys,' she said. She felt choked with pride for her daughter. 'Superb. The audience loved you.'

There was a commotion in the passage outside. 'Let us through! Let us through, we're family!'

Connie recognised that voice immediately and quailed. Trudy Evans pushed her way in, together with Phoebe, her protective arm around the older woman.

'Hey, Lynnys! Here's your Gran.'

Lynnys jumped up to hug her grandmother. 'Gran, I'm so glad you felt well enough to come. Did you enjoy it? Sit down by here.'

Josh gave a warning cough.

'It's all right, Josh,' Lynnys went on quickly. 'It's a wooden chair.'

'Lynnys, *bach*, I did enjoy it,' Phoebe said breathlessly. 'And I'm proud of you.'

Connie tried to retreat behind Josh's shoulder, but the room was so small there was no way to avoid being recognised.

'Oh, Gran, I want you to meet Mrs Lamar,' Lynnys said. 'This is my grandmother Phoebe Daniels, Mrs Lamar. I've told her so much about you.'

Connie met Phoebe's gimlet eyes, and saw stark hostility in them, but she managed to speak calmly.

'How do you do, Mrs Daniels.'

'Hello,' Phoebe said shortly, and then turned her head away.

'Well! I'm blowed!'

Connie was aware Trudy was staring at her in astonishment, and she prayed the girl would have some sense and not give her away.

'This is Trudy Evans,' Lynnys said. 'Trudy, this is my friend, Mrs Lamar.'

Trudy gave a wide grin. 'Well, well, I feel I know you already, Mrs Lamar.'

Connie gave a little cough. 'I think I should be going now, Josh.'

'I'll call a hansom for you.'

'No, no. I'll walk down to the station and get one there.'

'I don't like the idea of you being out on the streets alone at this time of night,' said Josh anxiously.

'Huh!' The exclamation came from Phoebe, and everyone looked at her, but she sniffed indifferently and began to fidget with her reticule.

'Goodbye for now, Lynnys,' Connie said warmly. 'And congratulations on a triumphant night. I hope I'll see you again.'

'Oh, please continue to come along to the studios,' Lynnys pleaded. 'I value your opinion.'

As she left the theatre Connie felt choked up with tears. There was a pain around her heart. Her beloved daughter was so near and yet so far away. But she must be thankful for what she had. At least she could share something of the girl's life.

Her mind dwelt on Josh's publicity talk. Lynnys had an astonishing talent, and probably she would at some point in her career go abroad, and Connie knew she would not be able to follow. Make the most of her now, her heart said. One day she will be lost to you for ever.

22

Norman Mathias patted his waistcoat contentedly as he strolled out of the dining room and into the smoking lounge of his gentleman's club in Wind Street, feeling very satisfied with the dinner he had just eaten.

Membership of the club was perhaps an extravagance on his part, but his expectations were good. Uncle Donald had left behind a fortune, which would be his when old Dolly went – well, his and Brynley's of course. Dolly was failing, he could see that, and he might not have to wait long, but there again, he was prepared to wait as long as it took.

He signalled to a waiter to fetch him a glass of port and then, evening paper in hand, he made his way to a vacant chair near the enormous fireplace. He hadn't been seated but a moment when someone approached his chair. Norman looked up to see a familiar face.

'Evening, Oscar,' he greeted amiably. 'How's everything at the bank? Any spare fivers, eh?' It was a joke he invariably made whenever he met his bank manager, Oscar Bennett. Oscar gave a weak smile, as he always did when Norman cracked that particular joke.

'Glad I ran into you, Norman,' Oscar said, and took a chair nearby. 'I've been waiting to have a word in private.'

'A professional word?' Norman smiled, anticipating new business.

'Yes,' Oscar replied. 'But my profession, not yours.'

'Oh!' Norman was intrigued. 'I haven't run up an overdraft, have I, without knowing it?'

'Listen.' Oscar looked about him before leaning closer. 'I shouldn't be talking to you about this. It's against banking rules. I could get in deep hot water.'

Norman frowned at his companion's words. 'Well, perhaps you'd better not say another word, then.'

Oscar licked his lips. 'We've been friends for a long time, Norman, and I thought you should know.'

'Well, what is it?'

'It's your aunt, Mrs Dolly Mathias.' He looked round about him again and seemed satisfied they were out of earshot. 'She withdrew fifty thousand pounds in cash from her account a few weeks ago.'

'What?' Norman jerked forward, the newspaper falling onto the floor.

'I tried to get out of her what the money was for,' Oscar said apologetically. 'But the stubborn old girl wouldn't give away a thing. I can't help feeling she may be becoming – well, incompetent to manage her affairs.'

'Fifty thousand pounds!' Norman could barely keep from spluttering. 'Why didn't you inform me of this earlier?'

'It's a delicate matter,' Oscar went on, shaking his head. 'I could hardly tell you officially. Even now it's risky.'

Norman scarcely heard him. The amount didn't exactly empty Uncle Donald's coffers, but still it was an enormous sum, especially in cash. What was the old girl thinking of?

He set his jaw determinedly. He couldn't allow this kind of cavalier behaviour with his inheritance. He must look into it, and as soon as possible. He took his watch out of his waistcoat pocket. Half past eight. Dolly never went to bed early. He knew she spent many long evenings entertaining her friends.

'I must leave you,' he said hastily to his companion, getting out of his chair.

Oscar Bennett rose too looking anxious. 'Avoid letting anyone know where the information came from, will you, old man?'

'Of course, of course.'

The waiter arrived with a glass of port. Norman took it from the tray and threw the contents into the back of his throat in one gulp. He needed that.

'Thanks for your help, Oscar,' Norman said gratefully. 'Any time you need legal advice, I'm your man.'

He hurriedly left the club and hailed a passing hansom. It was just after nine o'clock when he arrived at his aunt's house in Sketty. As usual all the lights were on. His aunt had never heard of economy.

The door was opened by Dolly's maid.

'Good evening, Mr Mathias, sir,' Elsie greeted him, and did not seem surprised at his late arrival. 'Madam is in the drawing room with Mrs Coombs.'

'Elsie, wait a minute,' Norman said as the maid retreated towards the back of the house. 'Tell me, how has my aunt seemed lately? I mean, have you noticed any odd behaviour?'

Elsie blinked. 'No, sir. Madam seems her usual self.'

'Quite so,' Norman nodded quickly. He did not want to start any wild speculation. Elsie flashed him a look of curiosity but continued towards the kitchen.

When Norman walked into the drawing room his aunt was sitting chatting to Mrs Coombs, with whom he had a slight acquaintance.

Dolly looked up in surprise. 'Norman! What brings you here at this time?' She gave him a knowing smile. 'I bet a fiver it's to do with money.'

Norman was disconcerted. 'Really, Aunt! Mrs Coombs will think I'm mercenary.'

He nodded amicably at the other woman. 'Mrs Coombs, how are you?' She was some years younger than his aunt, and quite well-to-do from what he understood.

'Very well, thank you.'

Norman sat down hesitantly. This was awkward. He needed to question Dolly about the money, but hesitated in front of a third party.

On the other hand, the thought struck him; Maisie Coombs might be an ideal witness that his aunt was incompetent if she witnessed erratic behaviour. Perhaps it was best to plunge forward and get it over with.

'Aunt Dolly, I must ask you about something,' Norman began, touching his moustache nervously. 'It's come to my attention that you've

297

withdrawn a considerable sum of money in cash. Where is that money now?'

Dolly flushed with obvious embarrassment and glanced apprehensively towards Maisie. 'Really, Norman! How could you in front of my friend. You're embarrassing her.'

'I'm not the least embarrassed,' Maisie said. Norman saw intense interest gleam in her eyes. 'Don't mind me. I'm the soul of discretion, I assure you.'

'Piffle!' Dolly exclaimed. 'You're an inveterate chatterbox, Maisie.' She glanced angrily at her nephew. 'Oh, Norman, look what you've done. This will be all over town by luncheon tomorrow.'

'Why did you withdraw all that money?'

'I don't want to talk about it. It's a private matter.'

'Dolly, is it something to do with that woman, Sybil Lloyd?' Maisie asked suddenly. 'Something she predicted a couple of weeks ago?'

Dolly gasped and whitened, but remained silent.

Maisie drew in a satisfied breath. 'As soon as money was mentioned I thought as much,' she said.

Norman was totally at sea. 'Who is this Sybil Lloyd? What has she to do with my ... my aunt's money?'

'I'm not saying Mrs Lloyd has Dolly's money.' Maisie shook her head emphatically. 'All I'm saying is that she put the idea into Dolly's head.'

'Who is she?' Norman was getting irritated. 'What idea?'

'She's a so-called clairvoyant; a charlatan, of

course,' Maisie declared with a sniff. 'I've mistrusted her from the beginning. She's such an upstart!'

'What did she predict?'

Dolly remained mute, her expression guarded and angry. Norman looked questioningly at Maisie.

Maisie shrugged. 'She said Donald predicted a sure-fire investment would come Dolly's way, and he urged her to invest.' Maisie made a little moue. 'Of course, the woman was convincing, I'll admit. The voice that came out of her mouth did sound like Donald's. It was quite uncanny.' She frowned. 'But it was a trick, I know it was.'

'Aunt? Have you anything to tell me?' Norman could feel his patience wearing very thin. 'Can you give me a rational explanation about the money?'

Dolly remained stubbornly silent. Watching her with growing exasperation he decided Oscar was right. Not only was Dolly throwing money about like confetti, she was also dabbling in the occult. If that wasn't evidence of incapacity, he did not know what was.

He looked at Maisie. 'Where can I find this woman?'

'I forbid you to speak to her,' Dolly said at last, her voice shaking. 'You have no right to interfere, Norman. I'm not dead yet.'

'Mrs Coombs,' he said. 'I appeal to you.'

Maisie told him what he wanted to know.

Elvi had left for work at Dr Howells' surgery. Sybil had an early appointment with a dressmaker in

299

Craddock Street in the town and was in a hurry to get there. She was annoyed therefore when the doorbell for her rooms rang just as she was carefully placing a hatpin. She must get herself a maid, she decided. She could certainly afford it now.

She opened the door and stared at the middle-aged man on the step. He wore a black bowler hat and a black coat with pinstripe trousers, the crook of a black umbrella hung over his arm. He looked like some clerk. He certainly did not look like a client and Sybil felt annoyed.

'Yes?'

'Are you Mrs Sybil Lloyd?'

Sybil tilted her nose in the air. 'I might be. Who's asking?'

'I'm Norman Mathias,' the man said with a snappy air. 'I'm Mrs Dolly Mathias' nephew.'

'Oh!' Sybil was taken by surprise.

'I want a word with you.'

His tone was rather abrasive, even demanding. Sybil could not think what he wanted with her. She remembered then Dolly saying that her nephew was a lawyer.

'What about?' she asked suspiciously.

'It's not a topic I wish to discuss on the doorstep,' he said. 'Is there some reason you don't want me inside your home?'

Sybil raised her eyebrows. 'I don't know you,' she retorted smartly. 'And I can't think what you might want with me.'

'In one word, Mrs Lloyd – money.'

'I beg your pardon!'

'Am I to come inside in a civilised manner or not?'

'Well! Really!' But Sybil stepped aside so that he could enter the hall. 'You'd better come into the sitting room.'

Sybil marched haughtily into the room, Norman Mathias hard on her heels. What an unpleasant man! And he certainly had a bee in his bonnet about something. Sybil decided she would not ask him to sit down. The sooner he left the better.

Sybil posed before the fireplace. She knew she looked elegant and immaculate, and felt a match for anyone. She lifted her chin and stared down her nose at him.

'Now then,' she began. 'What did you want to see me about?'

'I've been given to understand you advised my aunt to make an investment.'

'I did no such thing.' Sybil had no idea what he was talking about.

'You gave her a so-called message from beyond the grave from my uncle, Donald Mathias,' Norman Mathias insisted. 'She acted upon your advice and handed over fifty thousand pounds in cash.'

Sybil blinked at him, her mouth agape. She remembered Bernard's attempt to help Dolly out of a financial hole, therefore the talk of thousands of pounds disappearing was sheer nonsense.

'Do you deny it?' he persisted.

Sybil struggled to find her voice to defend herself.

'I most certainly do! I'm a clairvoyant of the highest degree of power,' she said breathlessly. 'Which I don't deny.' Sybil took a deep offended

301

breath. 'I did pass a message on from your dear departed uncle.' She shook her head. 'I'm not responsible for the contents of messages. I'm in a trance during a séance and don't know what passes between my clients and spirits from the other world.'

'Poppycock and balderdash!' Norman Mathias exclaimed angrily. 'You're no more than a fraud, woman; a charlatan of the first order. You should be shown up for the faker that you are.'

'How dare you?' Sybil was incensed with fury. 'Get out of my house.'

'Oh, no! Not until I get back the fifty thousand pounds you swindled from my aunt.'

'You're a madman, sir,' Sybil hooted. 'You must know your aunt hasn't a bean to her name. I was told in confidence...'

'My aunt is a very wealthy woman,' Norman Mathias interrupted rudely. 'Who has been passing these rumours about her finances? Who is your accomplice in this heinous swindle? Answer me, woman!'

Sybil stood confused. Instinct warned her to say nothing of Bernard. It was obvious Norman Mathias was out to make trouble. Lawyers were devious and cunning. She must be careful for her own sake. She would be ruined if she was publicly denounced as a fraud.

'Don't you speak to me in that tone and in my own home, too.' She glared at him. 'I'll call a constable if you don't remove yourself immediately.'

'I might call a constable myself,' Norman Mathias retorted angrily. 'A crime has been committed here. You say you're not responsible, but I wager you are involved, and you know who has the money.'

'This is absurd,' Sybil declared. 'If your aunt said I stole money from her she's rambling in her head. I'll have her up for slander, and you too.'

'My God! You really are brazen-faced,' Norman Mathias exclaimed. 'Fifty thousand pounds is missing, and that's a fact. I ask you again, if you don't have it, who does?'

An unpleasant thought came into Sybil's mind. Had Bernard lied to her about Dolly, used her for an underhand purpose?

She hadn't given up hope that his intentions towards her were honourable, and recently had been ready to overlook his lapse with Elvi. After all, men were men, and Elvi might have misled him. She only had the girl's account of what happened between them. Elvi could be lying to cover her shame at enticing the man on.

But with Norman Mathias standing here accusing her of fraud and worse, dark suspicion was forming in her mind. She would say nothing further to this lawyer, at least, not until she had spoken with Bernard. Someone was lying and she must get at the truth to protect herself.

'I have no more to say,' Sybil declared loftily. 'Except that I've not spoken to your aunt since the night of the séance and was never alone with her. If she says any different, the woman is lying, so there!'

'I warn you, Mrs Lloyd, there will be an investigation,' said Norman Mathias curtly. 'I intend to place the matter in the hands of the police. Expect a visit from them shortly.'

Sybil swallowed hard, her heart thumping in her breast. The last thing she wanted was to get involved with the police. Everything had been going so well lately. She had made more money in a few weeks here than she made in twelve months in Fleet Street. Was it all coming to an end? She could not bear the idea of going back to the hand-to-mouth existence she had known before.

But there was even more at stake now, her freedom. Whatever Bernard had done, he had involved her. She had to know all to be able to defend herself.

'Get out!' she shrilled at the lawyer. 'Get out and take your foul accusations with you.'

She followed him to the sitting room doorway, and watched as he crossed the hall and let himself out of the house. She stood there for a moment more, too shaken to take a step in any direction.

She had never felt more alone in her life. She so envied married women, who had husbands to fend off unpleasant episodes, protect them from the harshness of life. She had no one, and she had so set her heart on Bernard. He was such a strong man, capable and worldly. But he had disappointed her; deceived her, perhaps.

She went shakily back into the sitting room. She would not be able to rest until she had spoken with him and received an explanation.

When Bernie entered his house in Walter Road later that day he found Sybil Lloyd waiting for him in the hall. For weeks he had endeavoured to avoid her, certain she would challenge him over that encounter with Elvi in the kitchen. But she had not approached him on the incident, so either the girl had not told her mother, or else Sybil was biding her time.

This made him uneasy and he felt a spasm of annoyance now at having to face her. There was an unusual whiteness about her face which indicated she was very much concerned, and immediately he was on his mettle.

'Bernard,' Sybil began. 'I'd like a word with you. It's rather important.'

'I've just returned from business,' he said hurriedly. 'I'm weary. Can't it wait?'

'No, Bernard, it can't.'

She never spoke brusquely to him as a rule, and he saw immediately that she was not to be put off.

'Very well,' he said in a tired voice.

Seeing that a confrontation was inevitable now he stepped towards her sitting room, rapidly concocting excuses in his mind to account for his behaviour with Elvi. Normally, Sybil hung on his every word. He had guessed her aspirations for him a long time ago so he was certain he could pacify her now.

'No, Bernard,' Sybil said quickly. 'I'd prefer to speak to you privately in your rooms. I don't want Elvi to overhear.'

'I see.' So, it was about the girl, he thought. Nothing of consequence had happened in the kitchen, to his regret, so what was that little bitch Elvi accusing him of?

He ascended the stairs, Sybil climbing behind. A locked door cut off his apartment from the rest of the house, and he opened it now. Minnie Dart came immediately into a small vestibule to greet him.

'Good evening, sir. I'll take your coat. Oh!'

She was startled to see Sybil.

'Dart, show Mrs Lloyd into the study, will you, while I change my jacket,' Bernie commanded. 'And fetch me a stiff whisky.' He looked at Sybil. 'Would you like a drink?'

Sybil shook her head. He turned away as Minnie Dart indicated Sybil should follow her.

As he changed in his bedroom he considered his best defence. He could accuse Elvi of barefaced lying; even suggest the girl was jealous of the close friendship between himself and her mother, and had accused him out of spite. Or else, he could say Elvi had thrown herself at him, and as a red-blooded man, he had been momentarily tempted. Sybil would readily believe that, and perhaps would be moved by his honesty.

He decided in the end he would play it by ear, and see what Sybil had to say first.

When he went into the study she was sitting before the desk, twisting a lace handkerchief in her fingers. She looked extremely upset; one tendril of hair was hanging out of place, so unlike her. He decided sympathy was the best approach.

'Well, Sybil, my dear, what's troubling you?' He sat at his desk, smiling at her.

'I've had a very disturbing visitor earlier today,' she began, her lips trembling. 'A lawyer by the name of Norman Mathias. He made the most outrageous accusations.'

'Mathias?' Bernie was immediately alert.

Sybil nodded. 'The nephew of Dolly Mathias.'

She swallowed hard. 'He accused me of stealing her money. Fifty thousand pounds.'

Bernie controlled his expression with difficulty. 'How absurd! The poor old girl doesn't have that kind of money. I told you, remember?'

Sybil gave him a direct look. 'Yes, I do remember.' He thought he saw a gleam of suspicion in her eyes, and was immediately wary. 'But her nephew says that's untrue,' she went on in a challenging tone. 'She has pots of money according to him.'

'There's a misunderstanding here, I think,' Bernie said casually.

He stood up and walked over to the fireplace, his mind turning and turning like the wheels of a steam engine. He hadn't known about this interfering nephew, and wanted to kick himself for not checking first. Dolly had seemed such a natural target. Had he made an irreparable blunder?

'Norman Mathias is threatening to go to the police.' He heard the rustle of her silk gown as she stood up. 'Bernard, what's going on?'

He turned to her. 'What do you mean, Sybil? What makes you think I know anything of this?'

'You used me, didn't you?' she accused sharply. 'Used me to persuade Dolly Mathias to part with her money in an investment. I think you should explain this to her nephew. He thinks a crime has been committed.'

'The very idea is absurd.'

'I'm under serious suspicion, I tell you,' Sybil exclaimed loudly. 'I could be done for fraud.'

'Well, you are a fraud, aren't you!' Bernie lost his temper. 'You're making money hand over fist

307

with these fake séances of yours; milking my rich friends out of their money. Dolly Mathias is just another of your victims.'

'I've not had Dolly's money, as well you know,' Sybil shrieked. 'You've got that, and I'm beginning to think you've stolen it not invested it.'

'You'd better be careful what you say, woman,' Bernie thundered. 'I'm your landlord and I could have you out on the street instantly.'

'No, you can't.' Sybil tossed her head. 'I have a rent book fully paid up. I know the law.'

'I'll bet you do,' Bernie growled. 'Skating on thin ice as you have been for years.'

'You've got to put me in the clear as regards that money,' Sybil insisted angrily. 'You owe me that.'

He took a step towards her. 'I owe you nothing, you cheap mare. Your character is not so white. I know about the string of men you've associated with over the years.'

'You viper!'

He grabbed at her arm, giving it a little twist until her face contorted with pain.

'Listen to me, you stupid woman,' he rasped. 'You'll keep your mouth shut about my connection to Dolly if you know what's good for you. I can't afford to have any conjecture made.'

'Mathias said the police would be calling on me shortly,' Sybil said, trying to pull her arm free. 'What am I to do?'

'They have no proof that a crime has been committed.'

It was plain to him that Dolly had not revealed his name to her nephew otherwise the police would have been knocking on his door before now. She still believed what he had told her when he had sworn her to secrecy. She had no papers to show where the money had gone, no share certificates or other evidence. Nothing to connect him.

However, he now saw that when the time came to disappoint her, tell her that the bottom had dropped out of the stock, Dolly might put two and two together, and report it to her nephew. Bernie ground his teeth. Somehow he must avoid that.

Still, he would deal with that later. Sybil was the problem now. He must put the frighteners on her to shut her up.

'If you're foolish enough to mention this to anyone,' he warned, 'remember, it's your word against mine, and you're a fraudster.'

'I should've listened to that woman, Mrs Lamar, when she warned me about your plans for Elvi.'

'What?'

He could not believe his ears. Connie had betrayed him! He felt his blood boil. He would deal with Connie in due course, and she would be very, very sorry.

He gave Sybil's arm another sharp twist that made her cry out.

'Listen, if you don't keep silent I'll manufacture evidence against you that could land you in prison,' he warned. 'I'll hand you on a plate to the police. You don't know who you're dealing with in me.'

Sybil whimpered as he released her arm, and

pushed her towards the door. 'Get out of my sight,' he growled. 'And in future keep out of my business.'

Sybil fled from the room and immediately Bernie dismissed her from his mind.

Another worry was taking precedence. That prying nephew of Dolly's could break down her silence at any time. He must talk to her, size up the state of her mind. He had no doubt he could regain her confidence, charm her; play on her greed, persuade her that everything was going well, and that she must keep their secret if they were to make a fortune together.

If she could not be persuaded, well, there were other methods.

23

When Josh called in at Hibbler's studio one morning later in the week he was pleased to see Connie. He realised he needed to get her on his side in his plans to expand Lynnys' horizons, and to see her here again was encouraging.

He had been fabricating and exaggerating when he had told the reporter that Lynnys would be leaving on a European tour. However, thinking seriously on the idea, he realised that London was the place for this talented girl.

Connie thought that appearing at Swansea's Empire Theatre was the height of fame. The theatre was excellent and had attracted many famous performers over the years, but at this stage of her career Lynnys needed the breadth of opportunity that only London could give.

He watched Connie's face as the girl sang and knew she might be easily won over. But London might cost more money than he could muster. He would put the squeeze on Bernie again. A dangerous move, but he felt ready for it.

He and Connie chatted while Lynnys took a break to discuss technique with her tutor on the other side of the room.

'Any news about that poor girl beaten by Bernie?' he asked casually.

'She's still in a coma at the hospital.'

'So serious? Are the police asking questions?'

'We've no idea,' Connie said. 'Herb made sure that there's no connection with the house.'

Josh felt satisfaction. Here was something new he could use against Bernie.

'What does Bernie say for himself?'

Connie shook her head in wonder. 'He's not been near the Pleasure Palace since it happened. It's not like him to be without a woman for any length of time.'

'No,' he said thoughtfully. 'Bernie's not a man to deprive himself of anything.'

She looked at him, worry in her eyes. 'I can't help feeling pity for that poor girl he has at his house in Walter Road. God knows what state she's in. That mother of hers is useless or worse.'

'What girl?'

'Haven't I mentioned her before?'

'Maybe, but refresh my memory,' Josh said.

Connie explained Bernie's feverish obsession with the girl, Elvi. 'The mother's a fool. I warned her, but she threw me out.'

'Maybe I should investigate this myself.'

Connie grabbed at his arm. 'Oh, no, Josh! If you go there Bernie will know I've told you. God knows what he'll do. Since he beat that girl I'm mortally afraid of him.'

'I'll be discreet,' Josh promised. 'I'll call when he's at the shop. I'll size up the mother at the same time.' He looked at her. 'I'm not normally a vindictive man, Con, but somebody ought to put a stop to Bernie.'

Josh decided that the walk up to Walter Road from town would do him good, and following

312

Connie's directions he found the house without difficulty. It was a good looking property which must have cost Bernie a pretty penny. Obviously, he was doing well; better than he let on.

As he approached the front door Josh thought back to those early years. Bernie owed him more than he could ever repay. The man's madness in killing that guard had affected many lives, particularly his own. He had had to run for his life and liberty, leaving behind everything and everyone, particularly the girl he had loved. His life had not made much sense after that.

Bernie on the other hand had sat tight and had grown fat and wealthy and Josh had no qualms about blackmailing him. He would squeeze him dry if he could.

Life was looking better now. At last, in Lynnys he knew he had found something worthwhile, and could make a decent and respectable life for himself. Who knows, he reflected optimistically, he might even find someone to love again.

Josh rang the bell and waited. It was quite a few minutes before someone came to answer the door. A blonde, fashionably dressed woman held the door only slightly ajar and peered out at him. 'Yes, what do you want?' He detected fearfulness in her voice.

'Well, I'm not sure...' Josh began. An uneasy feeling stole over him as he looked at her. 'I'm looking for someone.'

The woman lifted a lace handkerchief to her lips and appeared to be about to burst into tears.

'You're a policeman, aren't you,' she said, a hysterical ring in her voice. 'Norman Mathias sent

313

you. I've nothing to say to the police, nothing. I'm completely innocent. Please go away.'

'No, I'm not a policeman,' he said. 'I'm an acquaintance of Bernie Pomfrey. I believe he owns this house?'

She opened the door a little wider. 'Major Pomfrey is the landlord here, yes,' she said. 'He has the apartment upstairs.'

Josh was studying her features as she spoke, and he felt his mouth drying up with something like shock, his heart pounding.

'May I come in for a moment?' he managed to ask.

'Well, I don't know...'

'Please!' He had to get inside somehow.

'The Major's not here at the moment,' the blonde woman said swallowing sobs. 'He's at business. His maid is out. I hardly think he'd want a stranger...'

'I'm not a stranger.'

'I'm sorry...'

'Sybil!' Josh could not hold back any longer. 'Sybil, it's me! Josh.'

'What?' She stared at him uncomprehending.

'Josh. You must remember me, Syb. I know it's a long time ago, but I've never forgotten you.'

She continued to stare at him and then her eyes became wide and round. 'Oh, my God! It is you!'

Her eyes fluttered up into her head showing the whites and her mouth went slack. As she was about to collapse Josh reached for her and prevented her sinking to the floor.

'Syb!'

He half-carried, half-dragged her across the

314

hall, through a doorway which led into a large sitting room, and lowered her onto a sofa. She moaned slightly as he rested her head on a cushion. And then he sank on to a chair nearby, leaned back, feeling weak himself, and stared at her pale face.

Sybil Lloyd. She had been just eighteen years old when he had been forced to scarper to London. Loving her, he had longed to take her with him, but it wouldn't have been fair; not leading the kind of life that faced him on the mean streets; ducking and diving, eking a living as best he could.

He glanced at the expensive-looking gown she was wearing. It seemed she had done all right for herself. Her left hand was resting on her breast and he saw a wedding band on her finger. So, she had found someone else after all. He could not blame her for making a life for herself.

She was beginning to stir. He looked at her face. The prettiness was still there after seventeen years, and yet, there was also a certain hardness around the mouth. He realised with a deep shock that she was no longer *his* Sybil, the girl he had loved. She was someone else now. Someone he did not know.

She opened her eyes, stared around bemused, and then her glance fell on him.

'Oh, my God! I didn't imagine it then.'

'No, Syb,' he said with gravity. 'It's me.'

She struggled into a sitting position. 'I can't believe it.' Her lips tightened. 'Why are you back? What do you want with me?'

He shook his head. 'I had no idea you lived

315

here, Syb.'

She stood up too abruptly and he was afraid she would fall again. She clasped her hands tightly in front of her.

'You've got a bloody nerve showing up here,' she exclaimed loudly. 'How you have the gall to face me after what you did, I don't know.'

He stood up too. 'I was on the run, Syb. I couldn't take you with me.'

'You deserted me, you swine!'

He was glad she was recovering her composure for they had much to talk about.

'I didn't mean to. I loved you.'

'Love!' She turned her face away as though thoroughly disgusted. 'You hypocrite!'

'It was Bernie's bloody fault,' he said savagely. 'If I'd stayed I might have been imprisoned or even hanged for a murder I didn't commit.'

She turned to face him, her mouth contorted. He did not know whether it was with contempt or fear. 'Bernie? Are you referring to Bernard Pomfrey?'

'Yes. We did a job together,' he admitted. 'But, Bernie, the murdering swine, killed a guard, and for no good reason. Somehow he stayed in the clear, but the police got on my trail. I had to bugger off as fast as I could.'

He took a step towards her. She was no longer his Sybil, but he still remembered the love he had felt for the girl he had known back then.

'I loved you, Syb. It took me a long time to get over you, and I never forgot.'

She sat down again, her head lowered so that he could not see her face properly.

'Serves you right!' she muttered. 'Life wasn't exactly a bed of roses for me afterwards, you know.'

'You found someone, though,' he pointed out. 'You married.'

'Married!' She gave a bitter laugh and looked up at him, anger flashing in her eyes. 'No, I never married. Not much chance of that under the circumstances. I wear this ring for appearances only.'

He felt confused. 'Who is Elvi?'

She looked at him, her expression still resentful. 'Your daughter, Josh,' she said harshly. 'The child you abandoned along with its mother.'

'What?' His legs were suddenly weakened and he flopped down on to the chair again. 'My daughter?' He could not believe the words he was uttering. 'I have a daughter?'

'I never married because no man wants a woman with a brat hanging on her apron strings,' Sybil said. 'I had to scrape a living any way I could.'

He stared at her apprehensively.

She shook her head. 'No, I didn't go on the streets, Josh.' Her lips curled mockingly. 'I've more self-respect than that.' She lifted her chin. 'I followed in my grandmother's footsteps and set up as a clairvoyant.' She looked around. 'It didn't pay until I took up Bernard's offer. I'm doing all right now.'

'Where's my daughter?' Josh said thickly. 'I want to see her. Does she know about me?'

'She thinks you're dead,' said Sybil brutally. 'She doesn't know she's ... illegitimate. That's another reason why I've always worn a wedding ring.'

A terrible thought struck him, turning him cold with apprehension; the reason why he was here at all. He leapt to his feet.

'Has that swine Bernie laid a hand on my daughter?'

Sybil looked up startled and then guilty, Josh thought and feared the worst, thinking of the girl Bernie had beaten into a coma. 'I'll kill him if he has!'

'He's tried,' she admitted. 'But luckily he was interrupted.'

'Where were you, Syb?' he demanded, looming over her. 'You should've been protecting her.'

'He tricked me!' Sybil exclaimed in a peeved tone. 'I had no idea then what he's capable of.'

'What happened?'

Josh sat down, listening with growing wrath as she told him of Elvi's awful experience in the kitchen. He was raging by the time she had finished so that he could hardly contain himself.

'I'll swing for that bastard!'

'Oh, Josh, he had me fooled, but now I'm beginning to think Bernard Pomfrey is a dangerous man. I've been accused of theft, and I didn't do it, but I think he knows more about it than he'll say.'

'Is that why you thought I was a policeman?'

'Yes. An elderly lady, a client of mine, has fifty thousand pounds missing. Her nephew has accused me. I'm sure Bernard has done something underhand.'

He did not doubt it for a moment. 'Tell me every last detail,' he said. 'Leave nothing out.'

Sybil related the events leading to her predicament. 'He threatened me,' she said. 'I'm frightened of him.'

'You have cause to be.'

That was the second time recently that he had heard a woman say she feared Bernie Pomfrey. Bernie was becoming overconfident and careless with it and therefore even more dangerous.

'So Bernie got you to set up the old girl beforehand,' he remarked. 'An old confidence trick. He's had that money all right. I'd stake my life on it.' He rubbed his jaw thoughtfully. 'You should get out of this house, Sybil, and take my daughter with you. It isn't safe here any longer.'

She stood up and walked stiffly to the fireplace. 'But things are going so well as regards clients and the séances, Josh. I'm making a lot of money.'

Josh shook his head in wonder at her crassness. 'It's over, Syb. Do you think this lawyer Mathias hasn't spread the word about you? You'll get no more upper-crust clients.'

'I'm innocent!'

'Mud sticks.' Josh rose from his seat and went to her. 'Sybil, be sensible. Look for new lodgings today and then do a moonlight flit. It's better Bernie doesn't know where you are, or at least where Elvi is.'

'I'll think about it,' she said reluctantly.

He realised he could not force her. 'Look, I've got rooms in St Helens Road.' He told her the address. 'Don't hesitate to get in touch if you need me.'

She smiled weakly. 'Thanks, Josh.' She held out

her hand. 'Goodbye.'

He took her hand and held it for a moment. 'I would've liked to see my daughter before I go.'

'She's at work at the moment at a doctor's surgery nearby.' She gave a light laugh. 'She has silly dreams of becoming a nurse.'

'Don't take chances with her, Sybil,' he said earnestly. 'Bernie has plans for her; he's obsessed. He's capable of anything.'

'I'm her mother, Josh; mother and father all her life. I know what's best.'

'I hope so, Sybil,' he said in a hard voice. 'Because if anything happens to her ... if that swine Bernie gets his hands on her, I'll blame you, and I won't be responsible for my actions.'

She gazed at him defiantly, and he wondered apprehensively if she really understood the danger Elvi was in.

Josh wasted no time after leaving Sybil. He hailed a hansom and headed for Bernie's shop. Even though he had not met his daughter yet, he wasn't prepared to leave Elvi's fate to chance, even if Sybil was.

He entered the premises to find quite a few customers being attended to. Dawson, the head assistant, gave him a harassed glance, but Josh waved his hand dismissively and headed straight for Bernie's office.

He barged in, his rage barely in check. Bernie glanced up from papers on his desk, his face darkening as he recognised Josh.

'What the hell do you want, Rowlands? If it's more money you can just bugger off.'

'I want you to keep your filthy hands off my daughter.'

'What?' Bernie looked astonished. 'Your daughter?' He smiled then. 'I don't think I've had the pleasure ... yet. Who is your daughter anyway?'

'Elvi Lloyd and I'm warning you, Bernie, keep away from her.'

Bernie leaned back in his chair. 'Little Elvi! Your daughter?' He laughed heartily. 'Well, this is a nice surprise.'

Josh could have bitten off his tongue in chagrin, realising too late, that in his fury he had made a bad mistake in admitting the relationship. He was now vulnerable.

'Life is full of surprises, Bernie,' Josh said harshly. 'Unpleasant surprises, which you'll find out if you lay a hand on my daughter again. I know about the incident in the kitchen at Walter Road.' Josh clutched tightly at his walking stick. 'By God! I could kill you.'

Bernie's face clouded. 'You've been to my house?' He rose abruptly. 'What the hell for?'

Josh struggled to control himself. He had made one mistake, he could not afford to make more. He had Bernie just where he wanted him, and he mustn't let his outrage spoil his advantage.

'A little bird told me about some unfortunate girl you had at your house,' said Josh 'A girl you had big plans for.' He smiled grimly. 'I wondered if she'd suffered the same fate as the kid you beat almost to death at the Pleasure Palace.'

Bernie looked startled.

'Oh, yes, I know about that, too.' Josh smirked at having the upper hand again. 'It might interest

321

you to learn she's in a coma at the hospital. If and when she wakes she'll be able to name you, Bernie. You'll be finished.'

Bernie wetted his lips. 'You've been poking about eh?' he said. 'Talking to that double-crossing bitch, Connie.' He sat down looking smug. 'I'm not worried about the girl,' he said casually. 'She can't name me. I'm known as Mr Smith at the Pleasure Palace. And if I know Herb, he made sure the house was kept out of it.'

'You're sure of Herb, are you?'

Bernie laughed. 'Herb does all right out of the house with backhanders, which he thinks I don't know about.' He nodded. 'He knows which side his bread is buttered. Besides, I've got the goods on him, so he knows better than to cross me.'

Bernie's confidence made Josh feel uneasy. 'You think nothing can touch you, Bernie,' he said angrily. 'But I know about the fifty thousand pounds you half-inched, and you left Sybil to carry the can for it.'

Bernie's face whitened for a moment and then suffused with blood. 'The stupid bitch told you about that?' he snarled. 'She needs to be taught a lesson.'

'Threatened with the police, she was scared,' Josh said. 'What did you expect?'

'Nothing can be proved against me.'

Josh smiled. 'You're forgetting, I know where the bodies are buried, remember?'

'In the eyes of the law you're as guilty as I am,' Bernie growled. 'If I swing for that guard, so will you.'

'But I can tell the police about the girl in the

coma and how she got that way,' Josh reminded him. 'I want another twenty thousand, Bernie, and I want it by next weekend. I want ready cash this time. I'm not prepared to wait until the cheque clears. I don't trust you and you may not have all that time left.'

'Go and take a running jump!'

'Suit yourself!' Josh laughed grimly. 'But it's you that'll take the jump, Bernie, if the kid never recovers. And there are other interested parties who'd like to know your identity. Think about it. I'll call in the shop on Friday next.'

Bernie sat for a while chewing his thumb nail after Josh Rowlands had left. A mountain of rage was growing in him. That was the second time Connie had talked to the wrong person. First she had tipped the wink to Sybil about his interest in Elvi, and now she had given Josh Rowlands the low down on what went on at the Pleasure Palace. Connie must be taught to keep her mouth shut and soon.

Bernie went over to the filing cabinet in the corner of the room, opened the top drawer and took out a half bottle of whisky together with a tumbler and brought them back to the desk.

He needed to think. Rowlands had him over a barrel, for the moment, but he would part with no more money. It was high time he got hold of Elvi.

Bernie smiled to himself. Josh Rowlands might not be so keen to own her as his daughter once she had been made into a dirty little whore. It would give him a great deal of pleasure to teach her the trade, and it would be sweet revenge on Rowlands, too.

But first there were other scores to settle. Connie needed her face broken and he was ready to do it. He would mark her so badly no man would look at her again, including Herb Collins.

Bernie let himself through the back door of the Pleasure Palace. It was quite late, well gone midnight, so he could be sure that all of the girls were occupied upstairs, and as he expected the parlour was empty, no sign of Connie.

Avoiding the office he went quietly up the staircase and along the passage to Connie's bedroom door, which was behind a curtain at the end. Quietly, Bernie turned the knob and eased the door open. The room was in semi-darkness, lit only by a gaslight turned very low.

Connie was in bed. He could tell she was asleep by the regular rhythm of her breathing. He considered for a moment. He had come here to punish her, punish her good, but there was no reason why he should not have some fun first.

Being very careful not to disturb her yet, Bernie closed the door and placed the back of a small wooden chair under the knob. Now Connie could scream as much as she would, but no one could get in until he had finished what he had come to do.

He took off his coat and cap, loosened the belt of his trousers, and then stood by the bed. Yanking the bedclothes off the bed, he threw himself onto her stretched out form, putting his hand over her mouth.

She awoke with a stifled scream, fighting like some wild animal and he was astonished at the strength with which she fought him.

'It's me, you double-crossing bitch,' he murmured hoarsely in her ear, struggling to restrain her. 'Don't fight me or it'll be the worse for you.'

She was still for a brief moment. Faint light revealed her face under his hand, eyes staring at him in terror. He was pleased at her reaction. She'd know what real terror was by the time he'd finished with her.

'You've been gabbing your mouth off, haven't you,' he rasped. 'Splitting on me to Sybil Lloyd that I'm after Elvi. Was it jealousy?'

Connie began to struggle again, trying to free her mouth, and he struck at her savagely. He remembered the night he had beaten the girl and a feverish excitement swept over him, more powerful than his desire for sexual intercourse. He had revelled in that beating, knowing he was out of control but did not care, because it satisfied a new and demanding hunger and he had wanted more.

'I'm going to punish you, Connie, like I punished that stupid girl. Maybe you'll end up in a coma, if I don't kill you first.'

He grasped a handful of her hair and rising from the bed, dragged her up with him. As soon as he released her mouth she let out a howl, but that was cut off as he ploughed his fist into her face.

She staggered under the blow, whimpering, but his grasp on her hair held her upright.

'Shut up! That's for ratting on me to Josh

325

Rowlands,' he snarled. 'You've made trouble for me, do you know that? Cost me money, maybe. But you won't do it again.'

He tore her nightgown from her, exposing her breasts, and then began pounding at her. Connie screamed in pain and fear, lifting her arms to protect her body, but they were no match for his fist.

He heard a man chortle with excitement, and realised it was himself. He let go her hair then and she crumpled into a heap on the floor.

'I'm going to beat you to a pulp, Connie,' he said with satisfaction. 'No man will want you. They'll look at you in disgust. Even Herb will turn away. Your own mother won't recognise you.'

'Bernie! For God's sake, let me be,' Connie muttered through swollen lips.

For an answer he aimed a kick at her ribs. She tried to roll away out of his reach, but his boot caught her on the back, and she screamed again.

Bernie was aware that someone was rattling the door knob and shouting. It sounded like Herb Collins.

'Bugger off!' he yelled. 'I'm teaching this cheap lay a lesson she won't forget.'

'Bernie!' Herb bellowed. 'Open this door. You touch her again and I'll kill you.'

'Kill a man?' Bernie hooted. 'You only kill women, Herb, remember.'

The door shuddered as Herb threw his weight against it. Bernie eyed the chair back. It was flimsy but it would hold for a while. He looked around for Connie. She had dragged herself towards the small fireplace and was rising up from the floor with difficulty, her face bloody.

'Don't come near me again, Bernie,' she warned with difficulty. She reached down into the grate and picked up a fire iron, brandishing it at him. 'I'll crack your skull open, you beast.'

With a snarl of rage he rushed towards her, grabbing the fire iron and wrenched it from her grasp. He was tempted to strike her with it, but that would be too quick. He wanted more sport, much more. He contented himself with slapping her across the face with his open palm and then seized her by the throat, pinning her against the wall.

'You're mine to do with as I will, Connie,' he rasped close to her face. 'You've always been mine, and do you know what, I've despised you for it over the years.'

She stared at him as though mesmerised. 'You won't get away with it, Bernie. I'll give you up to the police.'

He laughed. 'Is that so? You'll have trouble talking with a broken jaw.'

His hand tightened on her throat. He could easily squeeze the life out of her now and was again tempted, but he had no intention of swinging for the likes of her. Disfiguring, crippling, would be a greater punishment, one she would have to live with for the rest of her wretched life.

He raised his hand to strike her again but suddenly the door behind him splintered and gave way, and the next moment he was being seized roughly from behind. He had one second to recognise Herb's furious face before a clenched fist crashed into his own.

'You bastard! I'll kill you!'

He staggered back under the blow, while Herb moved in on him fists flying. He was as tall as Herb and managed to get in a few punches himself, but he knew he was no match for the ex-boxer. One vicious blow to the side of his head made him dizzy, the pain sickening him, and he fell to his knees, letting himself collapse on to the floor, realising it was the safest place for him.

'I'm going to give you a taste of your own medicine, Bernie,' Herb panted.

Bernie saw a kick coming and tried to double over to protect his body but before Herb could deliver the blow, Connie was at Herb's side, attempting to pull him away.

'Leave him. He's not worth it,' she mumbled thickly. 'Get me away from here, please, Herb. I need a doctor.'

Herb loomed over him for a moment more but Connie's pleading made him stand back. Bernie swallowed hard, pushing himself up on his elbows. That had been close. He decided it would not be wise to get to his feet just yet, and was relieved that he had got off fairly lightly.

He glared up at them from the floor. 'Get the hell out of my place,' he managed to yell at them, even though winded. 'You're finished here, the pair of you.'

Herb gave a snarl. 'You're lucky I don't burn the place down with you in it,' he said savagely. 'You've got it coming to you, Bernie, and you'll get what's owing, I promise.'

'Get out!'

'I'll get some things,' Connie said, moving awkwardly towards the wardrobe.

'You take nothing,' Bernie rasped out from the comparative safety of the floor. 'Everything in this house belongs to me.'

Herb grabbed Connie's wrap from a chair and put it around her shoulders.

'Come on, Con,' he said. 'We'd better go before I do him a mischief.' He shepherded Connie towards the door, and then looked around at Bernie. 'I'd watch your back from now on, if I were you Bernie, because you're a marked man.'

'Huh! You don't scare me, Collins,' Bernie retorted. 'The guts went out of you a long time ago. You're no more than a woman-killer. Nothing!'

Connie could hardly walk as Herb helped her along the passage and down the staircase, the pain in her face almost overwhelming her. She wondered with apprehension what damage Bernie had done, but gave up a silent prayer that Herb had saved her from much worse. Bernie had been well on the way to killing her. She had seen it in his face as he beat her.

'I'll take you to your sitting room while I find you some clothes to put on,' Herb said.

Connie clutched his arm. 'Don't leave me alone, please. I'm afraid.'

'He won't touch you again,' Herb said. 'And if he tries anything I won't use my fists on him next time, I'll use a knife.'

'I think he's gone out of his mind.'

'No, he's just being Bernie. The swine!'

Connie waited apprehensively in her sitting

room until Herb returned with clothes borrowed from some of the girls.

'These will do for now, while you see a doctor,' Herb said. 'But I'll be back to the place to collect all our belongings, and Bernie had better not be here when I do.'

'Leave everything of mine,' Connie said. 'I want nothing more from this place. I've had enough. I'm getting out of the game, Herb. I'll scrub floors if I have to.'

'I'll look after you, Con,' said Herb tenderly. 'You know the way I feel.'

'I want to dress now, Herb,' Connie said evasively. 'I'll be ready to leave this place in ten minutes. Come for me then.'

Herb left the room with lingering glances at her.

Connie sat down for a moment, shaking. What a fool she had been all her life, she reflected. And what good was love when it blinded you to the truth?

When Herb returned she was ready. He had a small case with him. 'I'll get you to Doc Benson's place straight away,' he said. 'After that we'll need to find somewhere to stay until I can get something permanent.'

Connie suddenly thought of Lynnys. She would not be able to face the girl for a while, not looking as though she had been run down by a hansom. It would surely raise questions in the girl's mind and she could not bear to lose her daughter's respect.

'Herb, I want you to see Josh Rowlands and tell him what's happened to me.'

Herb's face darkened. 'What's between you and him?' he demanded to know.

'My daughter,' Connie admitted wearily.

'What?'

She was beginning to tremble uncontrollably and knew shock was setting in.

'Please, Herb, no more questions. I feel faint. Help me!'

Herb made sure Connie was secure at the doctor's lodgings, and stayed long enough to learn that no great damage had been done to Connie's face, though what damage there was would take time to heal.

Wrath against Bernie still burned in him like acid, eating away at his innards. Something would have to be done about Bernie, something permanent.

But he would not be such a fool as to attempt it himself. It was too risky. There were others in the town that would do the job for him, others like Charlie Pendle.

It would be tricky. He had no connection with the man or any of the thugs who worked for him. It could be dangerous even making enquiries about him, so he had heard. Nevertheless, he had information which Pendle wanted, and he wanted nothing in return for it. It would be enough for him to see Bernie six feet under where he could do no more harm.

24

There could be no disguising the bruising to his face but Bernie was ready for the stares of curiosity from his shop staff the following morning.

'Good gracious!' Dawson exclaimed at the sight of his battered face. 'Major Pomfrey, sir, what has befallen you?'

'I was attacked on my way home from my club last night,' Bernie remarked, making his tone casual and matter-of-fact. 'The swine tried to relieve me of my wallet.'

Dawson's eyes were round. 'Did he get much, sir?'

'There were two or three of them,' Bernie lied deftly. 'But I fought the blighters off and they scuttled away empty-handed.'

Dawson looked appalled. 'Have the police any idea who they were?'

'None,' Bernie said shortly. He moved swiftly towards the office. 'I don't want to be disturbed for an hour or two, Dawson,' he went on. 'And I won't be available this afternoon either. Carry on.'

'Yes, sir.'

Bringing out the bottle of whisky from the filing cabinet, Bernie sat down at his office desk to think. There was a lot to think about. He had to replace Herb Collins as manager. Fred could stand in for the time being, but he didn't have enough brains to take permanent charge of the house, the money and the girls. Replacing Connie would be easy enough. Any one of the girls could do it.

But there were even more pressing matters. Dolly Mathias was becoming more of a danger to him every day. He knew he had to see her and regain her confidence, make sure she remained on his side. He would do that this afternoon, take her some flowers; flatter her a bit.

He had settled his score with Connie, not to his complete satisfaction, but nevertheless, the beating was a lesson she would not forget in a hurry.

And there was Josh Rowlands to deal with. Abducting Elvi would present no problem, he was sure of that. Sybil could be easily outwitted. With Herb and Connie out of the way, he could keep Elvi secure at the Pleasure Palace, treat her as he liked. She could scream as much as she wanted, no one would interfere, and no outsider would be the wiser because no one would know where she was.

Josh's daughter! He liked the idea. Elvi would suffer for her father's sins. It was poetic. He had been driven mad with desiring her, wanting her body over the months, and at last she would be at his mercy, although he would show none to Josh's daughter.

He had luncheon at his club, and made a great show of his facial injuries, claiming to have been victorious in defeating three or four men in a street robbery. Several members bought him drinks, and after calling in at a florist's, he hailed

333

a passing hansom and set off for Dolly's house in a pleasant frame of mind.

He was surprised when she opened the door herself, and then remembered that this was the day her maid normally took her half-day.

'Bernard, how lovely to see you.'

He was alerted by her tone which did not have her accustomed warmth and realised she was worried at his visit and he cursed Norman Mathias for his interference. He must put her mind at rest as quickly as possible.

She took the flowers from him. 'So kind,' she went on and then left the blooms as they were on the hall table.

'I call on you with some good news,' Bernie lied heartily as he followed her into the drawing room. Dolly sat down and Bernie did likewise.

She glanced at him then with mild curiosity. 'Whatever has happened to your face, Bernard?'

He related the story of the bogus robbery, embellishing his tale even more in an effort to distract her, but he saw she was only half listening to him.

'I'm glad you did call, Bernard.' Her tone was serious. 'There's something I must discuss with you.' She cleared her throat nervously and Bernie knew instantly she was about to ask for the return of her money. 'My nephew, Norman...'

'Before you go any further, Dolly dear,' Bernie interrupted quickly. 'I must tell you the good news. The value of the stock we bought has leapt forward as I anticipated. We have more than doubled our money, already. What do you think of that?'

Dolly looked taken aback for a moment and then the doubt on her face turned to pleasant surprise. 'Really? That's wonderful! I'm so relieved, Bernard dear. My nephew, Norman...'

Bernie did not give her time to finish. 'My inside informant tells me that the value is set to rise even higher.' He leaned back in his chair. 'It'll go through the roof, Dolly, through the roof.'

She wetted her lips. 'My nephew, Norman, thinks I'm being imprudent, Bernard.' She smiled wanly, the wrinkles in her cheeks stirring. 'He says I should never have made the investment, at least, not before consulting him.'

Bernie feigned surprise. 'Your nephew is a stockbroker, is he? He knows about these things?'

'He's a lawyer.'

'Ah! Yes, well,' Bernie let doubt sound in his tone. 'I'm sure he knows the law through and through,' he said. 'But I doubt he understands the mystery of stocks and shares. My inside informant is an expert, otherwise I would never have dealt myself.'

'I'm so glad you've proved Norman wrong,' said Dolly with approval. 'However, he gives me no peace over the matter. I feel it would be wiser for me to cash in my stock right away. That would ease his mind.' She clasped her hands and put them in her lap. 'Gracious! A hundred thousand pounds. Who would've thought it? Such an enormous sum. It's almost unbelievable. My nephew will have to eat his words and I can't wait to see his face.' She looked up at Bernie eagerly. 'How soon can I have my money?'

335

'You wish to cash in?' Bernie hid his chagrin and tried to look as incredulous as possible. 'But, my dear lady, you'd be throwing away a fortune, an absolute fortune. I can hardly believe you mean to do it. My expert tells me the stock has a long way to go before it's time to sell.'

'I'm sure you're right, Bernard,' said Dolly with a smile. 'But Norman has a point perhaps. A woman of my age should not be taking such risks. I'll cash in my stock.'

Bernie felt exasperation stir. 'This is madness, Dolly,' he said more gruffly than he meant to. 'The stock is as safe as houses.'

She frowned at his tone. 'I think I may do as I like with my own money, Bernard.'

'Of course, of course.' He checked himself. 'I'm thinking of you, my dear,' he said more gently. 'And the great opportunity you're throwing away.'

She shook her head. 'I'm only thankful things have turned out all right.' She paused and then went on. 'Norman wants to take the matter further; involve the police.'

'You sound as if you don't trust me, Dolly.'

'Of course I trust you.' Her old cheeks coloured slightly. 'It's Norman, you see.' She looked at him askance. 'You gave me no stock certificate or receipt as we had previously agreed. Norman thought that very strange practice.'

'It was a secret deal between friends,' Bernie said. He was beginning to realise she might not be talked around, and his mind was searching for another way out.

'So when will I get my money?'

'It's rather tricky to say, Dolly. You see, I lumped my money with yours, and I certainly don't want to disturb my portion. I could lose thousands.' He wetted his lips. 'It might take some weeks.'

'But anything could happen in that time,' she pointed out with some asperity. 'The bottom could fall out of the deal. I could lose my money.' She shook her head firmly. 'No, I'm determined to keep what I've already earned. I want my money Bernard, and I want it right away ... tomorrow.'

'That's impossible!' He was struggling not to lose his temper.

Dolly rose to her feet. 'Tomorrow, Bernard,' she said firmly. 'Or I'll have to speak to my nephew. You know he has already been in touch with the police. So far I've not mentioned your name to him.' She shook her head gravely. 'But you'll leave me no choice if I'm not reimbursed tomorrow.'

Fuming, Bernie leapt to his feet, towering over her. She looked up at him imperiously, her small frail form erect, her jaw set firm. He felt impotent rage swell in his chest, and itched to strike her down where she stood.

'You stupid old woman!' he stormed at her. 'Why couldn't you leave things alone?'

'Bernard!'

Furious with her stubbornness, he could not stop himself. 'Your money's gone,' he yelled. 'There is no money. How do you like that?'

She took an unsteady step backwards. 'What are you saying?'

337

'I'm saying you've been had for a fool,' he bellowed. 'You raddled hag.'

'Oh!' She stood quivering, and then raised a trembling hand to point at the door. 'Get out!'

'Do you think I'm going to leave you here to gab?'

His fury was growing moment by moment and along with it, panic. He had shown his hand, and there was no going back now.

She started to edge away. 'Don't you touch me. Don't lay a hand on me. I'll have the authorities on you, I warn you.'

'You ridiculous old cow. You won't talk to anyone.'

Without thinking twice about it he lashed out, his balled fist catching her on one temple. She was thrown off her feet by the force of the blow and landed in a crumpled heap near the fireplace, her head resting on the elaborate brass fender, and lay there without sound or movement.

Uncertain, he stood looking down at her for a moment and then striding forward bend over her to feel for a pulse in her throat. There was none, and he could tell by the way her head lay at a curious angle that her neck was broken.

He stepped away for a moment to think. Well, she wouldn't talk now. He was safe. Norman Mathias could stomp about and rave all he wanted, but there was now no proof against him.

He stirred himself. He should leave before the maid returned. But he hesitated. Something wasn't right. This death shouted out foul play. It ought to look like an accident.

338

He moved her frail body away from the fireplace and was glad to see there was no residue of blood on the fender. It was a clean break.

Old people often broke their necks falling down stairs, he reasoned. Lifting up the body he carried it into the hall and up the staircase. At the top he turned, and held her upright, her shoes resting on the top stair, her head lolling forward peculiarly. He positioned her as he thought would be right and then released the body. Noisily, it flopped down one stair after another, arms and legs flailing, and then it landed with a resounding thud on the marble floor below.

He smiled to himself. That should do it. Now all he had to do was slip away quietly and be thoroughly shocked when the news of Dolly's death broke.

He was just leaving through the front door when he remembered the flowers, and nipping back, snatched them from the hall table.

No one knew he had ever been here. He was in the clear.

Herb found lodgings for Connie close to his own rooms, where she could stay until she recovered, and where he could visit her daily to make sure she was all right.

Seeing her beauty damaged, and the pain she was in, his wrath against Bernie swelled, until he knew he could never rest until Bernie paid for what he had done. So, the following evening he went down towards the docks in search of contact with Charles Pendle.

There was one particular public house in that

area which was notorious as a meeting place for criminals. If he was to get in touch with Pendle, this would probably be the best place to do it, although he was aware that what he was attempting was very dangerous.

Not without some apprehension, he walked into the smoke-filled public bar of the Arches pub about nine o'clock, and scuffed his way towards the bar through the dirty sawdust which was strewn on the floor.

Even though he wore workingmen's clothing, he was aware of suspicious stares from some of the drinkers. A stranger was in their midst, and they didn't like it.

Herb was used to looking after himself, but he felt the nerves in his neck tighten in the face of such open hostility. He wondered if he was being a fool, but the memory of Connie's battered face soon strengthened his resolve.

He leaned nonchalantly on the wet bar as if he had every right to be there, while the barman scowled at him.

'What'll it be, mister.'

'Half a bitter.' He felt like something stronger, but knew he must keep his wits about him in a place like this.

The drink was brought, the glass dumped on the bar unceremoniously.

'If I was you,' the barman said quietly. 'I'd drink up and push off. We don't like copper's narks around here. It's not healthy, see.'

'I'm not a copper or a nark,' Herb said, lifting the glass and taking a long pull at the amber liquid.

The barman looked him over. 'You look like a copper to me.'

'I'm a boxer, down on his luck.'

'A boxer eh? What's your name, then?'

Herb wetted his lips before answering, reluctant to give his identity away. 'Herb Collins.'

'Huh! Never heard of you, and I know a bit about boxers.'

'Never made it big, I didn't,' Herb said, which was true. 'But I've cracked a few jaws in my time.'

The barman grinned. 'All right, but take a tip from me, mate. Don't go nosing around.'

'I'm looking for someone,' Herb said. He felt his mouth go dry at the hard suspicious look in the barman's eyes and took another pull at his bitter.

'I thought you said you wasn't narking.'

'I've got some information,' Herb went on. 'Which I think Charlie Pendle might be interested in.'

Herb was surprised to see the barman's face pale. 'Are you mad, mister?' he asked in a low tone. 'No one mentions that name lightly around here.'

'I want to talk to him,' Herb persisted.

'You're asking for a slit throat, you are.'

'I'm doing him a favour.'

'Do yourself a favour and push off now.'

'I'm not leaving until I make contact with him or one of his men.'

'Suit yourself. You've been warned.'

The barman walked to the other end of the bar and spoke quietly to a large rough-looking man

341

standing there. Herb had been conscious of the man's intense scrutiny since he had walked in. Was this the feared Charlie Pendle? He did not look much for all his bulk. Herb flexed his shoulder muscles. He could take this man easily if it came to it.

The man sauntered towards him and Herb turned from the bar to face him, his body tense, ready for action.

'You're not wanted around here, mate,' the man rasped. 'Bugger off!'

'You're going to make me go, matey?'

The man's eyes signalled the punch he was about to throw and Herb blocked it easily, throwing a powerful punch himself, his fist landing on the side of the man's jaw with a satisfying crunch. He went down full length on the bar-room floor and stayed there dazed.

Herb turned his back to the bar and faced the room. 'Anyone else want to try his luck?'

Two or three drinkers got to their feet, and took a few steps towards him. Herb took a deep breath. It looked like he had a fight on his hands after all, a fight he had better win. But before the men reached him, someone spoke up from the back of the room.

'All right. Leave him.'

Herb was surprised to see his would-be assailants step back hastily as a man came forward from behind; a young girl, pretty but cheap-looking, clinging to his arm.

The man was young himself, in his mid-twenties, Herb guessed; well-dressed for his surroundings. He was even-featured and slight of

342

build, certainly no boxer, but there was a deadly coldness in his blue eyes and a disturbing degree of arrogance in the way he walked forward which gave Herb pause for thought.

'What're you doing on my patch, mister?' For all his style, the man had a coarse local accent. 'Looking for trouble, or what?'

'Are you Charlie Pendle?'

'Might be.'

The young girl hanging on his arm was grinning at Herb as though she expected to see him humiliated. 'Get the lads to duff him up, Charlie.'

'Shut up, Kitty.' He spoke curtly to her. 'And get back to the table. Told you before, I have. Keep your nose out.'

'But Charlie...'

He rounded on her and lifted a fist threateningly. She scuttled away, while he turned back to look at Herb with eyes as deadly as sheet ice.

'You've got some guts coming down here to see me.'

'I've got information,' Herb said hastily. 'About the Pleasure Palace, and who really owns it.'

Charlie Pendle's eyes narrowed. 'And what do you want for this information?'

'Nothing,' Herb said harshly. 'I want to see a certain bloke get what's coming to him so I'm handing him to you on a plate.'

'A double-cross, eh?'

Herb ground his teeth. 'The bastard deserves it.'

Charlie Pendle studied him for a moment and then smiled. It was a humourless smile and, like his eyes, devoid of any warmth or feeling. It was

343

quite obvious the men around Charlie Pendle were afraid of him, and looking into the man's blue gaze again, he understood why. A psychopath if ever there was one. He had seen that look before in his days in the ring and a shiver ran up his spine. He was dealing with a very dangerous man.

'Righto,' Charlie said in an even tone which made Herb swallow hard. 'Let's talk.' He jerked his head towards a door at the other end of the bar. 'In the back room.'

He nodded towards one of the men drinking at a nearby table, and the man followed them into the back room.

Charlie Pendle sat at a desk in the room but did not invite Herb to sit. He was conscious of the other man standing behind him with his back to the closed door. He could rely on his own fists, but a knife between the shoulder blades was another thing. He stood tense and alert.

'The Pleasure Palace has been a thorn in my side for too long,' Charlie began, leaning back confidently in his chair. 'I'm going to dig it out.' He smiled. 'All right. Tell me what you know.'

Herb told him about Bernie Pomfrey's double life; on the face of it a respectable businessman but in fact a brothel-keeper who thinks he's too clever for the law.

'The place makes money then?' Charlie was looking at him with a speculative light in his eyes.

'Good takings,' Herb agreed reluctantly. 'Clean girls and most of the clientele are prominent figures in the town.'

'Opportunities to put the squeeze on, eh?'

'That wouldn't pay,' Herb said quickly. 'The quickest way to kill off trade.'

Charlie raised his brows and nodded. 'Makes sense.' He looked keenly at Herb. 'So, you want Pomfrey out of the way? Planning to take over, are you?'

'No, I've finished with the place.' Herb curled his lip. 'I'm sick of it.'

'Suppose after Pomfrey is dealt with, I take over and *insist* on you running it for me. What do you say to that?'

Herb swallowed hard. He knew men like Pendle kept his cronies under his thumb through fear. Either they carried out the dirty jobs he wanted done or they ended up in the river. Once in Pendle's pay he would never again be his own man, never be allowed to quit. But he must be careful how he answered.

'That's a generous offer, Mr Pendle,' Herb said with as much composure as he could muster. 'And I'm grateful. But I'm leaving Swansea for good.'

'What makes you think you'll get out of my patch without getting your throat slit?'

'That wouldn't be clever, Mr Pendle,' Herb said carefully. 'Bernie Pomfrey would know straight away that you're on to him. He's slick at disappearing into the woodwork. And knowing him as I do, he'd take all the profits with him.'

Charlie Pendle looked at him a moment more. 'You've got a brain, Collins. I could use a man like you. I need a reliable lieutenant to watch my back. Interested?'

Herb wetted his lips. 'Like I said, I'm leaving

this town.'

'All right.' Charlie Pendle stood up abruptly. 'Push off, but, keep your mouth shut about me, or anything said or seen here tonight.'

'Don't worry,' Herb said with heartfelt sincerity. 'I intend to be well away from Swansea before anything happens to that bastard.'

Late as it was Herb went straight to Connie's lodgings, where she was living under the assumed name of Mrs Connie Richards. She was not pleased to see him and wrapped her negligee more closely around herself.

'Are you mad, Herb, coming here at this hour?' she asked him pithily. 'I don't want gossip. I'm trying to start a new life.'

'I had to see you, Con. I'm leaving Swansea first thing in the morning.'

She looked astonished. 'Why?'

He bit his lower lip, and turned his face away.

'What have you done, Herb?'

'I went to see Charlie Pendle.'

'What?'

'Bernie's going to pay and pay dear for what he did to you, Con,' Herb said defensively. 'I've blown the whistle on him to Pendle. You and me will be long gone from here before it happens.'

'Before what happens?'

'Use your head, Con,' Herb snapped. 'Bernie's a dead man now Pendle knows who he is.'

'Oh, God, Herb!' Connie stared at him and he saw revulsion in her face. 'How could you do that to him?'

'It was easy,' he snarled, angry at her reaction.

346

Was she still in love with Bernie? Surely not. 'After what he did to you, he deserves all he gets. He could've killed you, Connie. Do you realise that?'

She nodded. 'I know.'

'I've still got some pals in Cardiff,' Herb went on. 'We'll do all right, I promise. I'll look after you.'

She shook her head. 'I'm not leaving Swansea, Herb. I don't know what made you think I would.'

'It's a new start.' He had banked on her going with him. 'I can't stay now. When Bernie gets it, everything will come out into the open; the double life he's been leading. The house will be investigated by the police, people arrested. I don't want to be around to answer questions. I can't afford to be involved.'

'I won't leave my daughter, Herb. She needs me.'

'She doesn't even know who you are.' He was angry with disappointment. 'Look, she can come with us if you like. I'll take care of you both.'

'Herb, be sensible. I know you're not a criminal yourself, but you work on the edges, and always will do. Lynnys has a chance for a decent life, with some success, perhaps.' She shook her head. 'I won't deprive her of it.'

'But, Con...'

'And besides,' she went on. 'I'm afraid to tell her the truth about myself, which I'd have to do if we went with you. She'd turn from me in disgust. I can't risk it.'

He stood looking at her, knowing it was useless

347

to fool himself any longer. He had loved her for years, and had never ceased to hope that one day she would turn to him. Now he knew it would never happen.

'I understand, Connie.' And he did, but it broke his heart nevertheless. 'I'll say goodbye, then,' he went on heavily.

She nodded and smiled weakly.

Unable to stop himself, he stepped towards her, holding out his hand. 'Connie, if you ever need me...'

She moved away. 'Goodbye, Herb, and thanks for everything.'

25

Trudy came from the scullery wiping her hands on a tea towel.

'Now don't forget,' she said to Lynnys. 'I'm doing a shepherd's pie for dinner and a bread and butter pudding for afters.'

Phoebe, who was sitting in her usual chair at the side of the range, where she spent more of her waking days, sniffed scornfully. 'Anyone would think she was cooking for the Lord Mayor of London, the fuss she makes.'

'Now, Gran,' Lynnys said as she stood before the small mirror above the mantelpiece running a comb through her long dark hair. 'Let's give credit where it's due. Trudy has taken a weight off my shoulders. I can get on with my training without worrying about you.'

'And don't let that Josh persuade you to race off elsewhere,' Trudy went on. 'You've got to get your grub in you to keep your strength up.'

Lynnys smiled widely at her words, and Trudy realised she must sound like a fussy mother hen. But she was quite proud of that. She had come a long way from her earlier life and felt so different; calm and satisfied. Perhaps it was due to the child she was carrying.

'I won't forget, Trudy,' Lynnys promised. 'I'm looking forward to my dinner already. I can't get over what a wonderful cook you've turned out to be.'

'We're all good at something,' Trudy said matter-of-factly. 'You've got your singing and I've got my cooking now.'

'Ummph!' The exclamation of disdain came from Phoebe.

Trudy let a smile curve her lips. Just a few months ago she would have gone off the deep end, offended at Phoebe's scorn, but now she knew the older woman better. Phoebe had always done the cooking in this house. Now it was beyond her physically so it was understandable that she was a little disgruntled. No one likes to feel useless. That was a lesson Trudy had learned herself.

'Oh, come on now, Gran,' Lynnys said, a mild scold in her voice. 'Trudy's cooking is very good. I reckon she could earn a living from it if she wanted to.'

'I've been thinking about that,' Trudy said as she cleared the table of the last remnants of breakfast. 'After my baby is born I'm going to try to get a job as a cook or housekeeper perhaps.'

'That's an excellent idea,' Lynnys agreed.

'It's nearly nine o'clock,' Trudy pointed out. 'Your hansom will be here soon.' She shook her head. 'It must be costing Josh a fortune.'

Lynnys smiled shyly. 'He reckons it's a good investment. Oh, Trudy, I hope so.'

'He's no fool, don't you worry,' Trudy said as she threw a chenille cloth over the table.

Lynnys paused before putting on her tam, a worried look on her face, and Trudy guessed why.

'Mrs Lamar still hasn't shown up at rehearsals then?'

'No, and I'm very concerned. Josh said she's indisposed. I'd like to visit her, but he says he doesn't know where she lives.' Lynnys shook her head. 'Somehow I just don't believe him. I'm afraid Mrs Lamar is disappointed in me, and doesn't want to know me any longer.'

'Good riddance!' Phoebe said bluntly.

'Gran!' Lynnys looked hurt. 'I respect Mrs Lamar's opinion on my singing.' She hesitated, looking glum. 'I really like her, and I hoped we could be friends, good friends.'

'You've still got me!' Phoebe exclaimed. 'I'll always stand by you.'

Lynnys put her arms around her grandmother and kissed her cheek. 'I know you will, Gran, and I love you for it. It's just that there's something about Mrs Lamar that makes me …. well, I don't know … makes me feel complete.'

Watching Phoebe's face, Trudy saw an expression of deep sadness at Lynnys' words, but her granddaughter seemed not to notice.

'Well, I'd better be off or Mr Hibbler will have something to say. Nothing irritates him more than tardiness in his pupils.'

When Lynnys had left Trudy sat down opposite Phoebe.

'When are you going to tell her the truth, then, Phoebe?' she asked firmly. 'She has a right to know Connie is her real mother.'

'It's none of your business, miss!'

'I know that, but Lynnys is my friend … and so are you, Phoebe,' Trudy said. 'It's plain Lynnys is drawn to Connie. What harm would it do for her to know who she really is?'

351

'Harm!' Phoebe looked angry. 'Would you like your child to know it was conceived in shame? How will your child feel when it learns its mother is a woman of the streets?'

Trudy hung her head. She had not considered that before. That kind of heartache was in her future, such as it was. So who was she to give advice?

Sybil was feeling very nervous of late, and had not held a séance since her awful quarrel with Bernard Pomfrey. She was even afraid to go out. She had seen no more of Norman Mathias, but how could she be sure she wasn't being watched by the police? It was so very unnerving.

She sat on the sofa in the sitting room, hands clasped tightly together, waiting for Elvi to come home from work. Of course, Elvi knew nothing of the spot of bother they were in, but funds were running a bit low, and Sybil now regretted overspending on luxuries. She supposed she ought to tell the girl the truth. And maybe Josh was right. They should find new lodgings.

Sybil jumped up when she heard her daughter's quick footsteps crossing the hall. Very often Elvi went straight upstairs to change but this evening she came into the sitting room and stood in the doorway staring at Sybil. Her young face was white with shock, and immediately Sybil was apprehensive.

'Elvi? What's the matter?'

Elvi swallowed hard as though holding back tears. 'Oh, Mam. Something terrible has happened.'

'What? What is it?' Sybil lifted her shaking hand to her throat. 'What have you heard?'

'It's Mrs Mathias. She's been found dead.'

Sybil could only gasp, her throat constricting with dread.

'Dr Howells was called out to her house this morning,' Elvi went on as she came further into the room and sat down on the sofa. 'She was found at the foot of the stairs by her nephew. Her neck was broken.'

'Oh, my God!'

Elvi lifted her fingers to her trembling lips. 'Mam! It's all my fault. I should've said something, warned her...'

Sybil stared uncomprehending. 'What are you talking about, Elvi?'

'I had a ... feeling...'

'What nonsense!' Sybil sat down again; her legs so unsteady she thought she might fall. 'It's nothing to do with us, girl.'

But even as she uttered those words a terrible suspicion entered her mind. She had been turning over in her thoughts every word that had passed between Bernard and her in their quarrel, and was more than ever convinced he had taken Dolly's money. The old lady's unexpected death was very convenient for him. Sybil dreaded to think what that meant.

'I've been thinking,' she said to Elvi. 'I know you're not happy here so I've decided we must find other lodgings. I'll look for a new place tomorrow.'

'Oh, Mam, I'm so glad!'

'I'll tell the Major as soon as he returns from

business later.'

Elvi bit her lip. 'Can't we just go and say nothing?'

That idea had crossed Sybil's mind, too, but it rankled that he had made a fool of her. She would not go quietly. He had led her on; there was no doubt about that. She needed to regain her pride, although she quaked at the thought of facing him, especially after their last encounter. The man had a violent streak in him and now she suspected he was capable of any outrage.

'No, we'd better do it properly,' Sybil said. 'Who knows, if we do a moonlight flit he might accuse us of stealing something.'

Elvi nodded agreement.

'You go and have something to eat,' suggested Sybil. 'And then go along to your room and stay there out of the way. I'll come and see you after I've spoken to the Major.'

It was almost seven o'clock before Bernard Pomfrey made an appearance. Sybil darted out in to the hall when she heard his steps.

'Bernard, I must speak with you.'

He looked angry. 'I told you to stay out of my sight, woman.'

'Don't you speak to me like that,' Sybil flared. 'I have my rights.'

His lips twisted in scorn. 'You're nothing but a cheap swindler.'

'Better that than a thief and ... and a murderer.' She hadn't meant to say that, and quailed at the look of pure hatred that appeared on his face.

'What did you say?'

354

She began to tremble to see the vicious light that sprang into his eyes, but now she had spoken she must go on.

'You must know Dolly Mathias is dead.' Sybil put a hand on the hall table to steady herself. 'Her secrets died with her. So convenient.'

He was silent a moment, glancing furtively up the staircase towards his rooms. Minnie Dart was there, and Sybil realised he would not want her as a witness to what was said next.

'What are you implying?' His tone was low.

'Isn't it obvious?' Sybil pressed on, although quaking inside. 'Someone had that fifty thousand, and it wasn't me.'

He stepped forward suddenly and, grasping her arm, dragged her roughly into her own sitting room. Sybil suppressed a scream of fright. She did not want Elvi to hear and make an appearance.

'Let go of me!'

'Listen to me, you dim-witted jade,' he rasped, still gripping her arm. 'People who stick their noses in my business get them bitten off. You wouldn't want me to mark that face of yours, would you?'

Sybil shook her head, terrified.

He smiled scornfully. 'I thought not. Mrs Lamar regrets the error of her ways, too. It'll be some time before she can show her face anywhere.'

Sybil was appalled. 'You touch me and I'll have the police on you,' she said, breathless with fear. She was only too aware that it was a feeble threat.

'Who'd believe you, a fraud and a suspected thief?' he mocked. 'You'd be wise to keep your accusations to yourself.'

'I'm giving you notice,' she said shakily. 'Elvi and I are moving to new lodgings. The quicker we get away from you the better.'

A fresh gleam came into his eyes, and he released her arm, pushing her away. 'Where is she?'

'That's none of your business.'

'Well, I'm making it my business. You can bugger off as quick as you like,' he snarled wrathfully. 'But the girl stays here. She's mine! I've waited long enough to have her and, by God, I will!'

'What are you saying?' Sybil shrieked. 'You leave my daughter alone. She's an innocent child. How dare you even look at her in that way?'

'Shut up!'

Without warning he reached forward and struck her forcefully across the face with his open palm. Sybil staggered back, to fall on to a nearby chair.

'I've got plans for young Elvi,' he said ruthlessly. 'She'll entertain me for a while until I tire of her.'

'No, don't you touch her, you beast!'

Without another glance at her he strode from the room and Sybil, holding her smarting cheek with one hand, struggled to her feet to follow him. He was making his way down the passage towards their bedrooms.

'Elvi!' Sybil screeched behind him. 'Secure your door!'

Sybil heard a chair being hastily placed under the door knob. Elvi had heard her warning, and Sybil gave up a prayer of thankfulness.

Bernard must have heard it too and gave a bellow of rage. He threw himself against the door panelling, but it held. Next moment he turned swiftly, and grabbed at Sybil, and holding her firm, slammed her face forward against the wall.

'Elvi,' he bellowed out. 'I have your mother here. If you don't want to see her get hurt, open this door now.'

'Don't listen, Elvi,' Sybil shrieked. 'Stay where you are.'

'Mam! Mam! What's happening?'

Before Sybil could utter another word, Bernard seized her arm, and wrenched it behind her back. The pain was excruciating and she could not stifle a scream of agony.

'I'll break her arm, Elvi, I swear it,' he shouted. 'Open this door.'

'What's going on, Major Pomfrey, sir?'

The new voice startled them both. Sybil turned her head painfully to see Minnie Dart in the passage, staring at them in astonishment.

'He's gone mad!' Sybil shouted to her. 'Fetch a policeman.'

'Stay where you are, Dart,' Bernard bellowed. 'This woman and her daughter have stolen money from me. They've got it hidden in this bedroom.'

'I'll fetch a copper, sir.'

'No. Get back upstairs and keep out of it,' he commanded. 'I'll deal with this myself.'

'We've stolen nothing,' Sybil yelled. 'He means to ravish my daughter. He tried to do it before.'

She screamed again as Bernard viciously twisted her arm to silence her.

'Oh, you wicked woman for saying such a thing about the Major,' Minnie Dart said. 'I always

357

knew you were a bad lot.'

'Dart, get upstairs now!' thundered Bernard. 'Or lose your job.'

Obviously jolted at his words, Minnie Dart turned on her heels.

'No! Can't you see what's happening before your eyes? He means to do my daughter harm, I tell you,' Sybil screeched. 'Help us! Fetch someone.'

But Minnie Dart scuttled away.

'Elvi! Open this door, or it'll be the worse for your mother.'

In dread and panic, Sybil heard the chair back being removed from the door. Bernard Pomfrey released his hold on her, and with a hefty push, sent her staggering sideways clear of the door. The next moment the door swung open and he was storming into the bedroom.

Sybil recovered herself and charged in after him. Elvi was cowering in the corner of the room near the dressing table, and it wrenched Sybil's heart to see such terror on her young face.

'You're coming with me right now,' Bernard said to the young girl. 'You won't need any clothes where you're going.'

He reached out and dragged her from the corner. Elvi screamed and struggled. In desperation, Sybil threw herself at him, fingers hooked into claws as she stretched up her hands aiming for his face.

'Leave her alone, you dirty beast,' she screamed hysterically. 'Take your hands off my daughter. Elvi! Elvi!'

Bernard turned on her and before she realised

his intention he struck at her with his balled fist. She caught the full force of the blow on her left cheekbone. There was pain and a sickening jolt of her head, and then there was darkness.

Sybil came to slowly, painfully, her face aching. She stared up in a daze at whoever was bending over her.

'Get up, you thief,' a voice said sternly. 'Where's the girl gone with the stolen money?'

Sybil recognised Minnie Dart's voice. She peered up at the woman's sharp features. Behind her loomed another tall form and for a moment she thought it was Bernard Pomfrey, and then realised it was a man wearing a helmet.

'Stand aside, please,' the newcomer said to Minnie Dart. 'Now then, what's all this?'

Sybil struggled up onto her elbows. 'Help me, constable. Bernard Pomfrey has abducted my daughter. He's got her upstairs. He'll ravage her.'

'She's lying!' Minnie Dart exploded. 'There's no one upstairs.' She pointed an accusing finger at Sybil. 'Her and her daughter stole money from my master, Major Pomfrey. The young one must have got away. The Major has gone after her to try to get it back.'

The constable hauled Sybil to her feet. 'What've you got to say for yourself?'

Weakened, she staggered and fell back against the wall. 'We've done nothing wrong, constable.' She struggled to find her feet, but her legs were like jelly. 'I must find my daughter or that monster will do her harm.'

'She calls herself a medium,' Minnie Dart put

in spitefully. 'Holds fraudulent séances, you know; gyps honest people of their money. The Major was properly taken in by her, I can tell you. And now she's robbed him.'

'I didn't! Oh, God!' Sybil wrung her hands in desperation. Where was Elvi and what was happening to her? 'While we're standing around arguing, my innocent daughter is being raped by that beast. If he's not upstairs with her then he's taken her elsewhere. Do something!'

'I think you'd better come along to the police station with me,' the constable said pompously. 'We'll have to contact Major Pomfrey and find out about this missing money. My guess is he'll press charges.'

Sybil stared at them both in desperation. No one would help her, and she dreaded to think what Elvi was going through at this moment.

Suddenly she was filled with rage at the horrific thought, and finding strength in her anger, rushed at Minnie Dart, hands outstretched. She knocked the mop cap from the woman's head and grabbed a handful of her hair, tugging at it furiously, while Minnie squealed like a pig with a knife in its throat.

'Where has Bernard Pomfrey taken my daughter?' Sybil demanded to know wrathfully. 'You must know. You'll tell me, or I'll tear every hair from your head and then I'll scratch your eyes out! Tell me, you miserable stick.'

'Now then, now then! Stop that.' The constable laid rough hands on Sybil to drag her off. 'That's bodily assault, that is.'

'I'll kill the scrawny cat if she doesn't speak up!'

'Threats against a person's life as well!' The constable sounded triumphant. 'You'll go down for that, missus. I'm a witness.'

'I don't care, damn you. I want to find my daughter!' Sybil twisted violently in his grasp. 'Don't you understand? She's in danger. Let me go!'

'You're coming down the station and you'd better come quietly or I'll send for the Black Maria.' The constable took Sybil by both upper arms restraining her forcefully, while she struggled. 'I'm putting you under arrest, missus, and you'd better not resist, because you're in enough trouble already.'

'Elvi's in danger, you imbecile,' Sybil shouted, and managing to free one arm, half turned and lashed out, catching him an open handed slap across his face.

'Oh, that's it!' The constable's expression showed fury and he withdrew his truncheon from his belt. 'Striking a police officer to avoid arrest is a very serious offence. You're going down for a long time, missus. It's Cox's Farm for you.'

The town's prison! Sybil was appalled. She was innocent of these charges. She opened her mouth to protest but he raised the truncheon above his shoulder.

'Now are you coming along with me?' he asked sternly. 'Or do I wallop you?'

'What the bloody hell is going on here?'

Everyone turned and looked down the passage at the newcomer. With a rush of relief Sybil recognised Josh Rowlands.

'Josh!' She tried to rush towards him but the

constable's restraining hands stopped her. 'Josh, Bernard Pomfrey has abducted Elvi,' she gasped out. 'He's taken her somewhere.'

'What!' Josh hurried towards her. 'When? How long ago?'

'I don't really know,' Sybil sobbed. 'He knocked me unconscious.'

'Now look here ... er ... sir,' the constable cut in officiously. 'This woman is my prisoner. No talking to her while she's under arrest.'

Sybil ignored him. 'Josh, please find her. He means to ravish her. He boasted he would.'

'Now, that's enough!' the constable said loudly. 'I hope you're not going to impede me in the course of my duty, sir,' he went on ominously. 'Otherwise, I'll have to arrest you as well.'

'Why is she under arrest, man?'

'Theft, threats against a person's life, and assault, and that just for starters. There's also the little matter of striking a police officer and resisting arrest.'

'Sybil?' Josh looked shaken.

'Never mind me.' She shook her head as the constable began to lead her away. 'Save our daughter, Josh. Go now.'

She tried to look back at him pleadingly as the constable led her away unresisting now. Josh was her only hope. She prayed he would not let her down as he had before.

As she reached the pavement she managed to turn to see him standing in the doorway. 'Bernard Pomfrey is dangerous, Josh,' she called out desperately. 'I'm sure he had a hand in Dolly Mathias' death.'

'Who?'

'Come along!' the constable insisted.

He strong-armed her along the pavement. Sybil went head down conscious of the stares of passers-by, but she could not care about that. Elvi! Where was Elvi and what was happening to her? Oh God! Would she ever see her daughter again?

She had been a selfish woman, she realised that now, and utterly foolish where men were concerned. She had never met one who was any good; not one who would stand by her and be dependable. Her only hope lay in Josh now.

Sybil dragged her feet in despair and reluctance, and with a grunt of irritation, the constable took the whistle from his breast pocket and blew it. Within minutes another policeman appeared.

'Find a telephone box,' her captor instructed his colleague. 'Call out the Black Maria. I don't trust this one not to try to make a run for it.'

Josh stood on the doorstep and stared after Sybil and the constable leading her away. He had been surprised to find the door open when he arrived and a heated argument going on. He had been even more astonished to see Sybil in the passage, dishevelled and in the grasp of a policeman.

And his daughter Elvi had been abducted by that bloody swine, Bernie Pomfrey. If he had laid a finger on her, he'd kill him where he stood.

Raging now, Josh turned back into the house. A thin sharp-faced woman stood there, a very satisfied look on her face.

'Serves her right!' she exclaimed to him, and

363

was about to mount the staircase but Josh darted forward and detained her.

'Just a minute. Who are you?'

She sniffed. 'Miss Dart, Major Pomfrey's maid. That woman should've been in prison a long time ago.'

'Where is he? Where's Pomfrey?'

'I don't know.' She looked impatient. 'Chasing after that girl to get his money back, I expect. Huh! To look at her you wouldn't think butter would melt in her mouth. Just goes to show. Like mother, like daughter.'

'I'm going to search his rooms,' declared Josh, and pushing her aside ran up the stairs.

'Here! You can't do that. I'll call another copper.'

Josh took no notice. Quickly he made a search of all the rooms, but there was no sign of Pomfrey or Elvi and no evidence that she had been there.

Miss Dart was still protesting at the door when he turned to leave. 'The Major will have the law on you,' she warned him.

'What other properties does he own?' Josh demanded to know. 'And where are they?'

'The Major owns property all over town,' Miss Dart said importantly. 'Not that it's any business of yours. He's a gentleman.'

'He'll be a dead gentleman when I find him,' Josh threatened. 'And you can tell him if he turns up here that I'm after his guts.'

'Oh! Such language! You're the Devil incarnate!'

Josh left without another word. He hurried down Walter Road, his mind churning. Bernie would take the girl some place where he knew he could do as he pleased with her and no one would interfere. The Pleasure Palace!

Josh rushed into the road and waved down a passing hansom. He had no idea how much time had elapsed since Elvi had been abducted. It might be already too late.

A great pain surged around his heart at the thought. By God! If Bernie had had his way with her, then blood would be spilled this day. He'd swing for the bastard, and gladly.

Elvi cowered on her knees near the head of the bed, struggling to hide her nakedness with a rumpled bed sheet.

She had thought herself in some terrible nightmare when, having brought her to this room in a strange house, the man she knew as Major Pomfrey, immediately tore her clothes from her body, despite her frantic screams and struggles, and had thrown her on the bed. Her flesh burned with the humiliation and shame of it.

Terror filled her heart and mind as she watched him undress, removing his waistcoat, shirt and vest first. He looked feverish; his colour was high and sweat glistened on his face as he looked towards her, eyes gleaming; teeth bared like some savage animal. She was reminded of pictures of an open-jawed wolf she had seen in a book, and quaked with fear.

She had not ceased to plead with him since he had bundled her out of the house in Walter Road. The last view of her mother had been to see her sprawled on the passage floor, and Elvi did not know whether she was alive or dead. No one knew where she was. There was no one to save her.

'Let me go, Major, please,' she begged once more, though without much hope.

'Shut up, you slut,' he thundered as he unbuckled his belt and undid the buttons of his flies. 'I'm sick of your whining.'

'Why do you call me that? Why are you doing this to me?' Elvi cried out. 'I'm a good girl.'

He grinned, a feral grin. 'Yes, you are, but not for much longer.' His trousers and underclothes removed, he walked towards the bed and knelt on it. 'Come here!'

Elvi turned her horrified gaze away from his naked loins. 'No, no, no!'

'Don't defy me, you stupid piece!' His face contorted with fury. 'It's no good fighting any more. You're mine. Accept it and maybe you won't get a beating.'

'Keep away! I hate you!'

With a snarl, he lunged across and grasped her arm dragging her towards him. Terrified at what he intended to do next, Elvi reacted with animal instinct, and reaching out, clawed at his face. Her fingernails scraped furrows in his cheek and he yelled loudly with pain. The next moment he struck at her with the back of his hand.

Elvi took the full force of the blow on her mouth, making her teeth cut painfully into her lower lip. She fell back, tasting blood and tensed expecting another assault, but he moved from the bed, his fingers exploring his injured cheek to look at his face in the dressing table mirror.

'Christ! Look what you've done,' he rasped, and turned his head to send her a malevolent glance. 'You bitch! You'll pay for this with bruises, my girl. After I've taken what I want, I'm going to beat you to a pulp.'

He bent over a china bowl and scooped up water to bathe his wound. As his back was turned, Elvi began to slide towards the opposite side of the bed. She must get out of this room, get away from him. He meant to harm her; kill her perhaps. As she moved she wound the bed sheet around her body as best she could.

He took a towel from the washstand to pat his face dry and as he did so he must have caught sight of her movement in the mirror for he swung around with an angry snarl.

'Oh, no you don't!'

He was on her in a moment, dragging her back to the bed. Elvi tried to struggle but he was far too strong. He flung her on her back and threw himself on top of her.

'Now, at last!'

'No!'

He was trying to force her legs apart but was hampered by the bed sheet, and frustrated, he let out a string of oaths Elvi had never heard before and did not understand.

Whimpering in fear and revulsion, Elvi clung desperately to the sheet while he tried to wrench it from her body. He was just about to tear it away when the door of the room burst open and someone rushed in yelling a warning.

'Boss! We got trouble!' a gruff voice said. 'Big trouble.'

'Get out, Fred, you damned fool!' Bernard Pomfrey shouted furiously over his shoulder. 'Can't you see I'm busy?'

'Help me!' Elvi screeched as she peered up at the newcomer. 'Please! Help me.'

Her assailant put his hand over her mouth to silence her, while the other man ignored her as though she wasn't there. Instead he darted forward and laid a hand on Bernard Pomfrey's bare shoulder and shook him. 'Boss, listen, for God's sake, listen will you!'

'Damn you, Fred!'

'Boss! A gang of men have burst their way into the house,' he gabbled. 'I couldn't stop 'em, boss; too many. They're downstairs now smashing the place up.'

'What?'

Fred looked at his employer with frightened eyes. 'Charlie Pendle's men, I think. One of them wanted to know where you were. Knew your real name, he did.'

'The devil you say!' Bernard Pomfrey hastily lifted his weight from her. 'Bloody hell!'

From somewhere below came the crash of glass smashing, and a woman screamed. Men were shouting and it sounded as though furniture was being broken up.

'Boss! Let's get out of here.'

To Elvi's intense relief Bernard Pomfrey got off the bed and immediately she scrambled away, still clinging to her sheet. She cowered back, watching the two men at the same time measuring the distance to the open door. Here was a chance to escape perhaps, if only she could slip out unnoticed.

'What did you tell them, Fred?' Pomfrey asked, and Elvi detected a quiver of nervousness in his voice. 'You didn't give me away, did you?'

'Told 'em I never heard of you, boss,' Fred said.

'Good man!'

He was reaching for his trousers from the floor nearby. Unnoticed, Elvi slid over the opposite edge of the bed to the linoleum, and knelt there, shivering in fright.

'They're searching the place though,' Fred went on. 'They'll be up here in a minute. We got to get out, boss, now.'

To Elvi's dismay, Bernard Pomfrey turned back to the bed. He pointed at Elvi.

'Get hold of her, Fred. She's coming with us.'

'She's just a bit of skirt, boss. She'll hold us back,' Fred said in agitation. 'We'll have to climb out of a window somewhere. We can't lug her with us, mun. It's Charlie Pendle's men, for crying out loud. They'll kill us if they catch us. I've no liking for having my throat slit.'

Bernard Pomfrey looked furious. 'By God! Someone's been talking and I think I know who. Bloody Herb Collins. He'll pay for this.'

There were heavy footfalls on the stairs below and more shouts. Some man was bellowing in fury: 'Pomfrey, you bastard! Where are you?'

'I dunno about you, but I'm getting out now, boss,' Fred said in obvious terror and ran to the door. 'Come on, mun. The room at the end of the passage. We can jump down from the window on to the low roof there.'

Bernard Pomfrey glared at Elvi as in terror herself she peered at him over the edge of the bed.

'Don't think you've seen the last of me. I'll be back for you,' he threatened in grating tones. 'And God help you then.'

The two men ran from the room, and Elvi heard their feet thudding away down the passage. She collapsed in a heap on the floor, weeping with relief. She had been saved from one terrible ordeal, but heaven alone knew what would happen next.

Now was her chance to get away. Elvi struggled to her feet, securing the sheet around her, and was creeping gingerly towards the door when the figure of a man appeared in the doorway blocking her way of escape. His lip was bleeding and so was his nose, and there was a wild look in his eyes as he stared at her.

'Pomfrey!' the man shouted. 'I'll kill you, you swine!'

Elvi stumbled backwards, falling on to the floor, and stared up at this new threat.

'Please, don't hurt me,' she pleaded tearfully. 'I don't belong here. I've been abducted.'

The man stared at her for a moment, the wild look still in his eyes, and then he rushed at her, and in the face of this new terror, Elvi screamed at the top of her lungs.

26

Josh paid off the driver of the hansom in Wind Street and hurried to the Pleasure Palace in Cambrian Place, wondering how he could manage to persuade the doorman to let him in without resorting to a fight. He did not want Bernie alerted to his arrival.

The heavy oak doors, normally kept locked and attended by Fred were wide open, with no doorman in sight. Stepping inside he was immediately aware of a rumpus going on; men shouting, a woman was screaming.

Quickly he glanced into the parlour to see that most of the furniture was overturned and that the ornate mirrors which adorned each wall were smashed. Debris was strewn everywhere.

Apprehensive for Elvi's safety at this turn of events, Josh made straight for the staircase and started up two at a time. He had not gone far when a man, unshaven and in rough working clothes dashed out from a passage, shouting at him.

'Hey, you!' The man rushed towards him. 'Where's Pomfrey? We want him.'

'You can have him when I've done with him,' Josh snapped, and continued up the stairs.

'You're one of his men, eh?' the man said, climbing after him, grabbing at his ankles. 'Charlie would like a word with you.'

'Bugger off,' Josh yelled kicking out. But he was unbalanced and tumbled down the stairs, taking the man with him.

At the bottom both scrambled to their feet, Josh cursing at the pain in his arm where he had landed heavily. The man threw a punch at his face which caught him on the mouth. His head rocked back, but before he could recover his balance his opponent took another punch on his nose.

The pain was agonising. Josh could taste blood and was suddenly enraged. Anything could be happening to his daughter in a room somewhere above, and this lout was standing in his way.

'I've had enough of you, mate,' Josh growled and kicked out viciously, his boot connecting with the man's groin. He went down on his knees howling. With both hands clasped together Josh hit him on the side of the head and the howling stopped.

With throbbing pain in his face and arm, Josh's dander was up good and proper now, and he raced up the stairs, yelling at the top of his voice.

'Pomfrey, you bastard. Where are you?'

He reached the top of the stairs and ran to an open door and stood there, still bellowing.

'Pomfrey! I'll kill you, you swine.'

He stared around the room and was then aware of the form of a young girl sprawled on the floor, wrapped in a bed sheet. She gazed up at him obviously terrified for her life.

'Please, don't hurt me.' Tears were rolling down her face and her mouth was bruised and bleeding. 'I don't belong here. I've been abducted.'

It was Elvi! He had found her. He rushed forward to gather her up, and she screamed in fright like a banshee. He knelt down beside her, but she tried to wriggle away from him, her eyes wide and filled with fear.

'It's all right, Elvi,' he said as soothingly as he knew how. 'I've come to take you out of here.'

She shook her head dumbly. 'How do you know my name? Leave me alone!'

'Your mother, Sybil sent me, kid,' Josh said. 'You're safe now. I won't let anyone harm you.'

She began to blubber like a baby, and Josh did not know how to comfort her, his own daughter. He saw in consternation that she was naked under the sheet and his mouth went dry with apprehension.

'Did Bernie...?' He did not know how to ask someone so young and innocent the question burning his lips, and clenched his teeth in renewed fury. Bernie would pay dear for this.

'I want to go home,' Elvi whimpered. 'I want my mother.'

Josh swallowed. This wasn't the time or place to tell the kid that her mother was under arrest. He must get her away from here and find somewhere safe. He thought of the small house in Cwmavon Terrace. Elvi would be safe there with Lynnys and Phoebe, at least until he could arrange an alternative. And there was Sybil to think of. He must try to do something for her.

'Come on, kid.' He helped her to her feet. The cotton sheet was thin, and Josh grabbed another one from the bed. 'Wrap this around you as well.'

He carried her from the room, and down the

staircase. The men who were in the process of wrecking the place were still downstairs, probably trying to force the safe in the office, Josh suspected. Well, good luck to them!

They left the house without further trouble and out in the street, Josh stopped. 'I'll find a hansom cab,' he said putting her down on her feet.

'Don't leave me!'

'I won't leave you, Elvi.'

Josh felt his throat tighten with an emotion he had never experienced before. This poor young girl was his child, and an overwhelming instinct to protect seized him. She needed him.

He suspected Sybil was in more trouble than she knew and might serve time. Elvi was now his responsibility. Strangely, he thought, he was not frightened of that as he might have been once.

He remembered her feet were bare. 'I'd better carry you to the main road.'

She pulled away.

'Now don't be afraid,' he went on soothingly. 'I swear I won't harm you. I'm your... I'm a friend of your mother. She's desperately worried for you.'

'I want to go home,' Elvi moaned.

In Wind Street Josh waved down a hansom, the cabby giving him stern looks to see what he carried, but Josh had no intention of explaining.

'Cwmavon Terrace, and be quick,' he ordered curtly.

Josh handed Elvi inside and climbed in himself.

'Why are you taking me to Cwmavon Terrace?' Elvi said. She was looking at him fearfully. 'I want to go home to Walter Road where my mother is.'

'Sybil isn't there at the moment,' Josh said carefully. 'And it's not wise for you to go back home just now. Pomfrey may be there.'

Elvi whimpered. 'I never want to set eyes on that horrible man again.'

Josh ground his teeth. He itched to come face to face with Bernie, but he must bide his time until Elvi was safe.

'He's a beast!' Elvi went on. 'I'm afraid!'

Josh felt his mouth go dry. 'Did he ... hurt you?'

'He hit me and tore all my clothes off,' Elvi exclaimed. 'I'm so ashamed!'

Josh opened his mouth but no further question would come. Perhaps he should leave it to Lynnys or Phoebe to get at the truth.

The hansom arrived at Cwmavon Terrace in a short time. Josh helped Elvi down and paid off the cabby, who was still scowling at him.

Ignoring the man's mutterings, he knocked on the door and waited. It was Phoebe who answered. She stared when she caught sight of the young girl in Josh's arms, wrapped only in bed sheets.

'Hey! What's this? Up to your old tricks, are you?' Phoebe exclaimed loudly. 'Push off. I'll have no more tarts under my roof.'

She made to shut the door, but Josh put his boot over the threshold.

'Hold on, Phoebe, please!' he begged. 'You've got the wrong end of the stick. This is Elvi. She was forcibly abducted from her mother and taken to a house of ill-repute. She's frightened out of her life.'

'What are you doing with her, then?'

'Must she remain on the doorstep practically naked?' Josh asked pithily. 'For pity's sake, Phoebe, let us in.'

Reluctantly, the older woman stood aside and Josh quickly carried Elvi down the passage to the living room. Lynnys and Trudy were there and both jumped up, looking astonished.

'Josh!' Lynnys exclaimed at the sight of him. 'What...?' She started. 'Oh, my goodness! That's my friend, Elvi.' Lynnys rushed forward. 'Elvi, for heaven's sake what has happened to you?'

Elvi whimpered as Josh set his burden down on her feet, sensing how her body was still trembling.

'Sit down by here, kid.' He looked pleadingly at Lynnys. 'Can you make her a cup of hot sweet tea? She's had a terrible experience.'

'But what has happened, Josh. How did she get into this state? Oh, Elvi!'

'I'll make the tea,' Trudy offered quickly. 'But talk loud so I can hear in the scullery.'

'Elvi, my dear.' Lynnys bent down to look closely into the other girl's face. 'Are you hurt?'

'She was abducted and taken to...'

'Yes, well never mind where she was taken to,' Phoebe cut in quickly. 'Why did you bring her here?'

'She can't go home. It isn't safe.'

'She looks as though she's in a stupor,' Lynnys said, taking one of the girl's trembling hands and rubbing it. 'Elvi, it's me, Lynnys.'

Elvi looked up dazedly into Lynnys' face and then tears began to glisten in her eyes.

'Oh! Lynnys! I'm so afraid. My mother's

landlord, Major Pomfrey, dragged me away from my home and took me to this awful house. My mother...' Her eyes opened wide and she stared up at Josh. 'My mother! Where is she? When the Major dragged me away, I saw her stretched out on the passage floor. What's happened to her? Did he hurt her, too?'

'No, she's not hurt,' Josh said carefully. 'Don't worry about her for the moment.'

Trudy came in with a tray of tea and put it on the table.

'Who's this bloke Pomfrey, then? I've heard that name before somewhere.'

'You know him better as Bernie Smith,' Josh said, giving Trudy a guarded look.

Trudy stared down at Elvi. 'Oh, my God! The poor kid.'

'Trudy, can you find something for Elvi to wear?' Josh asked. 'If Phoebe is willing, perhaps Elvi can sleep here tonight; maybe stay a few days? I have some business to attend to.'

'Well ... I don't know...' Phoebe began.

'Of course she can stay here,' Lynnys interrupted firmly. 'Elvi is my best friend. I'm going to help her all I can.'

'Thank you, Lynnys,' Josh said simply. He sank to his haunches beside Elvi's chair looking into her tear-stained face. 'I'm going to leave you now, Elvi. You'll be safe here, I promise.'

She caught at his arm apprehensively, her eyes large with alarm.

'I'll be back soon,' he reassured her with a rush of feeling. 'I have a bit of business to see to and I'll be talking to your mother, too. Now you mustn't worry about her. She's safe where she is at the moment.'

'But why can't I be with her?'

'I'll explain when I come back,' he said gently. 'Now you rest.'

Lynnys came forward to put an arm around Elvi's shoulders.

'We'll take care of you, Elvi. Don't be afraid any more.'

Josh prepared to leave the room, and signalled Phoebe to join him in the passage. She followed him out, a scowl on her lined face.

'See if you can find out if she's been ... well, you know, interfered with,' he said awkwardly. 'And ... and if so, call a doctor to her. I'll pay.'

'Why are you so concerned about this girl?'

Josh looked into Phoebe's eyes, wondering what her reaction would be. 'She's my child, Phoebe,' he said, a catch in his voice. 'A daughter I never knew I had until recently.'

Phoebe's expression showed how astonished she was at this revelation.

'She doesn't know I'm her father,' Josh went on quickly. 'Please don't say anything to her. I want to be the one to tell her myself.'

Phoebe looked pained. 'I'm no blabbermouth!' She sniffed disdainfully. 'Where's her mother?'

Josh bit his lip, reluctant to admit it. 'Under arrest.'

'What?' Phoebe looked scandalised.

'Sybil's not guilty of anything, I promise you,' Josh said hurriedly. 'She's being victimised. I'll explain later. I have to look for the swine who took Elvi, and when I find him...'

378

'Don't do anything foolish,' Phoebe interrupted sternly. 'The girl has problems enough without her father landing up in clink, too.'

Bernie paced up and down in his room in a run-down boarding house in a side street up near the potteries. It riled him to realise he must stay hidden. But for how long?

It was plain Charlie Pendle knew his real identity; knew about the shop, so he dare not show his face there or go home to Walter Road just yet or any of his other haunts.

He crashed one fist into his other palm at the thought of his helplessness. Damn Herb Collins for betraying him! He'd pay the swine back. But he couldn't grass up Herb yet.

And if it was now common knowledge that Major Bernard Pomfrey, besides being a respectable businessman was also a brothel-keeper, the police might be looking for him, too. The whole thing was blown wide open.

Bernie sat down on the bed, his hand at his jaw, thinking. He should get out of Swansea and fast, but he wouldn't go empty-handed. He had amassed a small fortune and he must find a way of getting at it without putting himself at risk. He thought again of the strong-box hidden at Walter Road. There was the fifty thousand in cash he had taken from Dolly Mathias, and also his bank passbooks for his private and shop accounts. He must get hold of that box somehow.

He jumped to his feet at the sound of someone at his door and relaxed as Fred came into the room, closing the door carefully after him.

379

'Well,' he barked impatiently as the man stood there hesitating. 'What's happening?'

'It's bad, boss,' Fred said, avoiding his gaze. 'I hung around down by the Pleasure Palace.' He nodded. 'You're right. Pendle has taken over the house. There were a couple of toughs on the door. I recognised them.'

'He's running my girls?'

Fred nodded, and Bernie let out an oath, and began to stride about the room. He owned the property, but he couldn't capitalise on it. It was too risky to go up against Charlie Pendle.

'What about the Lloyd girl? Was she still there?'

'While I was hanging about I saw that kid, Dilys,' Fred said. 'She'd picked up a bloke in Wind Street and was taking him back to the house. She looked scared. Somebody had given her a black eye.'

Bernie grunted. He wasn't interested in any girl other than Elvi. But maybe it was too late already. Chances were she wasn't what he'd call clean any longer, not with Charlie Pendle's men having the run of the place.

'What did Dilys have to say?'

Fred was looking nervously at Bernie. 'Josh Rowlands showed up at the house just as we got out,' said Fred. 'He took that kid, Elvi. No one has seen either of them since.'

Bernie sat on the bed. So Josh had got his daughter safely away.

Infuriated, Bernie slammed his fist on to the bedside table making an oil lamp rock on its base. Josh would hide her away and watch her like a hawk, Bernie guessed. He could forget Elvi

Lloyd. But there must be another way to get at Josh Rowlands.

Fred was looking agitated and restless and Bernie realised the man wanted to be anywhere but there. If he let Fred run out on him he would be stymied.

'What's the matter, Fred, losing your guts are you?' he taunted bitterly.

'Herb Collins has buggered off from Swansea, boss, and I ought to lay low myself,' Fred objected nervously. 'If Pendle learns I'm still working for you, I could end up in the river, and I've got a wife and kids to think of.'

'You'll do as you're told, then,' Bernie snapped, wagging a warning finger in Fred's face. 'You're scared of what Pendle might do to you. Well, you'd better start worrying what I'll do, if you cross me.'

'All right, boss.' Fred looked wary and sub-dued.

Bernie was not surprised to learn that Herb had got out. He was sorry not to get his hands on him, but contented himself with the thought that Josh Rowlands was still about.

Fred stood there looking at him, his expression unhappy, and Bernie was exasperated at the man's eagerness to leave.

'I'm not finished with you yet,' he snarled. A new idea had struck him. 'Get in touch with my housekeeper Minnie Dart in Walter Road. Bring her here, but be careful you're not followed.'

After Fred had gone Bernie thought deeply. Dart might help him salvage something if he made it worth her while. She could bring the box to him. He would have to trust her.

He cursed again at being in this fix. But he had been in worse holes, he told himself, and he would get out of this one unscathed somehow, and he now had Josh Rowlands in his power.

On making enquiries Josh found that, pending coming before a magistrate, Sybil had been moved to the women's wing at Swansea Prison as there were only meagre facilities for women prisoners at the police station.

Getting in to see her proved difficult. In the end he took a chance and obtained permission by posing as her brother-in-law. It was a risk but he felt he owed it to her.

The visitors' room held two or three small tables with chairs and was deserted except for him. Josh sat down and waited. When Sybil was brought in by a stern-looking female warden, he was shocked at her appearance.

She shuffled forward, wearing a shapeless blue calico dress that had had most of the colour washed out of it years since. Her blonde hair, once her pride and joy was limp, lifeless, and arranged in a bun at the nape of her neck. But it was the appearance of her features that raised pity in him. Her face was gaunt and she looked tired and thoroughly crushed.

There was panic in her eyes when she saw who her visitor was.

She stumbled towards the table. 'Josh! Have you found Elvi? Oh, tell me she's all right, for pity's sake.'

'Elvi's safe,' Josh assured her quickly. 'Safe and

relatively unharmed.'

'Oh, thank God!'

She looked as though she might sink to the floor before reaching the chair and Josh rose quickly and stepped forward to help her, but hesitated at a sharp warning grunt from the hard-eyed warden who had placed herself near the door.

'No touching!'

Sybil eased herself into the chair, looking white and sick.

'Are you all right, Syb?'

'This is a terrible place, Josh. I shouldn't be here.'

No, it wasn't fair. He longed to reach across and touch her hand to reassure her but dare not.

'What are the charges against you, Syb?'

'Resisting arrest and striking a police officer.' Sybil's face crumpled. 'But I had to,' she blubbered. 'I had to try to save Elvi and the officer wouldn't listen.'

'It doesn't sound so bad,' Josh said reassuringly. 'I'm sure a good lawyer can get you off.'

'There's more,' Sybil murmured miserably and then glanced apprehensively towards the warden.

Josh understood and looked at the woman too. 'Can we have five minutes alone?' he asked her. 'You can leave the door open and observe us from outside. I promise we won't touch and I won't pass her anything.'

'It's not allowed.'

'I need to talk to her about her defence,' Josh said in a reasonable tone.

'You're not her lawyer.'

'No, of course not, but I'm arranging a lawyer

for her.'

'Five minutes, mind, no more.'

The warden went outside into the passage, leaving the door wide open.

'Now you can talk freely, Syb,' Josh said in a low voice.

She shook her head helplessly. 'I'm in deep trouble, Josh,' she murmured. 'A lawyer named Norman Mathias has brought a charge of theft and fraud against me. He's convinced I took fifty thousand pounds from his aunt, Dolly Mathias.'

'What?'

'I never did, Josh, I swear it. Bernard Pomfrey did that. He practically admitted it to me.' She glanced towards the open door, and then whispered, 'Dolly Mathias' death was no accident. I'm certain Bernard Pomfrey had a hand in it.'

'Have you told this to the police?'

Sybil's face creased in panic. 'No! They think it was an accident. If I tell them what I believe, they could discover how she really died and they would blame me. I could hang. Josh, what am I going to do?'

The warden appeared in the doorway at that moment. 'Time's up.'

'Syb, try not to fret. I'll get you a lawyer, the best, believe me. And don't worry about Elvi. She's safe. I'll take care of her. She's my child.'

The warden laid a heavy hand on Sybil's shoulder, and she rose reluctantly. 'Come and see me again, Josh,' she begged. 'Don't abandon me like you did before.'

'I swear I won't, Sybil. I'll do everything I can to help you.'

Sybil was led away and Josh watched her go with a heavy heart. He would engage a lawyer immediately, but how could he find evidence against Bernie when he could not even trace the man's whereabouts?

Minnie Dart came into the rented room, closely followed by Fred. Bernie was irritated to see her nose wrinkle with distaste.

'Whatever is happening, Major Pomfrey, sir?' Her sharp featured face showed disbelief. 'I never thought to see you in a place like this.'

'You're not here to ask questions, Dart,' Bernie barked angrily. 'It's none of your business.' He checked himself, remembering he needed her help. 'I'm temporarily inconvenienced. That's all you need to know.'

'Yes, sir.'

'I have a task for you,' he went on. 'An important one, which will put things right.'

He explained about the strong-box hidden under the floorboards in his bedroom. Minnie Dart's expression showed total astonishment, but she kept her mouth shut.

'I want you to bring that box to me here as soon as possible. Fred will stay with you until you return with it.' He looked at each one in turn. 'I'll have a reward for both of you when the box is in my hands, untouched. Do you understand me?'

Both nodded.

'If I find the box has been tampered with,' Bernie went on ominously, 'you'll both find yourselves in deep trouble. Now, go.'

After Dart and Fred had gone, Bernie lay on

the bed, his hands under his head. Things were going well. Soon he would have plenty of cash and the means to get at his bank accounts. It might take a few days, but he could wait.

He would shake the dust of Swansea from his boots, but before he did that, there were scores to settle. Both Herb Collins and Josh Rowlands would rue the day they crossed Bernie Pomfrey. Rowlands' woman, the singer whoever she was, would end up with a badly scarred face and that was only the start of what he'd do to her. She wouldn't be worth two farthings to anyone when he had finished with her.

Minnie Dart and Fred returned within the hour. Bernie was relieved to see them, having been tormented with doubts as to how far he could trust either of them.

'Here it is, Major, sir,' Minnie Dart said as Fred put the strong-box on the bed.

'Good! You've done well the pair of you. You'll get paid, like I said.' He was itching to open the box with the key he always kept on his watch chain. 'Wait outside a minute. I'll call you when I'm ready.'

They both left the room and Bernie secured the door before opening the box. A quick rifle through it satisfied him that nothing had been disturbed. Dolly's money was still bundled up in brown paper strips with the bank's name on them, each bundle containing one hundred fifty-pound notes.

He took two notes out of one bundle and then pushed the box under his bed. He called out to them and they came in immediately, expectation on their faces.

'Here!' He gave each a note, and they both looked dumbfounded at the size of their reward. 'I expect you both to keep your mouths shut,' he told them curtly. 'Dart, I want you to close up the house in Walter Road. I'm leaving Swansea so you must look for new employment.'

'Oh! Sir!'

He ignored her stricken expression. 'That will be all, Dart,' he said. 'Now you may go.'

When the woman had left Bernie looked at Fred. 'Fred, I want you to watch Rowlands; find out where he lives, where he goes. There's a bit of skirt he's involved with; training her as a singer or something. I want you to trace her.'

Fred hesitated, looking sheepish.

'I already know who she is,' he said. 'Rowland's fancy piece lives in Cwmavon Terrace.' Fred mentioned the number of the house. 'I've seen him go in there a number of times. And I've seen his fancy piece. She's a beauty. Her name is Lynnys Daniels.'

Bernie felt a surge of anger. 'You've been holding out on me.'

'No, boss!'

Bernie let his anger subside, after all everything was falling into place. He now had the wherewithal to go wherever he wanted, do whatever he wanted. He would strike at Rowlands this very night by attacking his woman. Bernie felt good. Revenge was sweet.

'If I can't have Rowland's daughter then I'll do for his woman.' He grinned at his reluctant companion. 'I'll make him sick to his stomach to see what I'll do to her. I'll beat her to within an inch of her life.' He gave a laugh. 'Or even farther.'

'There's another bit of news, boss,' Fred cut in hastily. 'That Lloyd kid; her mother's been arrested. She's in clink.'

'What?' Bernie was uncertain for a moment. 'On what charge?'

'She's been charged with theft and resisting arrest.'

Bernie was pensive. He had thought putting her in trouble with the police was a good method of getting her from under his feet, now he wasn't so sure. Sybil would be screaming her head off, repeating all sorts of tales about him, and he had been indiscreet when he had almost confessed his connection with Dolly Mathias' death. Getting away from Swansea as soon as possible was more desirable than ever, but he wouldn't go without his money, or without taking his revenge on Rowlands.

'Is that all, boss?' Fred was hovering near the door.

'No, you've been paid well. I want you to keep watching Rowlands. There might be more to learn.'

'But, boss…!'

Bernie shook his head in warning. 'Don't get on the wrong side of me, Fred. It's not healthy.' He nodded towards the door. 'Now bugger off.'

Fred opened the door then hesitated. 'There's one funny thing though, boss,' he said, looking uncertainly at Bernie. 'Rowlands' fancy piece's surname is Daniels. But Daniels is Connie's real name, isn't it? What do you make of that, boss?'

Bernie was silent, puzzled and disturbed. That could not be a coincidence. There was something going on here that he did not understand, but he would. Connie was involved somehow and he sensed a chance to get back at her, too. All old scores would be settled tonight.

Connie was just preparing to go to bed when there was a knock at the door of her rooms. It was quite late and she was reluctant to answer. But when the knock came again with more urgency she knew she must answer before other roomers in the house were disturbed. She certainly could not afford to be gossiped about.

'Who is it?' she murmured quietly.

'It's Fred.'

Connie was taken aback. What on earth could the doorman at the Pleasure Palace want with her at this time of night, and how did he know where to find her?

Reluctantly she opened the door a crack and peered out at him.

'What do you want Fred?'

'I've got news.'

'It can wait until morning.'

Although Fred had always treated her with respect, despite her calling, and had never to her knowledge pestered the girls for sexual favours, she was uncomfortable with the idea of inviting him into her room.

'No, it can't wait, Connie,' Fred whispered through the crack. 'It's about your kid.'

'What?' Connie jerked the door open, staring at

him in consternation. 'What do you mean, my kid?'

'Her that's living at Cwmavon Terrace,' Fred said. 'I reckon she's your kid all right, and you should know what's happening. I've got daughters of my own,' he went on totally surprising her. She had never thought of him as a family man.

Connie's heart began to flutter. If Fred knew the truth then Bernie might know it too.

'Come in, Fred. Now what about my daughter?'

'Bernie's after her,' Fred said bluntly as he strode inside and closed the door behind him. 'He's going to do her a mischief.'

'What?' Connie's fingers flew to her mouth in dread.

'I had to warn you, Connie, because it isn't right.'

'But why?' Connie bit her lip in anguish. 'Does he know she's my daughter? Is that it?'

Fred shrugged. 'He believes she's Josh's fancy piece. He's out to take revenge on Josh by hurting your kid.'

He related how Josh had rescued the girl, Elvi, who Bernie had set his heart on, and went on to describe the ruckus at the Pleasure Palace.

'Charlie Pendle has taken over everything. Good thing you got out when you did, Connie,' he said. 'Pendle treats the girls like dirt, so I'm told. And he's out to get Bernie.' Fred shook his head. 'And Bernie's gone barking mad. He's dangerous.'

He told her about the strong-box.

'So Bernie is going to make a run for it,' Connie commented.

'Yes, but not before hurting your daughter. I reckon he'll try to do that tonight before he leaves Swansea.'

'I must go to her.' Connie put both her hands to her face. 'Oh, God! How will I stop him?'

'I'll wait outside while you get dressed,' Fred said. 'Then I'll walk you over to Cwmavon Terrace. It's the least I can do. Then I'm laying low for a while. I've got my family to think of.'

Connie dressed hurriedly, her hands shaking so much she could hardly pull her clothes over her head.

The thought of Bernie laying a hand on Lynnys filled her with horror. She knew how vicious he could be at the best of times, and now his back was against the wall, he was capable of any atrocity with his mind bent on revenge.

As she shrugged into her coat and pulled on a hat, she prayed she was in time and that she would be given the strength to stand strong against him and defeat him.

27

'I can't understand how Elvi got into this mess,' Lynnys said just as she and her grandmother were about go up to bed. 'Her mother must be worried out of her mind.'

Elvi and Trudy were sharing a bed. They had gone up earlier and Elvi was already sound asleep after Phoebe had given her a strong sleeping powder.

'Huh!' Phoebe was climbing the stairs ahead of her. 'That woman has got other worries.'

'What do you mean, Gran?' Lynnys asked, puzzled. 'Do you know her mother, then?'

Phoebe had been acting strangely towards Elvi all evening, and Lynnys could see her friend was confused by it, as she was herself.

'Never mind,' Phoebe said. 'But Elvi's in for a shock soon.'

'Now, Gran, if you're keeping something back, you'd better tell me,' Lynnys scolded.

'It's not my place,' Phoebe said defensively.

Lynnys was about to argue when there came a loud knocking at the front door.

'It must be Josh,' she said to Phoebe. 'I'll let him in.'

As Lynnys turned in the passage to go to the door she heard Phoebe descend the stairs behind her, and shuffle back into the living room. Lynnys smiled to herself. Phoebe would not go to bed now, tired though she undoubtedly was. She was afraid she'd miss something.

Lynnys pulled back the bolt and opened the door wide, expecting to see Josh, but instead a complete stranger stood on the step; a tall man wearing rough workingman's clothes.

'Are you Lynnys Daniels?'

Somehow his voice did not match the sort of clothes he wore, and Lynnys was immediately alert. She noticed the raw-looking claw marks on one cheek and the wild expression on his florid face and was wary.

'Yes, but who are you?' she asked sharply, drawing back a little. 'And what do you want at this hour?'

'I want you, you slut!' he exclaimed harshly, and reached forward to grab her arm.

Lynnys sprang back and shrieked, trying to shut the door on him, but he had his boot over the threshold and a hand against the door forcing it open. His strength was too much for her.

Lynnys ran down the passage towards the living room and to her horror he followed after.

Phoebe was sitting in her usual chair by the range, but struggled up hastily to see the stranger barge into her home.

'Here! What do you want? Get out!'

'Shut up, you old crone,' the man shouted. 'And keep back or I'll thump you.' He looked at Lynnys with hard eyes. 'I'll thump her anyway if you don't come with me now, you little tart.'

'What?'

'I know you're Josh Rowlands' fancy piece,' the man said. 'I've got a grudge to settle with him.

393

Now come here.'

The man lunged at Lynnys again and grabbing her arm in a painful grip, attempted to drag her roughly from the room. She fought back with all her strength, while Phoebe screamed like a banshee. Then Lynnys heard feet drumming on the stairs and Trudy, wearing only a nightgown, burst into the room and stood in the doorway.

'What's going on?' Trudy stared at the stranger and her mouth dropped open. 'Bloody hell! What are you doing here, Bernie?'

The man's grip was loosened momentarily as he looked Trudy up and down in surprise, and taking advantage of it, Lynnys moved quickly to put the table between them.

'Trudy?' He glanced from her to Lynnys and back again. 'What is this place,' he asked scornfully. 'A doss house for knocked up tarts?'

'Do you know this man?' Lynnys looked at Trudy in consternation.

'You bet I do. He's Bernie Smith or rather Pomfrey,' Trudy said angrily. 'The swine that put me up the duff, and then had me slung out.'

'What?' Phoebe gave another screech. 'Get out of my house, you dirty bugger.'

'Shut your trap!' Bernie lifted a balled fist and rounded on the old woman threateningly. 'I won't tell you again.'

'You leave my grandmother alone,' Lynnys shrieked at him, rushing forward to protect her. 'She's not a well woman.'

Bernie took the opportunity to seize her again, this time grasping her with an arm across the front of her body, holding her tightly against him and attempted to frog-march her out of the room and towards the passage.

Before they reached the door Phoebe staggered forward in their path. 'No! Take your hands off my granddaughter.'

For an answer Bernie put his free hand against the old woman's apron front and pushed her backwards. Phoebe fetched up against the sideboard, clutching at her chest, her face screwed up with pain.

'Gran!' Lynnys struggled in his grasp to reach her grandmother, but Bernie held her firm.

'You dirty rotter, Bernie,' Trudy yelled and threw herself at him, attempting to clamber on to his back, but her swollen abdomen hindered her.

'No, Trudy,' Lynnys cried out. 'Think of your baby. See to Gran first, and then go and fetch a policeman or call Billy next door.'

Lynnys struggled hard, digging her heels into the linoleum as Bernie forced her forward. They were in the passage then; the front door wide open as he had left it. Lynnys clung stubbornly to the living room doorframe. Instinct told her that once outside she would be completely at his mercy. She must hang on until help came in some form.

With a coarse oath Bernie struck savagely at her face in an attempt to subdue her, but Lynnys would not loosen her grip on the door post. She prayed that someone would intervene.

She could hear Phoebe moaning in the room behind and longed to go to her aid, but Trudy was there and Lynnys had learned to trust her.

She realised she would have to keep resisting

this man's attempts to abduct her until Trudy could fetch a neighbour or a policeman. But why had he picked on her?

'I'll break your bloody arm if you don't stop fighting me,' Bernie rasped in her ear. 'You're only making it worse for yourself, because when I get you alone you'll wish you'd never been born.'

'Bernie!'

The name was shrieked loudly by a new voice, and by the gaslight in the passage, Lynnys saw the outline of a female form at the front door. The woman came forward hurriedly, and to her astonishment Lynnys recognised Mrs Lamar, the last person she had expected to come to her aid.

The gaslight also revealed remnants of ugly bruising on her face, and Lynnys suddenly understood why Mrs Lamar had stayed out of sight recently.

Mrs Lamar edged towards them along the passage. 'Bernie, let her go!' she said in a voice that shook strangely. 'Do you hear me? Let her go, or by God, I'll do you an injury.'

Lynnys was astounded that they appeared to know each other. But then she realised she knew little of Mrs Lamar's life.

'Connie, well, well!' he responded and gave a harsh laugh, his hold on Lynnys tightening even more. 'So she *is* your kid. You kept that secret very well.'

Lynnys' struggles stopped momentarily as his words sank in. Your kid. What could he mean?

'Why are you doing this, Bernie?' Mrs Lamar's voice was quivering. 'Lynnys has never done you any harm.'

He gave a rasping laugh. 'I'm taking her in place of Elvi Lloyd,' he said. 'That bastard Rowlands took the girl from me, now I'll have his slut instead.'

Lynnys was appalled at this. Pressed against him she felt as well as heard a growl deep in his chest. 'I intend to have a high old time with her,' he spat out the words. 'Before I'll beat her to a pulp.'

'Bernie, have you gone mad? You don't know what you're doing. You don't understand who Lynnys is.'

'I know she's your bastard kid,' he said scornfully.

Lynnys felt shocked to the core to hear those words and stared at the woman she knew as Mrs Lamar. How could this be?

Phoebe had told her that her parents had died together long ago. Yet Elvi's strange pronouncement came into her mind and she felt even more confused. Could it be true, but why would her grandmother tell such a lie?

'And knowing she *is* your kid,' he went on. 'It'll give me great pleasure to have her the way I've had you many times. Now get out of my way, Connie.'

'No! I won't let you do this.' Mrs Lamar took up a stance. 'You'll have to beat me down too before you get out of this house, Bernie.'

'Have it your way.'

He barrelled forward, using Lynnys' body as a battering ram. Frantically Connie tried to strike at his face, while Lynnys struggled valiantly in his hold. Trudy was behind them, shouting, and Lynnys knew the girl was trying to do her part in the struggle, although she was worried for Trudy's baby.

Eventually, between the three of them they managed to force him back into the living room, while he cursed them ferociously.

'Dig an elbow in his ribs, Lynnys,' Trudy bellowed advice. 'Hit the swine where it hurts.'

Lynnys tried to take the girl's advice, but his grip on her was unshakable and she found she could not move her arms. Although the man was narrow of shoulder and paunchy, he seemed immensely strong, and she began to fear they would never defeat him.

And then Mrs Lamar kicked out catching him on the shin. He let out a howl of fury, and his hold on Lynnys slackened. She rammed backwards with her elbow and felt satisfaction when he howled again. She was out of his grasp in a moment, and sprang away from him, panting and trying not to burst into tears of relief.

'Damn you to hell, Connie!' he bellowed bending down to rub at his shin.

'I'll kick your other leg, you bastard,' Trudy threatened ferociously. 'See how you like that.' She moved forward purposefully, but Lynnys prevented it.

'Be careful, Trudy,' she warned. 'He could hurt the baby. Go quick! Put a coat on and call Billy next door. He can fetch a policeman.'

With a wary glance at Bernie, Trudy left the room, and Lynnys hoped she would be able to bring help soon.

Bernie had recovered from the pain in his leg and was watching them like a wolf watches sheep. His expression was hard and mean, and Lynnys sensed he would attack her again at any moment, although why in the world he should want to was beyond her.

She took her eyes off him for a second to take a worried look at Phoebe, who had sunk onto a chair near the range, her face white and drawn. She must go to her, Lynnys decided, despite the danger. She was about to do that when Mrs Lamar spoke out.

'Bernie, listen to me,' she said. 'Lynnys is my daughter but she's also *your* child. *Your* own daughter, man, doesn't that mean anything to you?'

Open-mouthed, Lynnys stopped and turned her gaze away from Phoebe to stare at Connie Lamar in consternation. 'What did you say?' she gasped out.

'It's true, Lynnys. This man is your father.' Connie shook her head, and cast her glance down at the floor looking shamefaced. 'I never wanted you to know.'

Lynnys dragged her gaze away from Connie's drooped head to stare at the man Bernie. This beastly, evil man was her father? She could not believe that.

'No!' she exclaimed in revulsion. 'My father is dead.'

'Dead?' For some reason Bernie found this amusing. 'Connie is nothing more than a dirty tart and has been all her life,' he said with a sneer. 'She's had hundreds of men and any one of them could be your father.'

'Bernie, for the love of heaven, how could you?' Connie's face was deathly pale. 'You were scared silly of catching venereal disease, and so you kept me for yourself. You wouldn't let another man touch me, not until you tired of me. By that time I was already carrying Lynnys. You can deny it all you want, but she is your daughter.'

He paused for a moment looking uncertain and then his lips twisted in a derisive smile. 'So, I fathered a bastard. So what? She's a slut too. She might as well be my slut.' He grinned nastily. 'I couldn't have found a better way to punish you, Connie, even if I'd planned it.'

Without warning he sprang at Lynnys again and, taken off guard by the distressing revelations about her origins, she was not quick enough to elude his grasp.

'Come here, you,' he bellowed. 'You're coming with me.'

Connie rushed forward to grapple with him, but he struck at her and she fell heavily before the range. Lynnys found herself being bundled roughly towards the passage again and, struggle as she might, she could not impede their progress towards the front door. She heard Connie shouting hysterically behind them.

'I'll kill you, Bernie! I swear it. I'll kill you. Take that!'

Lynnys heard the thud, and Bernie swore viciously. His right arm seemed to have weakened, for Lynnys was able to wriggle from his grasp in a moment and was free.

Turning from her, Bernie spun on his heel to

confront Connie who was standing in the living room doorway, a heavy fire iron raised above her shoulder.

'If you don't leave this house this minute, Bernie, I'll hit you again,' she said, and Lynnys could see she was shaking from head to foot, her expression showing fear. 'And next time it won't be just your shoulder. I'll smash your head in, you monster.'

'You've gone too far this time, Connie,' Bernie muttered wrathfully and took a step towards her. 'I should've finished you off the other day. I would have too, if that bugger Herb hadn't intervened.'

He moved forward menacingly and Connie retreated into the living room, waving the fire iron threateningly. 'Don't come any closer,' she warned him. 'I'll use it, I will!'

He gave a scornful laugh. 'You haven't the guts to do anything, Connie. You've always been weak.'

Next moment, before Lynnys realised his purpose, he sprang at Connie and wrenched the iron from her hand. Lynnys rushed forward to grab at his arm thinking he was about to strike the woman with it, but instead he threw it on the floor.

'I don't need a weapon,' he muttered gutturally. 'I'm going to finish you off with my bare hands.'

With that he took Connie by the throat with both hands and forced her back against the range. His attack was so savage that Connie had no time to scream or utter a word. His grip tightened and in horror Lynnys saw an expression of abject terror on Connie's face as her colour began to change, and her face contorted.

In desperation, Lynnys picked up the fire iron and swung it above her head. The idea of injuring anyone, let alone killing them, was abhorrent to her, but she could not let this man hurt Mrs Lamar, the woman who might be her own mother.

With a prayer asking forgiveness Lynnys let fly with the iron.

Josh waited in the darkened doorway of a dingy tobacconist's shop in a street of run-down lodging houses directly behind Swansea Market, a stone's throw from Cwmavon Terrace. He had been waiting some time, but knew his quarry would arrive eventually.

He was aware of boots hurrying on the cobbles, and withdrew into the shadows until the man he was waiting for came into view. Josh sprang forward then and grabbed the man by the arm.

Fred jumped back startled, his fist raised, but when he saw who it was he lowered his arm.

'Bloody hell, Josh! You didn't half give me a turn,' he gasped. 'Thought it was one of Pendle's men, I did. That's why I got to keep under cover, mate.'

Josh was in no mood to listen. 'Where is he?'

'Who?'

'Don't be a fool, Fred. You know who I mean,' Josh snarled. 'I want Bernie.'

Fred looked up and down the street. 'Can't hang about here, I can't, Josh. I only live up by there.' He pointed up the street. 'My wife and kids are waiting for me. I promised my old girl I'd quit working for Bernie.'

'I want him.'

'You're not the only one. Pendle's out to get him and anyone else who's with him.'

'Well, I want him first,' Josh said angrily. 'I know you've been helping him. Tell me where he is and I'll keep you no longer.'

Fred hesitated a moment and then shrugged. 'What the hell!' he exclaimed. 'I'm keeping clear of him from now on. I don't want my throat cut.' He glanced up and down the street again before going on. 'Bernie's in lodgings in Pottery Terrace, number twenty.'

'Thanks!' Josh made to move away but Fred's hand stayed him.

'I don't think you'll find him there at the moment.' He gave Josh a nervous glance. 'He's after your woman, Josh.'

'What?' Josh was baffled. There was no woman in his life at present.

'That young piece, you know, Connie's girl. He had me watch you. He knows about Cwmavon Terrace. I reckon he'll try something there tonight.'

As burly as Fred was, Josh grabbed him by the coat lapels, and yanked him forward, sudden fear making him rougher than he intended. 'You what?'

Fred pulled himself free of Josh's frantic grasp. 'He's jumping mad that you took that kid, Elvi Lloyd,' he explained. 'He's going to replace her with your young piece. He knows Connie is the girl's mother and he's out to get even with you both. I warned Connie, I did.'

'My God!' Josh stepped back appalled. 'My

daughter is at Cwmavon Terrace. If Bernie touches her again...' He glanced at Fred as he turned. 'Thanks, Fred. I won't forget this.'

Josh sprinted along the cobbles, feeling fear mount in his chest, making him breathless. Cwmavon Terrace was just a few streets away, but would he get there in time? It was pretty late. Bernie could have already been there and caused havoc. If anything had happened to Elvi...

Josh came to the end of Cwmavon Terrace and raced along the pavement to Phoebe's house. He reached the doorway to find it wide open and with dismay he heard a girl's voice screaming inside.

Josh did not hesitate. He rushed down the passage to the back room and came to a skidding halt at the sight that met his eyes.

Bernie was there, and he had Connie by the throat, while Lynnys stood behind them, a fire iron in her hands, already swinging it at his head.

Josh dashed forward and grabbed the iron from her, letting it drop on the floor. Lynnys fell back at the sight of him, her eyes dazed and staring in terror.

'Bernie, you bloody swine!' Josh shouted, and grabbed at the man's shoulders to drag him off his victim.

It took all of Josh's strength to prise Bernie's hands from Connie's throat, and with a howl of rage Bernie turned on him, throwing a wild punch at his face. Josh did not have time to see whether Connie was all right, for Bernie's fist landed squarely on the side of his jaw and he staggered back against the table, dazed.

'You interfering bugger, Rowlands,' Bernie bellowed in fury. 'This'll be the last time you get in my way.'

He came at Josh at a run. Confused by the sharp pain in his face, Josh did not have time to lift his arms to defend himself. Bernie punched him in the lower abdomen, and as he doubled over in agony his opponent hit him again in the face.

Defenceless, Josh sank down onto the linoleum, in so much pain he could hardly see. He squinted up at Bernie standing over him, seeing the fire iron in the man's hand.

'You've been asking for this, Rowlands,' Bernie snarled. 'It'll give me great pleasure to bash your brains in.'

Bernie brandished the iron but the next instant Josh saw Lynnys grab at Bernie's arm, trying to restrain him.

'No, no! Keep back,' Josh gasped out a warning. 'Get out, get out all of you. Run!'

Suddenly from outside somewhere there came the sound of police whistles, and the next moment Trudy ran into the room.

'Billy has called the police,' she yelled out. 'Coppers will be here any minute.'

With an oath Bernie dropped the iron and whirled towards the door. Josh tried to struggle to his feet, desperate to stop Bernie getting away.

'You're finished, Bernie,' he panted, already on his knees. 'You'll swing for sure. I know you killed that old woman, Mrs Mathias. I'm giving you up to the law this time.'

With a snarl Bernie swung another punch at his

unprotected head, and Josh went sprawling again. He was aware that Bernie was running from the room, but there was nothing he could do to stop him.

Bernie was escaping Scot-free once again, and with him went Sybil's one and only chance of proving her innocence of stealing Dolly Mathias's money.

Lynnys recovered first and as soon as her attacker had fled she ran to her grandmother, slumped in a chair near the range.

'Gran! Gran, are you all right?'

Phoebe's eyes were closed, her face grey, dark circles around her eyes. She looked as though she was already dead or dying. Lynnys' heart began to pound even more at the sight and she prayed for Phoebe's life.

'Trudy, get the smelling salts,' Lynnys cried out. 'Quick!'

Trudy was at her side in minutes and the little brown bottle was thrust under Phoebe's nose. With relief Lynnys saw Phoebe's eyelids flutter after a moment and her head moved aside slowly to avoid the acrid smell, and then she stirred and moaned.

'Oh, thank God she's alive,' Lynnys said. 'Trudy, make some hot sweet tea, will you, there's a love.'

'Mam? You're all right,' Connie murmured.

Lynnys rounded on her. 'No thanks to you,' she shouted. 'You brought that dreadful man here to this house.'

'No, I didn't.' Connie was standing with a hand on the mantelpiece for support. Her face was white, and there were angry looking bruises around her throat where the man's fingers had tried to squeeze the life out of her. 'It's not my fault.'

'It's all your fault,' Lynnys accused hotly. 'You and your filthy trade!'

Connie gave a little cry, and put her fingers to her mouth.

'There's no time for recrimination,' Josh exclaimed in a weary voice. He was hauling himself up from the floor, his face looked battered and there was bruising and swelling around one eye which had already begun to close. 'Where is my daughter? Where's Elvi?'

'Still upstairs sleeping like the dead after that powder Phoebe gave her.' Trudy answered as she came into the room with a tray of tea.

'Thank heaven,' Josh said. 'If that madman had hurt her...' His face contorted in hatred.

At that moment heavy footsteps were heard running down the passage and two policemen appeared in the doorway, truncheons raised. The law had finally arrived.

'What's going on here?' one said loudly, looking around at them. 'We had a call that there was a fight going on.'

'You missed it,' Josh said bitterly. 'A man broke in here and attacked the women. He had a go at me when I tried to intervene.'

'He gave you a pasting by the look of you,' one policeman said almost jovially, lowering his truncheon. 'You'll have a thick head in the morning.'

'Why did he attack you?' The other man frowned and looked hard at the women. 'What was he after?'

Lynnys opened her mouth to blurt out the whole truth, but a glance from Josh silenced her.

'He wasn't after them,' he said quickly. 'He wants to silence me. I know enough about him to put him on the gallows.'

'Is that a fact? Then you'd better come down the station with us.' It was a command rather than a suggestion. He looked at Lynnys and the others again. 'Perhaps you had all better come along with us.'

'Surely that won't be necessary,' Josh said quickly. 'The old lady is ill. Look at her! And this young woman is expecting. None of them knows anything, officer. They just happened to get in his way. I can tell you all you want to know.'

'Right you are,' he agreed, although Lynnys felt his suspicious eyes on her and the others again. 'We know where to find you if we want to question you further.'

Josh moved towards the door and Lynnys could see he walked painfully. 'Let's get it over with,' he said wearily. 'That madman's still on the loose. You'd better leave a constable outside in case he returns,' he suggested, anxiously.

'I'll have a word with my sergeant,' the policeman said in an off-hand tone.

Lynnys followed Josh and the policemen down the passage and closed the door securely after they had gone, hoping that a constable would be sent to protect them.

She was grateful to Josh for his efforts to save her and Phoebe from the scandalous truth, but she would not delude herself about the future. It

408

was all bound to come out into the open and then her reputation, her life even, would be ruined. She could say goodbye to a singing career.

Anger surged in her heart as she turned back to go into the living room to face Connie Lamar.

'I'm wondering if Mam should go to the hospital,' Connie said to Lynnys. 'I'll go with her in a hansom.'

'I'm staying here,' Phoebe said weakly but resolutely. 'I'm not bad hurt.'

Lynnys looked at her grandmother uncertainly. Colour was coming back into her face, and her eyes had lost that hollow deathly look. She was concerned for Phoebe's health, but even so, she was also angry. Why had Phoebe deceived her all these years?

'Are you sure, Gran?' she asked stiffly, unable to keep reproof out of her voice.

Phoebe glanced up at her and then glanced away again. 'You can't blame me for trying to protect you against the truth, Lynnys,' she said tentatively. 'I couldn't let you go the same way as your mother.'

'Mam!' Connie sounded wounded. 'I would never have let that happen myself.'

'Huh!' Phoebe's strength was returning with every passing minute. 'Then how do you account for what happened here tonight? That filthy bugger tried to take my Lynnys, and we all know what for.'

Trudy gave a little cough. 'I'd better go up and see how Elvi is,' she remarked. 'You don't need me here.'

Lynnys was grateful to her. Trudy was becoming

more sensible and considerate every day. Despite the sordid life she had lived earlier, Lynnys felt certain Trudy would rise above the shame of it eventually and live a useful and respectable life with her child.

With a riveting shock she realised that Trudy's child carried the same blood that she did. The child was her half-sibling. It was unbelievable!

She turned to Connie Lamar. 'Gran's right. You have a lot to answer for,' she said angrily. 'How do you think I feel knowing my mother is a common prostitute and my father is a homicidal brute?'

Connie took a step towards her. 'Lynnys, please, let me explain.'

'Explain?' Lynnys was furious. 'How can you explain your disgusting way of life? How can you hope to excuse the sordid way I was conceived?'

Connie flopped down on a chair at the table. 'I've left that life behind for good, I swear it,' she sobbed and then put her arms on the top and laid her head on them. 'All I want is to share a small part of my daughter's life,' she cried between sobs. 'I don't ask for more.'

Lynnys stared at her lowered head, listening to her sobs. She had admired the woman she had known as Mrs Lamar, and had thought she had understood her; thought there was empathy between them. Now she wondered how she could ever have thought that.

'There can be no excuses.' She glanced at Phoebe. 'Nor for you, Gran. I don't know which hurts the most, that my mother is a woman of the streets or that you, my own flesh and blood, lied to me.'

Phoebe rose shakily to her feet. 'I took you in as a baby, only weeks old, and brought you up in a respectable home,' she said in a weak voice. 'I did my best for all these years. You've been happy, Lynnys. Would you have felt happier growing up knowing the truth of it?'

Lynnys swallowed. She could not answer that. Or perhaps she could. She had lived humbly, making an honest living and she had lived proudly believing she had decent parents. She had been happy, it was true. Perhaps the truth would have spoiled her life from the start. But the fact that she had been kept in ignorance rankled.

'Gran, this was a terrible way to learn about myself,' she said sorrowfully. 'I'm less than I was.'

'No!' Connie cried out, lifting a tear stained face. 'Don't say that, Lynnys.'

'It's how I feel.'

'You're not responsible for who your parents are,' Connie went on. 'And know this, I loved you from the hour you were born, and I've loved you all along. That's why I asked Mam to take you and bring you up. I wanted a decent life for you.' She swallowed hard. 'I paid for my mistake by being denied your love all these years. Don't punish me any more.'

Lynnys turned away. 'Everything has changed,' she said miserably. 'How can I look anyone in the eye again? My singing career is over before it has begun. Standing up on a stage I'd be laughed at and ridiculed. The daughter of a whore.'

'Lynnys!' Connie's voice was full of pain. 'Oh my God! To hear those words from the lips of my own child. I can't stand it!'

411

'Then leave,' Lynnys whirled on her angrily. 'Leave and don't come back. I never want to see you again – Mrs Lamar.'

412

28

At the police station Josh sat facing a senior police officer, who wore an expression of deep distrust. He was also conscious of the presence of another uniformed officer standing silently behind him, and felt cold dread as though he was a prisoner himself. He thought again of Sybil, and the misery she was going through.

'Now, sir,' the senior officer began in a cynical tone. 'I'm Inspector Walden. I understand you claim you have information concerning a crime.'

'I don't claim to know,' Josh said sharply. 'I do know. The man who attacked us tonight is Bernard Pomfrey. He likes to call himself Major Pomfrey.'

'An army man, then?'

Josh gave a bitter laugh. 'Bernie has never seen the outside of a barracks let alone been inside one.'

'I see.' Inspector Walden's regard was keen, and Josh could not shake off nervousness, remembering his part in the warehouse robbery all those years ago. He was taking a risk. 'Well, Mr Rowlands,' the inspector went on. 'What is this information you have for us?'

'On the face of it Pomfrey is a respectable businessman, owning a gentleman's outfitters,' Josh said. 'But he's also the proprietor of one of the most profitable whore-houses in the town, the

413

Pleasure Palace in Cambrian Place.'

Inspector Walden looked interested. 'We've been looking to raid that place for a while; close it down,' he said. 'But time and again some big wig or other has thrown a spanner in the works.'

'You'd be surprised at the well known figures in the town that frequent the place.'

Inspector Walden grunted and his eyes narrowed. 'You seem to know a lot about it.'

Josh shrugged. 'I've been a punter there once or twice,' he admitted cagily. 'And I made it my business to find out who owns it.'

'So, this is the crime you're talking about, keeping a disorderly house?'

'No,' Josh said evenly. 'I'm talking about kidnapping, grievous bodily harm and possibly murder.'

'What?'

'Bernie Pomfrey half-killed a young girl a few weeks back; beat her almost to death. I understand she's still in a coma at the hospital.'

'Pomfrey did that?'

Josh nodded. 'He also abducted my daughter from her own home, and imprisoned her at the Pleasure Palace for immoral purposes.' He ground his teeth at the memory of Elvi's terror. 'I got her out of there during a fracas when a local criminal, Charlie Pendle, burst in and smashed the place up.'

'Charlie Pendle!' The inspector looked startled.

He signalled to the police officer standing silently near the door. There was a whispered consultation between them, while Josh sat fidgeting. This was taking too long. Bernie was free and heaven alone know what he planned next.

'Never mind about Pendle,' Josh exclaimed loudly, interrupting their whispering. 'You're wasting time. That bastard Pomfrey is getting away.'

The police officers paused and looked sternly at him, and then Inspector Walden waved a hand dismissively and the uniformed officer left the room hurriedly.

'Get Pomfrey,' Josh went on angrily. 'He duped an old lady, Dolly Mathias, out of fifty thousand pounds. I think he also had a hand in her death.'

'What do you know about that?'

Josh jumped to his feet. 'Look! I know where Pomfrey is lodging, but I'm certain he's ready to do a bunk. We can catch him with the money on him if we hurry.'

Inspector Walden rose to his feet too, his shrewd eyes studying Josh's face.

'All right, Mr Rowlands. We'll take a look at his lodgings but you'd better come with us.' He shook his head. 'I have a lot more questions for you.'

It had been a great risk returning to his house in Walter Road, but Bernie finally decided it must be done. The best way to leave Swansea was by rail and he must do that tonight if possible. There was usually a very late train going to West Wales. He was not fussy about a destination just as long as he got away. The police may already be looking for him, but a well-dressed traveller with baggage would be less conspicuous.

He hung around the vicinity for a while making sure the house was not being watched and then made his move. Dart had followed his instructions. The house was securely locked up. Nothing had been touched. He took time to bath. The water was cold, but that could not be helped. He boiled a saucepan of water to shave, changed clothing and then packed a small suitcase. He also set aside an empty Gladstone bag. That would carry the contents of the strong-box, his future.

There was no food in the larder, but he decided he would not have time to eat anyway. Hunger was better than capture, especially when a man had blood on his hands.

He left the house through the back entrance and began the long walk to his lodgings in Pottery Terrace on the other side of town.

He was filled with bitter resentment that his revenge against Josh Rowlands and Connie had been thwarted. But if he could get away free and clear, time was on his side. He would not forget either of them, and some time in the future he would settle the score.

It was getting worryingly late when he turned the corner from the High Street into the narrow side road that was Pottery Terrace. He pulled up short in consternation to see by the glow of a street lamp a group of men with a horse-drawn vehicle outside his lodgings. The Black Maria!

Bernie hurriedly dodged back out of sight, and then peered cautiously at them around the corner of a building. He swore fervently under his breath. How had the police tracked him down so quickly?

As he watched two men emerged from the

house. One wore a black bowler hat and a long black coat. The other man was instantly recognisable and Bernie uttered a coarse oath at the sight of him. Josh Rowlands! He should have finished Rowlands off earlier when he had the chance.

Then he noticed that the man in the black coat was carrying his strong-box! Bernie withdrew quickly and leaned his back against the wall, fuming at the turn of events. That box held his money, documents, his whole future. And then another disturbing thought struck him. It also contained other incriminating evidence; bonds and jewellery from the warehouse robbery from years ago, stuff he had been keeping by him in case. And now it was in the hands of the police.

Flinging the empty Gladstone bag from him, Bernie hesitated no longer but turned and fled. He had to get to the railway station before the police realised he was still in the vicinity. The High Street was a direct route, but now he was afraid to chance being so exposed. The police might not recognise him, but they had Rowlands with them, who would spot him instantly.

Bernie turned down a narrow lane which led to the Strand. These dark back streets would give him the best cover. Despite the setback of losing his precious strong-box, he felt his blood stir with a strange excitement. He would outwit the buggers! He would outwit everyone.

'You saw the contents of that box, Inspector,' Josh said anxiously as he stood on the pavement along side the Black Maria. 'The bundles of notes still have the bank's paper strips on them. They bear the cashier's initials, did you notice? That proves Sybil Lloyd had nothing to do with the theft.'

'It proves nothing of the kind,' Inspector Walden said curtly. 'They could be in it together.'

Josh ground his teeth in consternation. It looked as though Sybil's ordeal would continue, at least for a while. Elvi must be told soon, and he dreaded the thought of it.

'Well, what are you doing to find him?' he asked angrily. 'He's probably making a run for it as we speak.'

Inspector Walden shook his head. 'I don't think so,' he said with confidence. 'He won't leave without this.' He indicated the heavy strong-box. 'He'll be back. We'll set a watch. We'll get him, mark my words.'

Josh wished he could feel as confident and was worried. While Bernie was on the loose and now a desperate man, both Elvi and Lynnys could be at risk.

It was chucking out time in the pubs along the Strand as Bernie made his way hurriedly. He regretted his fine clothes now, for they made him stand out like a sore thumb amongst the low life that frequented these places.

He paused by a street lamp to glance at his pocket watch. He had ten minutes to get that train. He took a firmer hold on his case and stepped forward again.

Suddenly two men in rough clothing emerged from a shadowy doorway a few yards in front of him. He had an impulse to stop and turn, but checked it. That would signal fear and they would be on him in a moment.

Instead he strode forward, ostensibly unconcerned, and passed them at a steady pace, even unwilling to give way on the narrow pavement. They shuffled past and Bernie held his breath for a moment, his ears almost twitching to listen to the sound of their hobnail boots on the pavement as they moved away.

But then their footfalls stopped, and Bernie quickened his pace, his heart beginning to pound uncomfortably in his chest.

'Hey! Bloody hell! It's him!' one man exclaimed loudly. 'I recognise him.'

Bernie broke into a run; heading for a narrow lane that would lead up to the High Street and perhaps no more than a hundred yards from the entrance to the railway station. He heard them give chase and increased speed, panting painfully as he ran.

But he wasn't fast enough. The sudden weight of a man flinging himself on to Bernie's shoulders almost had him on his knees. With a tremendous effort, fuelled by abject fear, he managed to throw the man off.

No more words were spoken but the one thought in Bernie's mind was that these two were Charlie Pendle's men, and he was now running for his very life.

Flinging his suitcase from him, he stumbled forward desperate to clear the distance to the High Street, but they were right behind him, no more than an arm's length away.

He wouldn't make it! That sudden insight made him turn to face them. Obviously, they wanted his life, but they would have to fight him for it.

Bernie threw a punch at the nearest face, feeling satisfaction when his fist met bone and he heard the man grunt in pain and reel back. He could battle his way out of this. He was reminded suddenly of how he had beaten that stupid girl senseless. He had enjoyed that, and the thought sent his pulses racing and his blood simmering.

Wordlessly, Bernie meted out as much punishment as he could, keeping his back to the dry-stone wall of the lane. It was when the two men attacked at the same time that one managed to get behind him. He felt the rough cloth of the man's jacket sleeve as he seized Bernie around the shoulders hauling him backwards off balance, and then by the faint light of a distant lamp Bernie saw the long steel blade glisten in the man's raised hand.

'Charlie says goodbye,' a voice hissed.

Bernie opened his lips to scream, knowing what that meant, but a hand was clapped over his mouth before he could utter a sound. His head was jerked back savagely and then he felt a searing pain across his throat. The agony seemed to last for an eternity, and then blackness overcame him, delivering him from it.

Leaving the police at last there was no question of going back to his own lodgings that night, not with Bernie still on the prowl and so Josh returned wearily to Cwmavon Terrace just in case.

Lynnys was still up and let him in. 'Well?' she asked, looking anxious. 'You've been a long time. I was worried. What happened with the police?'

Josh sank into a chair near the range, feeling exhausted.

'I took them to Bernie's lodgings. He wasn't there, but his strong-box was.' Josh shook his head. 'The police think he'll come back for it. But Bernie is too wily.' He looked up at her. 'I was worried that he might come here again.'

'Everything's been quiet,' she murmured. He saw a look of bitterness on her face. 'Except for my row with Mrs Lamar and Gran,' she went on.

She sat down opposite him, and he thought it best to remain silent for the moment. The revelations of the day must have knocked her for six.

'Josh, I can hardly accept that terrible man is my father,' she said at last, her voice quivering with barely controlled emotion. 'I've always pictured my father as being a good, hard-working man. I was proud of his memory.'

'I understand, kid,' he said gently.

'No, I don't think you do,' Lynnys said promptly. 'How could you understand what I'm going through?' She bit her lip and Josh could see she was fighting to hold back tears. 'Within the space of half an hour this evening I learned that my mother is a common prostitute and that my father. ... my father is a criminal brute.'

He bent his head, only too conscious that within hours he would have to tell Elvi about her mother and reveal his relationship to her. Would Elvi be as disgusted at the knowledge that he was her father as Lynnys obviously was about Bernie?

421

'Connie loves you, kid,' he said at last.

'Loves me? She's betrayed me!'

'I know it's a shock,' Josh said. 'But who your parents are can make no difference to you. You're the girl you've always been.'

Lynnys rose abruptly from her chair. 'That's where you're wrong, Josh. I was not born out of love, was I? No. I was created out of a sordid, filthy act. There wasn't a relationship between my parents.' She turned her head away and sobbed. 'He was merely her paying customer.'

'But that isn't your fault,' Josh persisted. She was taking it very badly and he felt sorry. 'Besides,' he went on, 'I know for a fact that Connie loved Bernie for years. It's only recently that she's turned against him, seeing some of the terrible things he's done, and now she's left him for good. Connie has given up that life, Lynnys. You must believe me.'

She turned eyes on him that were brimming with tears.

'Believe you? You're forgetting how we met, Josh,' she said accusingly. 'You weren't above using poor Trudy, were you?'

He bent his head again, knowing that was a justified accusation. How could he explain to this young girl that he was merely a man with needs to be met? But was that excuse justifiable?

'You've got nothing to be ashamed of, Lynnys,' he said at last. 'You'll get over this in time. I'll help you and so will Connie.'

'I've sent Mrs Lamar away,' Lynnys said in a stony voice. 'I never want to set eyes on her again.'

Josh stood up. 'You can't mean that, Lynnys,' he said. 'Connie loves you. All your life she made sure you never went without by giving Phoebe money to keep you.' He paused seeing an expression of consternation on her face. 'Don't look like that. She did it for love.'

'You're telling me I've lived all these years on her dirty money?' She shook her head miserably and began to wring her hands. 'That's too much to bear. I hate her! I hate what she's done to me. She's ruined my life.'

Josh was silent for a moment looking at her. 'Are you going to turn Phoebe out of her home, too, because of your pride?' Josh asked quietly. 'You took Trudy in even though you knew what she was.'

'That was different,' Lynnys said defensively. 'She's a young girl who didn't know any better.'

'So was Connie when Bernie trapped her into the game. He was a brute even then. She was only a kid herself, but she learned to love.' Josh gave a grunt. 'God alone knows why.'

'It's no good, Josh.' Lynnys shook her head. 'I won't change my mind about her. She's taken my singing career away from me. It's finished. It's all finished.'

'What?' Josh was astonished and dismayed. 'This is madness, Lynnys. You have a magnificent talent. You can't deny yourself that future.'

'What? Set myself up for ridicule and humiliation?' Lynnys asked sharply. 'If I remain as I am I might be able to hide the truth, but in the public eye my whole history will be laid bare. I couldn't stand that. I have my pride.'

'Bernie would be laughing up his sleeve if he could hear you now, knowing he'd spoiled everything for us all,' Josh said. 'He's the kind of man who takes pleasure in other people's pain.'

'I don't want to talk about it.'

'Bernie regards you, his child, as less than nothing, Lynnys, remember,' Josh said feeling anger. 'He always despised your mother for her weakness in loving him. Now you're about to prove him right.'

Lynnys turned away and walked into the passage. 'I'm going to bed,' she said dully. 'You can stay or go as you please.'

'Now wait just a minute,' Josh said, thoroughly angry now. 'I've invested a lot of money in you, Lynnys. Tuition, clothes. I think I deserve better than this.'

'Goodnight, Josh.'

29

Reluctant to open her eyes, Elvi lay for a moment more savouring the comfort of the bed. She was gradually conscious of the warmth of another body next to hers, and for a moment thought she was back in the bedroom at Fleet Street, sharing the bed with her mother.

But that could not be true. She seemed to remember an awful nightmare; a strange room, struggling with a terrible man. Where was she?

Elvi's eyes snapped open. By the faint light of dawn she saw an unfamiliar ceiling above her, and then the person next to her stirred and gave a little snore. Thoroughly alarmed she slid from beneath the bed covers, her feet making contact with cool linoleum. She stood and turned to look at her companion.

The red tousled head of a girl lay on the pillow next to hers, and then it came back to her. The girl had said her name was Trudy. Yes, that was it. Then she remembered being brought to this house by some man, a complete stranger. She recalled how terrified she had been, so terrified that memories of events were blurred and fuzzy in her head.

She realised uncomfortably that she needed to use the lavatory. She bent down and glanced under the bed. There was a chamber pot there, but she blushed at the idea of using it with someone else in the room, even if she was asleep. The lavatory was probably out in the back yard.

An old woollen dressing gown was thrown over a chair nearby and Elvi put it on. Softly, on bare feet, she left the bedroom and the still sleeping Trudy, and proceeded down the stairs. From the living room she heard water running in the scullery so someone was up and about.

Memories of the previous night were still hard to grasp, but she was sure there had been other people in the house, an older woman and another girl. Oh, yes, Lynnys. That's right! This was the home of her friend Lynnys, and she felt comforted at the knowledge.

Expecting to see Lynnys' familiar face, Elvi hurried into the scullery only to pull up short, uttering a cry of alarm to see a strange man at the stone sink, stripped to the waist, washing himself.

'Oh!' Elvi turned to flee, reminded of her recent ordeal.

'Elvi, wait! I won't harm you.' The man quickly struggled into his shirt and followed her into the living room.

Elvi stood in the doorway to the passage; poised to run back upstairs should he attempt to come near her. He held out a hand to her as though pleading.

'It's all right, Elvi,' he said. 'You're quite safe here. I'm ... I'm Josh, a friend of Lynnys.'

'Do I know you?'

'How much do you remember of last night?'

Elvi put trembling fingers to her lips. Memories of pain, images, sounds, were beginning to

426

coalesce in her mind, and then it all flooded back. Her clothes being ripped from her body; that dreadful man's hands on her, his leering face as he tried to ... tried to...

Elvi uttered a moan and swayed on her feet, feeling nauseated at the memory.

'Sit down, kid,' Josh said kindly. 'I'll make you a cup of tea.'

'No,' Elvi said. 'I want to go home. I want to see my mother. Where is she? Why isn't she here?'

Elvi had always suspected Sybil had no real affection for her. She was a nuisance, always getting in Sybil's way, always spoiling her chances with men. But surely, after what Elvi had just been through, surely her mother would be by her side.

And then another memory came to her. Sybil sprawled on the passage floor in Walter Road. Was her mother dead? Were these people afraid to tell her the awful truth?

'Mam!' Elvi rose to her feet. 'Where's my Mam? She *is* dead, isn't she?'

'No, no. I already told you last night, it's nothing like that,' Josh said. His tone was soothing and kind. And that too stirred memories.

'It was you, wasn't it?' Elvi said looking at him closely. 'You rescued me from that terrible place, that room, that man...'

'You must put all that behind you, now, Elvi,' Josh said. He hesitated a moment too long and immediately Elvi knew something was wrong.

'You're hiding something from me.'

Buttoning his shirt, Josh sat down on a chair near her.

427

'Yes, there is something you must know,' he said seriously. 'But I don't want you to worry, because I'm going to see to it that everything turns out all right.'

'You'd better tell me,' Elvi said gravely. 'I'm not a child, you know.'

Josh smiled. 'No, you're a very brave young woman, and you've been through an appalling experience. But you'll need more courage for what I have to tell you.'

Elvi waited, wondering at the strange way he looked at her and why he was hesitating.

'Elvi, your mother has been arrested.'

'What?'

'Sybil is in Swansea Prison, waiting to come before the magistrate.'

'What has she done?' Elvi clapped her hand over her mouth. 'Is it to do with the séances?' She shook her head. 'Oh, I knew she'd get into trouble over that. I told her it was wrong.'

'No, it's not that,' Josh said. 'Sybil was frantic with worry when Bernie ... that man, abducted you.'

'Was she?' Elvi was eager to know her mother's reaction. 'Was she really?'

'Of course, she was.' Josh looked at her in a peculiar way, as though he were surprised at her surprise. 'The police were called,' he went on. 'Well, the fact is your mother lost her temper with the police officer's stupidity, and she struck him while resisting arrest. She was also falsely accused of theft.'

'Oh! My goodness!'

'Now you mustn't worry, Elvi,' Josh said hastily.

428

'This morning I'm going to engage a lawyer to argue her case. I'm almost certain the theft charges will be dropped. The police have found evidence that the thief was someone else.'

Elvi studied him for a moment. 'Why are you doing all this for us? Are you ... are you one of my mother's gentleman friends?'

He looked at her keenly and she thought she saw disapproval in his face. 'Does she have many gentleman friends?'

Elvi nodded and then bit her lip, feeling she was betraying her mother again.

'From time to time,' she said defensively. 'Mam thought Major Pomfrey would be her friend.'

Josh was silent and thoughtful. 'Sit down, Elvi,' he said eventually, indicating a chair nearby. 'I need to tell you something.'

Elvi sat, wondering at the gravity of his tone and his serious expression. He sat for a moment; elbows resting on his knees, hands clasped together, head bent. She waited tensely while he gathered his thoughts. She could not guess why he seemed so concerned, unless he had not told her everything about her mother's plight.

'Is it something terrible?' she asked in a small voice.

He looked up and smiled. 'Well, that depends,' he said. 'Tell me, has Sybil ever mentioned your father to you, told you anything about him?'

Elvi shook her head. 'No, not really. She told me he's dead, but...'

'Yes?'

'I sense she doesn't know whether he's dead or not,' Elvi confided candidly. 'I've always hoped

429

he was alive and would come back one day. Then I'd have a real family.'

While she longed to have her father back in her life, she wondered if she could ever forgive him for deserting them in the first place.

'What do you think your father is like?'

Elvi smiled, feeling shy suddenly. No one had ever asked her a question like that before. 'I don't know.'

Josh wetted his lips. 'Do you think he might be someone like me?'

Elvi frowned, confused. What a strange thing to ask. She was more than grateful to him for saving her from the horror of that house, but she hardly knew him.

'I couldn't say,' she replied. 'I don't know you well enough to judge.'

'No, and you don't know how much I regret that, Elvi.'

'I don't understand.'

'Your mother and I knew each other well, years ago, when she was young, when we were both young.' He looked away as though ashamed. 'I got into trouble with the police, big trouble, and had to run away to London. I had no idea that Sybil...'

He stopped and looked down at the floor, as though avoiding her gaze. Elvi waited quietly, sensing that she would learn more if she kept silent and let him tell it in his own way. At the same time a tingle of excitement started around her heart. What was he trying to say? Suddenly she had the feeling it was of great significance.

'We didn't have a chance to say goodbye,' he

went on. 'So she couldn't tell me she was ... expecting a child, you Elvi.' He shook his head. 'I swear if I'd known I'd have taken her with me. Your mother meant a lot to me in those days.'

The sense of what he was saying sank in, and she was startled. 'You mean I'm illegitimate? My mother was never married?'

He nodded. 'I'm your father, Elvi.'

Elvi blinked at him. Many times she had wondered how her father might look; handsome and distinguished perhaps. Josh was handsome, sure enough, and the greying hair at his temples gave him an air of distinction, but there was also a hint of rakishness about him. Could she possibly have such a man for a father?

'You're shocked,' he said quietly. 'Or perhaps I'm a disappointment.'

'No, I'm just surprised. I never really expected ever to meet you.'

She felt even more confused suddenly. Her mother was in prison and her father was a stranger. What was to happen now? More importantly, what was expected of her?

'I don't know how you feel about all this,' he said. 'But I want to be part of your life; take care of you, as a father should.'

'You mean ... you mean you're going to marry my mother.'

It was Josh's turn to look startled, and she realised she had been silly and foolish to think that.

'No, Elvi. What we had, Sybil and me, has gone.' He rubbed his jaw thoughtfully. 'But I can still be close to you and protect you, if you'll let me?'

Elvi lowered her gaze. He must think her gauche and childish, and felt ashamed. Her father had come back into her life and she didn't know how she felt about him. He was still a stranger.

'You must stay here for the time being,' Josh went on. 'I'll do everything I can to get your mother released.'

'I want to see her,' Elvi said urgently. 'Can you arrange a visit for me?'

'I'm not sure.' Josh looked serious. 'You must be prepared, Elvi. Sybil may have to face charges that can't be brushed aside.'

Elvi put her fingers to her mouth. 'You mean she'll have to stay in prison?'

Josh nodded solemnly.

'But she'll never stand it,' Elvi exclaimed anxiously. 'I know her. She'll pine away.'

'Sybil is tougher than you think, kid,' Josh said. 'She's managed to bring you up alone. That must've been hard.'

'Yes, I suppose so.' Elvi bit her lip. 'I do want to see her. I miss her so much.'

It was true, and she was surprised. She had longed to grow up and find independence; leave behind Sybil and the dubious way she made a living. She had always been ashamed of it. But now parted from her mother, and Sybil in such desperate trouble, she realised how much she loved her.

'Please do all you can for her ... Josh,' she said shyly. 'For us both. We're your family.'

Josh smiled and Elvi thought she saw something glistening in his eyes. 'Thank you,' he said.

'Thank you for forgiving me.'

Josh faced Inspector Walden across his desk. 'Mr Prosser, Mrs Lloyd's lawyer, has been to see you, I understand,' he said. 'The charges of theft against her are to be dropped for lack of evidence.'

'Well...'

'Good heavens, man!' Josh exclaimed impatiently. 'The money has been recovered, found in Bernie Pomfrey's possession. What more do you want?'

The inspector pulled in his chin looking aggrieved. 'This is a serious matter, not to be taken lightly.'

'The woman is innocent of the theft,' Josh insisted.

'That's as maybe.'

'There's no maybe about it. When will you release her?'

The inspector gave a little cough, as though annoyed to be challenged.

'While it's becoming clearer that Mrs Lloyd may not have actually been involved in theft from Mrs Mathias,' he conceded grudgingly, 'there's still the question of charges of resisting arrest and striking a police officer.' He frowned at Josh. 'A very serious matter as far as we're concerned. These charges will stand, as I informed her lawyer. She goes before the magistrate next week and in the meantime she stays where she is.'

Josh ground his teeth in irritation. 'And what about Pomfrey?' he asked with asperity. 'He's still at large. He's a killer, Inspector. What are you doing to find him?'

Inspector Walden passed his tongue across his lips thoughtfully. 'He has been found.'

'What?' Josh sat forward. 'What's he got to say for himself? Has he admitted anything?'

'I should have said his body has been found.'

Josh was speechless, and he stared at the inspector with his mouth open.

'His body was dragged from the river this morning,' Inspector Walden went on. 'His throat had been cut.'

Josh was silent for a moment, ashamed to realise he felt deep relief. Elvi was safe now and so was Lynnys.

'So, Charlie Pendle got him after all,' he said at last.

The inspector nodded. 'Looks like it,' he agreed. 'But it'll be a bugger to prove. Pendle's ruthless, psychotic, maybe, but he's also very clever. Anyone who gets in his way either disappears or ends up in the Tawe.'

'A dangerous man.'

'Very. We're sure he's been responsible for similar deaths over the last few years, but nothing proved. Witnesses are scared for their lives.'

'What are Mrs Lloyd's chances?' Josh asked.

Inspector Walden shrugged. 'It depends on the magistrate,' he said. 'But I can tell you this. A prison sentence is certain.'

Josh came away from the police station feeling very glum. How would Elvi take the news, he wondered. There was no place for her at his lodgings, so she must remain at Cwmavon Terrace for the foreseeable future. Yet it seemed hardly fair on Lynnys and Phoebe, not to mention Elvi. The poor kid must feel abandoned. Josh decided Connie must be informed of Bernie's death and he went straight to her lodgings from the police station.

Physically, she was looking more her old self, the facial bruising almost faded away; new bruising around her throat still purple. Josh was struck immediately by the look of misery and hopelessness in her eyes, and could guess why.

'You're worried about Lynnys,' he said as he sat in her living room. 'There's been no word from her then?'

Connie shook her head. 'I've lost her, Josh,' she said sadly. 'She'll never forgive me. I don't know what I'm going to do. My only child has turned against me. Life doesn't seem to matter any more.'

'You must buck up, Connie,' Josh said more severely than he intended. 'You've been without her love for the best part of seventeen years,' he went on to point out. 'Will you miss what you've never had?'

Connie looked at him with pain in her eyes. 'That's a cruel thing to say, Josh.'

'I'm sorry,' he said humbly. 'But you're giving up hope too soon. I'm going to do my best to talk Lynnys round.'

'Don't worry about me,' Connie said. 'Just make sure she's safe from her father.'

Josh hesitated before answering. 'Bernie will never bother her again,' he said, and then related the news from the police.

Connie sat back in her chair, her gaze vague; her whole being still.

'Connie, are you all right?'

She looked at him then. 'I'm not sorry. Isn't that awful?' she said quietly, almost defiantly. 'I loved him for so long, but eventually he turned my love to hate.'

'Have you thought about your future; what you'll do now?'

'I'm never going back on the game,' she said defiantly. 'That life has already cost me dear; losing my child. I'll go down on my knees scrubbing floors if I have to.'

'Listen,' Josh began sitting forward in his chair. 'I have plans. Lynnys has the potential to be a big star, I just know it. But Swansea is not big enough for her. London is her best chance.'

Lynnys had declared her career over but he was determined to talk her around. His future depended on it too, and not only his. There was Elvi to provide for now.

'London?' Connie looked at him in surprise.

Josh nodded. 'She doesn't know it yet but I'm taking her there and soon.'

Connie's smile was thin and sorrowful. 'You know I wish her every success, even if I can't be part of it.'

'But I think you can,' Josh said. He had been thinking about this for a long time. 'Lynnys will need a chaperone; someone I can trust, someone like you, Con, who knows the pitfalls for a young girl in the big city. I can't be watching over her every minute. She needs her mother.'

Connie's eyes lit up for a moment and her face became animated, and then suddenly all the light went out of her gaze.

'Lynnys will never agree. She hates me.'

'She doesn't hate you.' Josh shook his head. 'Not in her heart, she doesn't. She's just hurt, that's all.'

Connie stood up. 'Josh, I know you mean well, but you didn't see the way Lynnys looked at me. She despises me. I just can't hope any longer.'

'I can persuade her...'

Connie shook her head. 'It's no use, Josh.' She stood and walked to the window to stare out. 'I'm going away from Swansea myself. It's for the best. I'll only be an embarrassment to my daughter if I stay, especially now that Bernie is dead. The investigation will drag out every sordid detail of our lives.'

'Don't be hasty, Connie.'

She swung around to face him, looking at him pleadingly.

'Josh, please get Lynnys away from Swansea as soon as you can. I don't want her involved in a scandal. She must have her chance.'

Josh left Connie's lodgings in a thoughtful mood. He had to find a way to persuade Lynnys to forgive her mother and to continue with her career. He sensed that the girl would need her mother's love and support if she was to be happy in her success.

He would willingly be a father to Lynnys, but he had his own daughter to consider too. Elvi was virtually alone in the world, for who knew how long Sybil would remain in prison. It was his duty as a father to take care of her, but would she let him? She had already made it clear she thought of him only as a stranger.

How complicated his life had become. He had always dodged responsibilities and ties; he now had to deal with the consequences of old relationships and face up to the reality of new responsibilities.

For a brief moment he regretted the passing of his old carefree life. But now he had found something more precious – he had a daughter. His values were changed. Elvi needed him and so did Sybil, in a way. He could not love her as he had once done, but he could be her friend, her true friend.

30

Josh passed through the gates of Swansea Prison with a heavy heart. Having talked again to Mr Prosser, her lawyer, he dreaded seeing Sybil, knowing she must be taking her circumstances very badly.

As she was brought into the visitors' room he was again shocked at the change in her in so short a time. She looked older and had lost weight, the plain blue calico dress she wore hung limply from her shoulders. Her blonde hair, pulled back in a severe style, needed washing. Her skin was pale and dull. Concerned, Josh wondered how she would cope with the months of imprisonment before her.

'How are you, Syb?'

'I'm up before the magistrate next week.' Her face crumpled. 'Josh, I'm afraid!' She gulped and he could see she was fighting to hold back tears. 'Mr Prosser told me I can expect a sentence of about two months or more for striking that officer.'

'He assured me he'll beg the court for leniency in view of the circumstances,' Josh said. 'You were only trying to save your daughter from abduction.'

'They won't believe me!'

He paused, wondering if he should tell her about Bernie, then decided she should know everything. After all, Bernie was the reason she was in this predicament.

'Pomfrey is dead, Syb, murdered.'

She looked at him astonished.

'The police know him now for the criminal he was. That will help in your case.' He hesitated before going on. 'He kept a brothel in the town and that's where he took Elvi.'

'Oh, my God!'

'She's unharmed,' Josh hastened to say. 'She's begging to visit you.'

'No! No!' Sybil shook her head vehemently. 'She mustn't come here. She mustn't see me like this.'

'Are you sure?'

Sybil nodded. 'Tell her I love her dearly and I'm sorry for my selfishness and foolhardy ways in the past. I'll make it up to her somehow.' She gave him a pleading glance. 'Elvi's too young to stay anywhere on her own.'

Josh reached across to touch Sybil's hand despite warning grunts from the warden.

'Elvi's my daughter, too,' he said. 'I'll take care of her. I'll arrange for all your belongings to be collected from Walter Road.'

'Where will she live?' Sybil asked anxiously. 'Is there room in your lodgings for her?'

Josh hesitated, passing his tongue over his lips nervously. 'There's something I must tell you, Sybil. I'll be moving back up the Smoke very shortly.'

'What?' she looked at him accusingly. 'You're deserting me again!'

'No, not really,' he said quickly. 'I'm managing

a brilliant young singer, Lynnys Daniels, a good friend of Elvi's as a matter of fact. To succeed she needs to be in London.' He hesitated, wondering how she would take his next words. 'I want Elvi to come with me. I'll never be parted from her again.'

Sybil looked distraught. 'You're not only deserting me but you're stealing my child, too.'

He shook his head. 'No, Sybil, it's not like that. Look, when you're released I'll come for you. You can join Elvi in London; make a home there. I'll help you.'

'She has agreed to go with you then?'

Josh looked abashed. 'I haven't asked her yet.'

'I don't want her to go,' Sybil said. 'I'll be here all alone.'

'Sybil, listen to me,' Josh said urgently, not wanting to upset her more. 'Time will pass quicker than you think. Then you can put all this behind you and start again up the Smoke.' He smiled wanly. 'Who knows, you might meet a good man in London.'

'No one will look at me now I've been in this place.'

'You were always a pretty girl, Syb. You'll be pretty again, believe me.' He looked at her in mock sternness. 'But there'll be no more séances, understand?'

Sybil nodded meekly and then her eyes filled with tears. 'Two months in this place. Josh, how will I survive?'

'You must have courage, Sybil. These bad times will pass. The main thing is Elvi is safe and Bernie can't hurt either of you again.'

A tear glistened on her pale cheek. 'I'll be so lonely.'

'I know,' he sympathised and risked touching her hand again. 'Keep your thoughts on the future and a new life, you and Elvi together.'

'Time's up,' the warden said shortly.

Josh rose reluctantly. 'Take care of yourself, Syb.'

'Josh, you won't forget me, will you?'

He smiled. 'No, never, and Elvi won't let me either. Our daughter is a lovely girl, Sybil. I'm so proud of her.'

'And she's clever, you know,' Sybil said pride in her voice. 'I expect she gets that from you, Josh.'

He grinned, his heart lifting to see a spark of hope in her eyes. 'See you soon, Syb.'

Elvi sat in the small front parlour at Cwmavon Terrace, the only place she could find some privacy, waiting anxiously for Josh to return after visiting her mother at the prison.

When he finally arrived she could tell by his expression that he had bad news.

'Where's Mam?' she exclaimed. 'Josh, you said they might let her go free.'

'They've dropped the charge of theft...'

'Oh, thank heavens!' Elvi exclaimed.

'The police won't drop the other charges,' Josh said gravely. 'Her lawyer believes she may have to serve at least two months. It depends on the sympathy of the magistrate.'

'What?' Elvi was appalled. 'But that's not fair! She was only defending me.' Elvi felt upset and helpless and wanted to hit back at something.

'Didn't you tell them that, Josh?' she asked sharply. 'Don't you care?'

'Of course I care,' Josh replied quickly. He looked hurt at her tone. 'I've done all I can, Elvi, believe me. Her lawyer will plead mitigating circumstances in her case. Who knows, the magistrate may be merciful.'

Elvi put her fingers to her mouth in distress. The thought of her mother languishing in a prison cell broke her heart. Sybil would never bear it.

'Mam doesn't deserve this.' She shook her head miserably and gulped. 'I want to see her.'

Josh shook his head. 'Sybil doesn't want you to go anywhere near the prison, Elvi, for your own good. She sends her love, and asks you to forgive her.'

'There's nothing to forgive.' She gazed at him through tears. 'Me and Mam have never been parted before. And I can't stay here indefinitely. Where can I go?'

'You mustn't worry. I'll take care of you.'

Elvi stared at him. 'Why did Sybil never mention you through all those years?'

'Maybe she was ashamed, unwed but with a child.'

'Life's unfair!' Elvi exclaimed. She was too choked up to say more, and flinging him a final glance she rushed from the room to find sanctuary in the bedroom she shared with Trudy.

Lynnys came out of the living room into the passage to find Josh standing uncertainly at the foot of the stairs. She was uncomfortable to see him still around. She knew her decision to give up her singing career had stunned him, but she did not have the heart or stomach to go on with it any longer.

'I'm surprised to see you still here, Josh,' she said defensively.

He gave her a quick glance before staring up the stairs again.

'What's wrong?' she asked.

'Elvi's very upset,' he replied. 'I've brought bad news about her mother. It looks very like she'll remain in prison for a few months yet.'

'Oh!' Lynnys was dismayed to hear that. 'Poor Elvi. It must be breaking her heart.'

Josh nodded and moved away from the stairs to walk past her to the living room. She wished he would leave. He was a constant reminder of shattered dreams.

'Oh, it's you,' Phoebe said acidly as they both entered the room. 'I thought we'd seen the last of you, Josh Rowlands.'

'I'll be around for a while yet.'

'Why?'

'Because I intend to talk sense into Lynnys here,' he said quickly. 'She's throwing her whole life away.'

'You're wasting your time, then,' Lynnys said with feeling. 'My mind is made up.'

'What about Connie?' Josh asked. 'She's your mother and she's in as much misery as Sybil Lloyd. She's separated from her child and no future to look forward to.'

'That's nonsense,' Lynnys denied. Her anger at being deceived still simmered in her heart and so she did not want to talk about Mrs Lamar or even think about her.

'You're breaking her heart, Lynnys,' Josh insisted. 'She's talking about leaving Swansea for good. There's nothing here for her without you.'

There was a muffled sound from Phoebe, but she did not speak.

Lynnys received the news defiantly. 'Good!'

'You don't mean that,' Josh said. 'Or you're not the Lynnys I've come to know and respect.'

'Well, you don't know me at all.'

'I think I do,' Josh insisted. 'Lynnys, listen. If you let your mother go like this you'll live to regret it. Believe me, I know about these things.'

Lynnys sniffed disdainfully. Josh Rowlands had a golden tongue, but he wouldn't influence her.

'Perhaps you have already guessed about Elvi and me,' Josh went on.

'What?'

'Elvi is my daughter,' he said quietly. 'The child I never knew I had, because years ago I turned my back on her mother and ran away. I bitterly regret that.'

Lynnys was surprised. 'Elvi's illegitimate, too?'

Josh nodded. 'And do you know that she hasn't uttered one word of blame to me, or blamed her mother? That kid's got a big heart.'

'She has less to be ashamed of than I do.' Lynnys lifted her chin. 'At least her father isn't an out and out criminal. And her mother isn't...'

'Her mother is sitting in a prison cell at this moment, facing a jail sentence,' Josh pointed out. 'That's hardly something to be proud of.'

Lynnys turned her glance away from his steady

445

gaze, unable to deny that. She looked instead at her grandmother, who was sitting, saying nothing, which was very unusual for her. Did Gran regret all those years she had turned her back on Connie?

'There's a lot to forgive,' she said quietly. 'And I don't know whether I can. That dreadful man who she says is my father – how can I live that down? How can I ever feel safe from him?'

'About Bernie...' Josh began soberly and Lynnys turned at the strange tone in his voice.

'What now?'

'Your father is dead. He died some time last night.' Josh hesitated, and wetted his lips before going on. 'He was murdered, Lynnys.'

She stared at him, utterly confounded. She flopped down on a chair nearby. This was something she had not expected. She felt nothing but loathing and revulsion for the man, and knew a sense of release at the news, but then felt very ashamed that the death of another human being could induce that emotion in her.

'Good riddance!' Phoebe exclaimed with gusto.

'Gran!' She could not condone speaking ill of the dead, even though the man had been a blackguard; a monster. 'Does Mrs La ... does my mother know?'

Josh nodded. 'She's concerned now for you, Lynnys,' he went on. 'There'll be an investigation, of course. The police will look into every nook and cranny of Bernie's life. And there's plenty of muck to find, believe me. Connie doesn't want it splattered on you, kid.'

Lynnys put her knuckles to her mouth and

446

bowed her head. 'Is there no escape from this?'

'Yes, there is,' Josh said quickly. 'You must get away from Swansea as soon as possible. You deserve a future, Lynnys, don't you see?' he said persuasively. 'Don't let Bernie destroy that for you.'

'Go away?' she shook her head in bewilderment. 'Go where?'

Josh seemed to hesitate. She stared at him, wondering at his expression of wariness.

'We must go to London,' he said shortly.

'We?'

'Me, you, Elvi and ... Connie.'

'What?' Lynnys jumped to her feet. She had thought he had meant moving to another town close by. London seemed extreme. And what did Connie have to do with this? 'Are you mad, Josh? Why London?'

'You *must* go on with your singing career, Lynnys,' he said with energy. 'There are so many opportunities up the Smoke; your career will expand as it should. I've been thinking about this move for a while...'

'Oh, you have, have you?' He was trying to manipulate her and she would not allow it. 'Since when have you been in charge of my life?'

'Since you made me your manager,' he said. 'All right! So I'm thinking of myself as well,' he admitted angrily.

'Huh! I'm glad you're being honest!'

Josh shook his head. She could see he was angry.

'I've put a lot of time, energy and money into training you for a career,' he said sharply. 'I've done some stupid, yes even dishonest things in the past. But that all changed when I discovered you and your marvellous talent.' He spread his hands as though in appeal. 'Lynnys, your voice is a God-given gift. You can't just throw it away.'

'I think he's right,' Phoebe said suddenly.

'Gran, I thought you were on my side. And besides,' Lynnys said strongly. 'I'm still a little cross with you for keeping me in the dark all these years.'

'Oh, for goodness sake!' Phoebe leaned forward and, taking the fire iron, thrust it into the coals in the range fire and rattled it against the bars, stirring up sparks. 'If that's all the trouble you get in your life you'll be lucky.'

'Gran?'

Phoebe looked up at her. 'I am on your side, my girl,' she said. 'Don't make the mistake I did. When I learned what your mother had become I washed my hands of her.' Phoebe looked wistful. 'I've often wondered that if I'd welcomed her here in her home with open arms, she might have altered her ways. Look how Trudy has changed.' She shook her head sadly. 'I didn't give Connie a chance.'

'Listen to your grandmother,' Josh put in eagerly, and Phoebe gave him a warning glance to be quiet.

'Never mind us forgiving her,' Phoebe went on. 'Maybe it's the other way around. We should be asking her for forgiveness, for turning our backs on her.'

Lynnys listened in astonishment. 'I can't believe I'm hearing this from you, Gran.'

'For seventeen years Connie kept our heads above water where money was concerned.' She nodded wisely at Lynnys. 'We'd have gone hungry many a time but for her. I've been too proud to admit that before, to my shame.'

Lynnys sat down on a chair nearby, her mind in a whirl. 'Looks as though I've no choice.'

'Oh, yes, you have a choice,' Phoebe hastened to say. 'You can keep riding your high horse, going nowhere fast, or you can find peace of mind and real love in the company of the woman who birthed you.'

Lynnys tilted her head down in thought. It had broken her heart to make the decision to give up singing. It was like deciding not to breathe any more. And it had been her dream for so long.

Was she letting silly pride spoil everything for her, as Gran said? Had she the right to judge the woman who had given her life?

She glanced up at Josh. He was looking at her hopefully, like a little kid waiting for Father Christmas to appear. Her pride was spoiling it for everyone.

'Josh, will you see Connie and give her my apologies for my bad behaviour? Tell her I'd like to see her.'

He grinned. 'Is London on?'

Lynnys bit her lip, knowing she was about to make the biggest commitment of her life. 'Yes,' she said at last, realising it was her destiny. 'Yes, I want to go on singing and I want to make a success of it. Will you help me, Josh?'

'You bet, kid!'

Connie was due to call around the following afternoon. Lynnys was on pins with nervousness and she realised she must be the first one to offer an olive branch and be wholehearted about it. She hoped she could do that and not appear distant.

Lynnys felt it right to ask Connie into the front parlour where they could be alone. Phoebe would want to make peace, too, but Lynnys decided she must see her mother alone first.

'Please come in,' she said shyly to Connie when she arrived on the doorstep.

She did not know whether she should offer a kiss on the cheek, but uncertain of the proper thing to do, stepped aside instead to allow her mother to enter.

'You don't know how pleased I was when Josh gave me your message, Lynnys,' Connie began. She sounded breathless and Lynnys guessed she was just as nervous. 'Thank you, Lynnys my dear girl, for this second chance.'

'Let me take your coat and please sit down,' Lynnys invited bashfully, conscious of the tremor in her mother's voice, as though she were near to tears.

Connie removed her coat and took a seat, pulling off her kid gloves. 'Thank you.'

Lynnys sat down too and then felt suddenly awkward. 'I'll make a cup of tea later,' she said and then rushed on. 'Let me apologise to you for the way I treated you and the unforgivable things I said.'

'No, no, you were quite within your rights.' Connie ran her tongue over her lips nervously. 'It

450

must have been a terrible revelation to learn that your mother was alive and that she was no more than...'

'Please!' Lynnys exclaimed in distress. 'Let's not speak of that. It's in the past, especially now that my ... my father is dead.'

'Oh, Josh has told you about that.'

Lynnys swallowed hard. 'Yes and I can't say I'm sorry.' She paused. 'That must sound dreadfully callous.'

Connie reached forward to pat her hand. 'Lynnys, my dear, it's very understandable,' she said gently. 'I never meant for you to know who he was. I felt ashamed. I didn't want him to know about you either, or have anything to do with you. He was a vile man, I know that now.'

Lynnys bent her head. It was hard being reminded of her shameful origins, and she steeled herself not to mind. This meeting with her mother was all about their future; trying to salvage something of their lives.

'Can you find it in your heart to forgive me, Lynnys, my dear?'

'Oh, please!' Lynnys looked up quickly. 'I must beg *your* forgiveness. Gran reminded me of that.'

A slight flush came to Connie's cheeks. 'My mother said that?' Her tone suggested she could hardly believe her mother would even acknowledge her.

'Gran wants to talk to you later, after we've had our chat,' Lynnys said. She stopped, feeling her own cheeks heat up with embarrassment. 'I don't know what to call you even.'

Connie smiled, and Lynnys saw love and

tenderness in her face, and felt warmed by them.

'Call me Connie, for the time being,' Connie said gently. 'Until we get to know each other better.' She hesitated, uncertain. 'That is, if you do want us to be ... friends.'

'Oh, I do,' Lynnys said with feeling. 'I'd like us to be more than friends. I valued your friendship before...'

'Before you discovered my disgrace,' Connie cut in quickly.

Lynnys shook her head. 'Let's not talk of that, Connie. Let's talk of the future.'

'I understand you'll go to London with Josh Rowlands to further your career,' Connie said. 'I fully approve of that, and I wish you all the success in the world. You deserve it, Lynnys.'

'London, yes, but...' Lynnys looked at her mother appealingly. 'Josh told me you're thinking of leaving Swansea,' she said. 'Would you consider coming to London with us?' She swallowed hard seeing the expression on her mother's face. 'Josh is very kind but I need ... I need my family with me. I need you.'

Lynnys was surprised to see tears in Connie's eyes. 'Oh, Lynnys, what a wonderful thing to say. For years I've dreamed of being close to you, being part of your life. I never ever thought that dream would come true.'

Connie rose to her feet, arms outstretched and Lynnys stood, too, and went to meet her. With a little sob, she moved into her mother's warm embrace; felt her mother's kiss on her cheek.

It seemed the most natural thing in the world. She loved her grandmother dearly, but it was

452

wonderful to be held in a mother's loving arms at last. At last she felt safe and protected.

They were both shedding tears as each stepped back. Lynnys looked into her mother's loving face, feeling a great surge of happiness engulf her. She could achieve anything now.

'Oh, Mam,' she said, a sob of happiness in her throat. 'I'm so glad I have you with me at last. I want us to be together always.'

'You couldn't be gladder than I am,' Connie said tremulously. 'I thank God for the return of my precious child. I thought I'd never know happiness again.'

Lynnys tenderly kissed her mother on her cheek.

'Gran must be on pins herself,' Lynnys said. 'She's in the living room waiting to see you. I'll make a pot of tea in the scullery while you both talk.' Lynnys looked earnestly into her mother's face. 'Gran can be crusty at times, but she really loves you, Mam. She's been lonely for you all these years, you know.'

Connie's shoulders shook and she gave a little sob, and Lynnys put her arm around her shoulders comfortingly.

'Come on, Mam,' she said gently. 'A cup of tea will do you the world of good.'

31

'How's Mam? Is she all right?' Elvi looked eagerly into Josh's face. 'Oh, I do wish I could've gone with you to the prison today.'

'I gave Sybil your letter, Elvi,' Josh said. 'She was very touched. She sends her love, too.'

'Why must I say all this to her through other people?' Elvi whirled away, suddenly impatient. 'She's my mother. I've a right to see and talk to her.'

She wanted to see her mother face to face, squeeze her hand; show how much she cared. Sybil had not been one for demonstrable affection in the past, but now it was different. Elvi was certain her mother needed comforting.

'You must respect her feelings, Elvi. Sybil has her pride.'

She opened her mouth to protest, but Josh held up his hand.

'There's something else we have to discuss, Elvi,' he said seriously. 'Your future. You see I'm moving to London very shortly, and I'm taking Lynnys and Connie with me.'

'What?' she stared at him, uncomprehending. Was he deserting them once again now that they needed him most?

'I'm Lynnys' manager and it's my job to further her career as best I can,' he went on quickly. 'I want you to come to London, too, and live with me, that is, until Sybil is freed.'

Elvi stared at him aghast. 'What? Leave Swansea? Leave Mam to face it all alone?' She shook her head. 'No, I can't leave her now. She'll think I was deserting her. I won't do it.'

He took an envelope out of his jacket pocket and handed it to her. 'Sybil won't see you, kid. Here's a letter from her to explain.'

Reluctantly, Elvi took the letter from the envelope and read it through, twice and then lifted her chin defiantly.

'This makes no difference,' she said shakily. 'I won't go with you and I will visit her.'

'She's ashamed for you to see her,' Josh said hastily.

'But I'm not ashamed.' She stared at him rebelliously. 'You deserted her once,' she accused hotly. 'But I never will.'

'Elvi!'

She realised she had wounded him and was sorry.

'I'm not blaming you or denying you as my father,' she said more gently. 'When Mam comes out of prison you can fetch us. We'll both need you then.'

He looked at her helplessly for a moment and then smiled. 'You've got plenty of guts, kid, and I'm proud of you.'

She felt proud herself. The independence she had longed for was now hers, and she felt the stronger for it, although she regretted the circumstances.

'Josh, I want you to get permission for me to visit my mother as soon as possible – tomorrow.'

He sighed. 'Okay, kid,' he said. 'I can see you're a young lady with a mind of your own.' He paused. 'Would you like me to come with you when you visit her?'

'No thank you, Josh.' Elvi swallowed hard. 'This is something I have to do alone. Mam and I have a lot of things to talk about. Private things.'

He looked solemn. 'Don't exclude me from your life, Elvi.'

She touched his arm. 'We'll be together in London when the time comes, Josh, I promise you.'

Elvi was nervous the following morning as she stood outside the prison gates on Oystermouth Road waiting with the other visitors. Would her mother agree to see her?

The small side gate opened and the visitors trooped in. As the gate closed behind her she glanced around at the grey and grimy stones walls of the prison and was struck immediately with a feeling of isolation and depression. A person could easily fade away and die in here, she thought, with a shiver. Two months could seem like a lifetime, and she was frightened for Sybil.

The women's visiting room was small; the few tables and chairs crowded it. Thankfully only one other person was visiting in the women's wing that day, and so it seemed less claustrophobic.

Elvi sat and waited anxiously and finally a warden brought a woman to the table. Sybil shuffled in, head down, her shoulders drooping in utter despair.

Elvi was shocked beyond words at the deterioration in her mother's looks and spirits. She hardly recognised her and could hardly speak for a moment.

'Mam!' Elvi rose from her seat. 'Oh! Mam.'

Sybil lifted her head, startled and stepped back. Her expression showed her utter dismay. 'Elvi, what are you doing here?' she cried out in anguish. 'I told Josh you were not to visit me.'

'Sit down, Mam.'

'No! You must go. I don't want to see you.'

'But I'm your daughter. You can't send me away now.'

The woman warden put a firm hand on Sybil's shoulder and she had no choice but to sit down on the hard wooden seat. Immediately she covered her face with her hands.

'Oh, that you should see me like this, in this awful place. I'm so ashamed.'

'You've nothing to be ashamed about, Mam,' Elvi said. 'None of this is your fault. It was that dreadful man, Major Pomfrey.'

Longing to embrace her mother, she reached across the table to touch her mother's face.

'No touching!' the warden announced sternly.

Elvi threw the warden a sharp glance, suddenly angry. 'But that's cruel! She's my mother. It's only natural that I try to comfort her.'

The warden sniffed and looked away.

Sybil lowered her hands from her face and gave a little moan. 'I'll never be comforted again,' she cried. 'Life is over for me after being in here and that's why I didn't want you anywhere near me.'

'You mustn't push me away, Mam,' Elvi said, straining not to burst into tears. 'I think the world of you, you must know that.'

'I don't know why you should,' Sybil sobbed. 'I've had time to think and reflect in here, and I realise how selfish I've been. I wasn't a very caring mother to you, Elvi.'

'And I didn't help, did I,' Elvi admitted gently. 'I didn't consider how hard life was for you; being deserted and trying to bring up a child single-handed. I know you did the best you could, Mam.'

Sybil gazed across the table at her with eyes made bleary from crying. 'I put you in so much danger, Elvi. I let evil touch you. I can't forgive myself for that.'

'That's in the past now, Mam. We'll begin again together.'

Sybil looked at her. Warmth was in her eyes although they were swimming in tears. 'I do love you, Elvi,' she said, a catch in her voice. 'You may not have thought so, but I only ever wanted what's best for you.'

'I know, Mam,' Elvi answered, swallowing her own tears. She had to stay strong for them both now. In a way their roles were reversed. She was now her mother's support.

'When you're released we'll go up to London together, Mam; make a good life for ourselves,' Elvi said reassuringly. 'I'll train as a nurse. My father will take care of us. He's promised me that.'

'Has he left yet?' Sybil asked in dull tones.

'They'll be leaving in a few days.'

'Go with them, Elvi,' Sybil leaned forward to say quickly. 'I don't want you touched by this awful mess I've got myself into.'

Elvi shook her head. 'I'm not leaving you,

Mam. I'll visit you every day while you're in this place and nothing will stop me.'

Sybil burst into tears afresh then. 'Oh, Elvi, I don't deserve you,' she murmured between sobs. 'But I thank God I have such a wonderful daughter.'

'Time's up,' the warden announced in a tone that would not be defied.

Elvi rose reluctantly. 'I'll see you tomorrow, Mam, and I'll fetch you a box of borax crystals to rinse your hair; put a shine back in it.'

Sybil blinked and rose from her chair. 'Oh that's thoughtful of you, Elvi. You're such a sensible girl. What would I do without you?'

They stood for a moment looking at each other.

'Everything will be all right, you'll see,' Elvi said with confidence. 'My father and I will make sure of that. God bless you, Mam.'

'Gran! You must come to London with us.' Distressed, Lynnys knelt on the mat before her grandmother's chair next to the range and took her hand in her own. 'You *must* come. I can't leave you behind all alone. If you don't come with us I won't go either.'

Phoebe patted her hand. 'Lynnys, *bach,* I'm too sick and too old to leave my home now,' she said gently. 'I've had my day. Now it's your turn. You and your mother. Make the most of it girl.'

'But, Gran...'

'Listen to me,' Phoebe said. 'I won't be alone. I've got Trudy and Elvi for company.'

'Of course I'll take care of her,' Trudy put in. 'I think the world of Phoebe, you know that.'

Lynnys glanced up at Trudy gratefully. The girl had practically taken over the running of their home these last months. Big with child though she was, her condition did not seem to slow her down. The house was spick and span and she always had a nourishing meal ready. Trudy had turned out to be a wonderful cook.

'I know you do, Trudy,' Lynnys assured her. 'But Gran is my responsibility, after all.'

'Look,' Trudy said. 'I don't have a proper family.' She smiled and tilted her head wistfully. 'I've come to think of you as a sister, Lynnys.' She smiled at Phoebe and put her hand on the older woman's shoulder. 'And Phoebe is as dear to me as if she were my own grandmother.'

'Trudy will be staying indefinitely,' Phoebe said firmly. 'After her baby is born she and her child will continue to have a home here with me for as long as she wants. There's nothing for you to fret about, Lynnys, *bach*.'

Lynnys could tell from Phoebe's expression that it would be useless to argue further. 'It breaks my heart to leave you,' she said gently. 'But I'll make Josh let me come home often. And I promise you'll want for nothing. I shall send money as often as I can.'

'Now I don't want to be a drain on you,' Phoebe said archly. 'We'll manage somehow.'

'Gran, you let Mam help all those years,' Lynnys pointed out. 'Now it's my turn.'

'You're a good girl,' Phoebe said, and Lynnys could see tears glistening in her grandmother's eyes.

'So the big day is tomorrow then,' Trudy said.

Lynnys nodded. She had butterflies in her stomach at the thought of it. What if she could not make a success at singing?

She would be letting Josh down and everyone else, too. 'I hope I'm doing the right thing.'

'Of course you are,' Trudy assured her. 'You sing like an angel. You'll be famous one day, mark my words. And when you're top bill at the Empire we'll come and see you, won't we Phoebe?'

Phoebe chuckled. 'And we want the best seats, mind. Those seats in the gods are hard on my old rump.'

Lynnys laughed with them. A new way of life promised to open out for her, and no matter how famous she became, she would never forget she had once lugged about sacks of potatoes for a living; in muddy boots and dirty fingernails.

Everyone had said their goodbyes, many times over it seemed to Lynnys, and now the moment had come to actually leave the house where she had lived happily if humbly. She would never forget her roots.

'The hansom cab is here,' Josh said from the doorway as Lynnys and Connie kissed Phoebe one last time.

'Hurry up,' Phoebe scolded them. 'You'll miss your train.'

Lynnys saw Connie's cheeks were wet as she followed Josh down the passage to the pavement where the cab waited.

Throwing a last kiss to her grandmother in her chair near the range, Lynnys followed. Josh and Connie were already in the cab as she stepped

461

out on to the pavement.

Elvi came and stood in the doorway to wave them off, a sad yet proud expression on her face.

Lynnys paused and then turned, giving her friend a warm hug and then looked into her eyes, seeing a trace of tears there.

'I hate leaving you like this, Elvi,' Lynnys said sadly. 'I wish you were coming with us.'

Elvi took her hand and squeezed it. 'My mother needs me more than ever,' she said with certainty. 'But we'll see each other again soon, Lynnys, within weeks. We'll be happy then with our families.'

'Oh, yes.' Lynnys leaned forward impulsively and kissed Elvi's cheek. 'I'm so glad we're friends, Elvi. We've been through a lot together and we always will be friends, won't we?'

'Always.'

The publishers hope that this book has given you enjoyable reading. Large Print Books are especially designed to be as easy to see and hold as possible. If you wish a complete list of our books please ask at your local library or write directly to:

Magna Large Print Books
Magna House, Long Preston,
Skipton, North Yorkshire.
BD23 4ND

This Large Print Book for the partially sighted, who cannot read normal print, is published under the auspices of

THE ULVERSCROFT FOUNDATION